Hidden Falls

Hidden Falls

Carla Danziger

iUniverse, Inc.

New York Lincoln Shanghai

Hidden Falls

iUniverse, Inc.

For information address:
iUniverse, Inc.
2021 Pine Lake Road, Suite 100
Lincoln, NE 68512
www.iuniverse.com

ISBN: 0-595-31596-8

Printed in the United States of America

To my family

PROLOGUE

▼

"Mrs. Kelly! Mrs. Kelly!"

Kris thought it was part of her dream, but now she sleepily lifted her head from the pillow and tried to focus on the male voice with the singsongy Norwegian accent calling her name. Ever since childhood, the familiar rhythm of her grandparents' language had comforted her. But not now. Not in the middle of the night. Not accompanied by loud knocking on the door.

"Mrs. Kelly! Please wake up!"

This time she recognized the voice; it was that of Oscar Larsen, the hotel proprietor. She squinted at her travel clock: ten-thirty a.m.? No way! By this time, according to her cousin Elsa's plan, they should have been hiking for a couple of hours. So much for the alarm she had so carefully set for seven; they had both slept right through it.

Kris glanced at the bed opposite hers. Not even Elsa's blonde head was visible from beneath the massive comforter. Just a few days earlier her cousin had declared, "I'm a journalist; the news doesn't sleep, so why should I?" At least she was finally getting the rest she needed. Especially after last night.

"Elsa. It's ten-thirty," Kris said as she pulled on her robe and padded barefoot toward the door, feeling a knot form in her stomach. Why was Oscar calling only her name, not Elsa's? Could one of the kids be trying to reach her here in Norway? They only had the phone number at Elsa's house in Bergen, not here at the Fjord Hotel. Neither of them would know she and Elsa had gone away for a few days. But they were resourceful, and what if there was an emergency?

The security chain hung to the side of the doorjamb. Strange, she thought. Hadn't fastening it been the last thing she'd done before getting into bed last night? She opened the door and stared into Oscar's face. The knot in her stomach tightened.

"Come quickly," he said. "Miss Jenssen's been hurt."

"Elsa? But that's impossible, she's asleep." As Kris spoke, a sense of foreboding swept over her. Why hadn't Elsa stirred in response to Oscar's knocking? Why was the security chain already off? She rushed to Elsa's bed and yanked at the comforter. It fell to the floor, sending into disarray four fluffy pillows that appeared to have been lined up underneath it.

"Oh, no…" It was a ruse. Elsa had gone without her. "Where is she?"

"Hidden Falls," Oscar replied.

"Hidden Falls?" Kris repeated, puzzled. Last night Oscar had described the trails to the falls, and she and Elsa had agreed to hike there this morning. "It doesn't make sense. What happened?"

"An accident, they said." Oscar ran his hand nervously through his salt-and-pepper hair.

"Has a doctor been called?"

"*Ja.* A first-aid team is on the way," he replied.

"I'll be right back." Kris whisked her clothes from a chair and ran into the bathroom, unanswered questions racing through her mind. Elsa had always been unpredictable, but stuffing bedcovers? At age sixty-five? Why? And how did she get hurt? How badly?

Kris slipped into her jeans and pullover, noticing their newly acquired lavender smell—the scent that filled the closets at Elsa's house. Before rejoining Oscar, she quickly brushed her teeth, trying to wash away the bitter aftertaste of last night's lingonberry nightcap.

Out front Hasan, the hotel's jack-of-all-trades, waited for them in a blue pickup truck, its engine running, passenger-side door open. Kris jumped in, followed by Oscar who slammed the door shut as Hasan pressed down on the gas pedal. The pickup rattled out of the hotel grounds and down the road that skirted the fjord. Low-hanging clouds shrouded the surrounding peaks in shades of gray. Damp cool air blew in through the open windows, dispelling the cab's fishy odor. Oscar apologized that his other vehicles were unavailable.

That was the least of Kris's worries. "How badly is Elsa hurt?" she asked. "A broken arm? Leg? Do you know?"

Oscar shook his head. "They only said she fell."

"Who's 'they'?"

"Hikers. The manager of the youth hostel called me; he said Max Guttmann sent them."

"Max?" Kris pictured the robust German tourist from the hotel. "Did Elsa go hiking with him?"

"No, he went fishing."

"I drive her and the others to the Ridge Trail," Hasan interjected as he ran the stop sign at the intersection.

"What others?" Kris asked.

Oscar answered for him. "Mrs. Dahl…Mr. and Mrs. Mueller…"

Kris wished she could fast-forward through Oscar's drawn-out list.

"Dr. and Mrs. Stephens…"

"That was everyone," Hasan said.

"I don't understand why Elsa went without me," Kris said.

"When I saw her at breakfast, she said you needed your sleep," Oscar said.

"*I* needed *my* sleep? She's the one who had the dizzy spell," Kris said, at the same time thinking that Elsa definitely had some explaining to do once this was all over.

The pickup sped across the bridge toward town. On the other side of the river, Hasan hung a sharp left; and Kris felt herself sandwiched between the two men's shoulders as she and Oscar slid toward Hasan. Out of the corner of her eye she saw a small gray church where worshipers were filing in for Sunday services.

In a few minutes gravel hit the chassis of the pickup, signaling the end of the road's paved surface. With the rattle of the truck making it difficult to hear, and with her hair blowing in her face, Kris gave up talking. Instead, she tried to calm herself, breathing deeply as she had learned in yoga classes, and thinking positive thoughts: Elsa was in good shape, except she did have that dizzy spell last night. But she must have felt okay this morning or she wouldn't have gone hiking. Kris took another deep breath and assured herself that Elsa would be all right.

They followed the river, passing small farms in the mist, then an arrow-shaped sign with the words "Mountain Youth Hostel" pointing into the woods. The road narrowed to a lane wedged between the river and the mountainside, finally ending in a clearing near where the river roared out of a deep chasm. Hasan parked beside an ambulance and a police car.

"Follow me," he said and led them up the rocky trail.

Small stones slipped under Kris's shoes, making it difficult to run. The thundering of falling water grew louder as she pushed herself forward.

Then, rounding an outcropping of rock, she saw Elsa lying on the ground in red knit top, black pants, and hiking boots; two medics huddled over her.

"How is she?" Kris shouted as she approached. She disregarded the frown on the face of one of the medics; the crashing falls drowned out the other's words.

Kris knelt beside Elsa, who lay as wet and still as the mossy stone surface beneath her. Someone had placed a white towel underneath her head. Wispy bangs reddened with blood fell across Elsa's battered forehead. Her cheeks were swollen, her eyes closed; her smile gone.

"Elsa?" Kris lifted Elsa's left hand, cold and limp, and moved the gold wristwatch to feel her pulse. Nothing.

"Elsa," she said, grasping the older woman's shoulders, though she knew now she would get no response.

Eyes clouded with tears, she lay her head on Elsa's chest. This couldn't be happening, she told herself, and burst into uncontrollable sobs.

CHAPTER 1

▼

Bergen, 24 hours earlier

Kris browsed the tourist materials at the Bergen train station, then selected the brochure titled *Sognefjord Country*, captivated by the familiar photo on the front: an aerial view of snow-capped mountains, their steep slopes plunging into glassy waters rippled by the wake of a hydrofoil. At the tip of the fjord, as if at the end of the world, a village was nestled between mountains and sea. This was the kind of refuge she needed, if only for a couple of days, where she could find strength in nature and begin to regain her emotional equilibrium. She checked her watch. Almost ten o'clock. Elsa said the trip—train and bus rides—would take them a bit more than two hours.

A loud squeaking sound repeated itself in an annoying rhythm. Kris looked for its source and spotted a tall, older woman in brown pants and beige linen blazer absent-mindedly spinning the postcard rack, her attention focused elsewhere in the terminal. Kris followed the woman's stare to a bench outside the shop, to where her cousin Elsa, wearing fitted black pants and a bright red leather jacket, was talking animatedly with Nils Dahl.

Still trim, pretty, blonde (with help), and effervescent in her mid-sixties, Elsa probably would still have turned heads even if she wasn't a television personality and noted newspaper columnist. In the few short days that Kris had been in Norway, she had quickly been reminded that her cousin was a local celebrity, although Elsa would be the last to say so.

"Squeak!" That was it! Kris couldn't take it any longer.

"Excuse me," she said, putting her hand on a row of cards and bringing the rack to a halt. The woman shot her an irritated glance, then looked back to Elsa and Nils. Kris pretended to study the scenic photos while she assessed the woman. Nordic features, straight brown hair, no luggage, probably a local. She guessed that the woman recognized Elsa and also Nils, the distinguished editor of Bergen's *Fjordposten*, one of western Norway's largest newspapers.

Perhaps it was the modeling Elsa had done in her youth that contributed to her posture, her presence. Kris had always looked up to her. Women Elsa's age, like this woman at the postcard rack, might just as easily admire—or envy her.

"The Bergen-Oslo train is now boarding on Track Number Two," the announcement blared over the public address system. Elsa took a few steps toward the shop; the woman made a sudden about-face, elbowed her way past Kris, and stooped to study a pile of pamphlets on a low shelf on the back wall. Kris noticed gray roots along the part in the woman's hair.

"Come here," Kris called to Elsa, going to the doorway and motioning to her to enter. But when an elderly German-speaking couple laden with bags crowded in front of Elsa, she simply mouthed back—"we'll meet you at the train"—and she and Nils headed toward the platform.

Kris watched the woman in the beige jacket rise cautiously, make her way through the other browsers, glance in the direction of the platform, then dart out of the shop, and disappear into a group of people leaving the station.

Strange, Kris thought.

"So, my *lille venn*. Are you ready for your fjord adventure?" Elsa asked when Kris joined them.

"Definitely," she smiled, warmed by hearing the nickname "little friend" that Elsa had often called her ever since she was a child.

They settled themselves in facing seats, Kris and Elsa opposite Nils, and the train pulled out of the station. In minutes overhead lights replaced sunlight as the train plunged into the darkness of the tunnel under Mt. Ulriken.

As the train gathered speed, Kris told Elsa and Nils about the woman who had been watching them. "That's why I wanted you to come into the shop."

"Those old Germans got in the way. I have no patience for that generation."

"Elsa, get over it. You can't blame every German for what happened during the war," Nils chided.

"I don't blame the young ones."

"Elsa, you really fascinated the woman in the shop," Kris said, eager to return to her original subject. She didn't want Elsa to begin this weekend reliving painful memories from the Nazi occupation of Norway more than half a century earlier.

"*Fjordposten* folks are well known around town," Nils said. "People recognize us, especially Elsa."

"*Nei,* you're the famous one," Elsa said.

"But she zoomed to the back the moment it looked as if you were coming into the shop," Kris added insistently.

"Okay, describe her," Elsa said, taking a new interest.

"Tall, large frame, not fat. Dyed brown hair, about your age."

"Grete," Elsa said.

Nils grimaced. "Oh, surely not."

"I told you she's going off the deep end again."

"Who's Grete?" Kris asked.

"My wife," Nils said, his ruddy complexion turning ruddier still.

"Why would…" Kris felt a poke in her side.

"I told you she needs help," Elsa said.

"You don't know that for sure. Anyway, there are many women who could fit that description," Nils said. "You have to stop imagining Grete hiding behind every corner."

"Okay. Go ahead, Nils, bury your head in the sand like an ostrich," Elsa said, then turned to Kris. "Did you find some brochures?"

Kris whipped out the Sognefjord brochure and set it on the table between their seats. The photo on the front was a larger version of that on the pamphlet Elsa had brought home the day before.

Elsa raised her half-glasses to her eyes. "Yes, you can see things better here. This is one of the smaller fjords—one of the 'fingers' of the Sognefjord, and that's the Fjord Hotel." She tapped the picture of a stately white building across the river from the village. "See what you're missing, Nils."

"I can't be in two places at once, can I?"

No, fortunately, Kris thought. She was glad he had a conference in Voss and that she would have Elsa to herself for a few days. They had a lot of catching up to do. Sunlight streamed in the window. The tunnel was left behind, as was, noted Kris, the tension over Grete.

Elsa had let her reading glasses, which were attached to a gold chain, fall back to her chest. She took a small blue tablecloth from her rucksack and spread it on the table. Next she unwrapped a wax-paper package of homemade bread, goat cheese, slices of tomato, a small jar of strawberry jam, and almond cookies, and put them all on the tablecloth.

"Wow, Elsa! You think of everything. You'd be a good Girl Scout—you're always prepared."

"Yes, I usually am," Elsa replied. She handed Kris a thermos of hot water and a small orange container filled with an assortment of herbal teas. From a second thermos, she poured coffee into two cups and gave one to Nils. The strong aroma reminded Kris of the enticing smell that had wafted into her room at Elsa's house for the last three mornings. She knew her cousin thought her strange that she loved the smell of coffee but disliked the taste. In fact, when Kris was much younger, Elsa used to tease her when she would refuse coffee: "What kind of Norwegian are you, anyway?" she'd say.

"I remember when you were in Scouts," Elsa was saying now.

"That was a long time ago."

"Yes, you were nine? ten? the first time I visited Seattle?"

"Somewhere around that age. It's all pretty much a blur to me now," Kris said.

From the dimpled smile spreading across Elsa's face, it appeared that the memory was clear to her. "You must have thought I was an old lady," Elsa said. "I was over thirty after all." She laughed.

Kris smiled back at her. She sliced a piece of the brown goat cheese and put it on a thick wedge of bread. The sweet, almost peanut-buttery taste of the cheese blended with the hearty wheat and brought her first memory of this taste of Norway back into focus.

"You brought us *gjetost* when you visited," Kris said. "Nana and Grandpa were so excited."

"Yes, I remember, too, and when your mother served it, you asked where the toast was because everyone, you thought, had been saying 'Yea, toast.'"

They chuckled, then ate in silence, looking out the window. Far different from the landscape of Washington, D.C.'s Maryland suburbs where she had spent now almost half her life, the passing scenery made Kris think of the Pacific Northwest of her childhood. Behind her sunglasses her eyes welled up as she remembered her grandparents and her mother, who had now been gone for so many years. And her father, who was alive but in so many ways gone as well.

The train's ascent provided kaleidoscopic views of mirror lakes, frothy rivers, waterfalls. Brightly painted cottages added splashes of yellow, red, and white to the greens and grays of the landscape.

A few years ago she, Jim, and the kids had made a brief detour to Bergen to see Elsa on their way back to the States after a sabbatical in Israel. Elsa had given them a tour of *Fjordposten*, and they had met Nils. Sitting across from her now, he was as she remembered him: stocky, with thin sandy-colored hair, narrow eyes, and a ruddy complexion. Although he and Elsa had worked together for more than forty years, his friendship with Elsa and her father went further back than that. Elsa had told Kris once that Nils had been her first love. But that was before they each married other people.

"Did you bring your medicine?" Nils asked Elsa, interrupting Kris's thoughts.

"Never mind." Elsa shook her head impatiently.

"What medicine?" Kris asked.

"Oh, nothing. He's just being a mother hen. Don't worry." Elsa poured herself another cup of coffee.

"She's been dizzy," Nils said.

"Have you been to a doctor?"

"Yes. She said it could be a number of things. Maybe blood pressure or an ear infection. I have pills to take; don't worry."

Now things made sense, Kris thought. Her cousin needed to get away for medical reasons. On the way back from the airport Wednesday, Elsa had insisted they wait a week for Kris to get over her jetlag before they made any trips outside the city. Then, already yesterday—Friday—Elsa surprised her by announcing she had booked them on a weekend excursion to the fjords. Long ago she had learned that Elsa often acted on whim, and when her mind was made up, there was no sense in trying to change it.

"You know it's fine with me if you just want to rest at the fjord," she said.

Nils grinned. "Elsa doesn't know how to rest," he said.

"Because you're such a slave driver," Elsa said.

"Rubbish. It's not me; it's you," Nils said. "Even when you were a teenager, your brother Per and I used to call you Miss Never-Stand-Still."

Elsa gave a half-smile. "Yes, you did."

"You should know your cousin by now," Nils said to Kris. "If Elsa gets an idea, she doesn't let go. She's like a pit bull."

Kris had the distinct impression that, under the table, he'd just put his hand on Elsa's knee.

"Oh, pooh. I'd rather be compared to a police dog, or better yet, a Labrador—it has such a good disposition."

"Pit bull," Nils repeated. "You're just like your father!"

"No, Lab. Wouldn't you say, Kris?"

"Not always. You certainly went after Tor Olsen."

"You mean Leif's son?" Nils asked.

"Yes, we met him at the airport when Kris arrived," Elsa explained.

"And practically the first thing she did was ask him if he's still a bachelor," Kris said. "I wanted to disappear."

Nils looked amused. "She didn't propose to him for you?"

"Oh, stop it," Elsa said. "The only thing I did was ask him to dinner so he and Kris could talk."

"For that very night," Kris added.

"I don't waste my time," Elsa said. "Anyway, he couldn't come."

Kris thought about the Jenssens' airport reunion with Tor, who had warmly embraced Elsa's father—Kris's Uncle Andy—and Elsa.

"Papa and Tor's father were in Grini together," Elsa had said when she made introductions.

When she was a child, Kris had heard from her grandparents, and later Elsa, of Uncle Andy's imprisonment in Grini—a Nazi internment camp near Oslo during World War II. She had read about the savage beatings, the torture—often deadly. Elsa's and Tor's fathers had been among the lucky ones who survived.

"Actually, they remained good friends until my father's death some years ago," Tor had said.

Tor's blue eyes and easy smile were accompanied by a strong hand-shake. Tall, with a red-blond beard and balding head, he had been wearing jeans and a short-sleeved shirt. He had a tattoo of a Viking ship on his upper right arm. He fit Kris's image of a hardy Norwegian who would work on an oil rig in the North Sea—which was what he did for the Norwegian company, Statoil. What she hadn't expected was his American English, which he spoke with only the slightest Norwegian lilt.

She remembered smoothing the front of her hair with her left hand, hoping Tor would notice the wedding ring that she still wore.

"He's single, isn't he? Divorced?" Nils asked.

"Oh, yes, for many years. He says he keeps running faster than the women," Elsa said with a laugh. "You met his parents when you were a girl, Kris."

"I don't remember that."

Kris thought back to the first time she had visited Norway. She had been sixteen. Twenty-four years had passed, yet memories of parts of that summer would never leave her. Her mother's fatal accident; her father's breakdown. Her stay with her grandparents, then a month with Elsa in Norway—a month of healing was the only way to explain it. But she couldn't remember Tor's parents.

"Sorry, it just doesn't ring a bell," she said, slowly shaking her head.

"Do you remember the trip we made with Mother and Father out to the islands?"

"Vaguely."

"I know you will remember it," Elsa insisted. "Remember the house by the bay and the raft that you 'sailed' on?"

"Raft?" The word jarred her memory. Kris pictured the wooden raft that had allowed her to temporarily forget her sadness. "I loved it, pushing it around with a big oar," she recalled. I think I spent all day on it." She remembered an energetic older couple who owned the house and the raft. "Didn't we have *kransekake* on their porch?" she asked, remembering the first time she saw and tasted the cone-shaped, multiringed almond cake decorated with drizzles of frosting and small ornamental red, white, and blue Norwegian flags.

Elsa smiled. "That's right."

"But I don't remember meeting Tor."

"No, he would have been in the navy or at university," Elsa said. "He's a good man. You need to meet some good men, be social again. He's about your age, no, maybe a few years older, in his early or mid-forties. And don't worry about that instant dinner invitation. He has known me since he was a boy. Nothing I say would surprise him."

"So when will he come for dinner?" Nils asked. "I know you don't take 'no' for an answer when you want something."

"He said he would call me on Sunday," Elsa said. She took a small blue-and-white pack of candies from her pocket. "Peppermint, anyone?"

All that with Tor had happened, of course, before Elsa booked this excursion, Kris reminded herself as she savored the peppermint. In spite of his raft and the kindness of his parents many years ago, she hoped that if indeed Tor called tomorrow, he would give up when no one answered the phone. She did not want to deal with Elsa's matchmaking, definitely not now, maybe not ever.

The conductor announced that Voss would be the next stop.

"I almost forgot 'old faithful,'" Elsa said. She pulled her camera from her rucksack.

"Not your old Minolta?" Nils said when he saw it. "Where's the new camera I gave you for your birthday?"

"I couldn't find it. Here, quick, take a photograph of Kris and me." Elsa handed the camera to him, then reached her arm around Kris, "Say *gjetost*."

Kris laughed.

Elsa recruited a boy from across the aisle to take a photo of all of them; this time Elsa snuggled close to Nils. Picture taken, she folded up her picnic kit and put it and the camera back in her bag.

CHAPTER 2

▼

The bus from Voss, where Nils had left them after the train ride, crossed a lush plateau before beginning its descent. Kris sat by the window taking in the landscape. Beside her, Elsa—her knitting needles clicking away—busily connected blue and white yarns, making another sweater for refugee children, and, all the while watching the scenery.

"So what's the story with Nils's wife?" Kris asked.

"She's paranoid sometimes. When their children were young, she was in a sanitarium for a while. She recovered, or at least we thought she had."

"Nils seems to think she's all right."

"Yes, that's one of the things on which we disagree. Oh, look!"

"I'd rather not," Kris said, noticing that the shoulder of the road outside her window seemed about two hundred feet below them. Each time the bus made one of the sharp zig-zagging turns, her stomach did too. The side of the bus appeared to overhang the edge. She wrapped her hand around the end of the armrest.

Elsa stopped knitting. "Your face is the color of the kiwi we had last night, Kristina. Heights don't bother me. Here, let me change places with you."

"Gladly." Kris took the aisle seat for the remainder of the trip. The bus let them off in front of the post office near the village wharf and the glistening fjord waters.

Across the small bay, the white three-storied Fjord Hotel with dormers and lace-like carved trim, and a red, white, and blue Norwegian flag waving on the front lawn, held the promise of the rejuvenating retreat for which Kris yearned. She took a long breath of the clean, fresh air. The temperature had to be in the seventies.

"Miss Jenssen? Mrs. Kelly?"

"Yes?"

"Welcome. I am Hasan. I am here to take you to the hotel." He reached for Elsa's black bag and Kris's overnighter.

Swarthy, thirtyish, and muscular, Hasan, Kris thought, looked more like a member of the original "Mission Impossible" team than a chauffeur. She guessed he was from southern Europe or the Middle East. He escorted them to a van with *Fjord Hotel* written on its sides. When Kris and Elsa were settled in the back seat, Hasan started the van and pulled out into the main street, heading in the direction of the hotel.

Kris liked the village at once—busy shops were housed in brightly painted wooden buildings with red and pink geranium-filled planters outside the doorways. Victorian houses lined a winding lane leading away from the shops and up the mountainside. A small gray church with flowers climbing a corner of its façade stood at the edge of the village, near the river. Kris recalled that the dragon heads decorating the gables were an old Viking symbol of protection. People strolled along the wooden promenade that ran a mile or two from the village to the hotel.

Kris started to relax; here she could begin to get a new perspective on life. As they approached the hotel, she admired its reflection shimmering in the water and a sleek white yacht moored at the end of the dock. The hotel entrance was at the back under an overhanging roof.

"Pool, exercise room, sauna," Hasan said, nodding toward the A-frame building across from the hotel.

Hasan opened the van door for them. Kris and Elsa stepped out on to the slate entryway.

"I smell roses," Elsa said.

"From our rose garden." The man who spoke appeared to be in his late sixties, with flecks of gray in his dark hair. Short, with a slight build, he wore gray slacks, a long-sleeved white business shirt, and sports coat. "Miss Jenssen? I'm Oscar Larsen, proprietor here. Welcome to the Fjord Hotel; it's an honor to meet you."

"Thank you," Elsa said, shaking his hand. "And it's an honor for me to meet you."

"Oh, I'm not so sure about that," Oscar said modestly.

It was sheer Elsa, Kris thought, watching her cousin's gracious acknowledgment and Oscar's reaction. Elsa knew how to charm, how to break the ice with people.

"And you are Mrs. Kelly?"

"Yes," Kris reached out her hand.

"Welcome to Norway," he said, giving her a hearty handshake as well. "And this is Dag." He gestured toward a friendly black Labrador retriever, who came bounding down the driveway, tail wagging.

"Hi, Dag," Kris said, scratching him behind the ears. He ambled along beside them into the spacious lobby and the reception area.

Like most Norwegians, Oscar spoke English well. He checked them in at the reception desk, marking their names in a large, three-ring binder about four inches thick, while a young clerk tapped their registration information into the computer. A TV mounted on the wall behind the desk flashed CNN news. Kris glimpsed Israeli Prime Minister Yitzhak Rabin making a statement about his hopes for the new round of talks between Israelis and Palestinians.

"Maybe in September, I will be again on the White House lawn," Elsa said, the excitement clear in her voice.

"Let's hope," Kris said, remembering Elsa's visit to Washington two years earlier for the historic signing of the peace agreement between the Israelis and Palestinians, brought about by Norway's having arranged secret meetings between the two sides.

Oscar accompanied them up the stairs to the second floor and a spacious room with flowered wallpaper, soft green carpeting, and twin beds covered with snow-white duvets. Two pine bedside tables matched an armoire near the door to the bathroom and a dressing table, on which sat a basket of fruit and chocolates. Glass doors opened on to a covered balcony with gingerbread trim and a breathtaking view of the fjord, village, and mountains.

Dinner, Oscar said, would be served at seven o'clock in the dining room; in the meantime, they should ring him at the front desk if they needed anything.

"Shall we sit on the balcony and have some fruit?" Kris asked after he left. She picked up the basket.

"You go ahead. I forgot to ask him something." With that Elsa was gone.

"Still Miss Never-Stand-Still," Kris said to the empty room. She put the basket back on the table and decided to unpack. She took out her photo of Charlie and Laura and, as she kissed it, felt a lump in her throat remembering their graduation seven weeks earlier. "Weren't they just born?" Jim had whispered as they had watched the twins march into the high school gym to the strains of "Pomp and Circumstance." Kris had cried, not just the usual parental tears of pride mixed with grief for the passing of childhood, but also for the family that used to be. Afterwards all four of them had stood together for this photo, taken by Elsa: Laura and Charlie in royal blue caps and gowns, Kris between them, Jim next to Charlie. Jim's hand on Charlie's shoulder was the only sign left of him now, for she had cut him out of the picture.

She should have seen it coming, but hadn't. She had told herself that Jim's attention to Janet, his graduate student assistant, had been no different than that he paid to their other guests at parties they hosted. Besides he was Janet's mentor. Then, the day after Christmas, Jim had told Kris that it was more than that; that he wanted a divorce. Her world had come crashing down on her.

At least now she could think of that night and the past several months without crying. Yet she still felt hollow inside.

Elsa's return to their room brought her back to the present.

"What did you find out from Oscar?" she asked.

"The weather forecast."

"It looks sunny to me."

"Yes, for now. We may have some rain tonight."

"Why didn't you just call him?" Kris asked.

"Oh, I didn't think of that," Elsa said.

"Are you feeling all right?" Kris wondered if perhaps Elsa's dizziness had returned.

"Obviously better than you," Elsa said. "What's the matter?" Her eyes fell on the photograph. "Oh!"

Kris put the framed photo on the bedside table. "I was just missing the way things used to be. I still keep asking myself why Jim did what he did, what I did wrong."

"You can't think of it that way," Elsa said, motioning for Kris to sit beside her on the bed. "It's nothing you did. It's just something that happened. And I know it hurts terribly. I remember when Sterling left me."

"For another woman?" Kris asked. Elsa had rarely spoken of the British film director to whom she had been briefly married in the late 1950s.

"Yes. I should have realized I was just his flavor of the month, or rather year. I was swept away by the glitter and glamour of film and our visits to Hollywood. Of course, it's different with you and Jim—you made a family together; you were married for many years. But I've lived long enough to know, Kristina, that sometimes people can't explain what they do for love, or what they think is love. They don't want to hurt anyone, but they do." She gave Kris a hug. "You've been through tough times before, and you'll make it through this, too."

"With your help. Thanks for always being there for me," Kris said, savoring her cousin's warmth.

"Now, come," Elsa said. She picked up the fruit basket and walked out onto the balcony.

"When your mother died, you didn't have the life experience that you have now, Kristina. I'm here for you as always, but you don't need me. You just need time to find yourself again. Remember, you're a Jenssen. You'll make it! You must start a new life. You must meet new men. Now Tor Olsen, he is a good man. You'll see."

"I'm sure he's very nice."

"Not just nice, but exciting! He is an adventurer or at least he used to be—climbing mountains, doing triathlons, scuba diving. You would find him very interesting."

"Sorry, not interested," Kris replied.

"We'll see," Elsa said, selecting a bright red apple from the basket. "We'll just see."

CHAPTER 3

▼

At five minutes to seven, Kris and Elsa went down to the dining room, where they were greeted by the savory smells of dinner.

The maitre d' gave Elsa a second look upon hearing her name. "Welcome, Miss Jenssen," he said, bowing and extending his hand. "We are honored to have you here. This way, please."

Kris was struck by the medley of languages and the preponderance of gray heads among the seated guests. At least here among tourists Elsa could enjoy anonymity—or could she? Kris felt eyes upon them as they followed the maitre d' across the room. Perhaps it was simply because of Elsa's striking appearance. She wore a long black skirt with a pink silk blouse belted at the waist, and gold accessories. She walked confidently behind the maitre d', seemingly oblivious to the other diners. Kris tried to do the same until she felt her earring leave her ear and heard it hit the wood floor. She stopped and scanned the floor, seeing only pantlegs, table legs, chair legs. If she would just give in to fashion and get her ears pierced, this wouldn't happen. What now?

"Is this what you're looking for?"

She looked up. An attractive black man with military bearing and an American accent smiled at her and handed her the circular gold earring.

"Thank you so much," she said gratefully, then hurried off to catch up with Elsa and the maitre d', who were already on the other side of the room. Making her way through a sea of tables, Kris stiffened at the sight of a woman with brown hair, wearing a beige linen jacket. Without altering her pace, she glanced at the woman's face as she passed. Indeed, it was the woman from the train station—and her eyes were fixed on Elsa.

Kris caught up with Elsa at a table set for five near the windows. Two of their tablemates were already seated: a distinguished-looking man with silver-gray hair and an exotically beautiful woman with dark, doll-like eyes set in an oval face. She looked, Kris thought, like the subject of a Modigliani painting. The man stood. Kris was struck by his erect posture. "Good evening, I am George Mueller and this is my wife, Yolanda."

Kris and Elsa introduced themselves. The Muellers oozed affluence. Kris put George's age at a well-preserved seventy. Yolanda, deeply suntanned, her black hair pulled back in a bun, was perhaps in her fifties.

Name cards designated their places—Elsa near the window, across from Yolanda. Kris opposite George. A fifth place was as yet unoccupied. In the center of the mauve tablecloth, a white candle burned in a frosted-glass holder shaped like a snowball.

It took Elsa less than a minute to engage the Muellers in pleasantries and establish that they were from Venezuela.

"Mueller is not a Venezuelan name, is it?" Elsa said. "Is it German?"

"Yes, it is," George said.

Kris felt the floor vibrate and looked up to see a large man approaching the table.

"Good evening," he said in a booming voice, pausing to introduce himself to Kris and Elsa. "I am Max Guttmann," he said. They went through perfunctory introductions. Max said he was from Munich. When he took his place at the end of the table, Yolanda and George each steadied their wine glasses, letting go only after the table had settled.

"George and Max have discovered they share a love of art, fishing, and German beer," Yolanda said. In spite of her Latin appearance, her accent, Kris thought, sounded British.

"No beer for us tonight though," George said jovially. "Will you join us in a glass of *Liebfraumilch*?" He signaled a waiter, who poured wine for all of them.

"Let us drink to the honeymoon," Max said, raising his glass.

"Honeymoon?" Kris wondered where his wife was.

"Ours," George said. He put his arm around Yolanda's shoulders.

"Congratulations!" Kris said.

"Yes, congratulations," Elsa echoed. "*Skoal*."

Out of deference to the occasion, Kris took a sip of the wine and felt Elsa's approving glance. Much to her cousin's dismay, Kris's mild aversion to alcohol was similar to her dislike for coffee.

A server brought them steaming bowls of creamy mushroom soup. Its appetizing smell reminded Kris how hungry she was.

"The food here is *wunderbar*," Max said, spreading his napkin across his broad midriff. "Have George and Yolanda told you about their children?" He slurped a spoonful of soup and swallowed; his double chins seeming to vibrate from the effort.

"We have an orphanage," George explained.

Kris wondered if he'd noticed her startled look when Max mentioned children.

"They are our family," Yolanda said. She smiled at her husband and reached for the bread basket to pass it around. Kris eyed Yolanda's shiny red fingernails and cluster of rings. One extraordinary flower-like ring stood out from the rest with its emerald center surrounded by petals of small brilliant diamonds. The conversation centered around the orphanage that had brought George and Yolanda together. He had founded it twenty years earlier; she had arrived there three years ago as a teacher, and they had fallen in love. The forty children were their family.

"I can't imagine taking care of so many children," Kris said.

"Our country, like Norway, has oil. I've been fortunate with my investments."

"Oh, I didn't mean it that way," Kris hastened to assure him. "I just meant that I had my hands full with twins."

"Twins?" George replied with interest. "How old are they?"

"Eighteen."

"No, madam. You don't look old enough to have children that age."

"Thank you." Kris smiled and blushed slightly at his compliment. Whether he meant it or not, she thought, George knew the right things to say. She liked him. He was affable, a kind of father figure. Perhaps it came naturally with nurturing children.

"What took you to Venezuela?" Elsa asked.

"The war," George said, breaking a roll in half. "Many of us—Jews and non-Jews alike—lost our homes. I was a displaced person—they called us DPs. I had lost my family; I wanted to start a new life."

Elsa nodded. "Yes, I'm afraid many people had to do that. And you are British, I presume," she said, looking at Yolanda.

"No, but I attended boarding school and university in England."

"In London?"

"Yes."

"I spent several years in London myself in the mid-fifties," Elsa offered. "Perhaps we were there at the same time?"

"Unlikely," Yolanda said.

"But, I feel as if we have met before," Elsa continued. "Perhaps we had a class together in London?"

Yolanda shook her head in the negative. She wiped her right eye in an effort, it seemed, to remove an irritant. "Excuse me for a moment, please."

"Shall I come with you, *querida*," George asked.

"No, my dear, it is not necessary," she said.

George's look of concern followed Yolanda out of the room.

Kris broke the awkward silence. "So, Mr. Guttmann, how did you come to choose the Fjord Hotel for your vacation?"

"Oh, I like fish, and I like art. You see, this place has both. I am a collector."

"Of art or fish?" Kris asked.

Max laughed heartily, his chins joining in. "I would be quite happy to collect fish, but they do not always cooperate. Art is another matter. Have you seen the fine works of art here?"

"Yes, I noticed them this afternoon." Kris recalled the oil paintings in the parlors just outside the dining room. "But I admit I'm not familiar with the artists."

"I will be happy to give you a lesson if you have time."

"Perhaps tomorrow."

"Are you an art collector or an art dealer?" Elsa asked.

"Both," Max said, spreading butter on a roll. "I am an art dealer so that I can afford to be a collector."

Yolanda returned to the table, assuring her husband that her eye was all right again. Kris noticed that the lashes of both eyes seemed to have received a thick new layer of mascara.

Through most of the rest of the dinner—boiled potatoes, summer greens, and cod with a cream sauce—Max entertained them with stories of his adventures searching for valuable pieces of art. Yolanda showed an impressive knowledge of European painters and contributed often to Max's stories. Kris listened, now and then stealing glances across the room at the woman from the train station.

Oscar came over to their table as they were finishing dessert—fresh berries with a dollop of whipped cream. "I invite you to the library at nine o'clock for refreshment. I shall talk about the hiking in this area."

Kris liked how Oscar, like most Norwegians when speaking English, used "shall"—the literal translation of the frequently used Norwegian "skal"—instead of "will," adding to their delightful lilt.

"Yolanda, that is for us," George said.

"And for us also, Kris," Elsa said.

"Until nine then," Max said as they all stood up.

Kris bade them a good evening. Pretending to be preoccupied with the view, she held Elsa back and waited until the others were out of earshot. Then she whispered, "She's here."

"Who?"

"The wo…"

"Hello, Elsa," a woman's voice interrupted Kris.

Elsa whirled around. "Grete? What are you doing here?" she asked.

"What are *you* doing here?" The woman said back to her.

Kris could only watch open-mouthed at this encounter between her cousin and the woman from the Bergen train station who was, obviously, Nils's wife. Elsa had been right.

"I'm with my cousin from America. Kris, this is Grete Dahl."

"Nice to meet you," Kris said, resisting the temptation to pull her hand away too quickly from Grete's clammy handshake. She had a chance now to get a better look at Grete's face, to note the worry lines across her forehead; the slight collapse of her lower cheeks, perhaps a sign of ill-fitting dentures.

"Nils didn't tell me you were coming," Elsa said.

"Because he doesn't know. It's a surprise."

Elsa looked as confused as Kris felt. "But Nils is in Voss." She walked as she talked, leading them steadily toward the lobby. It was as if she wanted to hear what Grete had to say, and at the same time, to get away from her.

"Yes, I shall be here with Nils," Grete said.

"Nils isn't coming here," Elsa said. "By the way, were you at the train station this morning?"

The creases deepened between Grete's eyebrows. "I came by boat."

"That doesn't answer my question. Come, let's call Nils."

"He will not be there."

"Let's try."

"No." Grete stormed off.

Kris put her hand on Elsa's arm. "What are you going to do?"

"I'm going to call Nils," Elsa said.

But, as Grete predicted, he was not in.

CHAPTER 4

▼

Oscar welcomed Kris and Elsa to the wood-paneled library. "Please be comfortable." He gestured toward two couches and four armchairs arranged around two beautifully set coffee tables. The floor was covered by a Persian carpet, its design woven in golds, black, reds, and turquoise.

The Muellers stood near the door admiring a painting. "Everything is exactly as I remember it," George was saying as Kris and Elsa joined them. Kris glanced at the picture of Bergen harbor.

"You have visited Bergen then?" Elsa asked.

"Yes, a few days ago," George said. "But I was also in Bergen shortly after the war on my way to South America. This painting reminds me of that time. This is how I remember it."

"Your comparisons as a visitor then and now would make a very interesting story," Elsa said. "Would you consider being on my show on Norwegian television? I would like very much to interview you."

"Oh, no, no thank you," George said, shaking his head. "I have already been interviewed on Norwegian television."

"Oh, really?"

"Yes, it was quite amusing," George said. "When we arrived at our hotel in Bergen, a reporter was asking tourists about their reactions to Norway, and I was one of those people."

"But you mean for only a few minutes?"

"Yes."

"Oh, but I mean a longer interview, perhaps an hour?"

Oscar, who had been listening, interrupted. "Miss Jenssen is famous in Norway for her interviews."

"I'm flattered," George said.

"We are on our honeymoon, Miss Jenssen," Yolanda interrupted. She linked her arm with George's.

"Yes," he agreed. "It's very kind of you to ask, but the only woman to whom I give my time and attention is my bride." He looked adoringly at Yolanda and clasped her hand.

Kris was drawn to the view of the mountains. As she walked away from Elsa and the Muellers, she heard Elsa say, "Perhaps you will change your mind." That was typical Elsa—not wanting to take "no" for an answer. The man who had found Kris's earring at dinner stood near expansive windows, holding the hand of a woman in a red polo shirt just like his. She approached the couple.

"Hi. I'm Kris Kelly. Thank you for rescuing my earring."

"Hey, no problem," the man said. He had an infectious smile. "I'm Bill Stephens."

"And I'm Rachel." Rachel's frizzy red hair ballooned out around her delicate ivory face.

Kris felt an immediate affinity with her fellow Americans. She learned that Bill was a U.S. Army physician, stationed near Naples, Italy, and Rachel worked in an office on the base but also created jewelry—including the long dangly silver earrings she was wearing. The couple said they were on holiday.

"I have to ask you," Kris said, unable to contain her curiosity, "why did you choose to come to Norway when Italy is so beautiful?"

Bill pointed to Rachel. "She chose. I had dreams of the Riviera."

"Oh, you big tease," Rachel said, hitting his arm playfully with her hand. "We both said we wanted to see Norway while we were in Europe. We wanted to go hiking. And look how warm the weather has been—it's almost like the Riviera."

"Yeah, sure. That's why Hasan's making a fire," Bill said, laughing.

At the end of the room Hasan knelt in front of the stone fireplace, wadding up newspapers and stuffing them inside a tepee of kindling. A second later he struck a match and the stack imploded in flames.

"Let us begin," Oscar said, calling the group together.

Elsa, the Muellers, and Max had already taken seats near the coffee tables. Kris chose a comfortable armchair; Rachel and Bill sat on one of the couches. Oscar beckoned a lanky young man standing by the bookshelves to join the group.

"This is Odd Engstrom," he said.

Sourpuss Engstrom might have been a better name, Kris thought. He wore jeans and a black leather biker's jacket and sported an earring in his left ear. He took a seat next to her, but his shaven head turned immediately toward the door where a wholesome young woman entered with a tray of cream cakes. She was followed by Grete who, Kris noticed, avoided eye contact with Elsa.

"We will have a small group tonight," Oscar said. "Many guests are tired by this hour. I shall tell you now about the hiking while Inga and Hasan serve you coffee and cakes, or if you wish *aquavit*, our famous liquor."

He walked over near the windows. "Please look this way," he said.

Outside the evening light spread across the mountains, long blue shadows accented steep rocky crags. The scene gave Kris a feeling of tranquility.

"You can see many waterfalls from here," Oscar said, "but the greatest you cannot see. Where you think you see two mountains coming together, it is one mountain deeply cut by nature. That is where you will find Hidden Falls."

He handed them maps.

"What's this word next to Hidden Falls," Bill asked. "Schoolteafossen?"

"That's *Skjultefossen*; it sounds like 'shultefossen," Elsa said. "It's a strange way of saying Hidden Falls."

"Ah," Oscar said. "Miss Jenssen, of course, you would know," he said to Elsa, and you, too, of course, Mrs. Dahl," he said, acknowledging his other compatriot. And then to the others. "It is true what Miss Jenssen says. I've been told that the original name of the falls was *Juvfossen*—the falls in the gorge—but, for many decades, locals always referred to it as '*den skjulte fossen*'—the falls that are hidden. As time went by, some folks coined the name, *Skjultefossen*—a word that, as Miss Jenssen says, sounds strange to Norwegians who aren't from around here. As more and more English-speaking tourists started coming here, we just started calling it by the English translation, Hidden Falls, and that makes it easier for everyone."

"Well, Hidden Falls is sure a lot easier to say," Bill quipped.

Several others in the room nodded in agreement.

His language explanation finished, Oscar referred to the map and described to the guests their hiking options. They could go by foot or hotel van two miles past the church to the ravine and the bottom of the falls. Or a mile uphill from the village to a trail that would take them to the top of the falls. From either point they would have the additional option of taking a connecting trail so they could walk from the top of the gorge to the bottom or vice versa.

"Which way is best for us?" George asked. "We wish to walk, but we are not mountain goats."

Kris joined the others in laughter.

"I would recommend the trail above the village; it starts near the Roma Restaurant," Oscar answered.

"Roma Restaurant?" Bill exclaimed. "You mean we've come all the way to Norway, and we still get Italian food?"

"Norwegians are just like everyone else—we like to have our pizza," Elsa said, smiling.

"They should take it back where it came from," Odd said under his breath.

Rather a rude remark, Kris thought.

"If you have any more questions about hiking, I will be happy to answer them," Oscar, who had apparently heard Odd's remark, said sternly.

"What is the weather forecast for tomorrow?" Elsa asked.

What was with Elsa and the weather? Kris wondered.

"Maybe a shower tonight, a few clouds in the morning. Then it will clear up and be warm like today."

Oscar left to get some additional materials, and guests began to talk amongst themselves. Kris tried to make conversation with Odd. "Do you do a lot of hiking?"

"Yes, when I'm not working," he said, not lifting his eyes from his plate.

"What kind of work do you do?" Kris persisted.

"Computer programming."

"That's a good profession to be in these days," she said. "Where are you from?"

"Bergen." He spoke through his teeth, hardly opening his mouth except now and then to accommodate his fork piled high with cake.

"My cousin is also from Bergen."

"Hmm," Odd mumbled, his barely moving lips iced with cream.

He was definitely not a talker, Kris concluded. She took a bite of her own cake, savoring the rich taste and texture, and listening to snippets of the conversations of the other guests.

"Our *OktoberFest* is world famous," Max was saying to Bill.

"We had lived near the Polish border," George was telling Elsa, who was again knitting without looking at her needles.

"How long will you be in Norway?"

Kris realized that Grete was speaking directly to her. She turned toward her and replied, "Not quite two weeks. It's a lovely country. Have you..." She let her words trail off as Grete's attention fixed on the two women across from them.

"Yes, I know how to appraise jewelry," Rachel was saying to Yolanda. "My father was a jeweler and gemologist. I learned from him."

"Can you tell me something about this ring?" Yolanda asked, extending her hand toward Rachel. "I don't like to remove it."

"That's okay," Rachel said. She leaned forward and studied the ring. "It's stunning; clearly an antique and quite valuable. I would need to inspect it more closely, though, to give you an estimate of its worth."

Yolanda looked pleased.

Hasan brought Kris the apple tea she had requested. Kris took the cup from his tray, noticing that he, too, was looking at the ring. Then, as if remembering he had a job to do, he turned to Odd and asked if he would like coffee.

"I don't want coffee or anything from you!" Odd hissed, to everyone's astonishment. "You shouldn't be here anyway, you foreigner! You come and take jobs away from the rest of us." He leapt from his chair, practically knocking the tray from Hasan's hands.

Kris pushed her feet against the floor, moving her chair back an inch, unsure what would happen next.

"I'm not taking jobs away from anyone," Hasan declared. He gave Odd a piercing stare.

"You don't belong here!" Odd shouted.

"Bigots don't belong here!" Elsa shouted back, stepping between the two men. She grabbed Odd's arm. "Shame on you! This is no way for anyone, especially a Norwegian, to behave."

Odd, several inches taller than Elsa, gave her a cold, menacing look and pulled his arm away. Kris immediately moved to her cousin's side; Hasan took a step forward. But it was as if Odd saw neither of them, only Elsa.

"I know who you are. I read the papers; I watch television. I know what you think about these people," he shouted. "You want to sell us out. You want people like him to get free help with our taxes and then take our jobs!"

"Do you want his job?" Elsa snapped.

"Who wants a job?" Oscar said, re-entering the room and just catching the end of Elsa and Odd's exchange.

Odd looked through him and stormed out the door.

"That was shocking," George said. Others agreed.

"Oh, my," Elsa said. "I feel dizzy." She put her hand on her forehead.

"You'd better lie down," Bill said, helping Elsa to the couch that he and Rachel had vacated moments before.

Kris helped Elsa stretch out and elevate her feet, while Bill held her wrist.

"You're pulse is a bit fast," he said. "You'd better just rest here a while."

After about five minutes, Elsa sat up. "I'm okay now, thank you. But I think I'll go back to my room."

"We'll go with you," Bill said.

"No, no." Elsa swung her feet around to the floor. "You both stay here."

"No way," Bill responded firmly. "Rachel's gone to get my bag. Kris and I will go with you to your room, so I can make sure you're okay. If you are, we'll leave you alone. Fair enough?"

To Kris's surprise, Elsa agreed.

In Kris and Elsa's room, Bill checked Elsa's vital signs, all of which were normal—as was her behavior. She insisted in no uncertain terms that Kris and Bill get back to the "party."

When they returned to the library, most everyone was gone, except for Rachel, Max, and Oscar, who was relieved to hear that Elsa was okay. They chatted until ten-thirty, when Kris excused herself.

She found Elsa sitting at the vanity, writing in her notebook. She looked cozy and relaxed in her silk pajamas.

"I think I was just tired," Elsa said.

Kris was reassured by the healthy color of her cheeks. "You've had quite a day, haven't you?"

"Oh, yes, that's for sure," she said. "That Odd upset me so much!"

"But, there are prejudiced people everywhere."

"That doesn't excuse him. He's too young to think such garbage. I must talk to him."

"Why?"

"To change his mind."

Kris sighed. "What makes you think you can do that?"

"I don't give up easily."

"What did Nils call you? A pit bull? By the way, did you call him?"

"I tried; he's still not in."

"I don't understand how Grete knew you were here."

"Maybe Nils told her. Who knows?"

"Well, I wish Nils were here. She scares me."

"Oh, pooh. Grete may be a bit crazy, but she's harmless. By the way, I found out that Hasan is from Bosnia. I'm going to try to finish that sweater and give it to him for a child in his family."

"That would be nice," Kris said.

"Tell me," Elsa said, "What did you think of the Muellers?"

"I thought your idea for an interview was good. George is charming; Yolanda is a snob—and maybe a golddigger."

"You think she married him for his money? What makes you think so?"

"For one thing, she's younger than him by a decade or two." Kris spoke to Elsa's reflection in the mirror.

Elsa looked thoughtful, as if she hadn't considered the idea until now. "She's not as young as she looks. I don't think she's much younger than me. She could already be sixty. He might be seventy; seventy-five."

"He doesn't look that old."

"Well, these days it's hard to tell. Anyway, I want to know why Yolanda was hiding behind the plant."

"What plant?" Kris thought back to their conversations with the Muellers; she couldn't remember any plants near them.

"Oh, nothing. I was just talking to myself."

"Do you really think you know her from somewhere?"

"Oh, I don't know." She sounded tired.

"Elsa, are you sure you're up to hiking tomorrow? Maybe you should rest."

Elsa was bright-eyed. "I'll rest afterwards. I want to go."

"Why don't we play it by ear?" Even as Kris said it, she set her alarm for seven. She had looked forward too long to hiking in Norway to cancel tomorrow's plan—unless it was absolutely necessary. After all, she could go on her own if Elsa needed to sleep in.

Elsa closed her notebook and walked with it to the armoire where she rummaged through her bag.

"I have a surprise for you." She handed Kris a small white box.

"What's the occasion?"

"You," Elsa answered. "I am glad you're here."

"You don't need to give me a gift; being with you is my gift." Kris gave her a hug. "You've been like a mother to me for so many years; I don't know what I'd do without you."

"Open the box," Elsa prodded with childlike excitement.

Inside was a medallion of gold Olympic rings on a gold chain. "Wow! It's gorgeous."

"It is from last year's Olympic Games in Lillehammer. I want you to have it, to always remember that you are a winner."

"Oh, Elsa," Kris said, at a loss for words. She put the medallion around her neck. Then, adhering to an old Norwegian custom, she shook Elsa's hand and thanked her with a slight curtsy. "*Tusen takk,*" she said. A thousand thanks.

"Come, I have something for us. Take a sweater and let's go to the balcony," Elsa said.

Kris relished the fresh, moist air, the silence, and the dark outline of the mountains against a shadowy charcoal-clouded sky. From pockets of fog on the fjord she could see the faint lights of fishing boats. Closer to shore, the yacht at the hotel's pier was illuminated by a strand of lights from the top of the mast to the pilothouse. It felt as if it was going to rain, but Kris didn't care. Nothing could dampen her spirits here. Even without the moon, night hovered between twilight and blackness. Far to the north, above the Arctic Circle, it would be daylight still.

"Come, sit down," Elsa said.

On the small table between their chairs, there were two glasses of a burgundy-colored beverage, each covered by a napkin.

"This is lingonberry juice from Sweden, a special treat. Let's drink to the future, *Lille venn*." Elsa said, removing the napkins and handing a glass to Kris; then holding up her own. "*Skoal.*"

"*Skoal,*" Kris repeated, touching her glass to Elsa's.

CHAPTER 5

▼

Now all of Kris's hopes for this trip were forgotten as she clutched Elsa's lifeless body, wanting to protect her from the thundering waterfall nearby but knowing it was too late.

"Mrs. Kelly. Come," Oscar coaxed. "They must prepare to take your cousin away."

Kris felt his hand on her arm, gently urging her to rise. Reluctantly, she loosened her grip on Elsa's shoulders and moved into a sitting position. Oscar knelt beside her as did a middle-aged policeman, who introduced himself as Sven Bjornstad, district sheriff.

She nodded.

"I give you my condolences," he said, extending his hand to her. "When the news is out about your cousin's death, many Norwegians will weep with you. Elsa Jenssen was our conscience. Truly one of our greatest journalists."

"Thank you," Kris said, but she hardly felt ready to accept condolences. She wanted answers. "What happened?"

"It is possible she fell from that ledge."

Kris followed the sheriff's gaze upwards. High above them the falls roared out of clusters of bushes and trees; several feet below the top a ledge jutted out from the rock wall. The drop was at least a hundred feet, rocks everywhere.

"But Elsa was an experienced hiker. I don't see how…"

"Madame, I have men up there now," Bjornstad said. "They tell me the trail and the rocks are still wet from rain."

The furrows in Oscar's brow deepened. He shook his head. "I shouldn't have let her go. She was a guest in my hotel. I had no idea this would happen."

Bjornstad gave Oscar a sympathetic nod and continued to address Kris. "Your cousin could have gotten too close to the edge and slipped off. I understand she had some trouble with dizziness last evening. Can you tell me about that?"

"It was just for a moment, and it passed very quickly. The doctor said she was fine afterwards. She wouldn't have gone hiking if she wasn't feeling well," Kris said, although she couldn't be sure she was right. "Where are the people she was hiking with? Surely someone can explain what happened."

"My men are trying to find them."

What if Elsa had a dizzy spell on the ledge? Kris looked away from the falls, but she could not block out the steady roar of the waterfall, the torrent that must have engulfed Elsa, and hurled her against the rocks. Maybe, Kris prayed, Elsa fainted. Maybe she was unconscious before she fell, numb to the blows and cuts of the rocks. Kris wiped her eyes and tried to focus on the sheriff.

"Who found Elsa?" she asked.

"Hikers. They asked Mr. Guttmann for help," Bjornstad said; he gestured for Max, who was standing next to another officer, to join them. He had a blanket wrapped around his massive body, from under his arms to above his knees. His plaid shirt and heavy pants were drenched. He held rubber hip boots under his arm.

"I am so sorry," he said to Kris. "I pulled her from the water, but there was no life in her." He pointed toward the pool where the water swirled from the force of the falls then quieted among the shelter of some boulders, before feeding into the river.

"Did you see what happened?" Kris asked.

His double chins shook. "No, those two boys called to me for help. They saw her first. When I got here, it was too late." He reached his thick hand toward hers. "I am sorry I could not save her."

Kris grasped his hand for a moment unable to speak. She stared at the outline of Elsa's body now covered by a sheet less than ten feet away. If only she had awakened earlier…

Hasan shouted to them from where he stood at the edge of the water. Kris watched as he lifted a long-handled fisherman's net and brought it dripping to Bjornstad. The sheriff reached inside and pulled out a small black box.

"Mrs. Kelly, could this be your cousin's camera?" he asked.

It was bashed in on all sides, lens shattered. Kris turned it over in her hands. The brand name was still legible. Yes, it was Elsa's. Now even those last photos together were lost. "Elsa called it 'old faithful,'" she said.

"Ah, perhaps that is the explanation, then," Bjornstad said. He looked toward the top of the falls. "Miss Jenssen may have stepped out on the ledge to take a picture and gotten too close to the edge."

Kris felt goose bumps rise on her arms.

Bjornstad handed the camera to the other officer, whom he introduced to Kris as his assistant.

"We're ready to take her to the ambulance," one of the medics called.

"Okay then." Bjornstad raised his hand and motioned for everyone to draw near. "Say nothing to anyone about Ms. Jenssen's death. This tragedy must be kept secret until the rest of her family has been notified."

Kris immediately thought of Uncle Andy. Elsa was his life. How could he ever accept such news?

"If we pass anyone on the trail," Bjornstad was saying, "you must not identify the accident victim. If anyone has already heard that she has been injured and asks you about it, say 'yes, she was injured and taken to the hospital.' Refer everyone, especially the press, to me."

The two medics lifted Elsa's stretcher. Bjornstad asked Max to lead the procession back down the trail. Kris glanced over her shoulder at the falls, then fell into step behind the others, thankful for Oscar's grip on her arm.

A figure appeared at the bend of the trail, stepped to the side, and watched them approach. Kris recognized Odd Engstrom's shaved head. The straps of his backpack looked like green suspenders against his leather jacket. A large camera case was slung over his shoulder.

She watched Hasan turn and give him a menacing glance. Moments later, she caught Odd's eye. Last night he had seemed so full of hate, now he looked sweaty, confused.

"I…," he stammered. His lips moved as if he were going to say more and then thought better of it. Did he know it was Elsa underneath the cloth? Kris shuddered and looked away. Bjornstad spoke briefly with him before assigning his assistant to talk with him further.

"That fellow and my cousin had an argument last night at the hotel," Kris said.

"Oh? Tell me about it," Bjornstad said.

Kris told him the story. The sheriff shook his head, "Unfortunately, we have a few of these chauvinist young folks around. Too young to know what such ideas can lead to. Your cousin was just the person to put him in his place."

In the parking area, two teenagers with large backpacks leaned against a second police car, chatting with an officer. Bjornstad introduced them to Kris, explaining they were the hikers who had found Elsa. The boys were Dutch tourists. They told her they had been hiking, had seen what they thought was someone's sweater floating on the water below the falls, but then discovered it was a person. They remembered seeing the fisherman—Max—and had run to him for help.

On the drive back to town, Kris and Oscar rode in the police car with Sheriff Bjornstad and his assistant, listening while Bjornstad checked in with headquarters and dispatched more officers to cover the trails up to the falls and talk with any hikers along the way.

"Here, Mr. Larsen, please describe to them who they are looking for."

By the time Oscar finished listing the people who had been with Elsa in the van—a black man with a red-headed white woman; an older couple, he with silver hair, she wearing a bright turquoise-and-yellow jogging suit; and a tall older woman with dyed brown hair—Kris was certain the police would have no trouble finding any of them.

"I hope we can keep this quiet," Bjornstad said to Kris. "Can you tell us the names of her next of kin?"

His words burned inside her. "My Uncle Andy, Elsa's father. He's the only family she has. He lives in a senior citizens' home in Bergen." She put her fingers on her lips to stop them from trembling.

"I can ask the Bergen Police to dispatch an officer and a counselor to him."

"No," Kris said. She could not let a stranger tell her uncle of Elsa's death. "Nils Dahl, the editor of *Fjordposten*, needs to tell him. Nils is the family's closest friend. In fact, it's his wife who was hiking with Elsa—she's the woman with the brown hair that Oscar mentioned."

They arrived back in town and crossed the bridge.

"Is that Mrs. Dahl?" Bjornstad said, gesturing toward a tall woman in a brown jacket and slacks, a rucksack on her back, who was walking along the promenade in the direction of the hotel.

"Yes," Kris and Oscar replied in unison.

The sheriff's assistant stopped the car, strode over to Grete, and spoke with her.

Kris watched Elsa look their way, shrug her shoulders, and accompany the officer to the car, a puzzled look on her face. She greeted Kris and Oscar with a nod as she joined them in the back seat.

"I understand you are Grete Dahl, the wife of Nils Dahl," Bjornstad said.

"Yes," Grete answered. Her face flushed. "Is Nils all right?" She looked wildly at the sheriff, then at the others.

Bjornstad held up his hand. "Be calm, Mrs. Dahl, as far as we know, your husband is fine, but Mrs. Kelly's cousin, Elsa Jenssen, is not."

"Why?" Grete asked, the wild look returning to her eyes. "I saw her a little while ago. What has happened?"

"She fell into the waterfall," Bjornstad answered matter of factly. "I'm sorry to say she did not survive."

Grete's hands flew to her cheeks. "*Nei, nei,*" she said. "It cannot be."

"I'm afraid so," Bjornstad said. He waited a moment, letting the news sink in. "We would like to understand what happened, and we heard that you were hiking with her. When did you see her last?"

Grete looked at Oscar. "His man drove us up the mountain, that was eight-thirty, and we started walking to the waterfall." Her voice quivered.

"Us?" Bjornstad asked.

"Yes. Mr. and Mrs. Mueller, Elsa, and me. But then Elsa said she will go another way, and she left us."

"Did you see her again?" Bjornstad asked.

"No. I thought I would because I went back on her trail, but I didn't see her. Mrs. Mueller also looked."

"How was Elsa when you started hiking?" Kris asked. "Did she seem ill?"

"No, she seemed very good. Stubborn as usual. She wanted to go her own way." She shook her head back and forth, "*Nei, nei*. It cannot be," she repeated.

The sheriff moved on with his inquiry. "So, you were here with her and Mrs. Kelly," Bjornstad said, making a statement rather than asking a question.

"No, it was by chance."

Liar, thought Kris. She rested her head against the back of the seat and studied the car's ceiling.

"Grete, I think Nils should be the one to tell Andy," Kris said.

"Oh, this is terrible. Poor Nils; he will be so upset."

Devastated was more like it, Kris thought. "He's not only Elsa's boss but he's been like a son to her father," she explained to Bjornstad.

The sheriff told Grete that he wished to keep the news of Elsa's death quiet until Elsa's father had been informed.

"That is good," Grete said. "I cannot tell him."

When they arrived at the hotel, Bjornstad's assistant went with Grete to try by phone to locate Nils in Voss. Dag poked his head out from behind the reception desk; Kris watched him saunter over to her. He nuzzled her hand. She scratched his neck underneath his collar and, for an instant, she was reminded of the many times as a child she had been comforted by the companionship of one of the family dogs. But today the solace was fleeting.

While Bjornstad and Nils accompanied her to her room, Kris described how Elsa had left her bed. When they reached the room, they found the door ajar, the beds neatly made; Elsa's silk pajamas and Kris's own pink cotton nightgown folded and set on top of their pillows.

"Oh, no," she cried, dismayed. "I wanted you to see that Elsa purposely made her bed look as if she was still sleeping in it."

Just then Inga, whom Kris had last seen serving coffee in the library the previous evening, walked in. "Oh, I'm sorry. I'm almost finished; I just went to get a trash bag."

Kris stood at the end of Elsa's bed. "Inga, please tell the sheriff what this bed was like when you came."

"It was a mess, everything out of place."

"Lots of pillows and stuff, right? Did it look as if my cousin had put things on the bed so it would appear as if she were still in it?"

Inga looked at her quizzically and shrugged. "I don't know what you are asking."

Slowly Kris realized she herself had disturbed the evidence by pulling the comforter off the bed.

"People sleep in funny ways," Inga said. "But, yes, I found something strange." She walked past Kris and lifted the pillow at the head of

Elsa's bed. Kris gasped at the sight of Elsa's wallet, keys, pills, film to be processed, and a small packet of peppermints.

"I found them here. I put everything back in the same place after I made the bed."

The sheriff picked up the film first. "She must have put new film in her camera," he said to Kris, who hoped the roll was from yesterday's train ride. He opened Elsa's thick wallet and flipped through her stack of business and credit cards. Next, he picked up the pills. "Do you know what these are for?"

"Her dizzy spells, I assume," Kris said.

"I'll need to take these things; they will be returned to you in due time," he told Kris.

Bjornstad, indicating Inga could go, reached out for the plastic bag she was holding. "I'll take care of it," he said.

Inga paused in the doorway. "I saw her this morning at six-thirty when I came to work. She was making a call from the public telephone in the lobby."

Who would Elsa have called so early in the morning? Kris wondered as Bjornstad collected trash from the waste basket. He stood for a moment, peering inside the bag and shaking its contents. He triumphantly pulled an empty film box from the bag. "She must have reloaded her camera this morning," he said. "And what's this?" He pulled out a bottle. "Lingonberry juice?"

Kris wrinkled up her nose. "Yes, Elsa and I had a toast last night before bedtime." She remembered the tart cranberry-like juice less than enthusiastically.

"Not your kind of juice?" Bjornstad asked.

"Not particularly. Too much sediment in it."

"Must have been on the shelf too long," the sheriff said. He smelled the bottle, put the cover back on, then threw it back in the bag. The phone rang. Bjornstad answered it. "Yes, yes. O.K. I'll take it now."

Kris stood frozen in place and listened to Bjornstad's side of the conversation.

"Mr. Dahl. Yes, this is Sheriff Bjornstad. I regret that I have very bad news for you about Elsa Jenssen." He paused. "I'm afraid, sir, that it is worse than that. I'm sorry to inform you that Miss Jenssen died from a fall in the mountains this morning."

Bjornstad was silent, apparently listening to the reaction at the other end of the line. He placed his hand over his forehead as if shading his eyes, then sighed. "No, sir. We are not mistaken," he said sadly. "Yes, we're trying to find that out. Your wife was with her for a while, but she didn't see it happen. Yes, Mrs. Kelly's right here." He handed the phone to Kris.

"Nils?"

"Kris?" He hesitated. "Is she really gone?" His voice shook.

"Yes, Nils," Kris said; she held the receiver tight against her ear. Nils didn't speak. Couldn't speak, she guessed. Tears rolled down her cheeks. "Nils? Nils?" she said softly.

"Yes," he answered almost in a whisper. "Let me talk with the sheriff again."

She gave the phone back to Bjornstad and listened to him tell Nils more details of what appeared to have happened. No, he had not yet found eyewitnesses. He would try to keep the news under wraps until Elsa's father could be notified. Could Nils break the news to him? Apparently Nils agreed to do so. Bjornstad told Nils to contact him as soon as possible after telling Elsa's father so that he could release an official statement to the media. Then he added, looking over at Kris, "I shall arrange for Mrs. Kelly to fly back with the body in the next few hours."

After a few more words of condolence, the sheriff ended the conversation. As soon as he finished the call, the phone rang again, and he answered it.

"Very good," Bjornstad said. "Take them to the library; we'll meet you there."

He hung up the phone and said to Kris, "The Muellers have been located."

CHAPTER 6

▼

Kris and Bjornstad entered the library a few minutes before the Muellers arrived. Yolanda was wearing the bright turquoise-and-yellow sports outfit that Kris remembered Oscar describing earlier.

"What happened?" Yolanda asked. "We heard Miss Jenssen had an accident."

Before Kris could respond, Bjornstad spoke. "I am sorry to tell you that Miss Jenssen is dead."

"No! How?" George grabbed the back of a chair to steady himself.

"I am so sorry, my dear," Yolanda said, reaching a hand toward Kris in a sympathetic gesture. Kris appreciated the handshake, but thought how, like the eyes of a doll, Yolanda's registered no emotion.

"We were just with her this morning. This is a terrible shock," George said. "What kind of accident was it?"

Bjornstad suggested they sit down. When they were all seated, he explained that Elsa had apparently fallen from the ledge above Hidden Falls.

"They shouldn't have allowed us out on those wet trails," Yolanda said, her voice strident. "Look at my boots; they still are not dry." She pointed to dark spots on the leather.

George slowly shook his head; his gray eyes looked pained. "It is so tragic, so difficult to believe. When did this happen?"

"Sometime before ten-fifteen," Bjornstad said.

"But we were with her less than an hour before that!" George said.

"Tell us everything you remember about your hike with Miss Jenssen," the sheriff said.

Alternating between them, Yolanda and George told how Hasan had driven them, Grete Dahl, and Elsa Jenssen to the start of the trail above the Roma Restaurant. Yolanda said she felt that Elsa was uncomfortable around Grete—though she referred to them as Miss Jenssen and Mrs. Dahl—and that, when the trail split into two, Elsa insisted on taking the path to the meadow rather than continuing straight on to the top of the falls with them. Elsa told them that the map indicated she could get to Hidden Falls from the meadow. The Muellers and Grete found a viewpoint above the falls, and then a slippery path to the ledge. At that point Grete announced she was going to look for Elsa, and since George wanted to rest, Yolanda joined her.

"And what time was that?" Bjornstad asked.

"About nine-thirty," Yolanda said.

"Then what happened?"

"Mrs. Dahl and I hiked approximately fifteen minutes, but we didn't find Miss Jenssen," Yolanda said. "When we arrived at the meadow, Mrs. Dahl decided to take the trail down the mountain, and I went back to meet my husband."

"Then neither of you saw Miss Jenssen again?" Bjornstad asked.

"No," George said.

"I'm afraid not," Yolanda said.

"What did you do after that?" Bjornstad asked.

"We followed the trail from the meadow back to the Roma Restaurant," Yolanda said. "And that's where your officers found us."

"So where did Elsa go?" Kris asked.

"Perhaps she left the trail," Yolanda suggested.

"When you saw Elsa, was she feeling all right?" Kris asked.

"She seemed to be," George said. "What do you think, *querida*?"

Yolanda raised her eyebrows. "I don't know. It was hard to tell. She wasn't very cheerful."

"That will be all then," Bjornstad said. "Thank you for your time, Mr. and Mrs. Mueller. If you think of anything else—anything at all, please call me." He gave them his card.

The bracelets on Yolanda's wrist jangled as she shook Kris's hand. "I am so sorry."

Then George clasped Kris's hand with both of his. "Your cousin was a lovely, charming, kind lady. This is a terrible tragedy," he said. His eyes were moist. "My deepest condolences."

His face blurred in front of her. "Thank you," she said, her voice cracking.

Bjornstad accompanied the Muellers to the door. Kris stared out at the mountains, wondering how Elsa had managed to disappear from her companions' sight.

✻   ✻   ✻   ✻

A few hours later, Kris sat at the vanity in her room. Oscar had insisted she have some soup and rest. She had tried. Now she had showered and prepared for the trip to Bergen and her meeting with Uncle Andy. She put the Olympic-rings medallion around her neck and looked at it in the mirror: It was Elsa's last gift to her, and she would treasure it always.

The helicopter was to arrive at four. She had almost everything packed, except for the things on the night table. She put the photo of the kids in her shoulder bag and reached for her travel clock—it read three forty-five. She started to fold the clock into its case; then stopped. The lever for the alarm was still in the "on" position. She pressed the digital reading for alarm set. Last night she had set the clock for seven o'clock a.m., but now she would double check.

To her astonishment, the alarm was set for ten-forty-five a.m. So, she hadn't slept through the alarm after all, nor turned it off in her sleep. It had been reset. And by ten-forty-five she was already out of the room, rushing with Oscar and Hasan to the waterfall.

Perhaps Inga had inadvertently changed the setting when she was cleaning the room? Kris doubted it. It must have been Elsa. But why?

Hearing the distant whir of a helicopter, she threw her clock in her bag and ran to the balcony. She watched the mustard-colored chopper come over the mountains and buzz above the water, the throbbing of its rotors growing louder as it neared the hotel.

When Bjornstad and Oscar came to get her, she was ready.

"Nils Dahl called me a short time ago," Bjornstad said. "He was with your uncle."

"Poor Andy," Kris said. "Did Nils say how my uncle's doing?"

"As expected, he's in shock. And, according to Mr. Dahl, waiting for you. You will be met at the airport in Bergen by a police escort who will take you to your uncle," Bjornstad said. He took the bags while Oscar gave the room the once over, even opening drawers and checking under beds to see if anything had been forgotten. Kris gave a last look around, locking in her memory the precious time she had spent here with Elsa.

On their way to the lobby, Sheriff Bjornstad told her that "Dr. and Mrs. Stephens"—Bill and Rachel—were in the lobby, and that he had told them about Elsa.

Wearing blue denims and matching "Go Army" T-shirts, Rachel and Bill greeted her solemnly.

"Kris. We're so sorry. We went for a ferry boat ride after our hike. We didn't know about Elsa," Rachel said, giving her a hug.

"I just can't believe it," Bill said, shaking his head. "I should have checked her vitals again before she left this morning."

"You cautioned her about overdoing things," Rachel reminded him.

"Right," he said. He rubbed the back of his hand where Kris noticed dark scratches. "I should have insisted that we hike with her."

"We had no idea the conditions were that dangerous. What a God-awful accident." Rachel wiped her eyes with a tissue.

"If only I'd known, maybe I could have helped," Bill said.

"Thank you," Kris said, once again appreciating the couple who had been so helpful to her cousin the evening before. "When did you see her last?"

"In the van," Bill replied. "Hey, what's with this?" Dag was sniffing eagerly at his pantlegs.

"Come here, Dag," Kris called. She ruffled the fur around his collar, then gave him a farewell pat.

"Mrs. Kelly, you need to go now," Sheriff Bjornstad said.

"Then let's say goodbye here," Bill said. He and Rachel again expressed their condolences, each giving her a brief embrace.

Oscar walked with Kris into the rose garden while Bjornstad went ahead with the bags.

A small crowd had gathered to watch the activity in the evacuated parking lot where Bjornstad's assistant supervised the transfer of a wooden coffin from a hearse to the helicopter. Kris grabbed Oscar's arm for support and tried to control her sudden feeling of nausea.

Oscar led her to a bench, where they sat surrounded by the scent of roses.

Some minutes later, Bjornstad approached them. "They're ready for you now, Mrs. Kelly," he said. He handed her Elsa's rucksack. "My men found this at the side of the trail near the ledge. We've taken an inventory, and I added her wallet and other things. I am returning everything to you, except the medications and the film. Those will be returned later."

Kris turned to say goodbye to Oscar. He grasped her hand. "We shall never forget Elsa Jenssen," he said. "May God protect you and bring you back in happier times. Call me if I can do anything for you." He gave her his business card. The events of the day showed in his face; he looked tired, drawn.

"Thank you, Oscar. You have been very kind. I promise I'll be in touch."

Sheriff Bjornstad offered her his arm, which she took gratefully. From the corner of her eye, Kris saw people watching. Ahead of her, the helicopter waited. Somewhere in her mind the whole scene was playing itself out as if she were watching a film and seeing herself in it. It was all surreal.

CHAPTER 7

▼

As the chopper flew west toward Bergen, Kris unzipped Elsa's rucksack and peered inside: a handkerchief, an apple, a bottle of water, bandages, first-aid cream, sunscreen, a ballpoint pen. Elsa's wallet, keys, and the other things they had found under her pillow were in a plastic bag. Kris thought about looking into Elsa's wallet, then decided to save that for Uncle Andy. The side pocket contained Elsa's press card, half a pack of peppermints, and another yet unopened. Elsa, always prepared, Kris mused.

She thought about her uncle and tried to imagine how Nils had broken the news to him. Now that he had been told of Elsa's death, could he bear the shock? Andy was eighty-nine-years old; his life had revolved around Elsa. Kris was eager to see her uncle, to try to comfort him, but she wondered if her presence would be of any help.

When the North Sea came into view, Kris knew they were nearing Bergen. Flanked by seven mountains, much of the downtown area stood on a peninsula. Immediately she recognized the medieval wooden buildings lining the quay of the inner harbor, Vågen, and the stone structures—Håkon's Hall and Rosenkrantz Tower—guarding its entrance. Houses with red-and gray-tiled roofs climbed the hillsides. Using the white lookout tower of Skansen and the funicular moving up Mt. Fløyen as landmarks, Kris tried to find Elsa's street through the trees.

At Lille Lungesgardsvann, the octagonally shaped lake in the center of town, tiny ducks scattered and people, out for a Sunday stroll, looked up at the noisy helicopter. It all seemed so unbelievable. Only yesterday morning she and Elsa had walked near the lake before going to the train station. And two days before that, only a few blocks away, they'd walked on the university campus during Elsa's lunch break to see the yellow building that had once been the Sydneshaugen School, Elsa's grade school. Elsa had recalled the day Gestapo officers took her two Jewish classmates away. "I was thirteen years old, and I could do nothing to save them," she said, adding that years later she learned the children had died in the gas chambers of Auschwitz.

The helicopter climbed over a mountain and landed at Flesland Airport on the outskirts of Bergen. The medic helped Kris out of the helicopter onto the tarmac; she slung her bag and Elsa's backpack over her shoulders and walked toward the terminal. Two Nordic giants, men well over six-feet tall, one in uniform, blond and clean-shaven; the other in civilian clothes, with more hair in his neatly cropped reddish-blond beard than on his balding head—walked toward her from a waiting police car.

Beyond them the planes parked at the jetways caught her eye. Only days before, she had arrived here from the States. Elsa and Uncle Andy had welcomed her with flowers, a bouquet of red roses, blue bachelor buttons, and white carnations matching the Norwegian flag in the middle.

"Kris?"

Kris stopped abruptly and looked into the face of someone she had met at the airport that day: Tor Olsen.

"Tor? What? How? Elsa…" She didn't know where to begin.

"I know," he said. "I'm so sorry." He hugged her and she hugged him back, his beard brushing her forehead. She was keenly aware of the pleasant scent of aftershave. Tor was a stranger, but at this moment she felt a bond with him. He had known Elsa; Kris knew he shared her sorrow.

She swallowed hard. "How did you know?"

"Nils told me."

"Nils?" Kris tried to sort through her confusion.

He took her bags. "I'll explain later," he said, stepping aside to make introductions. "Kris Kelly, this is Finn Nygaard, Bergen's chief of police."

"I knew your cousin," Nygaard said. "She was a real *Bergenser*, a proud citizen of Bergen, and we were so proud of her. My sympathy to you—and to us all."

Kris bit her lip and held back her tears.

"Thank you, Chief Nygaard," she said.

"Call me Finn; your cousin did."

"Okay, Finn," she said.

"We will get you through the red-tape quickly. Tor will drive you to your uncle's."

Finn meant what he said, Kris realized, quickening her pace to keep up with his and Tor's long strides.

At the terminal, she signed forms and promised to advise of funeral arrangements as soon as possible. In minutes she and Tor were in his sporty Volvo heading toward town.

"So, what about Nils?" Kris asked.

"Remember, I told Elsa that I would call today?"

"Yes." Kris remembered that she had hoped he wouldn't.

"I left a message on her answering machine this morning. Nils called me back. He said he'd stopped by her house to check on things. He told me about her accident. I couldn't believe it! I asked how I could help, and he suggested I meet you at the airport."

"I appreciate it," Kris said. Indeed it was comforting to have been greeted and driven by a family friend rather than officials.

"It's going to be tough for your uncle," Tor said.

"Yes, it is!" she agreed, looking out at the passing scenery. She recognized their route—the same one Elsa had taken just a few days earlier. Elsa had been so bubbly; Uncle Andy so exuberant about having seen Tor. "It's good that you had that unexpected reunion with him and Elsa at the airport last week. They were so glad to see you."

"Same here. I wish I'd been in touch more often," Tor said. "Elsa's folks were an important part of my parents' lives."

He stopped for a traffic light and shifted gears. The movement made the ship tattoo on his right arm appear as if it were rocking. "Tell me what happened up at the fjord, Kris."

She gave a brief account of what had happened since Oscar woke her up, watching Tor's face carefully when she told him about Elsa's prank. If he thought it was strange, he didn't say so.

"So she just went off on her own?" he asked.

"That's what they all said."

"Why would she do that?"

"I don't know. But apparently that's what she wanted, or she would have awakened me. I just can't believe Elsa slipped off a ledge—she was too sensible for that."

"Sensible people can make mistakes, especially if they're not feeling well."

"But…"

"Death is like a thief in the night, Kris. It robs you of someone, something precious, and it leaves you feeling empty."

She felt tears escape from her eyes and roll down her cheeks. Tor had said it exactly right. She reached in her bag for a tissue.

On the other side of a tunnel, Bergen waited for them. Black clouds moved in across the barrier islands, promising to blanket the city with the rain for which it was so famous.

After another ten minutes they arrived at Andy's senior citizens' home. Tor took plastic grocery bags from the back seat, saying that even when in mourning, people must eat.

The doors of the home opened automatically. Residents lived in their own apartments and shared meals and recreation in common areas. Kris and Tor walked through the spacious lobby where several residents watched television.

"That's Sigrid," Kris said, smiling at an old woman in a wheelchair moving slowly toward them.

The fragile woman's hollow eyes widened as she looked up at Tor. "Hello," he said in a friendly tone.

Sigrid's face lit up, but only momentarily. She turned to Kris and spoke in a raspy voice, "Elsa's dead."

Kris's eyes flooded with tears. "Yes," she said. "But she asked me to give you this." She gently hugged the old woman.

"That was nice of you," Tor said a few minutes later.

"If Elsa had been here, that's just what she would have done." She remembered what Elsa had said when they had come here on Thursday. "Some people here are lonely; their families don't visit so often. I am here a lot so I am like family to them. A kind word, a few minutes to talk doesn't require much, but it means a great deal to them." Kris forced herself not to think about her own father at that moment.

Andy's apartment was at the end of the second hallway.

"That's his door, the one with the troll face on it. He carved it himself," she said.

Kris felt her stomach turn—facing her uncle would bring reality crashing down on them both.

Tor pulled the troll's round elongated nose. A doorbell rang.

"Oh, good, it'sh you," Nils said, opening the door.

Kris and Tor stepped inside and put down their bags; each shook hands with Nils.

Hair tousled, shirt half tucked out of his pants, Nils reeked of beer; his complexion was far more ruddy than Kris remembered.

Kris put her hand briefly on Nils's shoulder.

"How's Andy?" she asked, wondering if her elderly uncle was also inebriated.

Nils pointed toward an open door. "He'sh in hish workshop."

Kris and Tor followed the scent of cherry-blend tobacco mixed with the smell of wood. In other apartments the room they entered would have been the bedroom. But here there was no space for sleeping. Shelves lined with wood carvings of all sizes—trolls, Viking ships, fishermen, and other creations—filled three walls. Tor gave a low whistle.

Andy Jenssen sat on a stool, hunched over a large table carved from a tree trunk. If he had heard them arrive, he gave no indication of it. In front of him was the wooden bust of a young man. He ran his hands back and forth across the sculptured cheeks of his re-creation of his son Per, who had been killed during the Nazi occupation.

Kris walked up beside him. "Uncle Andy?"

"Kristina?" He slowly looked up from the sculpture.

Kris clasped his heavily wrinkled hand.

"She's gone?" he said, raising his thick white eyebrows.

"Yes," she said. Kris bent to embrace her uncle, his hand still clutching hers. With his free hand he brought her head to his chest. She could hear the steady beat of his heart. For a moment she was a child and this was her father comforting her, making her feel warm and safe.

After some moments, Kris gently pulled away from her uncle. Tor stepped forward, his hand extended. As he did so, Andy pushed himself up from his stool. "Per," he said, clasping Tor's hand.

Kris's hopes for her uncle fell. Even if they had been back in the 1940s, it would have been hard to see a resemblance between the sculpted thick-haired Per and the balding, middle-aged Tor in spite of his youthful physique.

"*Nei*, no, I am Tor Olsen, Leif's son, remember me?"

Her uncle's smile slowly disappeared, but he continued to grasp Tor's hand.

"Ah, *ja*, Leif's son," he mumbled.

Kris breathed a sigh of relief.

"Let's go sit in the living room," Tor said to him.

"I'll fix coffee," Kris said. She glanced back at the two men slowly making their way behind her, Andy leaning on his walking stick, Tor supporting his elbow.

In the living room, Nils slumped in a chair, a bottle of beer in his hand. Tears hung on his cheeks. When she saw him yesterday, he had been self-assured; now he seemed a broken man. He could certainly use some nourishment. She picked up Tor's grocery bags and went into the kitchen. The bags held crackers and Jarlsberg cheese, grapes, freshly ground coffee, and cream. She found tea in Andy's cupboard. She put the coffee in the coffee maker and found a pot to boil water. While waiting for the coffee to brew and the water to boil, she sliced the cheese, placing the slices on the crackers and arranging them on a large plate with the grapes. She appreciated Tor's coming to the kitchen and helping her to assemble cups, saucers, sugar and cream. Together they delivered the refreshments to the coffee table.

Both her uncle and Andy eagerly took the cups of coffee offered to them.

An hour later, Kris had finished her account of what had happened. The men had asked her several questions and the talking together had seemed good for all of them. Because Tor had insisted they all eat something, only a lonely cracker with a slice of cheese remained on the plate on the coffee table. Andy's mind seemed clear again, and Nils appeared considerably more sober. Kris thanked Tor for his thoughtfulness in bringing the groceries. He was right; even in mourning, it was important to eat. She hadn't realized how much she had needed a snack.

She got up from her chair and retrieved Elsa's backpack from where she'd set it near the door, and brought it to her uncle. "This is for you," she said. "Elsa left it at the side of the trail near the ledge."

Her uncle took the bag and held it close. "*Ja*, that is Elsa's," he said. He held it on his lap, carefully unzipped it, and took out the contents one by one, placing each item on the coffee table. He paused and flipped through Elsa's wallet before passing it to Nils, who handed it to Kris.

"I cannot look," he said, choking out the words.

"Nils, did Elsa telephone you this morning?" Kris asked.

"No, but I wish she had," he said wistfully.

"Apparently she phoned someone very early."

"She could have been checking her messages," he suggested.

Kris hadn't thought of that. "That's probably it," she said. She opened Elsa's wallet.

Listening to the melodic Norwegian conversation of her companions who were discussing the array of items on the table, Kris studied the designs of several business cards in the wallet and wondered how the people they represented had touched Elsa's life—and how Elsa had touched theirs. She recognized the crown logo at the top of a travel agent's card, the same logo she'd seen at the Royal Crown Hotel when she and Elsa had walked through the lobby Thursday night. Indeed Crown Travel's address was the same as the hotel's. Rolf Berg, whose name was on the card, must be the agent Elsa used to book their fjord excursion.

"Uncle Andy," she said, holding up the card. "May I keep this one?" As she expected, he had no objection.

Andy reached his hand into all corners of the rucksack. "Where is her notebook?" he asked. "She always carries her notebook. Here's the pen," he said, holding it up.

"I saw her writing in it last night, but I didn't see it today," Kris said. She pictured the notebook; it was about five by seven inches with a red cloth cover. Kris doubted that it would have escaped Oscar's final check of the hotel room. "Maybe it's on the bottom of her overnight bag," she suggested. She had only added things to the bag, not taken anything out.

Tor retrieved the bag from the car. Andy searched it to no avail; Kris double-checked. The notebook wasn't there.

"Maybe Elsa had the notebook on her when she fell," Nils suggested.

"*Ja*, maybe," Andy said. He rocked in his chair for a while, smoking his pipe, and looking thoughtful. Finally he spoke again. "There won't be any funeral!"

Kris managed to swallow her gasp. Was this her uncle's way of denying the reality of Elsa's death?

"My Elsa willed her body to science."

"That's right," Nils added.

"I want an autopsy," Andy said.

"The coroner will do one. The scientists will do another," Nils said. "But we already know what happened." He struggled to retain his composure.

"Was Elsa working on a story related to the fjord?" Tor asked.

Nils shook his head. "*Nei*, she was working on a piece about neo-Nazis and the extreme Right. The trip to the fjord was for pleasure—to rest and to spend time with Kris. She was looking forward to it." His voice cracked.

"Then this freak accident!" Tor said, nodding in disbelief.

"Accident? Nonsense!" Andy banged his walking stick against the floor. "It wasn't Elsa's time yet. It wasn't Per's time. Per didn't leave this world accidentally, neither did my Elsa!"

The only sound in the room came from the ticking of a handcarved grandfather clock.

Kris could not bear the tortured look on her uncle's face. "The sheriff is investigating, Uncle Andy," she said hoping to comfort him.

"Those county sheriffs don't know anything," he said. "*Fjordposten* must investigate."

Nils's face was crimson. "We'll write the story; we'll let the police investigate."

Andy looked off into space. "The Elephant killed her."

Kris's heart sank. The Elephant, she had learned as a young girl, was the nickname some Norwegians had given to the much-despised Gestapo officer who had killed Per.

Nils rubbed Andy's shoulders. "No, no, not this time."

Andy seemed unpersuaded.

Assured that Kris and Tor would remain a bit longer with Andy, Nils explained to Andy that he had to go to his office to prepare the news about Elsa for the morning edition of *Fjordposten*.

"The truth," Andy persisted as Nils said goodbye. "You must find out what happened. You must demand the truth about my Elsa's death!"

CHAPTER 8

▼

Andy had kept up a brave front when Nils left, but Kris wondered how he would hold up when she and Tor went as well. It was already almost ten-fifteen. Twelve hours ago this nightmare was just beginning. She felt as if it had been twelve days. Maybe she should stay here. But where? Andy slept on his couch; he did not have another bed. Should she offer to camp on the floor and keep him company through the night? He was fading in and out of lucidity. They couldn't leave him alone.

"Uncle Andy, would you like to stay at Elsa's with me tonight?" she asked.

The old man's face brightened. "Yes, that is what I must do," he said.

Kris washed the dishes while Tor helped Andy assemble what he would need for the night. When they were ready to go, Kris noticed that Andy had put his things in Elsa's backpack.

The rain had turned to a drizzle. They drove into town and up the narrow streets to Fjellveien—"Mountain Way," a road that stretched across the side of Mt. Fløyen. It separated the forest coming down the mountain from the dozens of homes working their way up. After the funicular station, they turned on Skansemyrsveien, then into a driveway.

Through the birch trees, the street light dimly illuminated the sidewalk to Elsa's yellow house and its windowed entrance door. Kris led the way, reaching into her purse for the key chain and duplicate key that Elsa had given her. Tor followed with Andy. The old man's walking stick beat a slow, steady rhythm as it hit the pavement.

In the faint light, it would have been impossible to see the keyhole without the help of the miniature flashlight on the keychain. Kris opened the door and stepped into the entry way.

"Where's the light switch?" Tor asked, walking past her into the darkness. Before she could shine the flashlight in his direction, bells jingled. "What the…" he muttered.

Chuckling, Andy hit the light switch next to the coat rack with his walking stick. "She got you. That's my Elsa. You see, you can't sneak into this house!"

Kris had forgotten about Elsa's long string of brass sheep bells that hung from the ceiling near where the foyer intersected with the stairs. From the driveway the house looked to be only one story; but, built into the hillside decades ago, it had two floors below this one.

They took their shoes off in the hall, a custom that undoubtedly contributed to the spic-and-span condition of many Norwegian homes. Elsa had added her own touch—a collection of slippers for guests not wishing to walk around in stocking feet. Andy had his own favorite pair. Since Kris's slippers were in her overnight bag, she wore a pair of Elsa's. Tor chose the largest pair of unisex slippers in Elsa's collection, yet his heels hung out over the ends.

Two doors led from the entry hall. One to the living room, the other to the kitchen. Kris loved the cheery kitchen: its walls papered in a wild-strawberry design. Snow-white appliances and cupboards with bright red handles. To the left of the doorway, white café curtains bordered with delicately embroidered strawberries, leaves, and blossoms hung over the only window in the room. Below the window, a bright red tablecloth covered the table.

"Look," Andy said, going over to the counter to the right of the doorway. "That's my Elsa's bread, made with her own hands." He caressed the whole-grain bread in its wax-paper wrapper.

"You can have it for breakfast," Tor suggested.

"*Ja*, she would like that."

Kris felt Elsa's presence. It was hard to believe that she wouldn't be popping up early to share some of the bread with them. They continued through the kitchen into the dining area and living room with its contemporary Scandinavian furnishings. Through two large picture windows the twinkling lights of Bergen spread out below them. By the harbor, floodlights illuminated the medieval landmarks.

"During the war," Andy said, staring out the window, "we lived in Nordnes. You see it there?" He pointed to the left of the inner harbor. "We were having breakfast when a boat in the harbor exploded. The windows, they shattered. Glass flew. We hid under the table and held on to each other." He stopped, apparently lost in his memories.

Kris put her hand on her uncle's arm.

"*Ja*," he said after a moment or two. "The sirens sounded. We saw the fires down the street, and Elsa said, 'Come, Papa, we must help the others.'"

Andy walked back to the dining area. There his attention focused on the sideboard filled with photographs in frames of all shapes and sizes—the same photographs that Kris and Elsa had looked at together in the past few days. He pointed to a recent picture of him and Elsa taken on the 17th of May—Norway's Independence Day. Elsa was wearing her *bunad*—her national costume, a dark blue pinafore over a puffy-sleeved muslin blouse with a traditional Solje broach with heart-shaped dangles. "We were in the parade." He sighed. "*Ja*, that was our last picture together."

He picked up a silver frame displaying a photo of a tall blond teenager and a sandy-haired youth with a slight build, both panning for the camera.

"This is Per," Andy said, pointing to the blond. "He was eighteen."

Kris remembered Elsa holding the same photo in her hands Wednesday night. "I saw him shot, Kris," she had said. "It was more than fifty years ago, but it feels like it was yesterday. I can never forget it. I can never forgive the Nazis for what they did." Then Elsa had wiped away the tears and asked her the same question Andy was asking Tor now.

"And do you know who this is?" he said, moving his finger to the other youth.

Tor shook his head.

"Nils Dahl," Andy said.

From the expression on Tor's face, Kris guessed that he too had difficulty identifying the slender youth in the photo as the mature, stocky Nils.

Andy took the photo of Nils and Per and placed it next to a group photo of *Fjordposten* staff. For several minutes Andy spoke about the Jenssen family, showing photographs of himself and his late wife, Liv, with Per and Elsa, and of his parents and siblings. That brought him to the American branch of his family, his younger sister, Kris's grandmother, who had emigrated with her husband to America and settled in Washington state.

"And this is Kristina," he said.

Yes, there she was with pigtails and freckles at Mt. Rainier with her parents and Elsa. "You've changed your hair style," Tor said.

Kris rolled her eyes.

Andy chuckled.

Tor pointed to a photo of Elsa standing in front of a double-decker bus. "London? When was that taken?"

"*Ja*, that's the question." Andy scratched his shock of white hair. "Maybe 1955. She was a student and worked part-time for the BBC; that's when she met that British Casanova."

Kris knew he was referring to Sterling Broadridge. Elsa had told her that Andy had never liked him.

Tor stopped in front of Elsa's photos of Laura and Charlie, from birth to graduation. Most were of just the two of them, but there were also some with Elsa, some with Kris and Jim and with Kris's father. Kris thought about the many special events Elsa had shared with her over the years—sometimes in person, like her and Jim's wedding, the twins' first birthday, their graduation. By phone or letters with photographs, Kris had recounted to Elsa milestone events such as their first teeth, first steps, first words, their school activities, their accomplishments.

"Nice-looking family," Tor said. "Your daughter looks like you." His comment brought Kris out of her nostalgia.

She was used to that response. Laura had her auburn hair and green eyes. Since the twins were fraternal, people often focused on their likeness to their parents before noticing their likeness to each other.

As Andy continued his review of photographs on the sideboard, Kris became distracted by the photos that were not there—some of Elsa's favorites: a photo of Elsa and Nils on skis taken when they were in their thirties; another on a hike in the mountains last summer; a third from Elsa's sixtieth birthday party—Elsa in an off-the-shoulder red dress, seated in front of a birthday cake; Nils behind her, his hands on her shoulders. All seemingly innocuous photos; all missing.

"Now, I shall show you the rest of the house," Andy said.

Tor took Andy's arm and together they walked down the first flight of stairs. Kris followed, the wooden steps creaking beneath their feet. At the landing Andy entered Elsa's study. Kris knew this room, had "read" two of the walls: one was packed with framed awards and articles—visual testimony of Elsa's long and successful journalistic career; the other displayed photos. Those of the late and beloved King Olav; his father King Haakon who from exile in England had inspired the Norwegian resistance to the Nazis; and the current royal family, Olav's son, King Harald and his wife Queen Sonja, and their children. Elsa, like many Norwegians, had viewed them as an extension of her own family—probably the reason that the photo of her with the King and Queen was the largest on the wall. But not all the photos were of Norwegian royalty. There was the historic 1993 photo of Israeli Prime Minister Yitzhak Rabin and Palestinian Authority Chairman Yasser Arafat shaking hands on the White House lawn with President Clinton smiling approvingly behind them. There were also photos from Elsa's interviews with the two men and Israel's Foreign Minister Shimon Peres after they received the Nobel Peace Prize in Oslo a year later. The dates were clearly marked. And there were a number of photos of other world leaders, film stars, famous names and faces: people Elsa had interviewed, met on special occasions, or come to know during her marriage to Sterling Broadridge. The remaining wall space in the room was lined with an impressive collection of books, many on Norwegian and European history, the Holocaust, the Middle East.

Kris pictured Elsa here hard at work at her computer, surrounded by the memorabilia so important to her and fenced in by the books stacked on her desk. Perhaps Andy had the same vision—one too painful to bear. He turned around. "Tomorrow...," he said.

They walked down the hall, the air tinged with the scent of lavender, and descended a second flight of stairs, Andy holding the broad polished wood bannister. "I made this for Elsa," he said proudly.

On the lower floor was a separate apartment with another living room and, down the hall, a kitchenette, bedroom, and bath. Elsa rented the place to university students; her most recent tenant had moved out a few weeks ago.

"Elsa wanted me to live here," Andy said. "but I refused. I told her she must have her own life." He stared into space, lost in his own thoughts.

The view from the downstairs living room was obscured by the foliage outside. The upper half of the windows were curtainless in order to let in whatever sunlight filtered through the trees and bushes. Kris had passed through this room a couple of times with Elsa on their way out to the backyard and the path to the funicular station.

Going at Andy's pace they finally reached the upstairs kitchen again, the tour of Elsa's house complete.

"It's late. You two need some rest," Tor said. "The question is, are you going to be able to sleep?"

"I shall have a nightcap to help me," Andy said.

"What about you, Kris?" Tor asked.

"I'll be okay." Certainly her body needed rest, Kris thought, but her mind was still preoccupied.

"I shall fix you a nightcap also," Andy said, taking over his daughter's kitchen. He leaned his walking stick against a wall and rubbed his hands together.

Tor sat at the table across from Kris and winked at her, as if to say any distraction to keep Uncle Andy from dwelling on Elsa's death was worth their indulgence.

Andy shuffled across the tile floor, opening and closing cupboards. He took out two wine glasses from one and placed them on the counter. From another he retrieved a bottle of juice. He handed it to Tor to open.

Kris recognized the color. "Is that lingonberry juice, by any chance?" she asked.

"Yes, you don't sound so crazy about it," Tor said.

She just smiled; she didn't want to hurt her uncle's feelings. But he seemed oblivious to their conversation anyway. He bustled around—as much as he could bustle without his walking stick—taking a package of pills from a drawer and from the back of the counter a brass mortar and pestle; it was the one Kris had brought Elsa from the Arab market in Jerusalem. He popped a pill out of a cardboard package, stuck it into the mortar, and pounded it with the pestle.

"What are you doing, Uncle Andy?" Kris asked, trying to keep her voice calm.

"Fixing us a magic cocktail, like Elsa does for me sometimes."

Kris felt as if furry caterpillars were crawling up her back.

"And what are those pills?"

"Valium," he said.

"Did she always mash them like that?"

"No. Sometimes a spoon works, but not so well."

"Why not?" she asked.

"Eh, it tastes like it's got sand in it," Andy replied.

Sand. Sediment. Kris thought about the previous evening's toast with Elsa and tried to remember exactly what had happened before they had clinked their glasses together. When she accompanied Elsa out to the balcony, the glasses had already been filled with juice and were covered with napkins: one white, one red. Elsa had removed the red napkin from the glass it covered and handed that glass to Kris. The red napkin must have been Elsa's cue to which drink had the Valium. Her cousin had purposely drugged her! Kris felt sick to her stomach.

She also felt Tor's eyes on her.

Her uncle poured the powder into one of the glasses and put the other half tablet in the mortar.

"That's okay, Uncle Andy, I'll pass. I'd rather go to sleep naturally."

"I shall make one for you anyway. It shall be here for you if you need it." He repeated the procedure. Then stirred the contents of each glass with a spoon.

"You know, I would like to taste the juice without the sleeping pill," Kris said, "Tor, would you like some, too?"

"Sure."

Kris filled a glass with juice for Tor and gave herself about a quarter as much.

Andy raised his glass to theirs, "To Elsa, *skoal*," he said and drank up his potion.

Kris took a sip; the juice tasted tart, but it certainly didn't have particles in it like last night. She was convinced now that Elsa had made her one of her special nightcaps.

"*Ja*, I shall go to bed now," Andy said, picking up his walking stick. "Tor, shall you come back tomorrow?"

"Yes, in the morning," Tor assured him. He took two pieces of paper from the notepad next to the phone and wrote down his phone number on each, handing one to Kris and one to Andy. "Don't hesitate to call me if you need anything," he said.

"Good night, Kristina," her uncle said.

"Good night, Uncle Andy," Kris replied, giving him a hug. "Remember, I'll be just down the hall."

Tor took Elsa's rucksack and accompanied Andy back down the stairs to Elsa's room.

Kris heard her uncle say, "*Tusen takk*, Tor." She wondered what things would have been like today without Tor. His presence had been a comfort to her uncle and, she had to admit, to her as well.

When he returned to the foyer, she said, "My uncle's right. A thousand thanks. You've been a great support for us both."

"Glad I could help," he said.

"He seems to be bearing up pretty well."

"For now. We'll just have to wait and see." He looked at her with a steady gaze.

"You seemed bothered by that nightcap. Why?"

Kris told him about the drink Elsa had given her and her suspicion that it had been spiked.

"But why would she do that?" he asked.

"That's exactly my question."

He pushed his feet into his loafers. "You've had a traumatic day; you must be exhausted. Just because you and Elsa drank lingonberry juice last night, it doesn't mean that she put Valium in it. If she did, maybe she accidentally gave you the one she intended for herself. You need a good night's sleep. Are you sure you'll get one without taking something?"

She nodded. "Elsa always reminded me that I'm a Jenssen. I have to be strong. I'll be okay," she assured him.

They parted with a handshake.

CHAPTER 9

▼

Kris managed to sleep a few hours before waking, overwhelmed by a deep sense of loneliness. She lay in the darkness, missing Elsa, missing her family, listening to the stillness in the house. Even back home she found the wee hours of the morning unsettling, especially after Jim left. Since he had moved out eight months ago, she had developed the annoying habit of waking up in the middle of the night, often unable to go back to sleep. She pictured the house where she and Jim had raised the children, planned for their future. Now Jim wanted the house sold; their joint assets split. She felt an irresistible urge to reach out and talk with Laura and Charlie, to remind them that she loved them, and to tell them, as gently as she could, about Elsa. But they were away working at summer camps. Laura was supposed to have led a hike for a few days in the Adirondacks, and Charlie was canoeing somewhere in West Virginia for a week. They were to call Jim and her when they returned. If they called Jim first, it would be good if he could break the news to them.

She yanked the lamp chain. It was evening on the East Coast, probably a good time to find Jim at home in Janet's—his and Janet's—Georgetown apartment. Oh, how, she hated to make this call, hated the possibility that Janet might answer the phone. She tiptoed upstairs to the kitchen. Fumbling through the pages of her address book, she found Jim's new phone number—an alien number that made her feel as if she was calling a stranger.

"Hello." The voice was not that of a stranger; it was the man she had loved, and maybe still did.

"Jim, it's Kris." She kept her voice strong. "I'm calling from Norway; something terrible has happened."

"What's wrong? Stuck in a glacier?"

She refused to let his sarcasm rile her. She explained briefly, forcing herself to remain calm and matter of fact, fighting back the tears.

"Gosh, I'm sorry, Kris," he said when she finished. "Elsa was really something. Hold on. I've got to tell Janet."

She could hear his muffled voice but could not discern the words. She imagined Janet, her long straight black hair, her shapely twenty-four-year-old body now ballooning in pregnancy. When Kris was Janet's age, she had already been married to Jim for four years and was the mother of two-year-olds; she could never have imagined then that Jim would leave her when the twins were grown.

"Kris?" Jim said into the phone. "I'll talk to the kids. I can't do more than that."

"Thank you. I didn't ask you for anything else. Please give the kids my love," Kris said.

"You bet," Jim said. And that was it.

For a long time afterwards, Kris stared at the strawberry wallpaper and listened to the low hum of the refrigerator. Once upon a time she and Jim would have faced this crisis together; now she was on her own. She thought of Uncle Andy sleeping downstairs, his sorrow temporarily dulled by the Valium. Her drink still sat on the counter. Now she understood why she had overslept at the hotel, why she had felt so groggy when Oscar had knocked on her door. But why had Elsa drugged her? It didn't make any sense whatsoever, and it made her very uneasy.

She thought again about the change of her alarm setting and Elsa's stuffed bed covers. What was all that about? Elsa had been up to something; she knew that in her gut. And she knew that Elsa had not, as Tor had suggested, simply given her the wrong drink.

Wandering through the living room and back to her bedroom, Kris felt Elsa's presence everywhere, making her absence painfully palpable. Uncle Andy said that Elsa's death wasn't accidental. Even though his reasoning was skewed, what he said was something that had gnawed at Kris all day but which she had been unable, or perhaps afraid, to identify. Suppose Elsa's death hadn't been an accident? Suppose she had been pushed? But, by whom? And, why?

Kris fell into a troubled sleep. She awoke at seven to the sound of raindrops on the windowsill and the smell of coffee and cherry-blend tobacco. Unsure of the day's agenda, she slipped on a blue cotton knit skirt with matching top, and headed upstairs.

Andy sat at the kitchen table, looking out the window.

"Good morning, Uncle Andy," she said, kissing him on the cheek.

He reached his hand out to her. "Tor shall be here soon," he said.

The table was set for three. Andy had set a slice of Elsa's homemade bread on each of the plates; his slice was half eaten. He took another bite and washed it down with coffee. "The photos are gone," he declared.

"Which photos?"

"The photos of Elsa and Nils."

So it hadn't been her imagination last night, Kris thought. The photos really were missing.

"Was Nils here?" he asked.

"I don't know." Then she remembered what Tor had told her. "I mean yes. He stopped by to get Elsa's messages yesterday."

"Ah, *ja*, that explains it." Andy seemed satisfied that the mystery had been solved, and finished his bread.

"Why would Nils move them?"

"So that others would not see."

"You mean Grete? That if she saw them, they would just feed her paranoia and give her more reason to imagine they were having an affair?" Why was she asking so many stupid questions. She filled the teakettle with water and put it on a burner.

"It is not her imagination," Andy said.

"What?" Kris sat down across from her uncle and waited for his reply.

"*Ja*, Elsa could not help herself. She loved him even when she was a young girl and he and Per were in school together."

"Oh, I'm so blind," Kris said, putting her head in her hands. Elsa was naturally flirtatious. Her warm relationship with Nils was obvious and understandable, yet it never occurred to her that it was a romantic one. She tried to remember what Elsa had said to her about her and Jim's breakup: "It's nothing you did. It's just something that happened. Sometimes people can't explain what they do for love, or what they think is love. They don't want to hurt anyone, but they do."

Elsa of all people understood exactly what had happened. She was Grete's Janet. Kris felt as though she'd been struck by an avalanche.

"Here comes Tor." Andy pushed his chair back and grabbed his walking stick.

The teakettle whistled, and Kris let Andy go to the door while she went to the stove. How could she have been so naive about Elsa and Nils? Is that why Elsa let her sleep in yesterday? Was she afraid that Grete might make more accusations? Spoil the high regard she knew Kris had for her? Had Nils and Elsa made up the story about Grete's paranoia as a matter of convenience?

"Good morning," Tor said. His smile filled the room.

"Hi. Like some tea?"

"*Nei, takk.* Coffee for me. Tea is for the British and at least one American."

Andy chuckled.

"*Ja*, I have made the coffee already," he said. "Have you the *Fjordposten*?"

"Hmm."

Andy sat back at his place and moved his plate aside so that Tor could spread the front page in front of him.

Kris peered over Andy's right shoulder, where Tor, standing to her left, had placed his hand. The headline above a photo of Elsa said, "Elsa Jenssen Dies in Hiking Accident."

Together they read the article which gave the basic information: Elsa Jenssen was on a weekend vacation in the fjords. She had been suffering from dizzy spells, went hiking and separated from her companions. A nature lover, she apparently slipped while trying to take a photo of one of the region's most spectacular waterfalls and plunged to her death.

Andy banged the table. "But it wasn't an accident! Why didn't he say that?"

Tor pointed to a small box near the end of the story: "Because of the notoriety of Elsa Jenssen, Kripos investigators will visit the scene today to verify the accidental nature of her death."

Kris breathed a sigh of relief that Kripos, the Norwegian FBI, was now involved.

"There's more," Tor said. He turned to the inside pages.

"Be so good to read it to me, please," Andy said, his voice still edgy.

"Well, first here's an excerpt from one of Elsa's articles from last year." Tor read: *"We are a small country with a big conscience. Through the Oslo Accords, we have created an opportunity for the people of the Holy Land, whose history was profoundly affected by the evils of the Nazis, to look for a way to live together in peace. We must applaud and continue to encourage their efforts. We must also act in the Balkans. We must never forget the lessons of the Nazi period; we cannot stand idly by and watch people be destroyed. We must fight as peacemakers and peacekeepers—with the same resolve as our Resistance fought against an enemy more powerful than we were. Just as we proved under the Nazi occupation that a people need not let their spirit be broken, we must help the victims in the Balkans so their spirits are restored. And now we hear of a genocide against Tutsi refugees in Rwanda. Do not ignore it. Whether 50 years ago or five days ago, we must never forget the evil deeds of war criminals, and we must be ever vigilant to bring them to justice."*

"Wow!" Kris felt the tears well in her eyes. It had been one thing to hear Elsa voice her opinions in personal conversations; quite another to hear her "speak" to her readers. Now Kris heard in her memory, the voice of Sheriff Bjornstad: "Elsa Jenssen was our conscience."

"What does the editorial say?" Andy asked.

Tor read Nils's editorial, mourning a life-long friend, a first-rate journalist, driven by her love of country and a passion for justice, who spoke candidly to her large following of readers. Deeply touched by the dark period of the Nazi occupation of Norway and the Holocaust in Europe, she had pressed early in her career, through her articles, for prosecution of war criminals who had escaped the Nuremberg trials. She had covered the Eichmann trial in Israel. More recently, she had played a key role in raising Norwegian consciousness about "ethnic cleansing" in the former Yugoslavia, had urged Norway's absorption of Bosnian refugees, and had been a long-time proponent of Norway's humanitarian aid around the globe. She had been one of the first to laud Norway's role in bringing Israelis and Palestinians together. Nils wrote that as much as Elsa called for her country to play a role in helping around the world, she also had high expectations for the behavior of her fellow citizens at home. It had angered her whenever a Norwegian spoke disparagingly of new immigrants or refugees of other ethnic backgrounds. Going all the way back to the late sixties when the discovery of oil in the North Sea had brought an influx of guest workers from Pakistan to Norway, Elsa had no patience for those who referred to a Pakistani shop owner as a *pakisser* or *svartinger*. Ever since then she had championed newcomers. She would be the first to defend a foreigner's right to get a job in Norway and to try to become a contributing citizen.

"That's what she did at the fjord," Kris said. She told Tor and Andy about the incident between Elsa and Odd Saturday night.

Andy glowed with pride. "That's my Elsa."

After a moment, Tor continued reading Nils's tribute. "For Elsa, last year's Winter Olympics in Lillehammer were a celebration of the potential of every country to strive for the best it can be. If there had been an Olympic event for journalists, Elsa would have been our champion. She was the best, and we will miss her dearly. To her father Anders Jenssen, in his own right a hero of our country, we send our deepest condolences."

"That's it?" Andy asked, his voice quavering. He flung the paper on the floor, then stared into his plate. His fingers moved bread crumbs back and forth across the smooth surface.

"But it's a very fine tribute," Tor said, voicing what Kris herself had been thinking.

Without further comment, Andy rose from the table, waved Kris and Tor out of his way, and tapped his way resolutely across the tile floor to the phone. He dialed, paused, and then asked to speak to Nils.

"It wasn't an accident! Why didn't you tell the truth?" Andy asked in a raised voice, then waited for the reply. He shouted an expletive and slammed down the receiver. His stick fell to the floor. His head and shoulders drooped, and he grasped the counter. His lips moved silently, tears cascaded down his cheeks. Kris and Tor rushed to support him. He collapsed in Tor's arms.

CHAPTER 10

▼

Two hours later, Kris sat in the *Fjordposten* reception area—on a mission for Uncle Andy. A short time after his collapse at Elsa's, he had pulled himself together, insisting he was okay. Yet, worried about her uncle's health, Kris had pleaded with him to let Tor take him home to rest. He had consented only after she promised that she would try to persuade Nils to independently investigate Elsa's death.

The door to Nils's office opened, and he stepped out to greet her. "Welcome, Kris," he said with a sad smile, embracing her. Gone was his rumpled appearance of the night before. His business attire was impeccable, his hair was neatly combed, and his complexion no longer red but pink. "Come in, let's talk."

Two beige leather chairs faced a large teak desk. On the other side of it, behind the editor's black swivel chair, a row of windows faced east toward the university. A teak credenza below the windows held a neat pile of papers. Nils motioned to her to sit in one of the chairs; he sat in the other, facing her.

"You're here about Andy?" he asked.

"Yes."

"He's irrational. She's gone, and we can't bring her back. He doesn't want to accept it; none of us do. But we must," he said firmly.

In the taxi to Nils's office, Kris had lectured herself, practiced the reasoned appeal she would make to him. She tried now to stick to her script.

"Nils, how can we accept calling it an accident if it wasn't?" she asked. "At least until Kripos determines that it was an accident, *Fjordposten* should question what happened."

Nils gave an exasperated sigh and looked away. "Up in the isolated mountains? The Kripos chief told me a few minutes ago that it appears to be an accident." He looked back at Kris, then at the carpet.

"Well," Kris said, "Maybe even they can make a mistake. The FBI does sometimes. You're a newspaperman, Nils. Do you just take whatever the police say as final? Isn't it possible they could be wrong?"

"Sometimes. But not this time."

"If it had been you who died at the fjord, it wouldn't have mattered if everyone told Elsa it was an accident. She would have investigated it herself."

Nils nodded. "Yes, she was headstrong," he said.

"It wasn't just that. She loved you, Nils; you were her best friend, even more. She must have thought you loved her, too."

His face flushed. "So, she told you about us?"

"No, Andy did."

"Our relationship was private." He had lowered his voice.

She studied the face he was trying to keep expressionless. "I can't believe that you don't have any doubts about her death being an accident."

"Sheriff Bjornstad does."

"He does?" Well, well, she thought.

Nils rose and walked around his desk to his black leather chair. Sitting across from her, he put his elbows on his desk and looked her straight in the eye. "Bjornstad thinks what you told him about Elsa's bed and the fact that she left without you could be significant. That, and the fact that she left the others also."

"Really?" Kris said.

"Yes, he thinks she may have taken her own life."

Kris slid forward to the edge of her chair. "How dare he! How dare you! How can you sit here and tell me that? You know Elsa wouldn't do that!" Kris's eyes smarted. She quickly tried to think. Had anything in Elsa's demeanor suggested desperation? No, Elsa was too positive, too engaged with life to throw it away. "What did you tell him?" she asked Nils anxiously.

"That she had everything to live for."

"Thank you, I agree," Kris said, relaxing a bit. "But I simply cannot believe she'd be so careless as to slip off a stupid ledge."

"That is what I meant before. None of us wants to accept her death. But we must."

"But suppose she was pushed? She was a well-known person; maybe she had enemies."

Nils seemed about to lose his patience. "And just who are your suspects?"

"Well, there was that guy with whom she argued about foreign workers. He was obviously radical—maybe even neo-Nazi; he certainly dressed like one."

"You're grasping at straws, Kris."

He swiveled his chair to his right and gazed out the window. Kris waited in silence, looking at his neatly arranged desk. A framed photo was angled enough her way for her to recognize Nils and Grete with, she guessed, their children and grandchildren. The picture triggered a thought. "Nils, why did you remove the photos from Elsa's?"

He spoke to the window. "You wouldn't understand."

She was beginning to understand a lot. "What was Grete doing at the fjord the same time Elsa and I were there?"

"She says it was coincidence, that she wanted to do something while I was in Voss, and she decided to take the fjord excursion. She happened to come to the same place as you."

"And you believe her?" Kris asked.

Slowly he turned back to face Kris. "Why not?" he asked.

"Because she made innuendos. She seemed to think you would be joining Elsa at the hotel."

His cheeks glowed red. "She didn't tell me that."

"It doesn't matter because you already made a decision without that information."

"What do you mean?" he asked testily.

Had she lost all sense of propriety? Kris thought for a moment. She was in a foreign country, talking to a distinguished editor who had been Elsa's closest friend. But the accusatory words continued to pour out.

"You don't want an investigation, Nils, because of Grete. You're afraid she killed Elsa."

He stared at her.

"You and I know that she would have a motive," Kris continued, "but the police wouldn't know that. That's why you removed the photos. You thought if the police came to Elsa's house, they would see the pictures, and maybe suspect something more than friendship between the two of you. And what would happen if they did? Maybe they would conclude that it wasn't a coincidence that your wife and your lover were at the same place at the same time, and one of them wound up dead."

From the look on Nils's face, she knew she was right.

He removed his glasses and massaged the skin below his eyes. "That's nonsense."

"Maybe yes, maybe no."

"Look, Kris. Grete had her bouts with mental illness over the years. It's been painful for both of us, but I thought she was doing all right."

"Why did she spy on you and Elsa at the train station?"

"I don't know. I just can't believe she had anything to do with Elsa's death." He buried his face in his hands.

"If she knew about the two of you, she had a motive," Kris said. Her thoughts raced. Did Grete go to Elsa when she was alone in the hotel room, recovering from her dizzy spell? Did Elsa put her off, suggesting they hike together the next day so they could talk? It would explain Elsa's motive for ensuring that Kris slept in. "We know that Elsa went off on her own, and that after Yolanda and Grete got to the meadow,

Grete went off on her own. That could have been part of their plan, to separate and then meet. Only death had not been part of Elsa's plan."

Nils glared at her. "You can try to open the case on the basis of your suspicions about Grete, but there is no motive unless you can prove one," he said. "I will deny whatever you say. And, I can tell you, even your uncle will do the same. He will not allow his daughter's death to be smeared by scandal."

"Scandal? Elsa Jenssen was the antithesis of scandal."

"Precisely, which would make it all the more sensational. You don't need Andy and me. Just start a few rumors. Our competition—*Bergens Tidende*—would thrive on the speculation about Elsa Jenssen, of all people, being involved in a secret love affair. *VG* would love it, and can you imagine *Nå* and the other tabloids with headlines like 'Did Dahl's wife do it?' 'Did Dahl drive his star journalist to suicide?' Do you know what that would do to Andy? That's not the kind of investigation he had in mind."

She hated Nils for what he was saying. Is that what investigating Elsa's death would mean? His words made her feel like a traitor, eager to reveal his and Elsa's secret, defame her beloved cousin's name, and destroy her uncle.

"Elsa's dead, Kris. We can't change it. We have to pick up the pieces and get on with our lives."

"Get on with our lives? How can you say that?" His words shocked her.

The phone on Nils's desk buzzed. "Excuse me, this is my secretary," he said, lifting the receiver. "I thought I said not to interrupt me," he snapped. "Oh, it's you, Fred."

Kris wanted to get up and leave, but she didn't trust the weak feeling in her legs. She focused on the buildings outside Nils's window and listened to what he was saying to Fred.

"Hold space on the front page for the prime minister's tribute to Elsa. And for an update on the progress of the talks in Eilat and Taba. Run a photo with the article on the peace-keeping forces in Bosnia.

And in the lower right corner the photo of the Rwandan children with the address of where to send relief donations for Central African refugees. Look, I've got someone here in my office. Let's meet in an hour and go over what's come in on the wire service."

Nils hung up the phone and looked back at Kris from behind his desk. "Where were we?"

"Finished," she said, at last confident that her legs would carry her out the door. "I promised Uncle Andy I would convince you to investigate Elsa's death. Now I understand that is impossible. What do I tell him?"

"Don't worry. I'll call and make peace with him. We've been through a lot together." He escorted her out of his office. "We'll get through this. And you will, too."

"Mr. Dahl," Nils's secretary called to him. "There's a man on line one for you. He says it's urgent; it's about Elsa. He won't give his name."

Kris stopped abruptly. This she wanted to hear.

Nils took his secretary's phone. "Hello? Hello?" he said. "Hello?"

The urgent caller had hung up.

CHAPTER 11

▼

Kris had come by taxi in order to arrive at Nils's office quickly, but now she needed to walk and to think. On the first floor she found a corner in the lobby where she exchanged her high heels for the sneakers she had stuffed into her shoulder bag. She donned her purple rain poncho and stepped out into the gray, drizzly Bergen afternoon; the smell of salt water permeated the air.

At the pedestrian mall at Torgalmenningen, the drizzle changed to a downpour, and she ducked into the Narvesen news shop for shelter. She scanned the headlines of the *International Herald Tribune*: a heat wave gripped Washington, D.C., and the eastern United States; at least she was missing that. She took the paper to the counter where she saw *Fjordposten* prominently displayed by the cash register. Elsa smiled out from the front-page photo. Kris's eyes grew moist. She fumbled with her coins, paid for the *Tribune* and a Mars bar, stuffed them in her bag, and ran back out into what was now a substantial rain.

In her mind, she could still see the photo of Elsa, feel her presence. She wondered if Grete really could have killed her, and, if so, would Elsa have wanted Kris to expose the truth or to bury it? She stepped off the curb. Water flooded her right shoe. She froze in a flamingo-like stance, not eager to get her other foot wet. Tires squealed; she teetered. A red Fiat, a blonde woman at the wheel, streaked past, splashing her with water just as someone pulled her back onto the sidewalk.

"Lucky you stopped or you would have been hit," her rescuer, a woman, remarked.

"Yes, thank you, but I should have been watching where I was going," Kris mumbled shakily. She pulled herself together and continued on her way. The sweet smell of freshly baked breads drew her into a small bakery. Her misery called for a calorie-laden pick-me-up, but she had no appetite for the beautiful cream cakes. She chose a wheat roll instead.

At the harbor, business at the outdoor fish market was in full swing. Vendors under makeshift booths with colorful awnings sold fish of all kinds, fruits, vegetables and flowers, jewelry, souvenirs. Fishermen peddled shrimp straight from their boats. Kris threaded her way through the shoppers and sought refuge on Zachariasbryggen where the dock jutted into the narrow harbor. She sat near the statue of Shetlands Larsen, a sea captain who, the plaque said, helped Norwegian Resistance fighters escape the Nazis by smuggling them on his fishing boat to the Shetland Islands. Across from her, the colorful timbered buildings of old Bergen, known as Bryggen, lined the quay. Each was narrow, four stories high with a gabled roof. They were attached to each other in pairs, with passageways separating each pair. These quaint buildings, once Hanseatic warehouses, were now tourist shops, restaurants, art galleries, a museum, a hardware store and other businesses. She and Elsa had strolled there her first night in the city.

A seagull, perched on a post nearby, squawked loudly at Kris; she tossed it a piece of her roll, immediately drawing two other gulls. She remembered times she and Jim and the twins had fed seagulls and ducks many years ago. Then she and Jim had believed their marriage was forever.

That was apparently what Nils also believed—only he added a lover on the side. She tried to put herself in Grete Dahl's place. It was bad enough that Jim and Janet's affair had gone on for eight months without her knowledge, but what if it had gone on for years? Had she found out, she never would have stood for it. How long had Grete known about Elsa and Nils? She imagined the hurt, the bitterness, the hatred, the anger Grete must have felt. Even if Grete didn't know for sure, had her intuition and suspicion haunted her for so long that they exploded yesterday into one violent act above a waterfall?

Kris deeply missed Elsa, but she was also angry with her. Hadn't she known how much she must have been hurting Grete? If Grete had killed her, didn't Elsa bear some responsibility for driving her to it? Didn't Nils? After all, he had hurt both women. Kris threw the last crumbs of her roll to the gulls and plunked the bag into a garbage bin.

In spite of the rain and her wet shoe, she didn't feel ready to return to the loneliness of Elsa's house. She walked along the quay at Bryggen, past the red, yellow and ochre wooden buildings, glancing idly at the windows of the souvenir shops and the crowd in the central tourist information office. Finally, she found herself back at the cobblestone street that led to the Mt. Fløyen funicular. Next to the ivy-covered entrance, a huge wooden troll with a stupid grin failed to make her smile. Like the locals she had passed on the streets, the few passengers on the funicular who were not tourists were cool and aloof. How different the Norwegians were when you got to know them. But today she welcomed their distant manner. She wanted to be alone, to fade into the scenery.

At last she walked up Skansemyrsveien to Elsa's house. Bouquets of carnations, roses, freesia, and a variety of other flowers—wreaths and plants as well—lined the walkway. "Oh, Elsa, did you have any idea how much you were loved?" Kris asked aloud.

Behind her a car door slammed. Kris turned to see Grete Dahl in a gray raincoat hurrying toward her, looking distraught.

"I waited for you. I must talk with you."

Kris bristled. What could Grete want with her? "Let's get out of the rain," she said, opening the door and guiding Grete inside. They took off their shoes. She hung up their wet wraps and sent Grete into the living room while she ran downstairs to discard her wet stockings and put on warm socks.

A few minutes later she found Grete seated at the dining table. "Grete, would you like some coffee? Tea?"

"*Nei, takk,*" she said.

Kris sat across from Grete at the table. "What is it, Grete? How can I help you?"

"Nils thinks I killed Elsa." She choked out her words.

"Why would he think that?" Kris tried to sound astonished.

"Because of the way he looked at me last night. I know what he is thinking." Grete pulled at her hair and fought for self-control. "I know Nils loved Elsa, but he loves me too. When I heard she was dead, I could not help but think that now I have him all to myself. I am ashamed." She bit her lip and glanced up at the ceiling, swallowed, and looked back at Kris. "But it is the same, even with Elsa dead. Maybe it is worse."

Grete walked over to the sideboard and picked up the photo of Per and Nils.

"Per was Nils's best friend. I think Elsa made him feel that Per was still alive. Now he has lost both of them. I grieve for my husband's loss."

"It's very painful for you, isn't it?" Kris said, feeling sympathy for Grete.

"Yes, and that is why I come here. You must find out what happened. You must find out who killed her."

"But the police say it was an accident."

Grete stared at her. "Elsa did not act like herself. Something was wrong."

"But you were quite hostile to her on Saturday night. Maybe she was just annoyed with you."

"No," she looked off across the room.

"If you think someone killed her, why don't you tell Nils? He can go to the police with you," Kris suggested. It was perfect, just what was needed. The triangle of Nils, Elsa, and Grete wouldn't even come up, not with Grete being an instigator of the investigation.

"No. I cannot cause more pain, more publicity for Andy, for Nils."

"But, what can I do?" Kris asked.

"You must find out what happened."

"But how can I? I'm a tourist, a stranger here."

"You must try. You are Elsa's cousin. You are like her; you can find out many things."

Kris felt speechless.

"And now I must go," Grete said.

"Will you tell Nils that you came to see me?" Kris asked as she walked her to the door.

"No. He will only say that I am crazy."

Kris watched through the window as Grete disappeared into the gray afternoon. For the first time she felt relieved that Jim had broken their ties. It had hurt a lot, but at least now she had the possibility of healing; not so for Grete, not as long as Nils suspected her of murder.

CHAPTER 12

▼

By now it was almost five in the afternoon, and Kris realized she would arrive at Andy's much later than she had expected. At least she could call and apologize, let him know she was on her way. She wondered if Nils had already called him, wondered what he had said. He seemed to think he could appease her uncle. She doubted it. Hadn't Nils himself told Elsa she got her pit-bull stubbornness from her father?

She used the phone on Elsa's desk. Tor answered, sounding upbeat as usual. She apologized for her delay. "The visit with Nils didn't go quite as I had planned," she said, doodling on a piece of scrap paper.

"But Nils was here. Everything's fine."

"What? Did he tell Andy he's not doing an investigative article?"

"Hmm."

Kris grimaced. That "hmm" was so annoying. It sounded like indifference, but was apparently a common Norwegian affirmation.

"Andy's okay with that," he added.

"You're kidding!" Five consecutive exclamation marks flowed from her pen on to the paper.

"No. He and Nils talked, and then we spoke with Sheriff Bjornstad."

"And?" Surely, there was more to it than that, she thought.

"He explained what happened. Here's Andy."

"Kristina?" As always, she felt warmed by his voice, which reminded her of her grandfather's.

"Uncle Andy, how are you feeling?"

"All right. I had many visitors. They brought food, flowers. Everyone loved my Elsa."

"Yes, I know. You must see all the beautiful flowers here, too," she said. She searched for a segue to ask her uncle about Bjornstad. He brought up the subject himself.

"The sheriff told me what happened. My poor Elsa. She fell; that's that."

Kris could almost see Andy leaning on his walking stick and shaking his head.

"Even Kripos says it was an accident," he continued. "Tomorrow we shall get the autopsy."

She couldn't lash out at him for agreeing with the others, nor tell him her doubts, nor what Grete had said. He needed to be at peace with himself, and if he wanted to believe Elsa's death was an accident, then so be it.

"You're a good girl; Elsa always said that. I will see you tomorrow."

"I'll see you sooner than that. I just have to get a taxi."

"No, I shall go to bed. I shall see you at Elsa's in the morning. Tor will talk to you now."

Kris's spirits plummeted. Now what was she going to do? She didn't want to spend the evening alone.

"The doctor wants your uncle to get some rest, the nurse here will be checking on him," Tor explained. "Would you like to have dinner with me?"

It would certainly beat being by herself. "Yes, that would be nice. Thank you," she said.

"Can you be ready by six-forty-five?"

"Sure," Kris said. After she hung up the receiver, she rested her head on Elsa's desk, using her folded arms as a pillow. If the case was closed for Uncle Andy, why couldn't it be for her? What could she do anyway? Maybe she just needed to stay a few more days for Andy's sake, then go home. No, she couldn't just pack up and leave. Not with her doubts. She sat up and surveyed the desktop before her.

Bills. You never think when you open them that someone else might end up paying them, she thought, looking at Elsa's collection in a copper holder. She took the stack and flipped through window envelopes—credit card companies, utilities, insurance, subscriptions. She stopped at one plain, thick envelope with B.A. written in the right hand corner, and peeked inside. Airline tickets. She pulled them from the envelope. Flights scheduled in September. Bergen–Oslo on Braethens SAFE, Norway's domestic airline; Oslo–Rekjavik–New York on Icelandair. New York–Buenos Aires on American. New York? Elsa was planning to go through New York next month and hadn't even mentioned it. Why? And why Buenos Aires? Kris wondered. A secret vacation? With Nils? That might explain it.

She put the ticket envelope to the side so she could take it with her and returned the other envelopes to the copper letterholder, keeping them in the order she'd found them.

There was no time to go through the stack of papers in Elsa's in/out baskets. She needed to take a nap, shower, get ready for dinner. Her one last surrender to her sense of order was to pick up the paper clips strewn across Elsa's desk pad and add them to others in a purple plastic cup next to the small box of scrap paper. She took the airline tickets with her and left, promising herself she would return later. This is where Elsa had spent much of her time. Kris remembered the light shining from under the door in the wee hours of the night. If Elsa didn't die accidentally, maybe clues to why not lay here.

After a thirty-minute nap, she showered, then blow-dried her hair into gentle waves that bounced off her shoulders. She made up her eyes carefully with eyeliner and mascara, and covered the circles underneath with foundation. It was a subtle improvement. She thought of Yolanda Mueller's elaborate makeup and golden tan. If she were to try to make herself up like that, she would look like a clown. That was one of the problems of being so fair-skinned: without a bit of makeup, she looked completely washed out; with too much, she looked like a first grader who had played with her mother's cosmetics.

The rain had stopped, and the breeze through the open window was mild. She put on black pants, a soft cotton teal V-neck top, gold earrings, and her Olympic medallion.

Despite feeling she was falling apart inside, Kris wanted to look good on the outside, to show Tor she had things under control. After Grete's visit to her this afternoon, she desperately needed to talk with someone. Tor seemed like a reasonable person; she liked his calmness, the way he treated her uncle. Elsa's high regard for him made Kris feel that he was someone she could trust—even if she had rejected Elsa's matchmaking schemes.

When the doorbell rang at six-forty, she was not only ready but had prepared a snack of apples and cheese.

"Good evening," Tor said. "You look very nice."

So did he, Kris thought as she thanked him. He wore navy slacks, a white button-down shirt open at the neck, and a light-weight jacket. He smelled nice too, she noted, catching a whiff of his spicy after-shave.

"Do you want to bring the flowers in?" he asked.

"No, not right now. I've been thinking I'd like to leave them here for now in remembrance of Elsa, for passersby to see. Do you think they'll be all right?"

"Sure. They're hardy—like most of us Norwegians."

She smiled.

"Are you hungry?" he asked.

"A little. So I fixed us some hors d'oeuvres." She offered him the plate of apples and cheese on the kitchen table.

"Hmm. Good idea," he said, taking a slice of apple. "We could take these outside and do an inventory of the flowers, you know, who sent what, so Andy can acknowledge them."

She agreed at once and was only sorry she hadn't thought of it. Tor took a kitchen chair outside and Kris set the food on it. Together they read the messages and names on the cards and wrote down what was sent. For the first time since Elsa died, Kris felt she'd done something useful.

When they had finished, she chose a huge basket of wildflowers, sent by Elsa's *Fjordposten* colleagues, to put on the dining table. As she and Tor passed through the hallway, he playfully batted at Elsa's row of bells. They jingled loudly.

They decided to walk to town. Kris led the way downstairs so that she could get her fleece from her room on the way out through the basement. Tor waited in the hall, unaware, she hoped, of her discomfort at being in the bedroom area alone with him. Would she ever stop thinking like a faithful married woman?

The lower part of the house smelled damp and seemed bathed in an oppressive, ominous gloom, in part, Kris observed, because outside the thick hedge shut out the late Nordic daylight. "It's eerie, isn't it?" she said, goose bumps rising on her arms.

"It's just the leftover feeling from the rain. Don't worry. There aren't any trolls here." He grinned, opened the door, and gestured for her to go ahead of him.

The short flagstone path took them through a wooden gate in the hedge and to a well-worn trail between the houses of Skansemyren and Fjellveien. In front of them, over the rooftops, the bay shimmered in shafts of evening sunlight breaking through the clouds.

"My God," Kris exclaimed.

"You can just call me Tor."

"Ha, ha." Kris acknowledged his humor. Tor was, after all, the name of the god of thunder in Nordic mythology. "Really, look!" She pointed to the far side of the bay, across the bridge from the university. An other-worldly tri-level red and white Lego-like structure, with two huge cranes on one side and another on top, rose out of the water on three giant concrete pillars. From so far away, it appeared almost as high as the mountain behind it. "I swear it wasn't there before," she insisted. "It looks like the launching pad for the Starship Enterprise!"

"That's what it is," Tor said.

She laughed.

"Actually, I hadn't thought about it in that way before," he said. "It's an oil platform in the dry dock at Laksevåg. It must have been towed it in today from the North Sea."

"I've seen pictures of them before, but in real life, they're much more awesome. That"s what you work on?"

"And sleep on."

"You don't mind being out in the middle of the sea on that thing?"

"*Nei*, it"s a community out there, a mini-city. I'm at home on the sea; besides we stay out there only two or three weeks at a time."

"Then what?"

"Have a break. Sometimes two weeks, sometimes three. This time I've got four weeks."

"Nice. What do you do with your time?"

"I find plenty to do." He didn't elaborate.

They had followed the trail down an incline to Fjellveien and the funicular station.

"Last chance to change your mind. Want to ride?"

"No, I'd rather walk," she replied. They took the sidewalk which, like the road, crossed above the funicular tracks and continued into a grove of tall trees where the view disappeared in the vegetation.

"How did you get into offshore work anyway?"

"My father. When I was a teenager, Norway discovered oil off the continental shelf. Dad worked for Mobil on shore. Before I started college he arranged for me to go with him in a helicopter—that was a big deal then—to visit their operations in the North Sea. And that was it. I decided that day that I wanted to become part of the new frontier."

"How American!"

"No, Norwegian. Think of the Polar explorers, Amundsen, Nansen. They were exploring new frontiers."

"So was Thor Heyerdahl when he sailed across the Pacific in the *Kon-Tiki*."

"Right. My folks actually named me after him."

"You're kidding."

"No. He made it an extra popular name, whether it's spelled with an 'h' or not."

A stairway led them further down the hill; the rooftops of the town drew closer. The shouts and laughter of children playing grew louder as the number of stairs dwindled. Off to the right a playground nestled among fir, birch, and maples. The two-foot fence surrounding the playground was dwarfed along the length of its downhill side by tall bushes, creating the illusion of a secluded garden. How her children would have enjoyed this when they were small, Kris thought.

Youngsters played on tire swings and climbed on a red-and-green wooden boat set in sand. The boat was about fifteen feet long with a small cabin. Two children disappeared inside, successfully concealing their whereabouts by crouching in a corner, away from the doorway. Kris soon spotted "It" by a tree stump, confirming her suspicion that a game of hide-and-seek was underway. "Jorunn? Karl? Where are you?" the little girl called.

"Do they remind you of your kids when they were young?"

"Yes." Had he read her mind? She remembered he'd seen their graduation photo the night before.

"What do you do when you're not being a wife and mother?"

"I do research for authors, check facts, background material."

"Kind of a word detective," Tor said.

"Yes, I guess you could say that," Kris agreed.

"Were you an English major?"

"No, a Scandinavian languages major. But I never finished my degree. Got married instead and didn't find much demand for what I did know at that time. My current work just sort of evolved."

The walkway ended at Skansen. Elsa had explained to Kris that the white tower—a Bergen landmark—had once served as a lookout for fires, and that the defunct fire station next to it was now used for neighborhood meetings. On the other side of the road, huge green pots of red geraniums and a few wooden benches marked a pleasant Bergen overlook. A couple admiring the view continued on their way, leaving the area empty; this was the opportunity Kris had hoped for.

"Could we sit for a while?"she asked.

"Why not?" Tor said.

The inner harbor lay just below them. Clouds sailed eastward over the mountains and the swath of lavender blue sky steadily broadened on the western horizon. The sound of a guitar drifted up from the wharf. Kris looked around to make sure no one was within earshot. Two teenagers were huddled inside a red British-style telephone booth to the left of the tower, engrossed in their phone conversation.

"Were you with Andy when Nils convinced him that *Fjordposten* didn't need to do an investigation?" Kris asked.

"No, Nils asked me to leave them alone. I went down the hall and visited with your friend Sigrid."

Kris couldn't help being amused by the thought of Tor chatting up the elderly woman. But her thoughts about that quickly vanished and returned to what Tor couldn't tell her—what Nils may have said to convince Andy to forget about more investigations.

"So when you went back, Andy was okay about Elsa's death having been an accident?"

"Right. Then we called Bjornstad. What's all this about, Kris?"

"I'm wondering if Nils intimidated Andy into accepting the accident theory."

"What do you mean—theory?" Tor asked, turning toward her, resting his left knee on the bench, stretching his left arm along the back.

Kris told him about Nils and Elsa's affair, about Grete's behavior at the train station on Saturday morning and her surprise appearance at the hotel, about Grete's mental instability. And, about her own suggestion to Nils that Grete could have killed Elsa, and that he wanted to cover up this possibility.

Tor listened intently. "That's sensitive stuff. What did Nils say?"

"He got angry, of course. He denied that Grete could have done it and said that to even raise the question would scandalize my uncle's reputation and Elsa's memory."

"He's right." Tor looked out in the direction of the rig and rubbed his beard for a few minutes, then looked back into her eyes. "Don't you think this theory about Grete is a stretch?"

"Well, the other thing is that she came to see me this afternoon."

"Nils had told her about your visit?"

"No, she came on her own. *She* says she doesn't think Elsa's death was an accident."

"Why?" Tor looked incredulous.

"She said something was wrong, that Elsa didn't act like herself."

"That could mean anything. You said she hadn't been feeling well."

"But how do you explain Elsa's stuffing her bed? Changing my alarm? And, I might add, fixing me a nightcap just like Andy did last night? If she didn't put anything in my drink, why was I so groggy that morning? And what about her missing notebook?"

"It sounds to me as if Elsa wanted to be alone for some reason, and she didn't want you to worry. As for the notebook, maybe she put it down somewhere in the hotel. Or maybe, as someone suggested, she tucked it under her arm when she took the picture of the waterfall."

Kris sighed. "Then tell me why she would drug me so she could take photos of a waterfall? It doesn't make sense."

"This isn't the United States where you have violent crimes every day. It's not like that here. We have our crime—robberies, some gangs in Oslo, other things. But at most we have about forty murders a year in the whole country; that's a lot less than places like Washington or New York have in a couple of months."

"But, you do have some crime here, and Elsa could have been a victim." She returned his gaze, aware that he was studying her.

"You have to have a motive. You suggested Grete had one. Have you changed your mind?"

"Well, I thought I had. But now I think about how weird she acted at the station and at the hotel, and I'm wondering if I can believe what she told me today. At least, she *seemed* genuine."

Jim would have been sarcastic; Tor seemed willing to suspend judgment and hear her out.

"Odd Engstrom would be another likely suspect," Kris said.

"The skinhead you told Andy and me about?"

"Yes. I'd like to know where he was when Elsa fell."

"Motive?"

"Hatred, perhaps. He knew that Elsa wrote on the subject they argued about, he knew she was an influential voice opposing his beliefs. Why not silence her if he sees an opportunity? He could have been angry about their argument, felt Elsa had humiliated him. Imagine he sees her standing on a ledge, concentrating on taking a photo, her back is to him. He sneaks up on her." Kris could imagine the scene as if she were there, the terror of the split second when Elsa felt hands on her back, pushing her, and realized there was nothing to hang on to, nothing to keep her from falling.

She shook herself. "It's just too awful to imagine!" She put her hands over her eyes.

Immediately, Tor's hand, the skin slightly rough, gently pulled them away.

"Hey, hey," he said. "You're upset about what happened to Elsa. That's natural, but don't try to fool yourself. You're not objective; you're angry. You don't want to accept her death."

So much for her rational image, Kris mused. She took a tissue from her bag and wiped her eyes. Tor couldn't know that her tears had come not only from her thoughts about Elsa but from his caring gesture. "Let's go eat," she said.

CHAPTER 13

▼

Kris and Tor descended the narrow cobblestone alleyways to the harbor and Bryggen's row of buildings that used to be medieval warehouses. As they were passing a shop window trimmed with Norwegian flags, heavy handknit sweaters, trolls, hand-painted wooden bowls, and other pieces of Norwegian craftsmanship, Tor stopped abruptly.

"There's someone here I'd like you to meet," he said, ducking as he stepped through the open doorway.

A young blonde woman with a pixie haircut and an angelic face bounced over to them. "Hi," she sang. She and Tor embraced.

"Lise," Tor said, "I'd like you to meet my friend, Kris Kelly. Lise's my…"

"It's a pleasure to meet you," Kris said, extending her hand. She didn't want to hear whether Lise was his girlfriend or fiancé or lover. It really didn't matter.

"I am very happy to meet you, too."

Lise was a full two inches taller than Kris, with long slender legs and the perfect young figure for the mini-skirt she was wearing. "Tor told me Elsa Jenssen was your cousin. I'm sorry about her accident. She was so wonderful!"

"Thank you," Kris said, trying to graciously accept the sympathy, but wanting to escape. "Why don't I look around the shop and give you two a chance to visit?"

"No time, we're on our way to dinner, remember?" Tor said. He kissed Lise on the cheek. "See you."

"It was nice meeting you, Mrs. Kelly."

"Yes, same here," Kris said, even though the "Mrs. Kelly" made her feel old. "Lovely *girl*," she remarked to Tor when they were back out on the street. Nothing like sounding catty, she thought. Youth was "in" judging from Tor's and Jim's taste in women; she'd have to accept that.

"This way," Tor said, turning into a wooden passageway between old timbered warehouses.

"This reminds me of something from a set for a Hollywood western," Kris said.

"Yeah, my friends and I used to play cowboys and Indians around here."

"You're kidding. Cowboys and Indians in Norway?"

"Yeah. It's not so surprising. Norwegians have always been great fans of the Americans, especially after World War II. When I was growing up, I heard a lot about America. I also used to devour Karl May books."

"Karl May?"

"Oh, I forget you Americans don't know him. His books are fantastic! He was a German writer in the late-nineteenth century. He wrote great stories about the wild West. Very realistic, yet he'd never been there."

"Unfortunately, America's treatment of the Indians is a tragic part of our history," Kris said. "But was it the excitement of the Old West stories that inspired you to study in the United States?"

He nodded. "It inspired me to push my parents to let me spend a summer with relatives in Minnesota. After that experience, I wanted to study there."

"It seems like every Norwegian has relatives in the States—thanks to our immigrant ancestors. I read recently that there are as many Norwegian-Americans in the States as there are Norwegians in Norway. Something like four and a half million."

"Sounds right. Or as they say in Minnesota, 'Yah sure, ya betcha,'" Tor said merrily as they reached the end of the passageway.

They turned into a cobblestone courtyard where the sounds of a happy evening crowd greeted them from the open door of a pub. Kris followed Tor inside. A male voice shouted Tor's name above the country music. Three men and two women, all probably in their thirties, sat at a table not far from the door. One of the men motioned them to come over.

"Engineers and roustabouts from Troll—one of the rigs I worked on," Tor explained to Kris. "Let's say 'Hello.'"

She felt his hand lightly touch the middle of her back, bringing her with him to his friends. He spoke first in Norwegian, shaking hands with all of then, kissing both women on the cheeks. Then he made introductions in English. The group seemed interested in the fact that Kris was American, and she decided to speak English rather than get into explanations of how it was that she knew Norwegian. She raised her voice to be heard above the din.

Neither Tor nor she made any mention of her relationship to Elsa Jenssen. From the way some of them were sizing her up, she guessed they assumed she was his date. Perhaps they were curious that he was with someone close to his own age.

"Why don't you join us?" the one called Peder asked.

"No thanks," Tor answered. "We have reservations upstairs."

Peder gave them a knowing look.

"Well, watch out for him," the woman named Astrid teased.

Kris tried to laugh, "Thanks, I will."

They left the crowded bar through a thick wooden door and climbed a flight of stairs to a cozy restaurant where a hodgepodge of conversations in English, Japanese, French, and Norwegian mixed with classical music playing in the background. The timbered walls painted in a muted green with peach trim along the ceiling beams and doorways were adorned with copper utensils and tapestries between the generous array of windows. A model of a Viking ship hung between the two brass chandeliers. The kitchen smells reminded Kris that she was hungry. The waiter seated them at a corner table set with white linen placemats and napkins, removed the "Reserved" sign, and lit the candle between them. He returned shortly with their drinks: orange juice for her, beer for Tor.

"I hope you didn't mind those guys downstairs," Tor said as the waiter walked off.

"No, not at all, it's fun to see people enjoying themselves."

"We do a lot of that. And I hope that, in spite of everything, you'll have a good time this evening," he said, raising his glass to hers.

She sipped her juice and tried to relax. This was the first time in ages that she had been in a restaurant alone with a man other than Jim. No, that wasn't quite true. Tom, from Jim's department, professing deep concern for her welfare, had taken her to dinner a month after Jim moved out. Then he suggested they go to bed. Why was she even thinking of that idiot? She had been flattered by the crew's teasing a few minutes ago. The looks from Peder and the others indicated that they did not consider her an antique yet.

"I like this restaurant," she said. "Lots of atmosphere."

"Your uncle helped me choose it." Tor's face radiated the glow of skin constantly exposed to the elements.

"Uncle Andy helped you choose?"

"Yes. He wanted you to get an idea of old Bergen. During the Nazi occupation, the Resistance had a secret room and a powerful radio transmitter in that building across from us. It's the Theta Museum now, named after the group that worked out of there. They supplied important intelligence information to the Norwegian government in exile in England until the Germans caught them."

"How did they get caught?"

"Bad luck. The room was completely hidden with fake walls; the Germans missed it in every search. Then one of the soldiers walking on the roof, fell through some rotten boards right into the room."

"How ironic," Kris said. "What happened to the Resistance guys?"

"None of them were in the room at the time. They had an escape plan, and a few managed to get away. Others were caught by the Nazis and sent to concentration camps; not all of them lived through that experience, but at the end of the war, some of the Theta members came home."

"What was Uncle Andy's connection to Theta?"

"He knew some of them. Your uncle ran an underground newspaper—also a very dangerous activity in those days. You know, he barely escaped a death sentence."

"It's scary to even think about that," Kris said.

"My father used to say that your uncle said many times he wished it had been him whom the Nazis killed instead of Per."

"Poor Andy. He's known such sadness. Did he talk a lot about Per and Elsa today?" Kris asked, thinking how terrible it must be for him now to have lost both his children.

"Yes, he talked about when they were little. I think it cheered him up." Tor took another gulp of his beer. "Guess we'd better decide what we want to eat."

She surveyed the menu: salmon with leek sauce; fish plate of codfish, catfish, and salmon; fillet of reindeer served with brussel sprouts and lingonberries; mussels sauteed in wine sauce. She chose the salmon; Tor the reindeer.

Kris knew she owed Tor the benefit of a lively, at least not distracted, dinner companion, but she realized she would not be able to give him her full attention unless she made a phone call. She excused herself to the ladies' room, which she had noticed downstairs next to two telephones.

She opened the Bergen phone book to the E's and ran her finger down the page until she came to Engstrom; there were a few with the initial O, but only one Odd Engstrom. She copied down the number and address, then dialed. There was no answer.

She took Oscar's business card from her bag and dialed the Fjord Hotel, putting several crowns into the phone to pay for long-distance.

When someone answered "Fjord Hotel," she recognized Inga's voice. Since she had no idea how she could explain to Inga why she wanted to talk with Odd, Kris disguised her voice and added a British accent. She asked for Odd Engstrom and was told he had checked out earlier in the day. "But I must speak to him," she lamented. "Have you a telephone number for him?"

Inga hesitated.

"He has my camera, and I must have it back," she insisted.

"Very well," Inga gave her the number, which matched the one she had. At least she knew she had the right number; she would just have to try later.

She looked at her watch; she had been gone ten minutes.

"Sorry to keep you waiting," she said when she rejoined Tor.

"It must be a popular place down there," Tor said, smiling.

She started to agree, but then decided otherwise. "I was on the phone, trying to track down Odd Engstrom," she confessed.

Tor's smile disappeared. "This thing is eating you up, isn't it?"

Her eyes met his, and she nodded in the affirmative.

"Give me your right hand," he said, stretching his across the table.

She did as he asked. "Can we shake on an agreement that you will put all of this out of your mind at least during dinner and try to eat and enjoy yourself?"

She tightened her hand around his. "Absolutely," she said.

At that moment the dinner arrived.

The salmon was delicious; Kris's first bite melted in her mouth.

"You know," Tor said, "during the war, there was such a shortage of everything, Norwegians made shoes out of fish skins."

"You're kidding," Kris said. With her fork, she gently pushed part of the skin of the salmon away from the meat. "How's it possible?"

"They would dry the skins, then shape them, and sew them, and attach them to a wooden base. I saw some once."

"Unbelievable," Kris said. It amazed her to imagine how this thriving country had once suffered so much from Nazi occupation.

"My mother told me she also made herself paper shoes in those times," Tor continued.

"The folks back then really proved that necessity is the mother of invention, didn't they?" Kris said.

"Hmm," he agreed.

"By the way," she asked, changing the subject, "why did Astrid say I should watch out for you?"

He grinned, then looked into his beer. "Oh, I'm still trying to live down the reputation of my younger years," he said.

"You mean you've reformed?"

"Hmm. But I won't bore you with the details."

She liked the way his eyes twinkled when he smiled. "You wouldn't bore me," she said.

He rubbed his beard, as, Kris had noticed, he tended to do a lot. "Well, we've spent enough time talking about me. I'd like to know more about you."

Kris fidgeted in her chair. She started talking about her work, and soon found, that in response to Tor's questions she talked about the family, especially the children. When he asked her about her husband, she moved smoothly into recalling their visit to Norway after their six-month sabbatical in Israel. She had planned then to keep the subject focused on Norway, but found Tor responding to her mention of Israel.

"Did you learn Hebrew?" he asked.

"Only a few words like *shalom, tohdah, sheket.*"

"Hello, thanks, and be quiet."

"How did you know?" she asked, astonished.

"I worked on a kibbutz once."

"Given your profession, I would have thought you'd have spent your time in other parts of the Middle East, like where the oil fields are."

"There, too," he said. "I was in Saudi with Aramco." He told her about his years in the Middle East, his work with Mobil in Houston, and about his graduate studies at Stanford.

After dinner they walked along the quay, beyond the warehouses and the Bergen Museum. It was the same walk Kris had taken with Elsa the first night she had arrived. Only a few clouds remained in the sky; a breeze had come up off the water. Seeing the Royal Crown Hotel reminded her of the travel agent's card from Elsa's wallet and the fact that she'd forgotten to call him today. They entered the grounds of Bergenhus Castle where spotlights illuminated the stone walls of Håkon's Hall (Håkonshallen, as Tor called it in Norwegian) and Rosenkrantz Tower with its distinctive gray-green cupola. Tor repeated, what Elsa had told her previously, that the former had been the royal ceremonial hall in the thirteenth century and the latter an important fortification during the same period.

"Last night your uncle talked about a boat exploding in the harbor," Tor said.

"Yes, I remember."

"That was in 1944. It was a Dutch boat—the *Voorbode*—that the Germans had commandeered for war service. They overloaded it with dynamite and detonators—a lethal combination. It killed more than a hundred Norwegians and injured thousands. The blast blew the roofs right off of these buildings."

"You'd never know it now," Kris said. They stood in the shadow of Håkonshallen, looking up at its arched windows, its long, pitched roof.

"I used to come here a lot with my folks," Tor said.

"Tell me about them."

"They've both passed away, but they were great. They loved America. They used to talk about how the Brits and the Americans had saved Europe, and how the Marshall Plan helped Norway get back on its feet. My mom used to say if it hadn't been for the Allies ending the war, my dad would have died at Grini."

Kris shuddered. "How long was your father there?"

"Three years. He was tough; I guess that's what got him through the camp and the torture he suffered."

"It must have been horrible."

"Hmm. He never talked about his treatment. It's my mother who told me."

"Why was he at Grini?"

"He lived near Oslo in those days. He was caught smuggling Jews to Sweden."

"He was a brave man."

"He would have been the first to tell you, 'not any braver than most Norwegians.' He would also have said, 'We should have done more.' The Danes did a far better job than we did in helping Jewish citizens." Then, as if he felt he had belittled his father's heroism, Tor added, "He was a good man."

"You must miss him."

"Yeah, and my mom, too." Tor burrowed his hands into his pockets. "My father died of a heart attack when I was studying in the States. That was a shock. I came back for the funeral and stayed, figured my mom needed to have me close by. Your family, Andy and Liv and Elsa, were great. They gave us a lot of moral support. I started working on the North Sea rigs. Then, less than six months later, my mom was diagnosed with cancer. Three months later, she was gone."

"I'm sorry."

"That's okay. It was a long time ago."

"Elsa told me that I met your parents once," she said.

"How's that possible?" he asked.

She told him about her visit to his parents' house with Elsa so many years ago and her infatuation with the raft.

"You remember the raft?" He threw his head back and laughed. "I built that raft when I was ten, and I was so proud of it. It was my *Kon-Tiki*."

Kris smiled, imagining a young Tor pretending he was sailing off to Polynesia on his homemade raft.

"Tell me about *your* parents," Tor said.

"They were the reason I came to Norway that summer. My mother was killed in a car crash. My dad had been driving, and he felt so much guilt, he just couldn't cope at first. I stayed with an aunt and uncle and their kids; then Elsa suggested I should stay with her for a month, and everyone agreed it was a good idea. She was a godsend. She and Norway helped me begin to feel that I could survive."

"What about your father?"

"He had a lot of therapy and recovered—as much as anyone can recover from such a tragedy. He went back to work and tried to be the best dad he could be. And he was! And a good grandfather, too, to my kids. But then, when he hit seventy, he started to decline." She tried to keep her voice from shaking. "He's got Alzheimer's. He rarely recognizes me anymore." She waited to regain her composure before adding, "I understand what you meant yesterday when you said death is like a thief in the night, robbing you of something, someone precious. It's not only death that does that."

"I guess not," Tor said. "I'm sorry about your father, Kris."

They took the funicular up the hill to Elsa's stop.

"Have you told your husband about Elsa?" Tor asked.

"Yes," she answered. "He was going to break the news to our son and daughter."

"Will he join you here?"

Of course that was a logical question, Kris thought. "No, he can't really get away right now," she said. It was the truth; she didn't need to add that he wouldn't come in any case.

They re-entered Elsa's house through the basement; Kris had kept her bargain over dinner, but now she needed to talk about what had happened to Elsa. "Do you want to stay while I call Odd Engstrom?" she asked Tor when they were back in Elsa's kitchen.

"Wouldn't miss it," he said.

She read him Odd's address.

"That's in Laksevåg," he said, "near where the drydock is."

It was eleven o'clock. Late, perhaps, but she figured she would have a better chance of reaching Odd now. Indeed he answered on the first ring. Kris identified herself and, surprisingly, he responded civilly.

"I was wondering if I could talk with you about my cousin's accident," she said.

"Okay. We could meet now," he said to her surprise.

"Just a minute, please." She covered the receiver and repeated his words to Tor.

"You've had a long day. Are you up to it?" he asked.

She had to admit that she would be in better shape in the morning.

"We're meeting Andy and Nils here at ten tomorrow. Do you think we could meet him at noon?"

Tor nodded.

Kris spoke again into the receiver. "Is noon tomorrow all right?" she asked.

"Yes. I will come to you," Odd said. She gave him her address. "He was certainly accommodating," she said after hanging up.

"Let's see how he is tomorrow," Tor said, rubbing his beard. "Remember, as far as you know, this man, no matter how much you distrust him, has done nothing wrong. You'll need to keep cool."

"I will."

"I should be going," Tor said. "Are you sure you don't mind staying here alone? I could ask Lise to keep you company."

"No, that's quite all right," she insisted, telling herself she would be okay in the empty house. God forbid, she didn't need someone half her age "babysitting" her. "I'll be fine. Thanks for dinner. I had a nice time."

They shook hands.

"The feeling is mutual," Tor said. "Have a good night. See you tomorrow."

Kris locked the door and leaned her head on it for a moment, thinking how much she had enjoyed his company. She returned to the living room. The last of the late Nordic sunset glowed a pale pink above the dark barrier islands. Across the bay in Laksevåg, a red beacon on the oil platform flashed on and off.

A few minutes ago, she had felt exhausted, but now alone in the house, she felt reluctant to go to bed. At home, watching a good comedy often relaxed her; perhaps she could find one now: maybe an old British *Fawlty Towers* or a rerun of *Seinfeld*.

Unfamiliar with Elsa's television, she played with the remote controls and finally got it to work, tuning in a late news broadcast.

She recognized the lobby of the Royal Crown Hotel where she and Elsa had walked Wednesday night. The reporter was interviewing tourists, finding out where people were from, getting their reactions to Bergen.

"You're kidding me," she said aloud. To her surprise and delight, George Mueller appeared before the camera and, after some initial confusion, graciously answered the reporter's questions about where he was from and when he had arrived in Norway.

"Are you on vacation, sir?" the reporter asked.

"Yes," George said, looking quite satisfied with himself, "I am on my honeymoon in your beautiful country with my bride. She is over there."

The camera panned to Yolanda Mueller partially hidden by a large plant.

Kris looked again at the TV's control panel. This was a tape; she had triggered the VCR. This must be the interview George Mueller had mentioned Saturday night in the library. Elsa had pretended not to know anything about it, yet she had taped it. The map of Norway with temperature readings flashed on the screen, and an attractive meteorologist in a coral dress forecast good weather for the fjord region with the possibility of evening showers. Special mention was made of the Peer Gynt Weekend celebrations in eastern Norway. Kris remembered that on her first evening in Bergen she had come upstairs after unpacking and joined Elsa who was watching this particular weather forecast on television.

The fact that the tape had begun at the interview with George Mueller indicated it had been rewound to that point. Kris tried to remember what Elsa had said at the fjord about Yolanda: "I want to know why she was hiding behind the plant."

Kris replayed the tape, freezing it where the camera showed Yolanda behind the plant. Whether she was hiding or simply obscured from view by the large plant was debatable. She had been in full view when the camera had first captured her and George coming out of the elevator together. Kris stared at the still shot until the tape started running again, then she turned it off.

Pit bull, nothing, bloodhound was more like it, Kris thought. Yolanda Mueller must have been the reason Elsa had decided they should go to the Fjord Hotel. It had nothing to do with weather, doctors, or the need to relax. But how did Elsa know Yolanda would be there and not still at the Royal Crown? And why the secrecy? Kris could no longer think. She needed to sleep.

Bed never looked more inviting. Dropping her bag on the floor, she had no energy left to take off her clothes, only the gold medallion, earrings and watch, which she put on the nightstand. Snuggling under the top blanket, she turned off the lamp and let her head sink into the pillow, savoring the light scent of lavender.

When she awoke abruptly a few hours later, the luminous digits of her clock indicated a few minutes past two. Something had awakened her. Was it the discomfort of having fallen asleep in her clothes, the longing to slip into a nightgown and crawl under the rest of the covers? No, it had been a sound, something between a thud and a bang. Had something dropped? Had she set something too close to the edge of the kitchen counter?

Through her open doorway, the nightlight from the bathroom down the hall threw grotesque shadows along the wall. Last night Uncle Andy had been here. But now she was all alone in Elsa's big house. Just knowing that could make her mind play tricks.

She held her breath and listened. Another sound, a slight shuffle upstairs. Adrenalin charged through her. She sat up and listened again. When the bells at the top of the stairs jingled, she was off the bed, her shoulder bag in tow.

CHAPTER 14

▼

Heart racing, Kris slipped along the dark side of the hall to the stairway leading to the lower floor. Instinct told her to run for her life. Afraid that the aged stairs would creak and give her away, she felt for the thick bannister and slid down it, landing silently on her bare feet. She heard the creaking of the stairs above her, then the distinct sound of footsteps moving toward the bedroom area.

Who was it? Someone who knew that she was alone in the house? But who, other than Tor, knew that? She felt her way carefully across the dark room. She heard footsteps go into Elsa's bedroom overhead, then the hall, moving in the direction of her room.

Her trembling hands, wet with sweat, slipped on the doorknob. She wiped them off on her pants and willed them to stay still. This time, she turned the knob with one hand, and slowly, almost noiselessly, opened the door wide enough to squeeze through. Just as quietly she closed it behind her, then turned and ran—the flagstones cold under her feet. She pulled the gate open, stubbing her toe as she did so. Holding back a cry of pain, she hid on the outside of the hedge, peering back through the bushes at the house. She reached down to momentarily wrap her fingers around her injured toe.

The light went on in the downstairs living room, and she could see, not very well, a man in a hooded sweatshirt; the hood casting a shadow over his face.

Had he heard her? When the door opened, Kris flew down the path. She stopped when she reached Fjellveien, and listened. Was that the sound of a gate closing? Had she left the gate in the hedge open? The funicular would not be running at this hour; she'd have to go the way that she and Tor had walked earlier. Ignoring the pain in her toe, she ran up the street, keeping away from the street lights and in the shadows of bushes and trees, praying that there was no broken glass in her path.

Mercifully, the few lights in the park were off or burnt out, providing her the cover of darkness. Her heart thumped loudly. Above the sound of her own panting it was impossible to hear if someone was behind her.

Reaching a step sheltered by an overhanging bough, she stopped and looked back the way she had come. She fought to stop her knees from shaking and her teeth from chattering. She could see the lights of Bergen below her, too far away. She was almost out of breath. She would have to find somewhere to hide. She ran down the last few stairs, hopped over the low fence, and into the silent playground.

The boat stood solid and unobtrusive in the shadowy darkness. She welcomed the feeling of sand under her feet, ran to the boat, and hid in the cabin, taking in deep silent breaths to regain control of her breathing and her nerves. It was unlikely anyone would find her here if she was quiet. Clutching her bag, she listened for footsteps. All she could hear was the gurgling of the fountain at Skansen.

Five, ten, fifteen minutes went by. He would have passed by now if he was after her. Did this mean she wasn't being pursued after all? Chains banging against each other signaled that someone was down by the tire swings. He must have stayed on the road and come down the hill on the other side of the playground. A few minutes later, Kris heard the unmistakable sound of footsteps nearby; then they stopped. Whoosh! She felt the movement of air as if a blanket were being shaken or a fish net cast. Could someone be imprisoning her here? The cloth fell on the back of the boat, away from her hiding place. She folded her hand around Elsa's keys and the flashlight; she would defend herself by wielding her bag or using the sharpness of the keys as a weapon.

"Come to me," a youthful male voice said in Norwegian.

Who was this pervert? she wondered. She needed to make her move now, not let him corner her here in the boat.

She jumped out of her hiding place, her flashlight aimed toward the voice that had just spoken. A shirtless young man turned around, fists out, ready to fight. His date, her open blouse exposing her bare breasts, let out a shriek. This was hardly the confrontation Kris had anticipated. She felt such relief to be facing young lovers rather than someone intent on doing her harm that she had to control an urge to burst into hysterical laughter.

"Excuse me," she said and walked past them toward the exit of the playground. She had dismissed her first urge to ask for their help; they were intent on their own urges. And in any case, would they have believed anything said by a woman who came out of a children's boat in the middle of the night?

Kris ran to the telephone booth at Skansen, brightly lit by streetlights. For the first time since she'd run from the house, she realized she was shivering from cold, not fear. She missed her fleece jacket. Below her the streets of Bergen were empty. A neon clock on top of one of the office buildings blinked the current time: three-ten a.m., and temperature: thirteen degrees Celsius. She tried to calculate to Fahrenheit; it must be somewhere in the mid-fifties. A brisk breeze added to her discomfort. Her feet were cold, but at least the ache in her toe was gone.

Her fear and pain of a short time ago were now replaced by anger as she realized that the intruder must have known of Elsa's death and have been looking for her valuables. She pulled out of her bag the piece of paper with Tor's phone number on it and dialed, praying she wouldn't get an answering machine. After four rings, a sleepy-sounding Tor answered.

"There's someone in the house."

"What?"

"It's Kris," she said. She told him quickly what had happened.

"Where are you?" Now he sounded wide awake.

"Skansen."

"I'm coming. I'll call the police and get a car to Elsa's right away. I'll pick you up in ten minutes."

"No, I'm going back. I want to see what this creep is up to."

"Don't be crazy." As if he knew that statement would not deter her, he added, "The funicular isn't running. Suppose that guy is hiding somewhere, waiting for you?"

"He's not after me; he's after Elsa's valuables," she said. Kris had heard back in the States about cases where families returned from funeral services to find their homes robbed by thieves who simply read the funeral notices in the paper and looked up the address of the deceased. Even without a funeral, news of Elsa's death had been on the front pages of the papers, and all over radio and television. It wouldn't be difficult to find out her address. And, of course, with all those flowers out in front, which house was Elsa's was a dead giveaway. Kris knew she couldn't just sit and wait for Tor.

"I'll be careful," she promised.

"Don't go back into the house by yourself," he cautioned. "I'll be there as fast as I can."

Before leaving the booth, she rummaged in her bag hoping to find something to keep her warm. Why couldn't she have stuffed a hat, a scarf, something into it? A pair of socks at least. She felt the candy bar she'd bought at the train station a few days ago and that she'd completely forgotten. Eagerly, she fished it out, peeled back the wrapping, and bit into the soft chocolate. If only she had shoes in her bag as well. She remembered Tor's story at dinner about how people made fishskin shoes during the war. Too bad she didn't have any fishskin, she thought wryly, and then brightened. Tor had also mentioned paper. That was it!

She took out the envelope with Elsa's tickets, put them with her own in her document pouch, and set the empty white envelope on the phone book next to the chocolate. Thank goodness she'd kept the five-by-seven-inch manilla envelope in her bag; it was empty because the graduation picture she kept in it was on her bedside table at Elsa's. She put it on the phone book as well. She would make herself paper shoes. Yes, it might work. *The International Herald Tribune*—yet unread—could also serve a purpose. Rubberbands? She always kept a few at the bottom of her bag. She recovered three big ones. Perfect.

Leaning against one side of the phone booth, she lifted her right foot, wrapped a page of the newspaper around it, and then slipped her padded foot into the manilla envelope. She fastened it with a rubberband. Next she wrapped her left foot with newspaper, pushed it as far as possible into the white business envelope and secured it with two rubberbands. She opened the remaining newspaper and draped it over her head and shoulders, and held on to it with her hands. Necessity was indeed the mother of invention. "Ready or not, here I come," she said, pushing the phone booth door open with her shoulder.

She went around to the left of the tower and scuffed her way up a small street, past the darkened houses. A tiny hedgehog popped out from underneath a trash bin and skittered across the street and into the bushes. A cat sitting outside one of the doors bristled and ran as Kris rustled by. So far her noisy shoes were holding. If only Charlie and Laura could see their mom now, she thought. The street dead-ended at stairs that took her close to the bend in the road coming from Fjellveien. She rested at the guardrail, away from the street light, studying the tree-corridor for anyone lurking in the shadows.

Headlights at the top of the hill warned her that a car was coming her way. Hide! she told herself. But where? On the opposite side of the road, maple saplings grew out of a large stump. She skipped across, hearing, then feeling her white shoe tear underneath, but the rubberbands held. She pulled off her newspaper cape, stuffed it under her arm, and crouched behind the stump just as the headlights struck the guardrail.

From the speed of the car, it was unlikely that the driver would be looking for anyone on the side of the road. The brakes squealed as the small red car slowed to make the turn; the driver wore a hood. Kris was sure it was the man who had been at Elsa's house, someone up to no good; otherwise, why cover up the license plate so it couldn't be read? In moments, the car was out of sight.

Kris guessed that it must be at least ten minutes since she had called Tor. She was too cold and uncomfortable to stay where she was; the only thing to do was resume walking. She wrapped the newspaper around her again, gritted her teeth, and headed up the hill. She felt the pavement through the hole in the newspaper wrapped around her left heel.

A few minutes later another car approached. She ducked into the shadows. This car moved slowly, its high beams blinding her. Only when it was almost next to her, did she recognize the Volvo and step into the light, waving feverishly.

Tor halted the car and leapt out. He wore running shorts, a light jacket over a T-shirt, and untied sneakers without socks.

"Boy, am I glad to see you," she cried.

"Thank God, you're okay," he said. "I came as fast as I could."

"You just missed the guy I saw at Elsa's."

He grasped her shoulders, his hands on the edges of the *Tribune*. His eyes stared into hers as if making sure that she indeed was all right.

She leaned her head on his safe, warm chest before she caught herself and pulled back. "Sorry," she said, embarrassed. "It's just so good to see a friendly face."

"No need to apologize." He took her newspaper and put his jacket around her.

She told him about the speeding car. "I tried to read the license number but there was something covering the plate."

"You're cold. Let's talk about it in the car." He held the car door open for her. "By the way, I like your shoes," he said.

Tor turned the car around at Skansen, and they headed back up the hill. "I came the back way. The police are already outside Elsa's. When they told me you weren't there, I kept going. I'm glad I found you!"

The police officers were waiting in Elsa's driveway. Kris discarded her makeshift shoes before getting out of Tor's car.

"We've circled the house twice. There's no sign of forced entry," one of the officers reported.

"Did you see anyone?"

"No one."

Kris unlocked the door and let Tor and the officers precede her, while she slid her feet into the warmth of her terrycloth slippers. A cursory walk through the living/dining room and kitchen turned up no obvious signs of a break-in.

At the officers' request, Kris recounted what had happened. When she told her listeners about the boat, Tor said, "So now you know what 'love boat' Norwegian style is."

It was the only humorous moment; none of them found the idea of an intruder in Elsa Jenssen's house the least bit funny. Kris was sorry that she couldn't give them a better description of the man she had seen.

They went through the house together, floor by floor, room by room. Nothing seemed out of place: no dresser drawers with contents strewn on the floors, no open file cabinets, no missing computer.

When they finished their search, they returned to the kitchen. "Mrs. Kelly, are you sure there was someone here?" the officer in charge asked.

"Positive," she said.

"But you say nothing appears to be missing?"

"Mrs. Kelly is a guest here," Tor interjected. He argued that Kris couldn't know if anything of value were missing and suggested that Elsa's father and friend conduct a careful search in the morning.

The officers agreed Tor's idea made sense, said they would submit a report, and that if anything was discovered missing, police headquarters should be notified.

"Thanks, Tor," Kris said after they left. She stood by the living room window, looking at the lights of Bergen and the beacon on the platform at Laksevåg, but she could also see Tor's reflection in the glass. He sat in an easy chair, rubbing his scruffy beard, his long legs resting on the ottoman in front of him.

"Thanks for sticking up for me," she said.

"It was a stretch. Kris, are you sure there was someone? This is a big house to be alone in."

"You mean you don't believe me either?" She spun around and faced him. "I don't know whether to be hurt that you doubt me or angry that you think I'm imagining it all."

"Don't be either. I believe you really believe you heard something."

"Thanks. That makes it a lot better. I saw someone, Tor—both here in the house and on the road, just before you picked me up. Believe me, someone was here!"

"But why?"

"I don't know. But there's got to be a reason."

"We'll see what Andy and Nils find in the morning. Now, we need some rest. I'll sleep here in the living room so you won't be alone in the house."

"Thanks," she said. "I appreciate it." She started to extend her hand then raised it and brushed her hair away from her eyes. Had he noticed her change of mind? She had wanted to say something more about his coming to help her, but she couldn't. His doubts about her story both hurt and angered her. "I'll bring you a blanket and pillow," she said.

Once she had Tor settled in the living room, she took a long, hot shower, washing away dirt, dust, and newsprint. The water running down her cheeks joined with her tears. It didn't matter that Tor was in the house. She was still alone.

She thought back over the evening. If the intruder had torn the house apart, it would have verified her story and not left even Tor doubting her word. There was something sinister about so neat a criminal. In spite of the warm water, chills ran up her back. The man in the sweatshirt could have been Elsa's killer. Did he return to find something of his that she had? To cover up a clue that might give him away?

Kris quickly toweled herself dry and slipped on her nightgown. Then, wrapped in her robe, she opened the door to the hall—the hall that a few hours ago had been her escape route. She was thankful that Tor was upstairs—awake or asleep—it didn't matter. She had work to do; she returned to Elsa's study. Call it intuition or whatever, she couldn't deny her gut feelings. This room had been the hub of Elsa's activities; there had to be something here—maybe some sort of sign from Elsa—that would help her understand what was going on. Carefully she scanned the walls for anything out of place. The awards, the photos of the royal family, of the movie stars, and others remained in position. If only they could tell her what they had seen in this room. The books on Elsa's desk appeared stacked as before. The piles of papers were intact. She looked at Elsa's desk more closely.

"Yes!" she practically shouted, feeling a rush of energy. Why hadn't she noticed the two paperclips on the desk pad before? She had picked up every single one before she left the study in the afternoon. She thought back to her stop here a short time earlier with Tor and the policemen. No, none of them had made any movements toward the paperclips. Still...two paperclips were hardly proof. Her eyes fell on the bill holder. The bill at the front was from an insurance company rather than the credit card company, whose bill she had purposely kept there—the way Elsa had left it. Someone had changed the order.

Now Kris knew. Knew without looking, why the intruder had come. She turned on Elsa's computer. It went through a few motions; "system failure" flashed on the screen, then it went blank. "Oh, no!" she shouted.

Tor came running down the stairs, three steps at a time.

"What happened?"

"Someone was *definitely* here. Look!" She stepped away from the computer.

Tor took her place. He typed a series of commands on the keyboard trying to bring the hard drive back to life; nothing happened. "Did Elsa say she had computer problems?" he asked at last.

"No. And I heard the keyboard clicking when I went to bed Friday night. She would have said something if her computer had crashed on her."

Tor went through several more keyboard gymnastics before giving up. "We'll have to get an expert in." He looked around the terminal. "She must have kept backups."

Kris pointed to the bare top of the filing cabinet. "She kept a container of disks there. Someone was very thorough."

"Yeah, but why?"

"Maybe Elsa's computer had her murderer's name on it," Kris mused.

"You don't know that she was murdered."

What else did she expect him to say?

"It may have nothing to do with how Elsa died," Tor continued, leaning against the wall, careful not to disturb the pictures hanging there. "Someone could have feared the information she had. You know journalists protect their sources, but if a journalist dies and has their sources' names on the computer, who protects them then?"

A good question, Kris thought. "I've no idea. But we have something else to ask Odd tomorrow. At the fjord, he said he was a computer programmer."

"You said you saw the man. Did he look like this Odd?"

"I really couldn't see him well. But how could I have been so stupid as to give Odd Elsa's address?"

"He could have gotten it from the telephone book just as easily," Tor said.

"Maybe. It just bothers me that the answer to Elsa's death may have been right here all the time and we missed it! Maybe there's something else here. I'm going to check inside Elsa's desk. Do you want to look in the filing cabinet?" She ignored his sigh.

"Don't you ever sleep?"

"Not when I have a cousin who has died, and the next day her computer documents are destroyed."

She pulled at the top, center drawer. It stuck after a couple of inches. "Well, I've found Elsa's stash of peppermints," Kris said. Several rolls of the candies were crammed into the front of the drawer. "Want one?" she asked, opening a roll, peeling back the wrapper, and offering Tor the first candy.

"Breakfast?" he said, taking it.

Kris also popped a peppermint into her mouth.

"See anything in the files?"

"If that guy went through here, he did it very neatly. It's hard to tell if he took anything." Tor said, sounding irritated.

"Let's concentrate on what's here; then maybe we can figure out what—if anything—is missing," Kris said. She left the mint drawer and went through the three side drawers: newspaper clippings, office supplies, packs of letters—including her own—held together by rubber bands. The letter she had written to Elsa in January, pouring out her heart about Jim's infidelity, was loose on top of the stack. Nothing here for a thief.

One by one she took the rolls of peppermints from the top center drawer and put them on the desktop, then pulled. The drawer still stuck. She slid her hand inside the drawer and rearranging unseen obstructions, pulled the drawer all the way out. Underneath some crinkled sheets of paper, she found a worn scrapbook. She took it out and rested it on her lap.

Given her current mood, probably the last thing she should do was to look at Elsa's souvenirs. Nonetheless, she thumbed through the yellowed pages, through photos of Elsa at Trafalgar Square and Piccadilly and other places in London and the British Isles, pictures of Elsa in her twenties.

"What's that?" Tor abandoned the filing cabinet and pulled the other chair alongside hers.

"I'm curious. Elsa has all those albums on the bookshelf over there, but this one she kept in the drawer," Kris said. "Why?"

Handwritten notes sprinkled the pages along with memorabilia—menus, theatre programs, newspaper articles Elsa had written for a London newspaper and for *Fjordposten*. Midway through the book, a postcard had been stuck between the pages as a bookmark. Kris put it on the desk. The page it had marked held a 1956 program for an amateur production of Agatha Christie's play *Ten Little Indians*. The top of the program featured a photo of the cast and stage crew. Elsa Jenssen's name appeared opposite that of one of the characters.

"Looks like Elsa was an amateur thespian during her London days," Kris observed.

She searched the photo for the Elsa of almost forty years ago. Even before she checked the name in the caption, she identified the young Scandinavian woman. She pointed her out to Tor. Towheaded in her youth, Elsa stood out from the others in a row grouped by height, except for one petite young woman in the front. The woman was identified in the caption as Anna "Shoshana" Grizinski. With her oval-shaped face, long dark hair, and doll-like eyes, she resembled a younger version of someone familiar.

"This girl looks a lot like Yolanda Mueller, one of the guests at the Fjord Hotel," Kris said, pointing her out to Tor. "This is incredible."

"You've overdosed on excitement, I think you need to sleep. Here's your bookmark." He handed her the postcard.

Kris took it and slipped it into its place. "Bingo! Look at this." The stark whiteness that surrounded the writing on the card contrasted sharply with the yellowed pages of the scrapbook. "This postcard is new. It's postmarked the day before I arrived in Norway. That means that Elsa must have been looking at this scrapbook last week!"

"Maybe," Tor said. "Or maybe she just threw it in the drawer and it got lodged between the pages."

"I don't think so. Let's go upstairs—I have something to show you."

In the living room, they watched the video tape she had discovered earlier. She let the Mueller segment run through once, then she rewound it to the point where Yolanda and George were coming out of the elevator. Kris paused the film.

"Okay, look at Yolanda Mueller. See those big eyes, the shape of her face. Now look here at the picture." Kris opened the scrapbook again. "There's definitely a resemblance, don't you think?"

Tor shrugged. "I know better than to disagree with a woman when I'm tired," he said. "And it's even more dangerous when *she* is tired. I'll say only that I think you have a better imagination than I have."

"I'll accept the part about us both being tired," she said. There was no point in arguing; Kris had her ideas and she would pursue them, regardless of Tor's opinion. They needed sleep to be fresh for the meeting with Uncle Andy and Nils. And for the visit from Odd—if he showed up. Just in case, she would be ready with a way to figure out whether he had been the intruder.

She placed the scrapbook on the dining room table and turned off the light. It was already dawn. "Good night," she said, noticing anew Tor's rumpled Manhattan Marathon T-shirt. "Thanks again for coming to my rescue."

"You had already rescued yourself," he said.

When Kris reached the stairs, he called after her, "But I'm available whenever you want to rest your head on my chest again."

She looked back at him and his bearded grin, and laughed.

CHAPTER 15

▼

Tuesday morning Kris was heartsick to discover that the gold Olympic-rings medallion she had left on her nightstand was missing. The thief must have taken it. Although it irritated her that the thief had also taken her Timex watch, she could always get another one. Maybe she could even get another Olympic-rings medallion—but it would not be the one Elsa had given her. She was relieved to find the cloth case containing a few favorite necklaces and earrings intact. Perhaps the thief had simply missed it because it was under a sweater in a drawer or maybe he hadn't even looked. She wished she had put the medallion in the drawer as well. She felt both sad and angry. She threw on slacks and a sweater and ran upstairs to tell Tor, wondering if he had already had breakfast.

The note on the table and a fresh pot of coffee told her that he had. "Kris. Went to my place to change clothes. Will pick up autopsy report. See you at ten. Don't worry. Bergen police are posted on both sides of the house. Tor."

Kris peeked out the kitchen window and saw a police car parked at the top of the driveway. From the living room window, after some effort, she spied a policeman standing beneath a tree.

She was touched by Tor's attention to her safety, and grateful for his absence so she could make a couple of phone calls. After eating a bowl of cornflakes, she double checked the information from her purse, and at nine made her first phone call.

It took only moments to get Rolf Berg of Crown Travel on the line.

"I am so sorry about your cousin," he said. "It is so tragic. I hope you got my flowers."

"Yes, they were beautiful. Thank you so much." After a proper pause, she continued. "I understand that you booked our trip to the fjord."

"Yes."

Could she pull off the next part? Kris wondered. She had to try. "My cousin was so grateful to you for getting us a reservation at the same hotel as the Muellers."

"Wait. Would you hold for a moment?" When the agent returned, he explained, "I am speaking from a private office. You see, we're not really supposed to give out information on other clients, but Ms. Jenssen was so well known, and…"

"Persuasive," Kris said, finishing his sentence. "She never took 'no' for an answer." Kris gave herself a thumbs up.

"Yes," he replied, sounding relieved by Kris's reaction. "You see, our office is in the Crown Hotel. Since the Muellers were staying here, Miss Jenssen thought they may have made travel arrangements with us."

"She *was* resourceful," Kris said, writing yes, yes, yes on the notepaper beside the phone.

"Yes," he agreed. "And lucky."

"Why's that?"

"Mr. and Mrs. Mueller already had their reservations for the Fjord Hotel; they made them before coming to Norway. It's luck because they came to me and asked me to move the reservations up by one day."

"Did Elsa say why she was interested in the Muellers?"

"She said they were old acquaintances, and she wanted to surprise them," he paused. "Did she?"

"It turns out it was a case of mistaken identity," Kris lied.

"Oh, that's a pity. In any case, if you don't mind, I would appreciate it if you don't mention this to anyone."

"Of course. Remember Elsa was a journalist and you were one of her sources. She would never give away a source, nor will I."

One down, one to go, Kris thought after she hung up. She had acted on a hunch and had been right. She thought about the photo from Elsa's scrapbook and wondered why Elsa hadn't just told her about Yolanda and why she wanted to see her. She was determined to find out the reason.

She dialed her next number. "Oscar? Hi. It's Kris Kelly calling."

"Mrs. Kelly. It is good to hear your voice." He sounded genuinely pleased.

"How are you?" he asked.

"I'm doing all right, thank you."

"I heard Miss Jenssen willed her body to science. Even in her death, she still gave to all of us," he said.

"That is very kind of you to say. Yes, she was amazing," Kris said. "Tell me, Oscar, how are you doing?"

"I spend my time helping Bjornstad."

"Really?" Was the sheriff on to something? Kris wondered. "Anything special?"

"Looking for jewelry. Mrs. Mueller's antique ring is missing. She thinks it has been stolen. I never had such a thing happen in my hotel!"

Kris wanted to say she also had jewelry stolen, but that was not what he wanted to hear. "I'm sorry to hear that. I hope it is found."

"*Ja.*"

"Oscar, I'm calling because I've decided that the best thing I can do is to continue the journey Elsa wanted me to take. I'm planning to return to the fjord. Do you have a room available for a few days starting tonight?"

"The hotel is full, but I always keep one room in reserve," he said. "You shall have it." She imagined him writing her name in his giant binder.

"Thank you. I'm hoping to see some of the guests that Elsa met; everyone was so kind."

"Yes, everyone is here," he paused, "except for Odd Engstrom."

"Oh, really?" She couldn't admit that she already knew that.

"He finally came back to get his things after a day."

"What do you mean?"

"He did not come back to the hotel on Sunday. He came only yesterday; he said he got too busy taking pictures and spent the night in one of the mountain huts."

Bingo, Kris thought. Picture taking, maybe, or perhaps he had run from his crime; then, the next day, mustered his courage to return to the hotel. In a couple of hours he would be here, and she hoped he would be surprised by all of her questions.

*   *   *   *

A few minutes before ten, Andy and Nils arrived. Kris hugged her uncle and greeted Nils cordially; neither she nor Nils spoke of their encounter in his office the previous day.

Nils told her that Tor had called him and that they had come early to check the house for missing valuables.

While Andy and Nils searched the house, Kris sat in the sunny dining room, reading through a stack of sympathy cards. When Tor arrived, the men joined her at the table.

"Some of Elsa's jewelry is missing, as well as some silver," Nils reported.

Kris told them about her missing necklace and watch.

"We'll make a list and give it to the police," Nils said.

Kris handed him one she had started.

Tor took the autopsy papers from a manilla envelope and handed copies to everyone. "The report says she suffered both a heart attack and a skull fracture," he said.

"A heart attack?" Andy repeated. "But she was so young."

"It could have been the fright," Nils suggested. "When she slipped..."

Or when someone pushed her, Kris thought.

"…and saw what was happening, her heart may have just gone." Nils's voice was almost inaudible.

"That's what the coroner concluded," Tor said. "Even if she was alive after the heart attack, the fall would have killed her. The blows to her head from the rocks were substantial." Andy reached over to the sideboard, picked up one of the photos of Elsa, and looked at it for a long time. "My poor, dear girl."

Nils, downcast, took a handkerchief from his shirt pocket and blew his nose.

"It's all so hard to believe," Kris said. "Everything's happened so fast. Elsa's gone and we can't bring her back, but we do need to find out who sabotaged her computer last night and why."

Tor gave his theory of a source trying to remain protected.

Nils hesitated. "I must tell you that I found some disturbing letters in Elsa's desk yesterday afternoon. She never told me about them."

"What do you mean by 'disturbing'?" asked Kris.

"Someone with extremist views threatened to kill her." As if anticipating Kris's next question, Nils continued, "The letters were unsigned, but the author was someone who condemned Elsa's support of foreign workers and refugees. I've turned the letters over to the police. Kris, I should have listened to you when you told me someone with those views might have had a motive for killing Elsa."

"I told you about Odd Engstrom, who Elsa argued with at the hotel," Kris said. "But he couldn't have had anything to do with the letters. He'd just met Elsa at the fjord for the first time."

"How do you know?" Nils asked.

He was right, she thought, how did she know that? "Well, I don't know, but we'll soon find out. Odd's coming here at noon to meet me," she said. She paused. "I think he was the intruder who was here last night."

"That's it. I'm calling Finn," Tor said, picking up the kitchen phone. His barrage of Norwegian was halted mid-paragraph; he looked over at Nils. "Finn's been trying to reach you." Tor held up his hand in a "hold on" gesture and listened, his eyes registering incredulity. Finally, he said to them all, "There was a pre-dawn fire in Laksevåg. They found the body of a man who they've identified as Odd Engstrom."

Kris felt faint. "But, but…" She had to talk with Odd about Elsa; what Tor was saying couldn't be true.

"Finn says Odd was an amateur photographer. They think he was developing photos when the heater in his darkroom caught fire. He was trapped in there and died."

"But I just talked with him last night; I can't believe this," Kris said.

"Hey, just a minute, Finn. I'm going to put you on speaker phone so everyone can hear."

Kris repeated what she had just said.

They all listened to Finn's reply. "You may have been the last person he spoke with. In addition to the darkroom, part of the living room burned, but we were able to salvage a lot of things." He paused. "We found a number of Elsa Jenssen's belongings."

"What?" Kris gasped, hearing the others voice the same question. She watched the color drain from Nils's face. Andy sat stone still, staring at his hands. For a moment her and Tor's eyes met.

Finn continued. "One of the things we found was a red cover for a notebook. We think it's the one that had been reported missing."

"What else?" Nils asked.

"Some floppy disks of hers, a letter addressed to her. There's also jewelry that may have belonged to her."

"What about a gold Olympic medallion?"

"Yes."

"That's mine. It disappeared last night," Kris said.

"We'll be sure you get it back."

"What about an antique emerald ring with diamonds in the shape of a flower?" Kris asked.

"Yes," Finn replied. "Was that yours, too?"

"No, it belongs to Yolanda Mueller, a guest at the Fjord Hotel."
She ignored Tor's questioning look.

"All of you also need to know that we found a lot of neo-Nazi propaganda," Finn said.

"Does this mean that Engstrom killed Elsa?" Nils asked.

"It is a very real possibility," Finn said. "But we can't know for sure. Not yet."

A pall fell over the room. Tor took the phone off speaker and spoke directly with the police chief for a few more minutes, then ended the call.

"I should have listened to you, Kris," Nils said. "You thought that fellow might have had a motive, but I didn't want to believe that her death was anything but accidental. I owe you an apology, and you, too, Andy. I should have called for an investigation into Elsa's death. If Engstrom killed her, he's been punished. If there hadn't been that fire, he would have gotten away with the crime."

"So it wasn't The Elephant," Andy said slowly. "It was a new Nazi, not an old one." He nodded his head thoughtfully.

"Why did you call him The Elephant, Uncle Andy?"

"Because of his ears." The old man cupped his hands behind both ears and pushed them forward. "They were large and stood out from his head like this." He rose from his chair. "Elsa has pictures, she took them last week when the two of you visited me."

Kris also stood up, concerned about her uncle's state of mind.

"Where are they?" he asked, looking around the room. "I didn't see them this morning. Maybe that thief stole them also."

"When did you last see them?" Tor asked.

"Last week when Kristina and Elsa came to see me; Elsa took them," Andy insisted.

Kris racked her brain, trying to remember Elsa's movements Thursday night.

"What photos do you mean?"

"Not photos! Drawings!" Andy said, pounding his walking stick on the floor.

"You mean the leather portfolio?" Kris asked, finally realizing what he meant.

"*Ja, Ja,*" Andy responded triumphantly.

Kris remembered how Elsa had rummaged through things in a dark corner of Andy's workshop, half-hidden by his toolbench. She had emerged with a dusty volume and promised to show Kris the contents, a collection of Andy's sketches, when they got home. But they decided to wait until the next day, and then, in the excitement of the fjord trip, the portfolio had been forgotten. "I don't think she took it out of her car that night," Kris recalled. "Do you have her keys?"

She found the portfolio in the trunk and brought it back, wiping the dust off with a damp sponge before delivering it to the dining room table with a muffled sneeze.

The aged artist pulled out portraits of his wife, Liv, Elsa's mother; of Per, and Elsa, even one of Nils, and of others whose names Andy called off as he turned over each drawing.

"Ah, here he is," Andy said finally. "Klaus Brunner—The Elephant."

He pointed to a page on which there were five or six renderings of a man's face and upper chest. The man appeared to be in his mid-twenties. His eyes and nose were unremarkable, but his oversized ears stood out unusually far from his head; his chin jutted out from his jaw. A swastika was emblazoned on the man's uniform. Written diagonally across the page in calligraphy was the word "murderer" in Norwegian.

The next three sketches presented the man from the front, the back, and in profile. The last drawing, a caricature, gave Kris chills: the man's ears had been made into real elephant ears and his nose elongated into a trunk that wrapped around his neck in a stranglehold, forcing his tongue out over his chin in a last gasp. Andy closed the portfolio, tears in his eyes. "I hope he met the cruel end he deserved."

Nils put his hand on Andy's shoulder. "I had forgotten about those drawings. Maybe when this is all over, we should arrange an exhibit of all your work. Elsa would be proud."

Uncle Andy's eyes lit up. "Yes, let us do it as a memorial to my Elsa, but first I must make her a sculpture."

"We're going to have a large memorial service for Elsa in about a month," Nils said to Kris. "We're sorry we can't do it while you're here, but Andy would like to have a small gathering for family and close friends this Sunday. How do you feel about that?"

"Good," she said. "What can I do to help?"

"Share your memories of her along with the rest of us," he said.

"But what about the arrangements?"

"Two of my staff have agreed to arrange for food and flowers," Nils replied.

"Surely there must be something I can do to help you, Uncle Andy," she pleaded.

"You are here; that is the main thing," he said.

Kris hesitated. "My return reservation to Washington is for Monday. Shall I try to stay a few more days?"

"You have your children in America," Andy said. "No, you must go to them. But first you must do what Elsa wanted you to do—to see Norway."

Kris couldn't believe her uncle's response. It was exactly what she had wanted to do. She couldn't see all of Norway, but she could return to the fjord, as she had planned. She needed to try to find out if Yolanda and Shoshana were the same person.

"I think then," she said, "Uncle Andy, that I'd like to go back to the fjord and retrace Elsa's footsteps, see what she wanted me to see."

"*Ja*, Elsa would do that," Andy said. "You are like her. If I were younger, I would go with you. *Ja*, you go back, and I will work on my sculpture."

He didn't have to say any more, Kris thought. This man, almost ninety, had his own way of working through his grief for his daughter.

"Would you like company to the fjord?" Tor asked.

"Well," Kris hesitated. She felt herself blush. How could she refuse him tactfully?

"*Ja, ja,*" Uncle Andy said. "Kristina, it is good for you to have a friend with you."

"Thank you, Tor. But it's your time off, and I probably won't come back until Saturday. Don't you already have other plans?"

"Plans can be changed," he responded.

CHAPTER 16

▼

At three that afternoon, Kris sat with Tor on the rear deck of an express catamaran, watching Bergen shrink to postcard proportions. In the wake of the startling discoveries about Odd, Tor had suggested that she would benefit from the relaxation of a cruise to the Fjord Hotel. It would take almost twice as long as driving, but there was no hurry now; Elsa's killer wouldn't get away.

Trying to relax after the trauma of the last two days was a good idea in principle, Kris thought, but she wondered if she'd really be able to do so. Being around Elsa, so charged with energy, had been exhilarating. Then Elsa was dead, and Kris had plunged into shock, confusion, anger, suspicion. Yet her gut feelings had been right—all was not what it had seemed to be.

Would things have been different if Elsa had not argued with Odd in the library? Or had he gone to the fjord already determined to kill her? Had he sent Elsa an anonymous note to meet him near the waterfall? That could explain Elsa's wanting her to sleep in on Sunday morning. But why would Elsa go alone, especially after having received threatening letters?

At the hotel, Odd had aroused anger, not fear. No doubt Elsa had not realized how dangerous he could be, nor had Kris. It was fortunate she didn't recognize him at Elsa's last night. If she had, she would have confronted him rather than run away. Would he have tried to kill her? The shiver that passed over her was not from the wind but from the possibility of what could have happened. Still, she wondered why he had looked so confused on the trail Sunday, and why he had he been so conciliatory about talking with her about Elsa. It must have been a ploy.

Once Bergen was out of sight and the boat was cruising between the coastal islands, most of the people on deck went inside. Kris and Tor sat on the life preserver bin and leaned against the bulkhead. She buttoned her open-necked blouse and zipped up her fleece against the cool breeze.

"Shall we go inside?" Tor asked.

"No, not yet. I like it out here."

"You have been very quiet. This has been hell for you, hasn't it?"

She nodded.

"It's not my business, but your husband should be here with you."

"He's part of the hell," she said. "Oh, shit! I mean, oops, sorry."

"I think I've heard that word once or twice on the rigs."

She smiled. "Look, Tor, I appreciate your concern about my husband," her voice faltered, "but he is almost my ex-husband."

He looked at her intently.

"He left me and is marrying one of his students. I just didn't want to talk about it before," she said, pulling herself further into her fleece.

"Whoa! I'm sorry," he said. "That's tough."

She nodded.

"It's rough when someone you love leaves you."

"You sound like you've been there."

"I have." He told her he had married in his late twenties. His wife had been a school teacher in Stavanger. "I thought I could have things both ways. The adventure of exploring for oil in the North Sea with the dangers and the money that came with it, and a loving wife who would be waiting for me whenever I came home. I didn't listen to her pleas to change jobs; I was too headstrong. After three years, she told me that was it."

"And so you lost the love of your life?" Kris asked. She hadn't meant her question to sound so dramatic.

He rubbed his beard. "It hurt," he said, "but she was not *the* love of my life. That's another story."

"That you don't want to talk about, I assume," Kris said.

"Not now."

"What about Lise?" Kris tried to sound casual. She focused on the flag at the stern.

"Lise?" He looked puzzled. "Oh, she knows about it."

That wasn't the kind of answer she had been looking for, but she could hardly ask for details.

"I admire you," Tor said.

"Me? Good grief, why?" Kris asked.

"You had your own ideas about Elsa's death, and you weren't ready to give up what you believed. I like that."

It's called Jenssen stubbornness," she quipped. "Now I'm getting cold. Let's go inside." They found two deep cushioned seats at the front of the observation lounge and made themselves comfortable.

"I don't know about you, but I had kind of a short night last night," Tor said, reclining in his chair. "I need some rest."

"Ditto," she said, smiling at the way he had said it. She leaned her head back, closed her eyes, and surrendered to the undulating motion of the boat, welcoming the sleep she felt overtaking her.

Sometime later, she was awakened by Tor's repositioning himself in his seat. His eyelids trimmed by red-blond lashes were closed; his mouth rested in a semi-smile. He was the picture of comfort, legs stretched out on the window ledge, arms arched, hands folded under his head. His chest and abdomen, absent of a middle-age paunch, moved up and down in a slow, steady rhythm under his knit shirt. Kris closed her eyes again, the image of the tattoo on his arm sticking in her mind.

When she opened her eyes again, she had the satisfied feeling of having had a rejuvenating nap. Tor flashed her a broad smile; a pair of binoculars rested on his chest.

"Bird-watching?" she asked.

"Sort of. We've just entered the Sognefjord."

The boat cut through a wide channel between gentle hills. Here there was no doubt that they were traveling on the sea, but as the miles passed, the channel narrowed, becoming more defined by rocky shores and steadily rising slopes. Ahead, mountains like huge sea monsters lying in wait, reached toward each other, giving the impression that passage beyond them was impossible. But as the boat approached, the stone monsters drew back, giving it a wide berth.

"My grandmother was from this area. I spent a lot of time up here when I was a kid," Tor said, nostalgia in his voice.

"And since?"

"Not as much as I'd like. But I know this fjord like the back of my hand. It hasn't changed much."

He handed her the binoculars. "Take a look."

She held the glasses up to her eyes. Small fishing villages hugged the shore.

"Here, look this way," Tor said, reaching one arm around her shoulder. Briefly covering her hands with his, he guided the binoculars upwards, bringing her focus to a farm clinging to the edge of a cliff hundreds of feet above them.

"It's amazing," she said, squinting to see a slice of green between the farmhouse and the cliff. "How can people live like that?"

"It's the Norwegian spirit—we like to challenge ourselves to live in rugged terrain," he said. "And, by the way, sometimes we get hungry. I smell hotdogs. Shall we eat?"

"Sure." Kris handed Tor back the binoculars. At the snack bar she ordered a *gjetost* sandwich and bottled glacier water; Tor a hotdog, potato chips, and soda.

"You're kind of a health nut, aren't you?" he said after they returned to their seats.

"Quasi. One of my principles is not to eat things that are composed of ground-up animal parts."

"Thanks for the appetizing comment."

"You asked."

"So I'll ask something else. What are your plans when we get to the hotel?"

"First, I want to talk again with the folks that saw Elsa Sunday—the Muellers, the Stephenses, Max Guttmann. Then I want to retrace her footsteps."

"Are you up to it?" Tor asked.

"It's not like I haven't hiked before."

"Hey, I didn't mean that as an affront to your fitness. I mean it's not going to be easy emotionally."

"Oh," she said, telling herself not to be so defensive.

They spent a long while not speaking, just looking out at the scenery. By the time they finished their dinner, Kris felt like the stone walls on either side of the boat were closing in on them. Tor explained that they had left the main fjord and they should reach the hotel at the end of this one.

"It's like being in a canyon," Kris said, looking at the steep green-gray slopes.

"Yeah," Tor said. "Three thousand feet above us and three thousand below us. Wading is not recommended."

They went to the front of the boat. The air was mild, warmer than in Bergen, and the wind subdued in the shelter of this narrower fjord. This was the way she was to have left the hotel with Elsa; instead it was the way she was returning without her. The blue-green water reflected the mountains that grew ever more shadowy as the evening sunlight retracted.

"There it is," Kris cried, recognizing the outline of the mountains and the village at their base; the white hotel at water's edge. She had returned to bring closure to what had happened here, to reconcile herself to her loss. Why then did she feel so apprehensive?

CHAPTER 17

▼

The homey elegance of the hotel embraced Kris and at the same time reinforced the emptiness she felt with Elsa's absence. Before leaving Bergen, she had called Oscar and asked him, since his hotel was fully booked, if he could recommend a place nearby for a family friend who would be accompanying her. Oscar had said he would arrange something. Now after greeting them warmly, he explained they would have rooms next to each other. Tor was effusive in his thanks to Oscar for his trouble. Kris wondered to herself if Oscar had sent some other guest to nearby accommodations in order to free up a room for Tor.

Her room, which Oscar insisted was "on the house," was not only a floor up from where she had stayed with Elsa but a step up as well. "I'm speechless," she said, as he showed her into a two-room suite. A bouquet of fresh roses on the coffee table bore a card that said, "*Velkommen tilbake.*" Welcome back.

The living room with flowered wallpaper, brocade armchairs, loveseat, and blue wall-to-wall carpeting was connected to the bedroom through a wide arched doorway. The bed, covered with a white lace spread over a red flounce, was only a few feet from the double doors that led to a balcony spanning the length of the rooms. The view was framed by one of the hotel's gingerbread-trimmed arches.

Before taking his leave, Oscar told Kris and Tor of the Muellers' invitation to join them on the terrace.

It didn't take Kris long to freshen up. She brushed her hair and reapplied make-up, unbuttoned the top couple of buttons of her blouse for a more relaxed, not-too-revealing look, and threw a cardigan over her shoulders. When Tor knocked on her door she was ready.

"You look refreshing," he said, "I mean refreshed."

"You, too," she said, knowing his wording had not been accidental. He looked good in jeans and a white polo shirt.

It was no wonder people had gravitated to the terrace; the air was still pleasantly mild, the fjord glassy in the twilight.

George and Yolanda sat at a table with Max and a fragile, elderly man in a wheelchair. Kris caught George's eye. He waved, stood up, and reached his hand out to her. "Mrs. Kelly, how good to see you again. How are you?"

"Better, thank you, Mr. Mueller," she said, shaking his hand. "As you may have heard, there's not going to be a funeral, so I decided to make a kind of pilgrimage to the fjord in memory of Elsa. This is Tor Olsen—a friend of the family."

Tor shook hands with George and Yolanda. "And this is the man who tried to save Elsa," she said, stepping aside so that Tor could also shake hands with Max.

George nodded toward the stranger in the wheelchair. "This is a new friend of ours, Otto Kohler."

"How do you do?" the man said in heavily accented English, making an effort to rise.

"That's all right, please don't get up," Kris pleaded. He reached a bony arm out and grasped her hand. His gaunt face was pale, the skin drooping loosely over his eyes and mouth, and his large earlobes moving with the occasional twitches of his small head. She guessed he was seriously ill, perhaps, with cancer. In the split second that Otto had considered rising from his chair, a plumpish middle-aged woman in a nurse's uniform had appeared and stood hovering over him, staring disapprovingly at Kris.

"It is fine, Helga," he said. The woman returned to a table at the end of the terrace. Then to Kris he said, "I regret to hear about the death in your family."

"Thank you."

"We heard about Mr. Engstrom," George said. "Shocking."

"Yes, it truly was," Kris replied.

She saw Hasan approaching. "Welcome back, Mrs. Kelly," he said.
"Would you like tea?"

"Yes, thank you," Kris replied.

"A sherry for me," George said.

"For me, too," Tor said.

After Hasan left, George asked Tor about himself. It was as if an electric current had passed through him when he heard that Tor worked for Statoil.

"I am also in the oil business. What do you do?"

"Geological engineer. We're working on developing new fields in the North Atlantic."

"I was also an engineer in my younger days. Now, I'm only an investor. Norway is a major producer of crude oil. We must talk…"

"Jorges," Yolanda interrupted, "please not now, or very soon you'll be talking about things none of the rest of us understand."

George smiled at his wife. "All right, my dear," he said. And then to Tor, "Let us talk later."

Tor readily agreed.

Kris could identify with Yolanda's feelings, remembering the times Jim would start discussing economic theory with colleagues, leaving her totally out of the picture. But she would have liked to have heard Tor and George's conversation.

"Where are you from, Mr. Kohler?" Tor asked.

"I am from Sweden."

Tor spoke to him in Swedish.

The old man responded with a few words, then switched to English. "I was born in Germany, but I have lived in Sweden many years."

Kris tried not to stare at him, then realized it didn't matter—he had just nodded off.

"Otto was lucky; he spent the war in Sweden," George said.

"Yes, Sweden," Otto repeated. He opened his eyes and raised his head, trying to stay alert.

Kris turned back to George. "In the library the other night, you said you were in Bergen several years ago…"

"Yes, that's correct. I was on my way to South America."

"From Bergen?" Tor asked.

"Oh, yes," George replied, brightly. "You wouldn't think so, would you? I had managed to get to Sweden when the war ended; the Swedes helped me get to Norway. I took a boat from Bergen to Liverpool, and then worked my way across the ocean on a ship."

"And how is it to be back after…how many years?" Tor asked.

"Forty-nine," George said proudly.

"Wow! That is a long time," Kris interjected.

"And it is wonderful to be back. Norway is still the beautiful country I remember."

Tor raised his glass of sherry toward George's. "To forty-nine years," he said. The two men clinked their glasses together.

Yolanda asked a waiter for another glass of liqueur. Kris studied her face, trying to imagine what she might have looked like forty years earlier. Had she been the young woman looking out from the photo in Elsa's theatre program?

"I understand they found your ring," Kris said to her.

"Yes, that strange young man stole it. The man who murdered your cousin!"

Kris looked down at the table. She had nothing to add.

Tor took one of Oscar's maps from his pocket. "Kris and I want to retrace Elsa's route on Sunday, try to understand what happened," he said. "Can you show us where she was?"

Max and the Muellers pored over the map. Otto looked on with momentary interest before nodding off again.

"She started out with Yolanda and me, and the other Norwegian woman. This is where Hans dropped us," George said. With his finger he traced the red line that led from the Roma Restaurant to the falls.

"You see we went along the plateau here, on the red trail, but then your cousin went this way." He handed the map back across the table to Tor and Kris.

The plateau trail branched off to another, delineated in blue, the main part of which criss-crossed the mountain, ending at the youth hostel. Other forks in that trail, however, led back to a path along the rim of canyon and the falls. Elsa could have taken any of them.

"Hans, will you join us?" George asked.

Kris looked up at the approaching stranger with bleached blond hair and bronzed skin.

Hans nodded to the group. He stopped behind Otto, brushed dandruff off the shoulders of the old man's jacket, and tucked in the blanket around his legs. He spoke softly to him, apparently checking if he was all right.

"This is Hans Schmidt, Otto's assistant," George said. Hans acknowledged George with a nod. Yolanda reached out her hand to him; he took it and kissed it in Continental fashion, his eyes moving over her. He shook hands with Tor; then with Kris, his eyes meeting hers, then moving steadily downward, penetrating her open-necked blouse, and stopping at her midriff partially hidden by the table. A shiver ran down Kris's spine. Far from flirtatious, Hans's gaze felt predatory.

She moved slightly closer to Tor and welcomed his casually stretching his arm out across the back of her chair.

"Hans, the sherry's good! Will you join us?" George asked.

Hans declined. He patted Otto's shoulder and told him he'd be back, took a cigarette pack from his pocket, and sauntered down the stairs toward the dock.

As gentle as he was with the old man, Kris guessed Hans was likely not so with women.

"Your cousin left us on the trail with blue markers," Yolanda said, drawing their attention back to the map. "She could have taken one of the smaller trails to the falls."

"Which one do you think Odd took?" Kris asked.

"We didn't see him."

"He could have hidden among the switchbacks here," Tor suggested. "We'll look tomorrow, Kris." He folded up the map. "That's a beautiful trawler out there," he said, nodding toward the yacht tied up at the pier.

"That is Oscar's *Fjordstar*," George said. "It is *wunderbar*! He takes us fishing in it. Why don't you come with us?"

"I'd like to. For how long are you here?"

"Until Saturday."

"Same as we are. So, let's do it. I'm busy tomorrow, but maybe the next day?"

"Yes. We can fish and talk oil," George said. "The women can go shopping."

The men laughed. Kris noted that Yolanda, like herself, was not amused.

Otto's nurse decreed that it was his bedtime, and the gathering broke up.

"It's nice that George and Yolanda have befriended Otto," Kris said to Tor on the way back to their rooms. "Not all honeymooners would do that. They'd want to be alone."

"Judging from how often Otto dozes off," Tor laughed, "they are alone even when they're with him. Hey, did you want to call Nils?"

Indeed she did. She invited Tor into her room for the phone call.

"I'm glad to hear from you," Nils said. He told her he had taken Andy shopping for just the right wood out of which to make his sculpture. Later, when he'd gone back to *Fjordposten* he had heard some alarming news. "Some of my staffers saw the photo of Odd Engstrom we're running in tomorrow's paper. They said they had seen him around our building. I told Finn Nygaard; he thinks Odd stalked Elsa."

"What?" Kris gasped. She repeated to Tor what Nils had said.

Tor shook his head and said what she had been thinking. "Why didn't she tell someone? The police could have staked out *Fjordposten*, could have caught him."

Nils apparently heard Tor's response, and added, "Or if one of the people here who saw him had just said something."

Before ending their conversation, Kris and Nils agreed to keep in touch over the next few days.

Kris felt drained. "I'd like to just sit out on the balcony and think. Would you like to join me?" she asked Tor.

"Sure."

He apparently understood her mood and didn't try to make conversation. They just sat there together, absorbing the peacefulness, watching twilight disappear and moonlight illuminate the patches of snow high on the surrounding mountains. It wasn't right, Kris thought. In this beautiful place especially, people should be protected from the kind of violence that took Elsa's life.

"Well," Tor said, after several minutes. "You wanted to get up early tomorrow. I think I'll say good night."

She walked him to the door. "Thank you for being here." She looked into his blue eyes. "More than a friend of the family, you are family. I appreciate your helping me. I just want you to know that." She gave him a quick, friendly hug.

He reciprocated. His arms wrapped around her and his beard brushed against her forehead. The tingle that rippled through her body unsettled her. He leaned down, kissed her cheek, and left without a word.

She closed the door and stared at the roses on the coffee table, trying to sort out the mixture of emotions she was feeling. She had come to Norway to gain perspective, but everything seemed out of focus. She arrived here, mourning her marriage; now she also mourned her cousin. Maybe her deep loneliness propelled her toward Tor, someone new that she could lean on. Elsa had told her to come to Norway to find her strength—strength to stand on her own. Kris was annoyed with herself, with her confusion, with the physical reaction she'd felt being close to Tor just now.

Could she ever risk caring about another man, being in his arms as she'd been with Jim? She had believed she was loved and desired; but she hadn't been, and for how long? Angry and hurt, she'd buried her physical desires with her dead marriage.

She needed to be patient. Her attraction to Tor, if she could call it that, was understandable. He seemed to care about how she made it through this ordeal. Having a male friend who was "just a friend" was probably a healthy step in her healing—if she could keep herself from becoming dependent on him. The memory of Lise reminded her that Tor had other interests, too.

CHAPTER 18

▼

Wednesday morning Kris was up at six; the alarm of her travel clock had worked perfectly. She planned to re-enact, as closely as possible, Elsa's actions the morning of her death.

She dressed in loose hiking pants with layers on the top—fitted tank top, T-shirt, sweater—and, at six-thirty, went to the lobby where the enticing smells of fresh baked breads and pastries from the nearby dining room promised a tasty breakfast. Her stomach growled. She stopped for some water from the drinking fountain, hoping it would help her to will away her appetite until she met Tor in an hour. The calm in the empty lobby reminded her of mornings at home before the kids and Jim awakened. Had it been like this when Elsa had come down here on Sunday and made her phone call? Had Bjornstad figured out yet whom Elsa had called? Had she indeed called home for messages?

"Good morning. You are up very early," Oscar said from behind the reception desk. "Mr. Olsen's in the fitness room lifting weights."

"You mean he's already up?" Kris replied. "I guess this means I don't have to worry about him oversleeping. Did *Fjordposten* arrive yet?"

"Yes, the copies are in my office. I'll get you one."

Before he could do so, the phone rang. Kris waited while he took the call. She watched as he opened the large binder in front of him and leafed through the dated pages showing a diagram of the hotel on each. There appeared to be a page for every day of the tourist season, from May to October.

"Yes, I can give you a room with two beds and a private bath on those dates," Oscar said. She watched him write the name of the party on the diagram, noting duration and date of the reservation. He entered the date the European style with day first, then month. "I will hold those for you awaiting your deposit," he said. When he finished the conversation, he wrote the information on the diagram of the room for each date it had been reserved.

"That's a very organized way to keep track of things," Kris said.

"Yes," he said proudly. "I designed it; I have used it for years. We also put the information in the computer so the staff can access it quickly. I don't trust those things, something can always go wrong."

He had a point, Kris thought, thinking of Elsa's sabotaged data.

"Let's see. Oh, yes, *Fjordposten.*" Oscar disappeared into his office. A moment later, he was reading the front page as he brought a copy to her. "Here it is." He pointed to a headline above an article on the lower right: "Extremist suspected in death of Elsa Jenssen." A photo of Odd appeared underneath. "I'm afraid this shall bring more reporters here. They disturb our peace."

The double glass entrance doors swung open, and Tor dashed in, wearing running shoes, shorts, and sweat-soaked T-shirt, his face dripping with moisture. He barely slowed his pace when he saw her.

"It's going to be a beautiful day, maybe even hot. Pick you up at seven-fifteen," he said somewhat breathlessly and disappeared up the stairs.

Kris shook her head. Working out before a hike? Maybe not such a bad idea. At least she should do some stretching exercises to avoid sore muscles later. Excusing herself from Oscar, she took the newspaper and briefly strolled through the parlors before returning to her room. Doing warmups on the balcony did not stave off the chill in the air, and she wondered at Tor's idea that it could be a hot day.

Tor picked her up at precisely seven-fifteen, showered and shaved, and smelling of his subtly spicy aftershave. He wore hiking shorts and boots and a Lillehammer Olympics sweatshirt.

They helped themselves to the smorgasbord and ate breakfast with the *Fjordposten* article between them. The lead paragraph implicated Odd in Elsa's death, noting he had been at the fjord the same time as Elsa. The article described the evidence found at the scene of the fire, and the letters found in Elsa's desk at her office.

Sheriff Bjornstad, identified as the officer in charge of the investigation at the fjord, was quoted as saying, "I stated from the outset that Elsa Jenssen's death appeared to be an accident. We never ruled out other possibilities. In fact, Odd Engstrom was to be interrogated yesterday."

Bergen Police Chief Finn Nygaard was also quoted: "It is standard police procedure to look carefully at circumstances of deaths that appear to be accidental. Bjornstad handled the matter correctly."

The paper gave a few other new details. The fire started in the darkroom before five yesterday morning. Apparently a heater, placed too close to chemicals stored on the floor ignited them, trapping Odd in the back of the small room. He died of suffocation. A passerby reported seeing smoke; otherwise, the entire house and the occupants in the adjacent apartments might have gone up in flames.

"Oscar's worried that reporters are going to swarm to the fjord," Kris said, finishing her muesli.

"They probably will. But, hopefully, we can beat them to the waterfall. Let's make our lunches."

Kris copied Tor and other guests at the buffet table, lining a plate with crisp sheets of wax paper, then adding slices of bread and the makings of a sandwich. She chose hers from a selection of cheeses and fish, while Tor piled his bread high with coldcuts.

At eight-thirty, Hasan drove them to the Roma Restaurant that, with its modern natural wood construction, looked something like a ski lodge.

A red "T" painted on the white bark of a birch tree marked the gravel trail at the edge of the woods about three-hundred feet from the restaurant. So this was it, Kris thought as she and Tor set out. This is where Elsa had begun the fateful walk that had led to her death.

The pungent smell of pine mixed with the sweet fragrance of birch. Crows cawed; small songbirds flitted in the underbrush. Kris felt transported back to her childhood, to the many walks in the mountains back home with her mother and father and the family dogs on trails like this, lined with tall grasses, blossoming clover, buttercups, cornflowers, lupin, occasional foxgloves.

After about ten minutes, she spotted a dying fir leaning over the trail ahead; at the same time, she felt Tor's hand grab her sleeve. Uprooted perhaps from a late spring storm, the fir, its needles brown, was propped up by two young birch trees bowed by its weight. "Stay here," Tor told her. He walked ahead and pushed the fir hard. Its supports wavered, but held firm. "It's okay," he said, motioning to her to continue. "But it wouldn't take much for it to collapse on to the trail, hopefully when no one's here. There are probably plans to remove it, but just in case, I'll check with Oscar when I get back. He'll know whom to call."

In another five minutes, they came to the first fork in the trail. A boulder to the left was painted with a blue strip; one on the right with red. Kris leaned against the one marked with red and took out her trail map and pen from her pack. She wrote down the time it had taken them to walk from the gravel road to this point.

Tor handed her a cup of water from the thermos. "How are you doing?"

"I'm in another world. It's so beautiful here," she said, taking the cup from Tor, then holding her hand still while a bee buzzed around her and then flew off. She drank the cool water and enjoyed the surroundings. "Uh, oh, bees' nest," she said, pointing to the gray mass hanging from a branch not far from Tor's head.

"They won't hurt us if we don't hurt them," Tor said, giving the nest a respectful look. "Which way do you want to go now?"

"The Muellers and Grete said Elsa took the blue trail, so we should too. Why don't you lead this time?" she suggested. She put the cup back on his thermos.

Kris followed Tor along the shady trail, wondering if he'd been sizing her up the way she was taking notice of his broad shoulders, muscular arms, and narrow hips. If Elsa had been with someone like him on Sunday, Kris concluded, no one would have been able to accost her.

Twenty minutes later, they entered bright sunlight and a grassy clearing, sprinkled with boulders. Far below they could see the glistening waters of the fjord.

"Here, put this on against sunburn," Tor said. He put an Atlanta Braves cap on her head, a Mets cap on his own.

Beyond the field of boulders, just where the forest started again, the blue trail intersected with the yellow one, the first trail Elsa would have come to after she left the others. Kris noted on her map how long it had taken them to reach this point and traced her finger along the yellow line indicating the trail. It would take them straight to the ledge, past a spur to the right—a diagonal route to the top of the falls.

"Shall we assume Elsa headed straight for the ledge?"

"Hmm. We know that's where she ended up," Tor said.

They followed the stony path through the trees, passing the spur. The sound of thundering water reminded Kris of the sound that had led her to Elsa on Sunday. She tried to substitute a mental picture of a happy, smiling Elsa for the one of the lifeless face and battered forehead that kept barging into her mind.

The noise of the water reached a crescendo. Kris could see the edge of the gorge ahead and the expanse of nothingness to the other side. A fluorescent rope stretched from one small pine tree to another; a sign in bold red and black letters warned hikers in Norwegian, German, and English not to pass. Beyond it, down another ten feet or so of trail, the ledge waited.

Tor ducked under the rope and lifted it for Kris. The ledge was much wider than she had expected; four people could have stood on it easily. Tor stepped onto the gray rock shelf and leaned against an out-cropping that seemed to glue the ledge to the canyon wall.

Kris tried to imagine Elsa coming down the path, stepping on to the ledge. Had Odd been waiting for her?

"Kris?" Tor called.

She wanted to run, to cover her ears, her eyes; to block out the sight and deafening sound of the falls. No, she told herself. She had to do this. What had Elsa done at this point? According to Bjornstad, she had taken off her backpack before going out on the ledge. Kris shed hers, setting it on the side of the path. She looked at Tor whose eyes were fixed on her. Taking a deep breath, she grasped his outstretched hand and stepped gingerly on to the ledge.

They could almost touch the cascading waters. Kris felt her knees shake. Tor let go of her hand, locked his arm around her midriff, and pushed her in front of him toward the edge of the precipice.

CHAPTER 19

▼

"It's all right. I'm not going to let you fall," Tor said, his mouth right next to her ear.

Kris stuck her head into the rising spray and looked down. Far below them the water churned against the rocks, in her stomach her breakfast churned as well. Even with her eyes closed, she could feel herself falling. She had wanted to experience what Elsa had gone through, but she had overestimated her courage. "Take me away, *please*," she yelled at the top of her lungs.

Instantly, Tor pulled her from the viewpoint. When they were off the ledge, he released his grip. She sank down on solid ground, holding her sides, trying to quell convulsive sobs. He knelt in front of her, pulled her forward so that her head rested on his chest. She smothered her sobs in his sweatshirt.

When at last she pulled away, regaining control of herself, she saw that Tor's eyes, too, were moist. Neither of them spoke; the crashing falls would have drowned out their words.

Kris put on her backpack, noticing that the loose soil on which it had been was full of flat pieces of shiny gray rock. She ran her hand through them and put a few in her pocket before getting up with Tor's unnecessary, but appreciated, help.

They ducked back under the rope and surveyed the steep trail up to the rim, then retraced their footsteps to the fork in the yellow trail and turned left. The spur took them to the top of the ridge and the apex of the red trail, the one they had started on near the restaurant and the one Grete and the Muellers had taken on Sunday. From higher up the mountain, myriad smaller waterfalls—the runoff from melting snow—merged into the rushing force that hurled itself over the cliff and into the gorge.

"Look at this," she shouted. Through an opening in the bushes at top of the falls, there was a perfect view of the ledge. From here, the cascading waters were only a sideshow. Had Odd stood here on Sunday and seen Elsa on the ledge?

Kris pulled the map from her pack. It had taken her and Tor about thirty-five minutes to hike to the ledge from the point where Elsa left the Muellers and Grete; it probably would have taken them the same amount of time to get here if they hadn't gone to the ledge first. Now she needed to see how long it would take to get back to where the red and blue trails divided. Twenty minutes later, she and Tor were at the place where they had paused earlier—not far from where the bees were still hovering around their nest.

Kris made a note on the map.

"Why are you doing this?" Tor asked.

"I'm not sure. But something tells me I have to. For Elsa."

"Hmm." He took off his sweatshirt and tied it around his waist. Underneath, he was wearing a Minnesota Vikings T-shirt. "I think we need a break. Let's go back to that open area; there's a meadow below it."

At the edge of a sea of buttercups and high grasses dotted here and there with wild strawberries and blueberry bushes, they found a boulder large and flat enough to stretch out with their backpacks and lunches between them. It was warm now, Kris chose the side of the rock shaded by birch trees; Tor took the sunny side.

"I much prefer a Norwegian heat wave to an East Coast one," Kris said, taking off her hat and loosening the laces of her hiking boots, then shedding her shirts down to just her tank-top.

"You don't have to stop now," Tor said.

She tossed her hat at him.

Despite the fact that they'd eaten breakfast a little more than two hours earlier, Kris eagerly ate her cheese sandwich. She had worked up more of an appetite than she'd thought.

"Are you sorry we went to the ledge?" Tor asked after they had eaten.

"No. I had to see it." Using her jacket as a pillow, Kris lay back on the rock, looking up through green and gold birch leaves to the azure sky and listening to the hum of the water and the sound of distant sheep bells.

"I know I'm still angry about Elsa's death, but..."

"But, what?"

"It bothers me that everything was solved so quickly. I've been thinking about it. It's almost, well, almost too convenient."

"The police got lucky. It can happen sometimes."

She turned and met Tor's eyes with her own. "I don't know. I have this feeling inside."

"You're on an emotional roller coaster, Kris. Your personal life is up in the air; you came to Norway to find some peace; then this tragedy happens. How can you know what feelings to trust?"

She shrugged. "Do you believe in intuition?"

"No."

"Well, I do."

"So?"

"I don't think we have all the answers to Elsa's death yet," she said.

A large bird circled overhead.

"What's that?"

"A golden eagle," Tor said. "Don't worry. It's looking for smaller prey than us. Look, I know it sounds cruel to say, 'You've got to get over it,' but you've got to. Come on, bring your cup, let's get some dessert."

He climbed off the boulder, took her hand, and helped her down. She thought about what Nils had said that day in his office, "We have to get on with our lives." Well, he had seen that things were not as clear as he thought they were. Maybe things weren't as clear as Tor thought either.

She followed Tor past long stalks of deep pink foxgloves to a clump of blueberry bushes. They picked berries, talked, and now and then looked up at the eagle. Finally, it glided to a perch atop an old snag.

"Tranquility base here. The eagle has landed," Tor said.

"Neil Armstrong, Apollo 11 Eagle, July 20, 1969." Kris replied. "I remember that day well."

"Me, too. Only the last time I talked with a woman about the landing on the moon, I had quite a different experience."

"Oh?" Their cups were full now. She fell into step behind him, eating berries as they headed back toward their boulder.

"It was the twentieth anniversary of the landing, and we were watching a replay of it on television," he recalled. "I got all excited and said, 'I remember that.' My date said, 'I don't. I wasn't born yet.' I can tell you that I lost a few more hairs right then, and my beard seemed like it would touch the floor."

Kris laughed.

"That experience cured me of dating women half my age."

"So you made an exception with Lise?" The words had just slipped out. And the bitchy, angry tone of her voice surprised her. Tor was right, she thought: she was on an emotional roller coaster, one moment submerged in grief, the next spitting fire. "I'm sorry. That's really none of my business," she said, embarrassed.

Kris had gotten used to his towering above her when they stood near each other. Now he had stopped in his tracks only inches away, his solid frame like a wall forcing her to halt. He yanked her cup away, disregarding the blueberries that tumbled out, stacked it on his cup and set them on a rock.

"Lise is my niece," he said matter of factly.

Kris's face burned. "I...I didn't know. I thought..." She tried to read the expression in his eyes.

"I was going to say that when I introduced you, but you interrupted me."

"I'm sorry," she said again.

"I'm not." He put his hands on either side of her waist and lifted her off her feet until her eyes were level with his, then he kissed her. She should have beat his chest, kicked him, made him let her go, but responding to the tingling in her body, she could only wrap her arms around his neck and return the kiss. She felt him gently loosen his hold, moving his hands from her waist to her back, guiding her as she slid slowly downwards against his body until her feet touched the ground. With all the willpower she could muster, she put her hands on his bearded cheeks and pulled away.

"I don't think I'm ready for this."

He held her chin in his hand as if to ensure that she wouldn't look away from him. "Maybe you are more ready than you think."

"Hey, you two, are you trying to melt all the glaciers around here?"

Kris and Tor turned their heads in the direction of the boulder where they'd had their lunch and from which the voice had come. "That's Bill Stephens and his wife Rachel," Kris said, waving. "They're guests at the hotel. He's the physician who checked on Elsa Saturday night when she had her dizzy spell."

"Hmm." Tor picked up the blueberry cups and handed her one, then put his arm around her shoulder as they walked toward Bill and Rachel who sat on the boulder.

Maybe they'd think her blush was sunburn. She felt as she did at seventeen when her father had found her necking with Jim in front of the television.

Bill and Rachel's poses made her laugh. They sat with arms crossed just below the "Desert Shield" on their matching shirts, their mouths set with a "Hey, so we know what you've been up to" look. They wore hiking shorts and their bare legs were crossed in the same direction. They jumped off the rock to greet Kris with hugs.

"It's good to see you," Kris told them.

"Same here," Bill said.

"This is my friend Tor Olsen."

"Well, yes, we hope he's your friend," Bill said, smiling broadly. The two men shook hands. "So, Tor, were you teaching Kris some of your Viking traditions?"

"Yes, I was just about to take her by the hair and pull her into my hut."

Bill slapped his thigh. "See, Rachel, we shouldn't have interrupted them. We could have had our rock back and maybe enjoyed a few X-rated scenes."

"Your rock?" Tor asked, good-naturedly. "We didn't see your sign on it."

"Bill calls it that because we found it on Sunday," Rachel explained.

Rachel and Bill had brought a blanket, tablecloth, sandwiches, fruit, cookies, coffee, and a bottle of wine.

"Wine?" Tor said. "And what are *you* planning for the afternoon?"

"You just wish you had thought of it, don't you?" Bill said. "Kris, watch out for this man."

Kris laughed. The banter had taken the embarrassment out of the moment. "Not to worry," she said. "Blueberries, anyone?"

They settled around the Stephens' tablecloth and chatted. Kris explained why she had come back.

"We heard about that crazy Odd and your cousin," Rachel said. "That's so horrible."

"Yes, it is," Kris agreed. She paused. "I'm trying to figure out how Elsa spent Sunday morning."

"You mean how she ran into Odd?" Rachel asked.

"Yes, that, too," Kris said. "Hasan said he dropped you off before he took Elsa and the others up the restaurant road."

"Right," Bill said.

"Did you see Elsa after that?" Tor asked.

"No, probably because it takes more than an hour from down there, back and forth on switchbacks up to here—at least it took us that long."

"Did you see anyone at all?"

"Well, Odd passed us up there," Rachel said, pointing to the top of the meadow. "He came from this direction."

"Did he say anything?"

"No, we said 'Hello.' He kind of nodded."

"So which way did he go?"

"That way," Rachel pointed in the direction of the part of the blue trail leading toward the Roma. "Then we got settled here on the rock, and we saw this turquoise and yellow figure coming through the trees."

"With another tree," Bill added.

"Bill!" Rachel chided. "He means the other Norwegian woman who was in the library last night; she was wearing all brown so kind of blended in with the trees. She went down the way we had come up, and Yolanda Mueller just sat on the ground for a few minutes."

"At first we thought something was wrong," Bill added. "But then she went back into the woods. And about twenty minutes later she returned."

"I wonder what all that was about," Kris said. When Yolanda told her story in the library the day of Elsa's death, she hadn't mentioned resting before going back to meet George. But maybe it wasn't important. Kris squinted at the opening in the line of trees where the yellow trail began. She tried to imagine the view from that point. "Did she see you?"

"I don't think so," Bill replied. "If you look from up there, it's not so easy to see this rock."

"Her husband came after about five minutes," Rachel said.

"He probably took a leak," Bill added. "He was hurrying to catch up with her."

"And then Odd came again," Rachel said.

Kris was confused. "Odd was with George Mueller?"

"No. He came about half an hour later, running like mad, even with all his gear."

"I guess we know why now," Bill added.

"Did you see anyone else?"

"No, believe it or not," Bill said. "We packed up our stuff and hiked to the falls."

"So you saw practically everyone?"

"But not Elsa."

"So where could she have gone?"

"Anywhere, if she went off the trail," he replied.

Had Elsa left the others so that she could hide somewhere? Spy on them maybe? Kris wondered.

"Oscar said Odd told him he had spent Sunday night in a mountain hut. Did you see any?"

"Negative," Bill said.

Kris took out Oscar's map and studied it again. "And there's nothing on here."

"That's hand-drawn," Tor said. "You need a real map." He took one out from his backpack. "The mountaineering association has placed huts within a day's walk of each other. We need to look to the higher elevations."

While Tor looked at the map, Kris scanned the terrain above them.

"Here," Tor said, pointing to a spot on his map. "This is about where we are. See this red and white square? That marks a hut. From where we are now, he'd have had to hike to the hut by going above the falls."

Kris saw the route went for some distance above the falls, then traversed the mountain eastward to the red and white square and continued on. "Odd was at the bottom of the falls when we brought Elsa out. That would mean he first hiked up to the falls, then down, then back up?" Kris asked. It didn't make much sense to her.

Tor studied the map. "He could have gone another way. Look, here not far from the youth hostel, there's a footbridge over the river. He could have followed the old railroad track—even the road—up the valley to the eastern end of the trail."

"Which way would be shorter?" Kris asked, wondering if Odd had hoped for a quick get-away.

"Could be the one above the falls, but shorter doesn't necessarily mean quicker," said Tor. "The upper trail is probably steeper, so it would take longer. The way up the valley rises gradually; it would be an easier, faster walk. Of course, it would depend on how fast Odd walked. The valley way probably would have taken him a couple of hours."

Kris thought about Odd. He had been at the bottom of the falls when they brought Elsa's body out. Had he pushed Elsa, then hidden until he saw Elsa's body had been discovered, then acted as if he were just coming upon the scene? Afterwards, he could have hiked to the cabin for the night, to think about his next move. That, she concluded, was a likely scenario.

"Did you go out on the ledge when you went to the falls?" Kris asked Bill and Rachel.

"No, we took the path to the top," Rachel said.

"What time was that?"

"Sometime after ten," Bill said.

"Then we went back down the mountain to town and took the ferry ride."

"If only we had seen Elsa. If only we'd taken her with us," Rachel said.

"Kris, we may never know exactly how Elsa and Odd met up and what exactly happened up there," Tor said, nodding in the direction of the falls. "You realize that, don't you?"

"Yes," she admitted. She also realized that the discussion had dampened the young couple's earlier levity, and if anyone was going to break the morbid mood it would have to be her. "I'm sorry to drag you all through this again," she said. She pointed to the panorama before them. "Elsa would want us to be enjoying this beautiful nature. Just look at it."

The effect of her words was immediate. She herself felt the relief, the kiss of the cool breeze, permission to enjoy the pristine nature.

"These mountains remind me of the Adirondacks," Bill said.

"Honey, that's because for you one mountain's just like another," Rachel said, stroking Bill's arm.

"Actually, Bill's on the right track," Tor said. "The Adirondacks and these mountains share similar geological histories. They were formed during the Precambrian period hundreds of millions of years ago."

Kris pulled out the rocks she had found at the ledge and held her palm out. "Are these that old?"

"Yes. They're gneiss," he said. "The mountains are full of it."

"Looks like slate, but sparkles like granite," Bill said.

"That's because of the heat and pressure deep in the earth at the time; igneous rock meeting metamorphic."

"Sounds like we have a Viking geologist here," Bill said good-naturedly.

Tor smiled. "Something like that," he said. "Hey, are you wearing those T-shirts just because you like them or were you in Desert Storm?"

Within minutes, Tor was asking Bill about Iraq, and the two were sharing recollections of Kuwait and Saudi Arabia. Bill talked about the Gulf War; Tor about his work with Aramco.

"So, how did you meet Bill?" Kris asked Rachel.

"Our grandparents. They knew each other."

"You mean they matched you up?" Kris asked.

"Not exactly. They arranged a reunion of their families and that's how we met."

"Were they alumni of the same school?"

"No, of the same war. Bill's grandfather was a soldier during World War II. His unit liberated Dachau in 1945. My grandfather was one of the survivors that he rescued."

"Wow," Kris said, trying to imagine the friendship that must have ensued between the two grandfathers.

"Hey, Kris, I'd say it's time for us to shove off," Tor said.

She would have liked to have continued visiting with Rachel and Bill, but she knew Tor was right. Their, or at least her, research wasn't over yet. She told Rachel she'd like to hear more of her story another time, and said her goodbyes to the couple.

She and Tor headed toward the trail leading down the mountain. They followed the switchbacks through woods and open areas; past rocks and debris spilled in a giant heap by a winter avalanche; past sheep and goats with bells around their necks, grazing in high pasture. The distant sound of the waterfall was a constant companion. After forty-five minutes, they saw the trail to the youth hostel. "Time for a rest stop," Kris said.

The hostel manager was too deep in conversation with a woman holding a microphone and a man with a TV camera propped on his shoulder to raise any fuss about strangers using his restrooms. When Kris came back into the hallway, she heard the hostel manager saying, "And the police came and blocked off the road. They didn't say who was hurt. We had no idea until we read it in the paper."

"But weren't you the person who notified the Fjord Hotel manager?" the woman asked.

"Yes, but the message I had was to tell Mrs. Kelly that her cousin was injured."

"Who is Mrs. Kelly?"

"Tor, let's go," Kris said. They left the hostel and the press behind, and followed the mountain trail to the bottom of the waterfall.

Surrounded by rock walls and bathed by the white spray from the falls, the area was awash in lush mosses. Beams of sunlight filtered through the moisture, spawning a rainbow halfway up the falls; the mist from the waterfall felt silky against Kris's face. She showed Tor the spot where she remembered Odd pausing to let the entourage with

Elsa pass. "If he pushed Elsa, why would he show up here and risk being connected to her murder?" she mused aloud.

"Doesn't the criminal always return to the scene of the crime?" he asked.

"Maybe."

They walked along the road back to town. As they crossed the bridge over the river, a small red car raced past them, veered recklessly into the opposite lane to pass two bicyclists, and then returned to its own lane barely in time to miss a head-on collision with a van.

"Idiot!" Tor shouted after him.

On the other side of the bridge, they took the promenade.

"Did you see who was driving that car?" Kris asked.

"Yeah, it was Hans," Tor replied, anger in his voice.

"He was driving a red Fiat," Kris said. "That's what the thief at Elsa's drove."

"Hey, just because he's speeding here doesn't mean he was in Bergen," Tor said. He put his arm around her and squeezed her shoulder hard, more, she thought, out of frustration than affection. "How many red Fiats do you think there are in Norway? How are you even so sure the other car was a Fiat? You saw it at night. You've got to accept that the case is closed."

"Right," she said; wrong, she thought.

CHAPTER 20

▼

Kris and Tor neared the end of the promenade. Across the expansive lawn the beautiful hotel beckoned; at the dock, Oscar did as well. He was standing on the deck of the *Fjordstar* motioning to them to come aboard.

He greeted them, shaking their hands, and escorting them into a luxurious sitting room—saloon, Oscar called it—and galley. In spite of the sun beating in through the windows, the room was pleasantly cool. Dag was curled up on a rug in the center of the saloon. When he saw Kris, he pulled himself up and bounded to her, licking her outstretched hand. She knelt and rubbed the Lab's back affectionately.

"You see, he's your friend now," Oscar said.

"I thought I was Kris's friend, too," Tor said, "but she doesn't do that to me."

Kris felt herself blush. "No comment," she said.

Oscar chuckled and brought them each a soda from the refrigerator. They sat with their drinks and chatted.

"This is a beautiful Romsdal," Tor said.

"*Ja,*" Oscar replied. "You know them?"

"I know them well," Tor said. "I've skippered them."

Tor explained to Kris that Oscar's yacht was named for the county to the north, which was world famous for building these fishing trawlers. In spite of having a large engine, the boat still had masts—a tall one in the foredeck, a small one at the rear of the upper deck, like in the sailing days when it was first designed.

"Would you like to see the rest of it?" Oscar asked.

"Yes," they both answered enthusiastically.

They followed Oscar through the galley, down a couple of steps past a bathroom and a door leading to the engine room, and down several more steps into a spacious master stateroom. The walls, cupboards, shelves, fold-down desk, and large double berth were all made of gleaming wood.

"I'll take this room," Kris said, flippantly. Indeed, she was half tempted to climb into the double berth with its cushy pillows. Even the built-in bookshelf offered history and travel books about Norway, a few Ibsen classics, and mystery novels for on-board entertainment.

Further on, there were two smaller cabins, one with two bunk beds, another with one.

"Do you do charters?" she asked Oscar.

"Sometimes. Mostly, we take guests fishing and sightseeing. I use it sometimes for vacations with my family."

"It must be easy to feel at home here for a couple weeks," Kris said.

"*Ja*," Oscar agreed.

Tor mentioned George's invitation to join them for fishing.

Oscar seemed delighted. "Will you come also?" he asked Kris, who was only too aware that Tor had not asked her.

"No, thanks," she said. "I think it's a 'guy' thing."

From the look on Oscar's face, she knew he had not understood.

"I don't think fishing is for me, but I'd love to go sightseeing sometime," she explained.

"Very fine," Oscar said.

They returned to the main deck. Tor and Oscar went up to the pilothouse while Kris lingered in the saloon to pet Dag. After several minutes she took the interior steps to the pilothouse. Tor and Oscar were sitting on the settee at the back poring over a chart on the table in front of them. They broke off their conversation when Kris arrived.

"Don't let me interrupt," she said, glancing at the squiggles on their chart, walking past them, and placing her hands on the shiny helm.

"Where shall we go?" she teased, looking at the panoramic view of the fjord through the row of windows above the console. On the console itself there were levers that looked like joy sticks, numerous buttons, a couple of microphones connected to radios. Radar.

Tor came beside her and explained all the gizmos and gadgets.

"I guess you do know these boats," she said.

"Maybe I can even learn some things about them from him," Oscar said.

Before leaving the pilothouse, Kris looked again at the mishmash of wavy lines and numbers that Tor and Oscar had been studying. She was used to reading land maps, not maps of the sea. At least she understood the demarcation "international waters" at one side of the chart.

Oscar and Dag accompanied them back to the hotel lobby.

"How about a swim and sauna?" Tor asked when he and Kris were on the way to their rooms.

"You're kidding, aren't you?"

"Only if you like sore muscles."

Twenty minutes later Kris stood in front of the mirror in her new black Gottex swimsuit that pulled in her tummy and pushed up her breasts. She remembered Laura's reaction when they had gone shopping together at the beginning of the summer, and she had tried it on: "Mom, you look so sexy! Go for it!"

Kris's shrinking to a size eight from a size twelve was one of the only benefits of the breakup of her marriage; she had giggled at Laura's comment and bought the suit. The self-confidence she had felt that day in the dressing room evaporated now as she thought about standing like this in front of Tor. In spite of her new shape, some things would never change after having given birth: the slight bulge of her stomach, stretch marks on her legs. Accept the fact that you're no longer twenty, she told herself. She put on a blouse and a wrap-around skirt over her swimsuit and went to meet Tor.

Sunlight streaming through the glass wall warmed the A-frame, giving the large room with its turquoise pool and huge plants a tropical atmosphere despite the smell of chlorine.

Tor slipped off his shorts and threw them on a lounge chair. Kris tried to keep her cool. Seeing him in running shorts was quite different from seeing him in a navy blue elastic suit that left very little to the imagination. Jim would never have been so brazen.

"Why don't you go ahead," she said, keeping her eyes on his face.

She slowly unbottoned her blouse. If he dived into the pool, she calculated she could do so too while he was underwater and avoid the feeling of unveiling herself.

"I'll meet you at the other end," Tor said.

"Okay."

Tor plunged into the water. Kris threw her blouse and wrap-around on to the chair and dived in after him. Brilliant, she thought, as she surfaced and shook her head to get the water out of her nose and ears. Why hadn't she gone down the ladder into the pool so her hair would have stayed relatively dry; now she no doubt looked like a wet dog. She joined Tor at the opposite end of the pool, and they swam laps together for half an hour. She had to admit it felt good to be immersed in the water after all the walking they had done.

Finally, Tor climbed on an air mattress and floated around the pool. "Want to join me?" he asked, winking at her.

"No thanks, but I'd like to know the story behind your tattoo," she said, swimming next to him.

"It's from my navy days. I must have thought I was Erik the Red or one of my other ancestors."

Kris laughed. Their eyes met. "I'm going to do another lap," she said, swimming quickly away, as if in doing so she could quash the tingly feeling she felt coming over her. She heard the splash from Tor rolling off his float. When she reached the edge of the pool, he caught up with her and put his arm around her waist.

"Sauna?"

"Sure, why not?" At least if she blushed in there he wouldn't be able to tell.

They climbed out of the water and wrapped their towels around themselves. Kris picked up her wrap-around skirt and blouse, and Tor his shorts and shirt, and they followed the signs downstairs to the end of the hall, past a massage room and a jacuzzi. An area with cupboards and tiled showers led to the sauna.

"Ever been in a sauna before?" Tor asked.

"Years ago. My favorite part was the smell of the wood," Kris said, putting her clothes in one of the cupboards.

Tor checked the sauna's heating controls. "It's about a hundred and ninety-five degrees Fahrenheit."

"Swell, I'll be cooked in thirty seconds!" Kris joked.

"Don't worry. I'll turn it down." He adjusted one of the knobs. "It's okay as long as you don't stay too long."

He held the door open, and Kris walked into a blast of dry heat and the sweet fragrance of wood. The sauna was more or less like the ones she remembered: about eight feet by ten, lined in birchwood, with three tiers of hot, dry shelf-like benches.

Tor took a dipper of water and poured it over a pot of hot rocks, causing a momentary burst of steam. He climbed to the bench on the third level and lay down on his towel.

Kris stayed on the first tier and, like Tor, put her towel on the bench and lay down. The terrycloth made the hot wood tolerable. Using her folded arms as a pillow, she closed her eyes.

"This place brings back many warm memories," she said.

"Ha, ha."

She smiled against the dry wood. "Not meant to be a pun. No, it's not so much the sauna as the dipper. My grandparents used to have a dipper near the well. My cousins and I would pump water by hand; we'd watch it shoot out a narrow trough and run down into a large bucket for the cows." Kris fell into a light sleep, dreaming of the stars and the big and little dippers and how they had always reminded her of the dipper of her childhood.

The timer buzzed. "Time's up." Tor said. Kris felt Tor's warm hand on her back.

"Wow, that was relaxing. I'm probably as red as a tomato, though," she said, as they walked into the anteroom.

"No, an apple," Tor said. "Now, tradition is that you should jump into the snow. But since we don't have any here, you can jump into a cold shower."

"I'm so hot, I could almost do that," Kris said. "But I think I'll settle for the jacuzzi around the corner. I'm willing to watch you go into shock though."

Tor turned on the water, but instead of stepping into the shower, he stepped toward her. "Come on, you know when in Scandinavia…"

"Oh, no!" She backed away from him, but he was quicker. He whisked her off her feet and carried her into the icy shower.

"Let me go!" she screamed, trying to wiggle herself out of his grasp. It was as if his arms were attached to her with Crazy Glue. The cold water stung her skin; she buried her face in his chest.

"What happens here?"

Kris stopped screaming when she heard Hasan's shouting. She glanced at him in time to see his angry expression change to one of amusement.

Tor brought her out of the stream of water. "It's okay. The water was just too cold for her."

Hasan gave them a knowing smile and left. With her hands Kris wiped her face and wrung the water out of her hair as best she could. Her bathing suit, which had dried out in the sauna, was again dripping wet.

Tor stood grinning at her. "I enjoyed that!"

"Yes, I know you did," she said with mock anger. "I'll get my revenge eventually."

She struggled with the buttons of her blouse and with her emotions; she wanted to say that it had been fun, that he had awakened desires she hadn't felt in months. But she couldn't bring herself to admit it. She finished with her blouse and tied the belt of her wrap-around skirt, which was already damp.

Tor had put his shorts back on over his swimsuit. The sight of his chest through his open shirt did nothing to quell Kris's feelings. He put his arm around her.

"Don't think that's going to get you back in my good graces," she teased.

They went through the pool area to get back to the hotel. Kris spotted Yolanda in a chic yellow two-piece bathing suit, sitting in a lounge chair, sipping the remains of iced tea. Her long black hair was brushed straight and fell gracefully over the front of her right shoulder. Hans sat in a chair to her right; there was an empty chair with a towel on it to her left. Kris scanned the pool; she caught sight of George swimming laps just as he looked up. She waved, and he broke the rhythm of his strokes to wave back.

Seeing the Muellers again reminded Kris of the reasons she had returned to the Fjord Hotel.

"Hello," she said to Yolanda, all but ignoring Hans.

"Good afternoon, my dear. You're looking much better. You have some color."

"Thanks," Kris said. "Saunas do wonders for the circulation."

"I was just teaching Kris some of our Nordic after-sauna customs," said Tor; he acknowledged Hans with a nod.

She heard Hans snicker under his breath.

"Oh?" Yolanda said, looking admiringly at Tor. "How very intriguing."

"More wine?" Hans asked Yolanda.

"Yes, thank you," she said. Hans's hand covered Yolanda's for an instant as he took her glass. She seemed well aware of his eyes passing

over her body, and for a moment her own eyes followed his movements as he walked away. Then she turned back to Kris.

"It must be difficult for you…without your cousin," she said.

"Yes," Kris replied. "But I'm trying to understand her. Do you
remember when she suggested you may have been in London at the
same time?"

Yolanda nodded, "Yes, quite unlikely."

"Are you sure? She thought the two of you may have acted together
in a play in London. Is that possible?"

Kris found Yolanda's laugh disarming. "Me, an actress?" she said. "I
assure you it wasn't me."

But Kris persisted. "She thought you looked very much like someone named Shoshana."

"A case of mistaken identity, my dear," she said coolly.

"Kris, we should be going," Tor said.

She felt his hand in the middle of her back, prodding her to say
goodbye and move on.

CHAPTER 21

▼

Kris turned down Tor's invitation to dinner, telling him she needed some time alone. He sounded disappointed, but didn't push her to change her mind. She had a much-needed nap, then ordered a light dinner from room service, enjoying the fresh air from the open balcony doors.

Although she had chosen not to have dinner with Tor, she thought mostly of him while she ate. Reviewing the almost twenty-four hours they had spent together, she couldn't deny her growing attraction to him. Was her way of mourning Elsa to escape into a flirtation? Or was this a genuine friendship developing out of the loss of someone dear to both of them? She felt torn between wanting to give in to her impulses and needing to stay on guard. She was annoyed that he interrupted her questioning of Yolanda. She also resented his skepticism toward her idea that the red Fiat that Hans drove at the fjord could be the same one driven by the thief at Elsa's.

Her thoughts turned to Hans and Yolanda. They had supposedly just met. How close were they? Given George's age, Yolanda might well be physically attracted to a younger man like Hans. It didn't really matter, Kris concluded, unless there was a tie between Yolanda and Hans and what happened to Elsa.

If she could reconcile herself to the idea that Odd killed Elsa, Kris knew she could "get on with her life" as Nils had said the other day, and "get over it" as Tor had said. But seeing Hans in the red Fiat on the bridge had stirred up her uneasiness again.

Could it have been Hans, not Odd, at Elsa's Monday night? Kris wondered. The police had found Elsa's things at Odd's and concluded that he had stolen them. But if Hans, not Odd, had been at Elsa's and taken her things, then that would mean that Odd hadn't died accidentally, but that Hans had killed him and framed him. But why? Maybe to protect Yolanda?

Perhaps Yolanda had lied today. Shoshana what's-her-name had been an actress, or at least had a thespian bent. If Yolanda was Shoshana, then today's denial was an act. Had Yolanda given her ring to Hans to leave at Odd's? Was it just luck that the ring wasn't damaged in the fire?

Kris had more questions than she had answers. She called Nils. He reported that things were moving along for the gathering on Sunday, and that Andy was deeply involved in sculpting a likeness of Elsa.

She told Nils about the hike, trying to emphasize the beauty of the nature and how much Elsa must have enjoyed it until her final moments. She told him about finding Elsa's ticket to Buenos Aires. "Did you know that she was planning to go to there next month?"

"Yes," he said.

Before Kris could ask if he had planned to go with Elsa, he added, "She was going to try to find Brunner—The Elephant."

Kris was dumbstruck. "She thought he was still alive?" she managed to ask at last.

"Yes. She thought there was a chance."

"But what was she going to do?"

"She thought if she could find him, she could expose him."

"How?"

"Media attention. She was inspired by your American television journalist, Sam Donaldson, who exposed the Nazi war criminal, Erich Priebke, in Argentina last year."

"I remember that. And I remember how excited Elsa was, but she never indicated she wanted to do the same thing."

"Priebke will probably be extradited to Italy to stand trial for the crimes he committed," Nils continued. "Elsa wanted that to happen to Brunner."

"For killing Per?" Kris asked.

"Yes, and for killing other Norwegians, and sending hundreds of Jews and non-Jews to the gas chambers in Poland." Nils's voice was strained with anger. "The Nazis, the SS, especially the Gestapo, were monsters; Brunner was no exception. Elsa researched what he did after he was transferred from Norway to the Eastern Front in 1943. She traced him to a Gross-Rosen, a concentration camp near the Polish border, then to Auschwitz, where the victims of his appetite for torture were fed to the gas chambers. He disappeared when the Allies came, and he escaped the Nuremberg trials. We assumed he either died—maybe even was killed by Israeli Intelligence, the Mossad—or escaped to South America."

Kris listened, fascinated.

"Remember Elsa covered the Eichmann trial in Israel in 1960."

Kris nodded. "She spoke about it often over the years, especially when she visited us in Jerusalem." Memories of that visit, of going with Elsa to Yad Vashem, the Holocaust memorial, flashed in Kris's mind.

"Elsa had her ways and her contacts," Nils went on, "including contacts in the Mossad, whom I think she somehow met when she was there for the trial. Don't ask me how she did it. Anyway, someone confirmed for her that the Mossad had not killed Brunner after the war. The fact that the Israelis captured Eichmann, so notorious a war criminal, gave Elsa hope that The Elephant could be caught. She came back to Norway very optimistic that he would be found. But years passed, and it didn't happen," Nils paused, and then went on. "Her hopes dimmed, but she never gave up. She had artists recreate ways Brunner might change his appearance through plastic surgery, how he might look as he aged. Members of the Jewish community in Norway helped her make contact with Nazi hunters in France, Austria, and Israel; Brunner was still on their most-wanted list."

"Had someone told her that Brunner was in Argentina?"

"I don't think so. I think she was just impatient. The fact that Eichmann and Priebke had both been located there made her want to go see for herself."

"But why didn't she leave that up to her friends in the Mossad?" Kris asked.

"She believed that after the Demjanjuk acquittal, Israel would not hold any more trials of alleged war criminals."

Kris remembered the controversial ending to the long trial in Israel of the Ukrainian emigre to the United States who was accused of being "Ivan the Terrible," a notoriously sadistic guard at the Treblinka death camp. Although evidence was presented to suggest that he had been a guard at Treblinka, the Israeli supreme court ruled the evidence insufficient to prove him "Ivan the Terrible." She recalled the outcry from Holocaust survivors when he was acquitted. The seven-year trial had taken a toll on the country. The consensus at the time was that Israel probably wouldn't, as Nils said, consider going through such a trial again.

"Elsa believed that during the decades between the trials of Eichmann and of Demjanjuk, Nazi war criminals lived in fear of the Israelis," Nils said. "'Why shouldn't their days and nights be filled with the fear of being found?' she used to say. But times have changed. We have to remember Israel has more immediate concerns—making peace with the Arabs, for example, a process in which Oslo has played a significant role."

"So," Kris said, now understanding her cousin's motives more clearly. "When Elsa saw that a fellow journalist had exposed a Nazi war criminal, she realized that she might have the power to do so as well."

"Yes," Nils replied. "She saw that Nazis had to be almost as worried about being shot by a camera as by a gun. The final result might be the same."

"But what did she plan to do if she found him? Would Norway ask for extradition?"

"No, the statute of limitations for Nazi crimes in Norway ran out thirty years ago. That was probably Elsa's greatest frustration."

"But if Israel is unlikely to try any more Nazis…"

"That was the problem. But Elsa decided she would find Brunner first, then worry about it."

"I'm stunned. Elsa seemed so involved in the present. I knew the past drove the issues she pursued, but I never dreamt she had become a Nazi hunter herself. Why didn't she tell me her plans?"

"You know Elsa could be very secretive. She probably thought you would say it was a foolish idea."

"Not if she had told me the reasons."

"She cared very much about your opinion of her. She told very few people about her plans. She wanted to do it quietly; if she were successful, then everyone would know."

"Wow, Nils, you've given me a lot to think about," Kris said, looking through the balcony doors to the mountain on the other side of the fjord.

"We'll all be thinking about Elsa for a long time to come," Nils said.

"Would you mind if I ask you a couple more questions?"

"Go ahead."

"I'm still wondering about Odd Engstrom's role in all this. Could you find out what kind of car he had?"

"Yes, that should be easy."

"The other thing is not so easy. Do you know anyone named Otto Kohler?"

"No, at least I don't think so. Why?"

"Well, there's a man here by that name. He lives in Sweden, says he lived there during the war, that he was born in Germany. He's an old man, and he seems quite ill. But there's something about him that bothers me, and maybe it's because he appeared at this hotel where Elsa brought me." Kris cleared her throat and continued. "He has big ears that kind of stick out from his gaunt face. It occurred to me that being

German, if he was lying about having been in Sweden during the war, he could be The Elephant. Do I sound completely crazy?"

"Kris, I don't know. Sweden is a long way from Argentina. But I've learned my lesson. I don't scoff at your ideas any more. How old is this man?"

"It's hard to tell because his illness may make him look older than he is. I'd guess mid-seventies to mid-eighties. Oh, and if it helps, he has a nurse named Helga and a sleazy assistant whose name is Hans."

"I'll see what I can find out, but I'll need some time."

"We don't have much. They're leaving Saturday."

"I'll call you tomorrow night at eight," Nils said, ending the conversation.

Kris sighed. Her next call, to Uncle Andy, was brief. He sounded glad to hear from her, and asked if she had gone to the ledge. She told him she had, and dreaded questions he might ask about Elsa's fall. But he only said, "Good, Kristina. That's good."

She asked him about his sculpture, and he told her he was making progress and needed to return to it. The call was over in a few minutes.

Her uncle was working out his grief in his own way. For her part, she would need time to digest all that Nils had told her about Elsa, but she had taken some positive steps to follow her hunches about Hans and Otto. Now she would have to wait.

CHAPTER 22

▼

Tired of being alone and needing to get her mind off the discussion she just had with Nils, Kris decided to go downstairs and see what was going on. Perhaps she could catch sight of Hans and try to imagine him as the intruder. But what would she do if she ran into Tor? She hoped she wouldn't so that she wouldn't have to wrestle with her emotions.

Strolling solo through the hotel parlors, Kris ached for Elsa's ability to walk confidently into a crowded room, seemingly oblivious to stares, graciously addressing those she knew.

Kris glanced at tables in search of a familiar face. Apparently a tour group had arrived that afternoon, adding significantly to the crowd.

Finally she decided to study the paintings, an activity that would allow her an opportunity to also observe the other guests from a safe corner of the room. She paused in front of a large nineteenth-century oil painting with mountains in the background, a river and small log cabin in the foreground. The artist's depiction of sunlight on the mountains reminded her of a Bierstadt painting of the Rocky Mountains.

"Good evening."

She cringed at the sound of Hans's voice. She forced herself to remain calm. He stood uncomfortably close to her, his clothes reeking of cigarette smoke.

"Good evening," she said finally.

"It is too nice an evening to be indoors, is it not?" he said, looking her up and down with his cat eyes.

"Not at all," she replied. "It's a lovely evening to be inside, to take time to notice what's on the walls."

"Or to look for the handwriting on the wall?"

"And just what do you mean by that?"

"That you need a man. One who is more sophisticated than that Norwegian."

"You're rude," she said. She tried to pass by him, but he blocked her way.

Hans smirked. "I do not think so. Come with me to my room, and we can have a drink together." He ran his fingers along her right cheek to her chin, then down her neck to her neckline.

"Stop it!" she ordered, gritting her teeth and grabbing his wrist.

"*Gutten abend*," Max boomed.

"You have discovered the paintings, I see," Max said to her, maneuvering his girth to Hans's side, forcing the unpleasant fellow to step back. "I would be happy to tell you about some of them."

"I'd love to hear about them!" she said, grateful for Max's arrival.

"And you, Hans, my friend?" he said.

"Not now. I should check on Otto. Until later, Kris Kelly. *Auf Wiedersehen.*"

"Thank you, Max," she said as Hans left the room.

"It is my pleasure."

Was he referring to his offer to tell her about the paintings or to his interrupting Hans's harassment of her? Had he noticed? Kris wondered.

"Now, this painting we are standing in front of is by Hans Gude, one of Norway's most famous painters from the national romantic period. And, I should add, one of many who studied in Germany during the nineteenth century."

Kris allowed herself to be transported back in time to imagine artists in an idyllic place like this, struggling to capture on canvas its inimitable natural beauty.

"And this one over here," Max continued, escorting her past a couple visiting over cocktails, to another huge painting in an ornate gold frame, "is by Eilert Adelsteen Normann. Again we have a Norwegian-German connection—Normann studied in Dusseldorf for several years."

In this painting, which the artist had flooded with sunlight, men rowed a dingy from a sailboat in a placid fjord. Women and children in nineteenth-century dress stood in the grassy foreground.

"Perhaps I can buy you a drink now?" Max asked after explaining several other paintings.

"Thank you, that would be very nice," she said. "Thank you."

She certainly preferred having a drink with Max to one with Hans. They went to the adjacent cocktail lounge, where he ordered two glasses of white wine.

"I am sorry," he said to her after the waiter had left, "I did not ask if you wish the white wine."

"It will be fine," she said. He had been too kind for her to start making a fuss about the order.

"How did you find out about this hotel?" she asked.

"A good travel agent who knows my interests recommended it to me this spring," Max said. He was using his stomach as a shelf, resting on it the base of the wine glass he held in his hand. She noticed his eyes focus on something behind her. "Your friend is coming," he said.

She felt a gentle tug on the back of her hair, then Tor's warm hand on the nape of her neck. "What's your secret, Max? She told *me* she wanted to have a quiet evening."

"With me, she *is* having a quiet evening. Please join us," he said.

Tor pulled a chair over from a nearby table. "She's even drinking wine with you? Kris, I thought you never drank anything stronger than tea?"

"Sometimes the occasion calls for wine," she said. She told herself she was too old to be having a school-girl crush, but she felt giddy. She wondered if Tor's smiling eyes—looking straight into hers—could read her thoughts.

"Max has been giving me a lesson in art history," she said.

"And, doing my duty to rescue a damsel in distress," Max said.

"Oh? How so?" Tor asked.

"He rescued me from Hans," she said. "Max, I wasn't sure you had noticed."

"But, of course, I did," he said.

"Hans was hitting on you?" Tor asked.

"Yes, I would say so," she replied. His command of modern American slang again amused her. Was he jealous?

"It is a fact of life, my friend," Max said to Tor, "that when a man sees an attractive woman alone he will respond to his desire to be with her. You would have done the same."

"Thank you, Max," Kris said.

She put her hand on Tor's arm. "Never mind Hans. What have you been up to?"

"Hmm," Tor grinned at her. She was sure he hadn't heard her question. More importantly he had gotten the silent message she tried to send through her touch. She felt the muscles in his arm relax.

"I understand you will come fishing with us tomorrow, Tor," Max said.

"Unfortunately, I can't."

"Don't pass it up on my account," Kris said.

"Oh, that's not it. I have to go to Stavanger."

"So suddenly?"

"I believe it is time to leave you two alone," Max said, rising from his chair. "It is a pity you cannot fish with us," he told Tor. Then to Kris, he said, "It was my pleasure to spend some time with you." He kissed her hand.

"I enjoyed your company, too. Thank you so much for everything." She watched Max walk away. In spite of his mass, he moved with an agility that she found surprising.

"Would you like this?" she asked Tor, holding her wine glass out to him.

"Sure. Wouldn't want to see it go to waste."

"So, what's happening in Stavanger?"

"Statoil meeting. Will you be all right while I'm away?"

"Why wouldn't I be?" Kris asked.

"I was worried it might be hard for you to be here without Elsa."

Kris hastened to reassure him. "But, I have to get used to it. And it's good to be alone sometimes."

"I don't want Hans bothering you."

"Don't worry," she said, moved by his protectiveness. "I plan to avoid him like the plague, which should be easy since they're all going fishing." She was not about to let Tor think she couldn't handle things by herself for a day. And with the plans she had for tomorrow, his absence could be very convenient. "How long will you be gone?"

"About twelve hours. Stavanger's only a couple of hours away by helicopter. I can take one from the valley early tomorrow morning, meet most of the day, and fly back. Will you have dinner with me tomorrow night?"

"Sure." Kris smiled. "I'd like that."

They walked hand in hand back to her room, and stopped outside the door. "I'm going to miss you," he said, looking into her eyes.

She held his gaze. "Today on the mountain, I wasn't ready for this," she said.

"Hmm," he said leaning toward her.

"Well, I've changed my mind."

She stood on her toes, placed her hands on his shoulders, and kissed him.

He wrapped his arms around her and returned her kiss.

CHAPTER 23

▼

The memory of their kiss was fresh in Kris's mind on Thursday morning. It had only confirmed the chemistry between them, making her thankful Tor had been called away on business so she could concentrate on other things for a while.

She breakfasted with Bill and Rachel in the hotel dining room.

"So where's Tor?" Bill asked.

"He had to go to a meeting in Stavanger."

"Probably not his choice of activities," Bill said.

"Would you like to come hiking with us?" Rachel asked. "We're not going anywhere near the falls, and a change of scene would be good for you."

Kris appreciated the invitation but declined it, saying she wanted to spend some time in the village and just take it easy.

The Muellers were coming in to the dining room as Kris was leaving, and she took a few minutes to chat with them. Yolanda and George hand-in-hand and Otto smiling up at her from his wheelchair, pushed by his nurse, dispelled Kris's suspicions about Yolanda's infidelity and Otto's past.

However, when she caught sight of Hans in the lobby in swim trunks and open shirt heading toward the A-frame, Kris had no doubts about her loathing of the man. While he exercised, she would execute the first part of her plan to find out more about him.

She strolled through the rose garden, making sure that if anyone was watching her it appeared she was literally just taking time "to smell the roses." She stopped now and then to breathe in the crisp air or to lean her nose close to the flowers. At the end of one row of deep pink roses, she followed a path into the parking lot, looking up at the mountains and acting oblivious to the vehicles she passed. She took a moment to lean against one of the cars and pretend to fix her sandal, stealing a furtive glance toward the hotel and especially the A-frame to see if anyone might be watching. She admonished herself for being so paranoid. The windows of the exercise room were obscured by a row of saplings. She doubted anyone could see her.

A red Fiat was parked at the end of the lot. Her back to the A-frame, she stopped for just a second, slipped out pen and paper from her bag and quickly wrote down the license number and the name of the rental company on the decal. She continued slowly around to the other end of the garden, acting as inconspicuous as possible, and went back into the hotel. She found the phone number of the rental car company in the local telephone directory.

"Good morning," Kris said to the cheerful representative. She feigned a British accent. "I hope you can help me. One of my husband's business associates rented one of your cars last week, and he thinks he may have left his briefcase inside. We were wondering if you could check the boot."

The solicitous young man asked for a description of the car.

She gave him the particulars. "My husband thinks his friend returned the car to you on Sunday or Monday."

He asked her to wait while he checked.

"That car, Madam, was returned on Friday and rented on Monday morning. We make thorough checks of all cars once they are returned, and we have no record of a briefcase being found."

"Well, is the car back? Perhaps you could take a look in it yourself?" She imagined the young man's growing dislike for her.

"No, Madam, the car is still rented. I assure you the briefcase is not in it."

"Oh, dear. Well, thank you for your help."

So, Hans had rented the car on Monday morning; he would have only needed two or three hours to get to Bergen. Somehow she needed to find out, without arousing any suspicions, if he was at the hotel Monday night.

In the meantime, she had other plans.

She drank tea on the balcony, writing down thoughts about Elsa to share at Sunday's service, and watching Oscar, Hasan, Hans, and Max get Otto and his wheelchair aboard the *Fjordstar*. Yolanda waved good-bye to them and walked toward town.

When the boat pulled away from the dock at ten o'clock, Kris sprang into action. She changed to a short-sleeve top, tucked it into her wrap-around skirt, and tied a long-sleeve shirt around her waist in case of a cool breeze. In the lobby, she ran into Oscar and Dag. On a whim she asked if she could take Dag on her walk.

Once they were underway, Kris had second thoughts that Dag might slow her down, but on the contrary, he kept her walking at a brisk pace in between his stops to sniff bushes, rocks, posts and some old men fishing from the promenade. On the main street of town, Dag basked in the attention of two children selling fresh raspberries, which gave Kris time to stop and buy a small containerful, before she and Dag continued on their way.

Hiking up the hill, she paused several times to pop luscious berries into her mouth and savor their sweet taste while Dag busily explored the side of the road. At last they reached the Roma Restaurant; she tied Dag to a tree away from the parking area and went inside.

A middle-aged man with black wavy hair and an Italian accent met her at the door. "*Velkommen, Bonjourno,*" he said.

She smiled. "Good morning."

"You are American. An extra welcome to you."

She thanked him and stopped him as he started to escort her to a table. She explained that she would like to have lunch but would first like to get some water for her dog outside. A last minute impulse to identify Dag as belonging to Oscar Larsen at the Fjord Hotel proved to be a good one. The man insisted that Oscar's dog must have VIP treatment. He excused himself and returned with a dish of water and a juicy bone which he carried in a plastic bag. He accompanied Kris outside.

If the man wanted to see for himself that the dog was no threat to restaurant guests, Dag's appreciative, wagging tail assured him. He insisted that they take Dag where he would be more "comfortable"— on the lawn in front of the restaurant. Once there, the man handed the bone to the excited Dag, who grabbed it and trotted off, no longer interested in the two humans he left behind.

"Are you the owner here?" Kris asked on their way back inside.

"Yes. I am Vittorio Rosellini."

"My name is Kris Kelly. I am Elsa Jenssen's cousin."

"Oh, my dear lady, I give you great sympathy. Ms. Jenssen was extraordinary!" He kissed his fingertips for emphasis.

Kris told him about her pilgrimage to retrace Elsa's footsteps.

Vittorio seemed deeply touched.

"Is there any chance that you may have seen my cousin on Sunday?" she asked.

He shook his head. "No, no, I am sorry. I did not. But maybe I saw her companions."

"Oh?" What did he mean?

"I remember them because the woman is *bella*. I thought that she is Italian, but she is Spanish."

"The Muellers?"

"Maybe. The man, he is older than the wife."

"What time did they come? Do you remember?"

"Oh, yes. It was quarter after ten. The tour busses they were coming also."

"Do you remember anything else?"

"Yes. The husband, he did not feel well. He was very red and the breath was so fast. His hand it was bleeding. I gave him iodine and a bandage."

Kris couldn't remember seeing a bandage on George's hand on Sunday.

"Did he say what had happened?"

"Yes, he said he tripped on the root of a tree and fell on a rock. It can happen so easy, especially with older people."

Vittorio seated Kris by a window with a view of the garden, Dag, and the fjord. She asked him if a man in a wheelchair or a muscular German who looked like a prize fighter had come to the Roma on Sunday.

"No," he said. "No, not Sunday; Tuesday, no, no, it was Monday. A man in the wheelchair and a nurse came with the Spanish lady and her husband. No fighter."

He handed her the menu and poured her a tall glass of water.

After ordering Vittorio's recommendation of spaghetti with venison, Kris gazed at the view, trying to piece together the fragments of information she had gleaned.

What had she hoped to learn from Vittorio? That Hans or Otto had been at the restaurant on Sunday morning? Just because the Muellers didn't meet Otto here at the restaurant didn't mean that he and his entourage couldn't have spent time in the village before going to the hotel. Hans could have gone hiking and found Elsa. Kris knew her idea was preposterous: how would Hans even have known that Elsa was on the mountain? Although Kris was more and more convinced that it had been Hans at Elsa's house on Monday night, she couldn't come up with any motive or opportunity for his killing Elsa.

Kris finished her meal and raved to Vittorio about how delicious it had been, even though she had no recollection whatsoever of how anything had tasted—which could not be said of Dag, who carried his bone all the way back to the hotel.

Hans's Fiat was parked at the hotel entrance, where he stood, hand on the lid of his open trunk, engaged in conversation with a young Norwegian. She forced herself to keep a straight face when she heard him say irately, "I told you there wasn't a briefcase here."

"I was certain of it, sir, and that's what I told the lady. But my boss told me I should check since you were here at the hotel. I am sorry for having disturbed you." The car rental employee was obviously embarrassed.

Kris passed the two men, giving them a casual glance. At that moment Hans pushed down the lid of the trunk, the front of his sport jacket flared open, and she glimpsed a holster under his upraised arm. At the same time, Hans appeared to notice her. She looked away, acting as if Dag, leash taut, was pulling her ahead into the hotel.

Kris returned Dag to Oscar and went to her room. So Hans had a gun. No doubt about it, he was dangerous. Again she wondered if he could have been on the mountain Sunday. If so, how did he avoid being seen by Bill and Rachel, Grete, Odd and the Muellers? Had Odd, in fact, seen him? Was that why Odd was dead? Maybe the Muellers had seen Hans, too. Could Hans have threatened George? she wondered. Is that why George was injured and upset on Sunday? She found herself wondering again if there was something going on between Yolanda and Hans. Did George know? Yet George's gracious invitation to Hans to join them the night she and Tor arrived at the hotel was hardly the behavior of a jealous or frightened man. It would take a lot to intimidate George Mueller, of that she was certain. A gun, however, could be quite persuasive.

She took a short nap and then went in search of the Muellers. She spotted them on the terrace, having coffee with Max and Otto—or at least with Max; Otto's eyes were shut. She asked a waitress to deliver a pot of herbal tea and a plate of cakes to their table, then approached them, smiling her friendliest.

"You all look so comfortable out here. May I join you?"

"But, of course," George said, rising. She sat next to him, across from Yolanda and Otto who had just awakened.

"You're looking much better," George said to Kris.

"The sunshine helps," she responded pleasantly.

"I was sorry Tor could not join us fishing today," George said.

"He was disappointed, too," she said. Sitting close to George for the first time, she could study his face, the wide pores of his skin, the lines of age on his relatively youthful-looking face, the faded, jagged scar under his jaw. "How was the fishing?"

"Very good."

"*Wunderbar*," Otto said. "I caught a sea trout." From the childlike tone of his voice, it may have been one of his most exciting activities in decades. No doubt he had help, but Kris was not about to put any dents in his fish story. Surely he could not be the Nazi she imagined; but just an unfortunate, unattractive old man.

"I stayed here and wrote to the children," Yolanda said, holding up a thick bundle of postcards.

"Individually? That must have taken a lot of time," Kris said.

"Yes, but they're my children," Yolanda said proudly.

Kris wondered if she had been too critical of Yolanda.

"Would you like to see our photos?" George asked.

Yolanda handed him her purse from which he pulled out a book-sized leather pouch. And one by one, handed Kris the pictures.

"Here are our youngest," he said. He showed her a photo of himself with two toddlers sitting on his knees. "That's Jose and this is Fernando."

"They're adorable," Kris said, looking at the smiling children clinging to their adoptive father.

They went through group pictures and family-style photos of George and Yolanda with the children, everyone looking happy and well nourished. Holding a photo of all of the children standing on the steps of a villa framed by palm trees, George pointed to each child, giving his or her name and age.

"Some of the children have come to us from terrible conditions," Yolanda said. "We give them a good life. Some of the older children have grown up in the orphanage; it is the only home they remember."

"And here we have Maria, Rosa, and Consuela," George continued. In this photo three girls between the ages of five and ten played with dolls in a room filled with bright colors and pictures—a room, Kris thought, Laura in her younger years would have taken to immediately.

"They're lovely girls," Kris said. "And what a cute room. Is that a Barbie doll house in the corner?" she asked, bringing the photo closer to her eyes. "Very nice," she said. She returned the photos to George. "They have a pleasant scent." She'd noticed it when she had taken a closer look at the last photo. "Lavender?"

"Perhaps," George said. "My wife knows those things better than me." He handed the photos to Yolanda, who put the pack of photos to her nose.

"Yes, it is something like that, lavender or maybe lily."

It was definitely lavender. Kris felt her eyes grow tear up—the lavender had reminded her of Elsa. She silently thanked the waitress for arriving at that moment with a stack of small plates and a platter of cakes. The expressions of delight from those at the table—especially Max—and the focus now on the cakes closed the subject of the children at the orphanage.

"Oscar is taking us to Bergen on the *Fjordstar* on Saturday. Will you come with us?" George asked.

Max coughed loudly, covering his mouth and trying to catch his breath. His face flushed; Kris instinctively jumped up and patted him on the back.

"Thank you. I'm quite all right," he said, recovering. "I did not know the coffee was so hot."

"Max is also coming with us," George said.

"Yes, if I do not die first," he joked.

"I'd like to come," Kris said, returning to her seat, "but because of my uncle, I may have to return to Bergen early."

Before being distracted by Max's coughing, Kris had noticed Yolanda's frown when George invited her to join them on the boat. She probably should get back to Bergen early; in any case, she didn't savor spending several hours on the *Fjordstar* with Yolanda.

"Will you be staying long in Bergen, Max?" Kris asked.

"Only a few days and a few galleries."

"What about you, Otto?"

"I will return to Sweden with Hans and Helga."

"Ah, here comes the sheriff," George said. "Perhaps he has your ring, *querida*," he said to Yolanda.

Sheriff Bjornstad, dapper in his blue uniform and carrying an attache case, doffed his hat to the group. "Good afternoon, ladies and gentlemen. Mrs. Kelly, it is good to see you again. I have something for you, ladies."

He reached into his case and pulled out an envelope from which he extracted a ring. "Is this yours, Mrs. Mueller?"

Yolanda's eyes lit up. "Yes, it was my mother's," she said. She accepted the ring from Bjornstad and immediately slid it on her finger. Kris noticed that she had tears in her eyes.

George kissed Yolanda's cheek. "Now everything is all right, *querida*."

"You were lucky," Bjornstad told her. "And, Mrs. Kelly, I believe this is yours." From a second envelope, he handed Kris her necklace from Elsa as well as her watch and earrings.

Kris turned the medallion over in her hand, looking at the five linked Olympic rings.

"The necklace has sentimental value for you?" George asked sympathetically.

"Yes, Elsa gave it to me."

"May I see it?"

She was touched by his interest and gave it to him to look at.

George held it in his left palm. Kris noticed below his thumb a scratch about an inch long. This must be the cut—now healing—that Vittorio at the Roma had mentioned. George lifted his hand to look at the necklace more closely, revealing the blue-black hue of his thumbnail.

"What did you do to your thumb?" she asked, trying to sound as concerned as she was curious.

"I fell on it."

"Ooh, that must have hurt."

"Only for a few minutes."

"George was trying to be a mountain goat," Yolanda said.

All heads had turned toward George's hand, and he seemed embarrassed by the attention. He returned Kris's necklace.

Bjornstad presented documents to both women to sign, acknowledging receipt of their jewelry.

"Sheriff, will you join us for coffee and cake?" George asked.

Max moved toward Yolanda, making room for the sheriff to pull up a chair. Bjornstad helped himself to a large slice of cream cake.

"I'm curious," Kris said to Yolanda. "I remember admiring your ring over the weekend. You always seemed to be wearing it. How did Odd steal it?"

"I can only think of one possibility," she said. "I left it in our bedroom in the afternoon when I took a shower. He must have come into the room then."

Either Yolanda was sincere or she really was an amazing actress, Kris thought. She decided to press.

"That's upsetting, isn't it? I thought our locks were secure."

"I expect they are," George said, looking somber. "I regret that I may have been at fault. I went downstairs while Yolanda was in the shower. I knew I would be right back; I may not have shut the door properly."

If that were the case, Kris thought, indeed Odd—or Hans—could have slipped into the room and taken the ring.

"But now you both have your jewelry again," Bjornstad said. "And the Bergen police have returned your cousin's jewelry to your uncle, Mrs. Kelly."

"Your cousin's jewelry? When did he take that?" George asked.

"When he broke into her house Monday night," Kris said. "Sheriff Bjornstad, you and your assistant spoke with Odd on Sunday when we were taking Elsa to the ambulance. Did you have any suspicions about him?"

"Did I suspect him of murder? *Nei*, not at all," he said, shaking his head. "But then we don't have much experience with homicide here. I know that isn't an excuse. All I can do is apologize to you that we literally let him get away with murder." He took a swallow of coffee and continued. "He was a dangerous man. You were lucky to get out of the house."

"You were in the house?" Yolanda asked.

"Yes, but I ran away the minute I heard noises." Kris shivered remembering her fright.

"Did you see him?" George asked.

"No, not really."

"It is all very tragic," George said, "but in the end, justice was done."

"Yes, the case is closed," Bjornstad said, pushing his hands on his thighs and stretching his back. "Oscar Larsen tells me you are all leaving on Saturday."

There were several nods.

"Then, I wish you a safe trip. I regret that your vacations were marred by such a terrible event." Bjornstad stood, said a few more parting words, shook hands with everybody and left.

With the sheriff's departure, Kris excused herself in order to get a good rest before dinner with Tor. On her way to the stairs, she saw Hans hustling Inga at the reception desk; at least his distraction would allow her to sneak past him to the stairs, she thought. But she was wrong.

"Oh, Mrs. Kelly," Inga called.

Kris had no choice but to walk up to the desk.

"Mr. Olsen telephoned to say he has been delayed; he cannot return until ten o'clock."

"Did he say why?" Kris asked, disappointed.

"Probably with another woman." Hans sneered. "Too bad."

"Why don't you just take a hike," she said. "Like to the terrace—Otto's probably looking for you."

He looked at his watch and slunk away.

"I can't stand that man!" Inga said.

"That makes two of us," Kris sympathized.

"I think he is a fox."

The other desk clerk, a girl about seventeen with a peaches-and-cream complexion, giggled. "You mean a wolf."

"Oh, yes, a wolf," Inga corrected herself.

"It must be difficult for you," Kris said. "I suppose Oscar wants you to be gracious to all the guests."

"Yes, I must behave politely to him. But I refuse to make up his room."

"Why?" Kris welcomed this opportunity to get more information about Hans.

"On Monday morning he asked for his room to be made up early. When I went there, he told me to get in the bed with him. He's disgusting. I told him to go soak his head."

"What did he say?"

"He got angry. I left fast. I told Martha, the head housekeeper, about him, but I didn't dare tell Hasan."

"Hasan? Why would you tell him?"

"Because we've been together almost since he started working here in March."

"I never would have guessed."

"We try to be discreet."

Kris noted they had definitely succeeded. "So what did Martha say?" she asked.

"She said she would make up his room. She's an older lady." Inga nudged her colleague. They both laughed. "She's not his type, she doesn't take any bad behavior."

"But she teased Inga the next day," the teenager said.

"Yes," Inga said. "She told me that I must have broken his heart because he didn't sleep in his bed on Monday night."

"Really?" Kris said, not believing her good luck. "Do you think that's what happened?"

"No, I think he went to a bar and found someone friendlier than me. He only came back at nine on Tuesday morning."

"I didn't realize the village had such a nightlife."

"It doesn't. He probably went to one of the larger towns, maybe up the valley."

"Tell her about the…you know," the girl urged.

"What? Oh." Inga lowered her voice and leaned toward Kris, "We think he's a cross-dresser."

"No!" Kris said in genuine disbelief. She could think of many names to call Hans, but that was not one of them. "Why do you think that?"

"Martha told us she found a woman's blonde wig in his closet."

"Very strange," Kris said, shaking her head. "I guess anything's possible. By the way, when did he check into the hotel? I thought I saw him on Saturday," she pretended.

Inga frowned. "No, no. He arrived Sunday with Mr. Kohler and the nurse." She tapped the keys of the computer and confirmed the information.

"Well, I should be going," Kris said. "Thanks for telling me about 'our friend.'"

The three women exchanged knowing looks.

CHAPTER 24

▼

A blonde wig. Kris sat on her balcony pondering the news that Hans had one in his closet. She tried to picture the blonde woman driving the red Fiat that almost hit her as she walked in the rain on Monday after leaving Nils's office. Could it have been Hans? But why? It made no sense. If it had been Hans at Elsa's, not Odd, then that meant he probably planted Elsa's things at Odd's. If Odd had already had Elsa's notebook at his house, there would have been no need to add the jewelry and software. No, Hans must have planted everything. Had he killed Odd and then set the fire?

All she could do was to file everything in her mental collection of clues and move on to her next step. But what was her next step, now that Tor wasn't coming back for dinner? On the one hand she was disappointed; on the other, it gave her more time to find things out on her own. She was still bothered by not knowing where Elsa had been prior to going to the ledge. It was only four-thirty. With the long summer daylight, she realized she could easily return to the mountain where she and Tor had gone yesterday and look again for places where Elsa might have gone. Only she wasn't eager to hike all the way back to the Roma again.

Kris phoned Oscar at the front desk and asked if it would be possible to borrow a hotel car and get a couple of sandwiches for a picnic.

After confirming that she had a valid driver's license, Oscar agreed immediately to both requests. "Just stop by the desk on your way out, and everything will be ready."

Kris felt charged by the idea she had come up with, but what about Nils? They had agreed to talk at eight. If she wasn't in, he'd be worried. Fortunately, she was able to reach him at his office. She explained that her plans had changed, and she would be out at eight. When she asked if he'd been able to get any information, the answer was affirmative.

"Odd didn't have a car; he owned a motorcycle," Nils reported.

Kris was sure now that her hunch about Hans was correct.

"What about Otto Kohler? Did you find out anything about him?" she asked.

"I have his address in Sweden. That's all. My sources at Interpol are still checking. Maybe I'll hear tonight, but it may be tomorrow morning. Now tell me why you wanted to know about Odd's car."

"Because I'm sure now that Odd wasn't at Elsa's."

"Then who was?"

She told him of her suspicions about Hans and what she had learned from Inga. And about seeing the holster under Hans's arm.

"Have you told Sheriff Bjornstad?"

"No. Besides it would just be my word against Hans's right now."

"Tell the sheriff."

"Okay." She wasn't about to tell Nils that she'd just been with the sheriff and not said a word. She hoped she could catch up with Bjornstad at the police station.

"Kris, do you think this Hans knows you suspect him?"

"No. How could he?"

"Is Tor with you?"

"No, but he'll be back soon." Soon was, she told herself, a relative term.

"Do not take chances, Kris. Don't be like Elsa." She heard the concern in Nils's voice.

"Don't worry. I'll be careful," she promised.

Goosebumps rose across the back of her neck. The best thing she could do would be to tell Bjornstad what she'd found out, and let him prove that Hans had been in Bergen on Monday. She was a mother, not a detective. When she called the police station, however, he wasn't in his office. The officer on the other end of the phone offered to take a message.

"No, thank you. It's a personal call," she said. She wanted to talk with the sheriff directly; she would have to wait to do so.

Her thoughts swept across the ocean. It would be late morning in upstate New York—a good time to try to reach Laura at camp. She lucked out. Laura was back from her outing and working in the camp office.

"Hi, Mom!"

She hadn't realized that one voice could do so much for her spirits. They talked for five minutes, Laura telling of her sadness about Elsa, wanting to be sure her mother was all right; Kris assuring her she was okay, then turning the conversation to what Laura was doing at camp. Before they ended the call, Laura told Kris she and Charlie were taking time off to meet her at the airport when she returned to Washington on Monday.

After the call, Kris felt an urgency to return to the States, to embrace her children, to step out of this nightmare she found herself in. But she had a few more days here, and she still needed to find some answers.

She found Oscar in his office behind the reception area, busily making notes in the large reservation book on his desk. "Am I interrupting?" she asked.

"No, no. Come in. I'll be right with you," he said, nodding toward the chair across from him. Kris scanned the paneled walls and the photos that appeared to date back to the turn of the century. In the corner, on mute, the television flashed the familiar faces of CNN reporters.

Oscar finally looked up. "How are you?"

"Better, thank you. And fascinated by those photos. Are those family pictures?"

"Yes," he said. He pointed to the different images. "These are my grandparents in about 1905, and these are my parents in 1935." He spoke with a melancholy that made Kris wish she hadn't asked.

"This is the hotel in 1890." His tone became more upbeat.

"That little house is this hotel?" Kris asked.

"Yes, the first one. But they built on as more and more travelers came this way. Here it is in 1914. This one you recognize, yes?"

She nodded.

"And this elegant man and lady are the founders."

"Are you related to them?"

"Oh, no, no. But I am the first proprietor not to be. I bought the hotel in 1970."

"You enjoy your work, don't you?"

He nodded.

"I've been impressed by how well you treat your guests, how you want to make sure they are satisfied. You did a wonderful job matching Elsa and me with our tablemates in the dining room. Max and the Muellers were very congenial company."

"But I can't take the credit for that," Oscar admitted. "Shortly after I showed you to your room, Miss Jenssen came and asked me if you and she could be seated with the Muellers."

So, that was it. Kris had suspected at the time that Elsa hadn't really gone downstairs to ask Oscar about the weather; now she knew the real reason.

"Did she tell you why she wanted to sit with them?"

"She said she was curious to know more about them. And that didn't surprise me—she was a journalist after all."

Kris smiled. "Well, it doesn't surprise me either," she said.

"Excuse me," Inga said, peering around the corner. "Mr. Larsen, can you come out here for a few minutes?"

Oscar handed Kris a generously sized plastic lunch bag. "Please make sure this is all right. I'll take you to my car in just a moment. Excuse me."

Kris peeked in the bag. Whoever had made up her picnic included cheese sandwiches, cucumber and onion salad, an apple, a banana, and plenty of lefse—thin potato pancakes sandwiched together with sugar and butter—a perfect dessert. There was also a bottle of water and a small carton of orange juice. In addition to paper napkins there was a small dishtowel, perhaps to use as a tablecloth. She stuffed the bag into her backpack along with her fleece jacket.

She could hear Oscar mediating a dispute between some guests and a tour bus driver. More out of curiosity than any wish to be nosey, Kris turned the huge reservation book around so that the open pages—each with a September date—faced her. Each page had a diagram of the three floors of the hotel; only the upper two had guest rooms.

She leafed back through the pages, finding the section for August and the current date. What a great invention, she thought. It showed where everyone was staying. On the third floor diagram, she checked to make sure Olsen and Kelly were properly entered. Yes, there she was, date of reservation same day as first day of stay. Kelly was written over another name that had been only partially erased. She tilted the page toward the light. Olsen? Oscar must have originally planned to give Tor her room. Tuesday's reservation date had been written slightly to the right of one that had been erased, hurriedly probably and not thoroughly. It had been a March date, so it wasn't Tor's reservation— the name Olsen in Norway was about as common as that of Smith in the States. The Olsen for whom this room had been reserved must have canceled or been moved to another room.

She checked the other days of her stay, finding the same sort of erasures and rewrites; no other Olsens besides Tor staying on the third floor. No Olsens on the second floor either. No erasures for today's date.

The Muellers and Otto, Max, too, had suites on the second floor. Otto's was close to the elevator for obvious reasons. The Muellers' and Otto's reservations had been made the first week of March; there was an erasure where the Muellers had moved their reservations up by a day; Maximilian Guttmann's reservation was made the second week of March, as was that of the Stephens. On the same floor she found only one other reservation made in March. People plan summer vacations in

March, she told herself. Did it matter that the people she had met here had all planned their trip the same month?

She heard Oscar's conversation winding up.

Quickly, she flipped back to last Saturday and found the Jenssen/Kelly reservation made on Friday. Then she found Odd's reservation made the same day as well—another indication that he had been stalking Elsa.

Kris turned the book back around the way Oscar had left it, open to September. When he re-entered his office, her hands were back on the bag of food.

"I am sorry. Sometimes it takes longer than one expects to satisfy guests. That business took longer than I expected."

"No problem. The lunch looks wonderful," she said. "A smorgasbord in a bag."

Oscar looked pleased. "Come, let me take you to the car."

A few minutes later, she was driving out of the hotel grounds in Oscar's blue Saab, feeling a sense of liberation. After a week of walking, traveling by public transportation, or in cars driven by others, she was happy to be driving herself. She knew that she had just made an important discovery in Oscar's book, but what it meant she wasn't sure. She hoped more fresh mountain air would clear her brain. Once at the Roma, she checked with Vittorio to make sure he didn't mind her parking the car there and promised to stop in after her hike.

CHAPTER 25

▼

Walking on the mountain at this hour had its advantages. For one thing, Kris noted, no morning dew on the high grass. For another, the late afternoon sunshine and shadows filled the woods with a certain peacefulness and her with an inner calm. She walked cautiously under the fir that still leaned tenuously over the trail.

At the split of the blue and red trails, Kris assessed what she knew. She and Tor had followed the marked trails yesterday, assuming Elsa had as well. But if Elsa had, then why hadn't anyone seen her? Where had she gone? Kris tried to imagine herself in Elsa's shoes on Sunday, leaving George, Yolanda, and Grete.

"Okay, guys, see you," Kris said to her imaginary companions and marched off down the blue trail.

She welcomed the silence, punctuated only by the distant hum of water. For the first time in many years she was hiking alone, without Jim, without the children, without anyone else, and she felt totally in her element. Although she thought she was concentrating yesterday, being with Tor may have been distracting—even before they kissed in the meadow.

This time she watched closely for animal paths intersecting with the main trail. She noticed one off to the left, but rejected it, convinced Elsa would not have headed in a direction away from the falls if her goal was to go to them. Other paths dead-ended in the bushes. Somewhere behind her she heard a twig snap, signaling the movement of an animal, two-legged or four-legged. Probably other hikers.

Aha! she thought. To the right, another track appeared to end in a thick overgrowth. Would Elsa's eyes have been sharp enough to detect the deer path on the other side? Kris found her way to it and soon was scrambling up an incline through boulders and thick trees. She could no longer see the trail she had left, which could mean that if Elsa were here on Sunday, she would have been hidden from view. Kris guessed that the deer who made this route would have been in pursuit of the water above the falls and the plant life it offered. Sooner or later, the path would intersect with the red trail above or possibly the yellow trail between the meadow and the ledge.

She kept her eyes to the ground, looking for some sign—she didn't know what—that Elsa may have taken this path. It would be difficult, she knew, to find any footprints on the mossy rocks and dry topsoil. She heard youthful voices, male and female, and stopped, trying to determine the direction from which they were coming. They were below her, she decided, on the yellow trail. She strained to see through the vegetation and caught sight of a young couple disappearing down the trail toward the meadow. If Elsa had come this way, she might have watched, heard the others; maybe she had sat out of sight somewhere, waiting. But waiting for what? or whom? Looking around, Kris saw the "somewhere" or at least where *she* was going to sit and have some of her dinner—a recess in a boulder, sheltered by spruce trees. It looked like an armchair sculpted by nature. She settled into it and ate her sandwich and banana, listening to the sounds of the forest and the falls, and wondering if Elsa, too, had sat there. Kris topped off her meal with the orange juice. From here she'd go to the ledge, or at least the entrance to the ledge, she decided.

She stepped back on to the path, looking at the ground as she walked. She probably would have missed the small piece of foil had it not been for a spot of sunlight hitting it at just the right angle. She picked it up. The foil was backed by light blue paper on which were the letters "mint" in black; the bottom part of the "t" was torn off. Kris's spirits soared: the colors were those of Elsa's brand of mints. It didn't matter to her that anyone could have dropped this piece of candy wrapper on the trail because she was convinced that Elsa had done so inadvertently.

Kris stuck the wrapper in her jeans pocket, almost jubilant that she had solved the mystery of where Elsa had been. But what happened once Elsa had arrived at the ledge? According to Bjornstad's theory, Elsa had intended to take a photo. Kris made her way down to the yellow trail and walked toward the ledge, which was still blocked off with plastic tape. She stopped and looked toward the top of the falls and thought she glimpsed a head above the bushes. Was it another hiker or just her imagination? Whatever the explanation, she suddenly felt particularly alone and vulnerable.

She felt the ground vibrate before she distinguished the rumbling sound from the roar of the falls. Instinct told her to run, curiosity forced her to look up; she did both. A boulder the size of a tire barreled over the rocks above her and crashed across the spot where she had stood moments before. Loose soil and gravel spraying in its wake, it spun over the cliff and into the gorge. Kris knew that huge rocks didn't just roll down mountains without heavy rains or snows to dislodge them. Someone had pushed it. She ran in the direction of the meadow.

"Ouch!" She felt a twinge of pain as a stone grazed the side of her head. Someone was targeting her. But who? She heard stones hitting the ground behind her.

"Stop it!" she shouted.

A rock the size of a tennis ball bounced off the tree in front of her. This was no joke. She pulled her backpack up over her head and neck. If a stone were to hit her backside, she'd survive; a direct hit to her head would be a different matter altogether.

Kris reached the meadow, huffing and puffing. It had to be Hans who was trying to kill her, or hurt her, or give her the scare of her life. But why? He had no way to know of her suspicions about him. Her eyes focused on the path behind her, she forced herself to take a few measured, deep breaths. She could not afford to get winded. Her heart was already pounding in her ears.

If only Inga hadn't given her Tor's message in front of Hans. He must have seen his window of opportunity and taken it. This was insane, Kris told herself. She had kids, she had a life in the United States. What in the heck was she doing here warding off some psycho?

The only comfort, she concluded, was that Hans must want whatever happened to her to look like an accident; otherwise, he could have just shot her with his gun.

She glanced at her watch. Seven o'clock. She had to keep moving; the nearest help was the Roma. With no sign of her pursuer, she ran up the blue trail. She had to stick to it. If she went off, no one would see her if she was in trouble. She guessed Hans was somewhere on the red trail. Would he be waiting for her where the trails intersected?

She heard the chatter of children, then saw two little boys with white-blond hair with a man and a woman, probably their parents, approaching her. With other hikers around, she'd be safe.

She could hear them speaking Norwegian. "Hi," she said.

"Hei," they said, passing her single file.

"Can you help me?" she said almost in a whisper.

The concerned couple halted. "What can we do? Are you hurt?"

She heard a distant rustling in the bushes. Was it Hans? She had wanted to ask the couple if they would go with her to the Roma Restaurant. But now she knew it wouldn't make her any safer. As long as she died in what appeared to be an accident, would it matter to Hans if a few other people, even children, succumbed as well? She no longer wanted help from this family; instead she wanted them on their way as fast as they could go.

"Oh, no, no," she said, faking a laugh. "I just wanted to make sure this trail will take me to the restaurant."

"Yes. Just turn right at the red markings," the man said. "Follow the noise of the Scouts down by the Roma. They're on their way to the meadow for camping tonight."

"Thanks." She waved and continued toward the Roma.

The junction of the blue and red trails lay just ahead. Where was Hans? Could she react quickly enough to whatever he had up his sleeve? How far would she have to get on the red trail before she could scream for help and be heard by the Scouts and their leaders? While she feared Hans might risk hurting a family of four, a whole troop of Scouts, she was sure, would be an entirely different matter. She picked up a big stick from brush at the side of the trail and pretended to use it to aid in her walking. She held the sharp point against the ground so if Hans approached, he wouldn't see it.

She reached the intersection without meeting Hans or being hit by any more flying objects. Now she could see and hear the Scouts in the distance, making their way up the trail toward the precipitous fir tree. If she walked at a steady pace, she would probably reach the tree about the time they did; if she ran, she might make it a few minutes before. If she could get to that point, she would be safe.

Or would she? Kris heard the sound of chopping from the area of the leaning fir. Her hopes plummeted. Hans. If he were to cut the two young birch trees, weaken them, the fir could crash to the ground and hit whoever was in the way—even if it was a bunch of kids. He could probably see her from here, just as she could see the trees. She started down the trail, yet she knew she couldn't keep going, couldn't risk endangering the boys. At the same time, she needed an escape route.

In her favor were the rocks, brush, and line of birch that would obstruct Hans's view of her until the last thirty feet or so before the fir. As soon as she reached that area, she fell to the ground and crawled on her hands and knees—the rough ground hurting her hands, her jeans barely cushioning her knees—back up the red trail to a point just past the junction, where staying to the far right would keep her out of Hans's view. She guessed she had another five minutes before he would notice she wasn't on schedule, another few until he would figure she hadn't stopped to tie her shoelace or do something else. And then it would take him a few minutes to get back to the trail, especially, if by that time, the Scouts occupied most of it. He still wouldn't know if she was somewhere on that part of the trail until he could see all of it.

She had already devised the second part of her plan. Making sure she was at a safe distance away but still within range, she lobbed a rock at the bees' nest she and Tor had noticed the day before. Bingo! It fell onto the ground near where the two trails merged, the angry, confused bees swarming out of it. She hoped that the angry bees would provide a distraction, if not a deterrent to Hans. The Scouts, and certainly their leaders, would know how to deal with bees. She ran toward the falls, brushing against some honeysuckle as she tried to keep to the side of the red trail.

Suddenly Kris felt a sharp pain as a bee dug its stinger into her upper right arm. She batted it away and spun around half expecting all the bees to be diving at her like the birds in the Hitchcock movie. But this was the only one. Maybe it had been in the flowers.

Stopping now and then to listen to the sounds around her and scratch her itchy arm, Kris sprinted toward the falls. So far, she only heard evening birds, no footsteps or branches breaking. Heart pounding, she was too mad to be scared, and too determined to get away from Hans to let her fears get the better of her.

By the time she reached the apex of the red trail, the roar of the falls drowned out all other sounds. She still believed she held the advantage if she could just find an escape route; she had to rely on instinct and her memory of the map Tor showed her, Bill, and Rachel yesterday. After a few false starts, she found a trail along the river above the falls. Following the curves of the rushing water, within about ten minutes she was out of sight of anyone who might stand above the falls looking for her.

Tor had said it should be about four miles from here to the mountain hut. Unless she could get across the water, she'd be stuck on this side to fend for herself if indeed Hans figured out where she'd gone. The promise of a roof over her head when night fell urged her upward. The itchy ache in her arm forced her to stop.

Thank God for all of Norway's rocks, she thought. She found one to sit on next to the river, out of sight from the trail. She splashed icy water on to the bee sting, which not only hurt but had enlarged to the size of a quarter. She had forgotten about the stinger; it was supposed to come out, but she couldn't see it. She drank the rest of her water and filled the bottle with the glacial runoff. She held the bottle for a few moments on her arm, but knew she couldn't afford any more time for first-aid.

She returned to the trail. Above her she could see where rocks divided the river into smaller streams, and where she could probably cross to the other side. She glanced over her shoulder, in the direction of the falls, and gasped. Footprints. Her own. All the way back as far as she could see. The other trails she'd been on were so rocky or mossy only an expert would be able to decipher footprints, but here the soil was damp and the prints fresh.

She hoped Hans was racing in the opposite direction, down the switchbacks toward the youth hostel. But she could not count on it.

A signpost with an arrow bearing the word *hytte* and a picture of a hut pointed across the streams to where another trail began. Kris turned the sign so it pointed to her side of the river, and continued making footprints until she found a place where they would disappear in gravel. Then jumping from rock to rock, she crossed the streams to the hut trail. She slipped behind a cluster of birch trees and looked back the way she had come, relieved not to see anyone coming up the trail behind her.

Kris climbed toward the treeline, keeping to the side of the trail that hugged the steep slope. She wiped her brow with the front of her T-shirt. The heavy feeling in her thigh muscles weighed on her resolve to keep going. Her right arm felt as if a hundred bees were poking their stingers into her skin. "The hut," she said aloud, "I've got to focus on getting to the hut."

After two hours of hard climbing the trail leveled out. Kris remembered reading about hikes "across the roof of Norway"—an apt description for where she was now. This part of the roof even had a few patches of snow. The view from up here was not unlike that from the helicopter she took on Sunday. Only then it had been afternoon; now evening shadows were settling across the fjords and moving up the mountains as the sun sunk lower in the west. She could see tiny people, a campfire, and squares in the meadow far below—no doubt the Scouts and their tents. But in the vast landscape between her and the boys, it was impossible to detect individual hikers who could be any-where among the rocks and trees.

It was already ten. She wondered if Tor had come back. She should have left him a note. At least Oscar knew she had gone on a picnic. Would they wonder why she wasn't back yet? Or think that she had stopped off in the village? In any case, they probably wouldn't think to look for her here.

She hoped Hans wouldn't either. The last time she'd run from him—at Elsa's—he hadn't pursued her. Could she hope for that this time? Was he playing a mind game with her? Make her run, then not follow. If that was the case, then she was safe.

Safe from Hans, perhaps, but not from the bee sting. Her arm was swollen from her shoulder to her elbow. She rummaged in her back-pack for something that might help; the smell of onions from her uneaten salad nauseated her. How could she have been so stupid as to not bring something against insect bites? The water bottle was tepid now. If only she had an ice pack. The moment the thought crossed her mind, she also thought about the snow. A few minutes later, using Oscar's dishtowel, she held a snowball against her aching arm.

According to her calculations, she had another mile or two to the hut. Her uphill pace had been slower than it would be on more even ground. Her arm sufficiently numbed, she set out again. The thought of the awaiting hut energized her.

Another fifteen minutes passed. The sky turned shades of pink and purple, a sign that the sun was sinking behind the horizon; evening had fallen on the landscape below. Kris put on her fleece to ward off the autumn-like chill, but her cheeks were burning, and her forehead and palms sweaty again. Her head ached. Her arm felt as if a rock had been grafted to it. She knew she must be having an allergic reaction to the bee sting, but she'd never been allergic before. Was she in danger of anaphylactic shock? Of losing consciousness? Didn't those things happen immediately, not three or four hours later?

Dusk clung to the mountain top. Kris kept her eyes on the trail anxious not to lose her way. Now and then sounds of small animals rustling in the bushes or the ghostly cries of an owl broke the silence. From time to time she paused for several minutes, trusting that if Hans were following her, he might trigger alarm among the wildlife. She had gotten away from him, at least for now.

She smelled the wood fire before she saw the hut and the light glowing from the window. Her longing to be inside competed with her rising fear. Had Hans gone the other way to the cabin? If so, why would he light a fire and give away his presence? Wouldn't it be more logical for him to hide, to make the hut appear dark and deserted, more approachable? Or did he want her to think friendly hikers were waiting inside?

She didn't have the strength to play this guessing game, nor could she keep going or spend the night outside. All she knew was she wanted to live, wanted to see her children again. She would have to use her wits and whatever weapons available to her to fend Hans off if indeed he was in the cabin. She staggered forward, fighting a round of dizziness, wishing she had kept the walking stick to help her keep her balance. Stepping as quietly as possible, she sneaked up to the edge of a window and peered inside. She saw the man's back just before she blacked out.

CHAPTER 26

▼

Kris woke to unfamiliar surroundings in a darkened room, where she lay on a bare but firm mattress with a wool blanket over her. She thought she smelled onions. Although she was in her stockingfeet, she had no memory of going to bed, of taking off her hiking boots, or even of arriving at this place. Then she remembered her hike up the mountain and peering in the window of the cabin. And then? She couldn't remember what had happened next.

She heard people arguing. Familiar voices. She looked across the small room and recognized Tor and Max. They seemed to be wrestling with each other. Candlelight exaggerated the shadows of the tall Norwegian and the gargantuan German.

"Not now," Max boomed. Hasan was there too, his back to her. Shorter and more compact than both Tor and Max, he tried to separate them. "Shake it," he shouted. "Quiet!"

Shake what? Kris wondered.

"All right, you guys, let's focus on helping Kris." This time she recognized Bill Stephens's voice. She closed her eyes. A moment later she felt his hand on her forehead.

When she woke again, the cozy smell of a wood fire brought back childhood memories of a cabin in Mt. Rainier National Park where she and her parents had taken Elsa for a weekend on her first visit to the United States.

She looked around. The candles were out, dawn in. Bill sat at the table. Max and Hasan were asleep in two of the other three beds. She couldn't see Tor; the person in the third bed was not him. She touched her right arm with her left hand. The swelling had gone down.

"It's coming," Tor called, bursting through the door, bringing the cool morning air with him, and speaking to Bill.

"I think Kris just woke up," Bill replied.

"Good morning," Tor said to her, flashing his bearded grin.

"Hi," she said weakly, feeling her mouth broaden into a smile.

He kissed her cheek, then sat on her bed and stroked her forehead. "How do you feel?"

"I'm not sure. What's going on?" she asked.

"It's a long story, but probably not as long as yours. Right now we're going to take a helicopter ride," he said. He put her hiking boots back on her feet while Bill checked her blood pressure and pulse. They both helped her get into a down jacket three times her size.

"Let's go," Tor said. He picked her up and carried her out of the cabin.

Bill called after them, "See you guys back at the hotel."

*   *   *   *

Settled in a comfortable armchair in the living room of her hotel suite, Kris felt lucky to be back safe and sound. A few more hours of sleep and a sumptuous breakfast delivered by Oscar had restored her energy, even if a long soak in a hot bath had only slightly eased the soreness in her legs.

She picked up the phone, called Tor, and told him she was ready to talk. A moment later she heard the key in the door; she'd given it to him after they got back from the mountain.

"Hei," he said.

She waved, overcome with the joy she felt in seeing him again. He looked deliciously trim in jeans and polo shirt, she thought, as he approached her, bent over, and kissed her on the lips. She welcomed his kiss, the smell of his aftershave, his hand momentarily on her shoulder.

"You gave us a real scare," he said, his eyes fixed on hers.

"I had quite a scare myself," she replied.

He arranged the other armchair at a right angle to hers, sat down, and folded her hand in his.

"How did you find me?" she asked.

"The owner of the Roma called Oscar a few minutes before I got back. He said he was closing and your car was still outside. He was worried. Bill and I took Dag and drove to the Roma. We hiked to the meadow; I thought if you got stuck on the mountain for some reason, you might go to our rock."

"You mean Rachel and Bill's rock."

He smiled.

"The sheriff and his rescue people were combing the area. Several of us wound up in the meadow where we found a bunch of Scouts camping out. They said they had been there for hours, but hadn't seen you. Frankly, I was scared shitless."

She squeezed his hand. "Why?"

"Because I didn't want anything to happen to you," he answered.

Kris couldn't tell if he continued his story because he thought his answer to her question simply common sense or because he wanted to avoid her pressing the point.

"I remembered our discussion the day before about the hut, although I couldn't figure out why you would go there. Bjornstad was skeptical when I told him my idea, but he agreed someone should check, and I think he was probably glad to have me out of his hair. He gave Bill and me a police radio and told us to keep in touch, then he sent his folks to the falls, around the youth hostel, and in between. Bill and I took the red trail, Dag leading the way. When he took off on the trail above the waterfall, I was sure we were on the right track. I called Bjornstad and told him where we were going. He got in touch with

Bill and Max, and they volunteered to come up the other side and meet us at the hut."

Kris was grateful for the efforts to find her. "Was Hans at the hut?" she asked.

"Not when we got there." Tor looked agitated. "Is that what you thought? When we found you, you were delirious; you kept mumbling, 'Hans. Got to get away from Hans.' Before I went to Stavanger, you told me you were going 'to avoid him like the plague.'"

She hadn't seen him look so serious since the day Elsa had died. He leaned forward in his chair, his eyes locked on hers. "So what happened?"

"I think he tried to kill me." Kris told Tor about the crashing boulder, the rocks thrown at her.

Tor's eyes filled with anger, and he let out a Norwegian expletive.

The phone rang, and Kris answered it.

"It's Nils," she said to Tor, who had begun pacing the floor.

"Kris, Oscar told me about the bee sting," Nils said. "How are you feeling?"

"Much better, thanks."

"I've got your information."

"Great. Just a minute." She motioned to Tor to pick up the phone in the bedroom and told Nils he would be coming on the line.

The two men exchanged brief greetings, then Nils began his report.

"Otto Kohler is the adopted name of Ernst Brunner. He was a minor Nazi war criminal who was tried at Nuremberg and served eight years in a German prison."

"I can't believe it!" Kris said. She tried to absorb what Nils had just said. In spite of the questions she had raised about Otto, she had not expected this.

Nils continued. "There's more—two things that would have been of interest to Elsa. Kohler is a man of some means. It's believed that he finances much of the neo-Nazi movement in Sweden. But the biggest news is this: Otto is the brother of Klaus Brunner, the man we used to call 'The Elephant.'"

"No!" Kris couldn't believe that she had heard him right. "Nils, do you realize what you're saying?"

"Yes, I do."

"It's crazy. Do you think Elsa could have known that Otto was arriving on Sunday?"

"I don't know."

"I'll bet she did. You said she was working on a story about neo-Nazis," Kris said.

"Yes, but she never mentioned Otto Kohler to me."

"But that doesn't mean she didn't know about him."

"That's true, especially given the thoroughness with which she did her research," Nils said. "But, you said he wasn't at the hotel when you and Elsa were."

"That's right."

"So if she had known he was arriving, she must have planned to meet him, or at least observe him, after her hike. And we know she never got the opportunity."

"As far as we know," Kris said. "Or maybe he knew she would be here, and he didn't want to meet her. Maybe Odd had contact with him. Maybe he let Otto know that Elsa was at the fjord, and then Otto ordered Odd to kill her." Kris shuddered as she made the suggestion that a withered body like Otto's did not preclude a mind still capable of ordering evil deeds. "And then maybe to close the loop, Otto told Hans to kill Odd."

"Wait a minute," Tor said. "Didn't you forget about motive?"

"Well, isn't it obvious? They were afraid Elsa was going to expose Otto's real identity."

"But I thought you hadn't met Otto before Tuesday night," Tor said.

"That's true," Kris answered. "I hadn't met him. But he could have been in the village on Sunday. Besides, Otto didn't have to be there himself at all if he wanted to get rid of Elsa. He could have just ordered Hans or Odd to do it."

Nils spoke again. "I also found out that Hans Schmidt is listed as employed by Otto Kohler as a security guard. He has a checkered background: worked in security for a high-tech company, served a short stint as a mercenary in Africa; some years are unaccounted for. He's also linked to the neo-Nazi movement. It's not surprising that he has a gun."

"Gun?" Tor said. "Who says he has a gun?"

"Kris saw it yesterday," Nils explained.

"She obviously hasn't finished telling me everything," Tor said.

"Then I'll say goodbye. But you two be careful," Nils said. "And, Tor, don't let Kris out of your sight."

"Don't worry, I won't."

They said goodbye to Nils with an agreement that they would talk again later.

Tor returned to the living room, a deep frown on his face. "What the hell? In a matter of hours, you discover Hans has a gun, you get boulders rolled at you. This is serious stuff, Kris. Is there anything else you haven't told me?"

"Of course," she said. She was still trying to digest Nils's news that Otto Kohler was Klaus Brunner's brother.

Answering a knock on the door sidetracked Tor from whatever he was about to say next, and he ushered Bill, medical bag in hand, into the suite.

"Hi! How's the patient?" he asked.

"Much better, thanks to you, I understand." Kris smiled at him.

"Glad to help."

"By the way, you guys, who was it that I saw through the cabin window?"

"That was Boris," Bill said.

"Who?"

"A Russian hiker. In fact, he may really be the one you should thank."

"How's that?" she asked.

"I'll tell you. When Viking man, Dag, and I reached you at the hut, Boris had just rubbed onion on your bee sting."

Kris laughed at Bill's description. "Why onion?"

"He said it's an old Russian remedy."

"If only I had known," Kris said, thinking about the onion and cucumber salad that had been in her lunch bag all along. "But I don't understand what happened. I've never been allergic to stings before?"

"Maybe it wasn't an allergy," Bill said. "Since you didn't get the stinger out, if you scratched your skin a lot, the sting could have gotten infected."

"How did this Boris find me?"

"He said he heard something outside the window and went outside to look."

"Well, God bless Boris," she said.

"And Viking man, too," Bill said. "He fussed over you a lot."

Tor shook his head. "Don't believe everything he tells you."

"Kris, I'd like to check your vitals one more time before declaring you recovered from your adventure. Is that okay?" Bill asked.

"Sure."

Bill took her temperature, blood pressure, pulse once more, and examined her head and neck. "It looks like that scratch above your left ear is healing. I put alcohol on it at the cabin."

"Scratch?" Kris located the sore spot. "That must be where the rock hit me."

"Well, you're in good shape for what you went through," Bill said, apparently assuming a stray rock was just one of the many hazards of being on the mountain at night. "But take it easy today. What are your plans?"

"No walks," she said. "I feel muscles in my legs that I didn't know I had."

"Why don't we spend some time on the *Fjordstar*?" Tor suggested.

"Is Oscar taking it out today?" Kris asked.

"I'll check."

Tor used the bedroom phone while Kris and Bill visited. He returned a few minutes later. "It's all set."

"So when is he going?" Kris asked.

"Not he, we. Just the two of us."

"Are you sure?" she asked, amazed.

"Don't worry, I have my pilot's license."

"That's not what she's worried about," Bill said, twitching his eyebrows in Groucho Marx fashion.

Kris laughed.

"A cruise would be good for you," he said, heading toward the door.

"Thanks for your help," Kris said. "I'm really glad you and Rachel are here."

"Me, too. It was one of those spur-of-the-moment decisions."

"How so?" she asked, her inner antennae going up.

"Oh, we just decided last month that we'd like to see Norway. We were lucky to get reservations."

"Yes, you were," she said, remembering that Oscar's book clearly showed they'd made their reservations in March. Why did he say otherwise?

CHAPTER 27

▼

An hour and a half later, relaxed on the settee in the pilothouse, Kris watched Tor steer the *Fjordstar* through the fjord. The beauty of these surroundings and the safety of being alone here on the boat with him, she realized, would have been impossible to imagine last night on the mountain. She only wished that there weren't so many questions still unanswered.

Tor seemed absorbed in his own thoughts until he pointed to a cove and eased the boat into a sunny spot. "We can stay here without any-one running into us," he said, shutting off the motor.

He sat down at the opposite end of the settee, picked up Kris's feet, and placed them in his lap; he did it without asking, an innocent and at the same time intimate gesture.

"You haven't finished telling me about Hans," he began.

"And we haven't finished talking about Nils's news about Otto," she answered.

"We'll get to that. I want to hear about Hans first."

Kris told him everything had really started Wednesday afternoon when they had seen Hans driving the red Fiat recklessly across the bridge. She told him about her rental car inquiry, the clerk coming to Hans about the nonexistent briefcase, about her seeing Hans's holster, Inga's revelation that Hans hadn't slept in his bed on Monday night, and Nils's report that Odd owned a motorcycle, not a car.

"I'm sure that it was Hans who was at Elsa's," Kris said. "At the time, I assumed it must have been Odd—he didn't like Elsa, he had her address, he was a computer programmer so he would know how to sabotage her computer. It just never occurred to me that it could be anyone else. And then the police found Elsa's things at Odd's, and it seemed pretty clear that he was the intruder—and maybe the murderer. But I think Hans planted the things at Odd's—the remnants of Elsa's missing notebook, the software and jewelry he stole from her house—and set the fire in Odd's dark room. I'll bet Odd couldn't escape the fire because he was already dead!"

"But why would Hans kill Odd?" Tor asked. "Aren't you forgetting that Odd had stalked Elsa and threatened her in letters? That's evidence that would suggest he had a motive to kill her."

"Yes, I know. And very convenient for anyone needing a scapegoat. Otto supports neo-Nazis, and the police found evidence that Odd was involved with that movement; maybe Otto ordered him killed for other reasons. It's just as I was suggesting to you and Nils earlier. Tying Odd's death to Elsa's was a convenient way to arrange things so that the police would be distracted. They would turn their attentions from the cause of Odd's death to that of Elsa's. No one would connect either of them with Hans. And keep in mind that if it hadn't been for the fire, no one, as far as we know, would have bothered about Odd and his connection with Elsa."

Tor gazed steadily at her. "So you think that s.o.b. thought you suspected him of Odd's murder so he tried to obliterate you with a boulder?"

"Yes, but there's got to be another reason."

"Why?"

"Because I think he also tried to run me over on Monday."

"In Bergen?"

"Yes. Remember I told you about the woman in the red car who almost hit me in the rain?"

"Yeah?"

"She was blonde. Hans has a blonde wig in his room and rented a red car."

"You went into his room?" Tor ran his hand over his shiny head, clearly exasperated.

"No, I didn't go into his room; Inga told me."

Tor looked relieved yet puzzled. "But Monday afternoon was before anyone broke into Elsa's. Why would he do that?"

"I don't know," Kris said. She looked out at the mountains. "I feel trapped. Caught in the middle of some story that I can't put together. Trying to understand what happened to Elsa and Odd, even what happened to me, what Hans's motives are, and where Otto, Yolanda, and George fit into this is like being stuck in a fjord with these rock walls around me and only one way out. And I can't find it."

"I know the way," Tor said. "Just say the word, and I'll take you out right now. You can see your uncle, then I'll put you on a plane and send you home. I don't want to see you go, but you'd be safer."

His eyes told her that he meant every word.

Isn't that what she had longed for last night on the mountain—to be back in the States with her family?

"Thank you, but I can't go, not yet," she said at last.

"Why not?" he asked.

Kris couldn't tell whether he was stroking her right foot intentionally or absent-mindedly. "I could tell you that it's because I'm not ready, or because I don't have all the answers, but it's really because I love your footrubs," she said.

He laughed heartily, and once again she felt wrapped in the warmth of his friendship.

"We're all leaving tomorrow," Tor reminded her, "so that means you have less than a day to get your answers. But don't think you're going to have any more adventures playing detective. You're stuck with me now until Hans is far away from you."

"That's fine with me."

Tor lightly squeezed the sole of her foot and ended his massage. "Let's go below and get something to eat."

He went ahead of her down the narrow ladder to the foredeck, then put his hands on her waist and lifted her over the remaining steps. She reached her arms around him as she felt her feet touch the deck.

"Last night I got the scare of my life when you disappeared," he said. "I realized how much I care about you."

He looked at her with a deep intensity in his blue eyes. She tingled with anticipation as their lips met.

After a long kiss, they went inside to the living room where they had visited with Oscar a few days before.

Kris watched as Tor washed his hands in the galley, poured orange juice for both of them, and brought the glasses and a plate of ginger-snaps to the table.

"I've been thinking," she said, "about our conversation with Nils. Do you suppose George and Yolanda have any idea of Otto's past?"

"How would they?" Tor asked.

"Otto evidently told George he spent the war in Sweden. George must have assumed that he's also Jewish."

"Hmm."

"Do you think we should tell him about Otto?"

"What would that accomplish?"

"I don't know, but it's all so surreal—to meet someone who was a Nazi. I worked closely with two authors who wrote about the Holocaust. I've met survivors in Israel and in the United States. I've read lots of material about the Nazis. I know how evil they were, but Otto seems like just a frail old man."

"He's a Nazi, Kris!"

"I know. And I'm wondering if that neo-Nazi story Elsa was working on was just subterfuge, and maybe her quest for the Muellers was a hoax. Maybe she really wanted to see Otto so she could make him an offer—to keep him out of her supposed story in exchange for information."

"What kind of information?"

"Where his brother was. She was only weeks away from going to Argentina in search of Klaus Brunner."

"Wait, hold it a minute!" Tor gaped at her. "Argentina?"

Kris shared with him what Nils had told her about Elsa's plans.

He shook his head. "Incredible! What was she going to do if she found him?"

"Nils said that wasn't clear since the statute of limitations has expired here, and it's doubtful Israel would try him."

"Why?"

"Because it was so torn apart by the Demjanjuk trial, it won't have another; it's too painful for the survivors."

"Tell that to the survivors," he said harshly.

She was taken aback. "Were you thinking of anyone in particular?"

"Yes. Of someone I knew once."

She took a chance. "You mentioned 'the love of your life' the other day. Does this have something to do with her?"

Silence. Had she gotten too personal?

"Yes," he said, his eyes focused on a distant memory. "It was over twenty years ago—when I was at Stanford."

"What was her name?"

"Dina. We lived together in Palo Alto for a few years, spent a summer on a kibbutz, picked oranges, went to ulpan to study Hebrew, hitch-hiked everywhere—to the beaches, the archeological sites, Jerusalem."

Kris wondered if someday she would be able to talk about Jim like this, when the pain now so fresh was buried under years of new memories.

"The day we went to the Holocaust memorial, I felt we shared a bond beyond ourselves. Her people had suffered beyond belief; my family, my country had also been touched by the Nazi cruelty."

"You must have loved her very much."

He looked at her. "Yeah. I even asked her to marry me, and I think she really wanted to…"

"But?"

"Her mother and father were Holocaust survivors. They liked me. They respected Norwegians and our resistance to the Nazis, but they said that Dina owed it to her grandparents to marry one of her own people. Her grandparents had died in the gas chambers of Auschwitz."

"I'm sorry," Kris said and thought how inadequate her words sounded.

He acknowledged her words with the slightest nod.

"Deep down Dina agreed that it was her obligation. Then my father died, and it seemed that fate meant for us to be apart. I came home."

"Did you keep in touch?"

"Yes, two years later she invited me to her wedding. She married a rabbi."

"That must have been painful for you. Did you go?"

"Yes, it was painful. No, I didn't go."

"You still feel strongly, don't you?"

"Yes, about what the Nazis did! My father used to say that 'the Nazis taught Norwegians to hate.' They taught a lot of people to hate. What they did affected not only my father's generation but mine too. But I got over Dina long ago."

"So you decided to stay single?"

"It has its benefits. After Dina, and then my marriage, I didn't want another serious relationship. I screwed around a lot, had a good time. Then AIDS came along, and I had to start worrying about who the women in my life had slept with before me."

Kris winced. "I never thought I'd have to worry about AIDS."

"Thought? Past tense?"

"Yes, when I learned Jim had slept with Janet—and maybe other women as well—I got tested. It was pretty scary until I got the negative results back."

"Yeah, I know what you mean."

"But you're a sociable guy—not someone I'd expect to be celibate."

He roared with laughter. "I didn't say I was celibate; I just practice safe sex."

Kris blushed. "So you're happy being a bachelor?" she asked.

"Let's just say, life's easier that way. No permanent commitment. It's easier to take risks if you're not attached to someone and vice versa."

That was one way of looking at things, Kris thought. "What kind of risks?"

"Working on oil rigs isn't without dangers. And I have some hobbies that some people consider risky."

"Elsa mentioned once that you used to be into mountain-climbing," Kris said.

"Still am," he said, stretching in his chair.

"What else are you into?" she asked.

"Hang-gliding, scuba diving. Other stuff. But why was Elsa telling you about me?"

"Remember when she asked you to dinner?"

"Hmm." He nodded.

"Well, she was trying to set us up."

"Oh, you mean make a match?" he asked, grinning.

"Yes. She said you were 'a good man.'"

"And what did you say?"

"That I wasn't interested."

"Thanks a lot," he said.

Kris gave him a flirtatious sideways look. "Nothing personal. I just wasn't ready," she said, thinking how quickly she had changed her mind in the last few days.

She closed her eyes and tried to reconstruct the origins of their meandering conversation. "We were talking before about Elsa's plans to go to Argentina. The bottom line is that she never got there."

"And now you say Hans is trying to kill you or at least wants to scare you to death. Why?"

"I don't know. Maybe Otto wants me dead. Maybe he thinks Elsa told me who he was. But wait. If Otto already served his sentence, as Nils says, then why would he care?" Kris felt confused.

"Hmm," Tor replied. "It may not have had anything to do with his Nazi past; maybe it had to do with his support of Neo-Nazis. In any case, Kris, you're safe here. Let's eat. Maybe it will re-energize our gray cells."

Together they unpacked the generous lunch that Oscar had ordered prepared for them: bread, several plastic containers of pickled beets and herring, shrimp, cucumbers, and potato salad, cold cuts and cheese, apples, and raspberries.

After lunch they did the dishes together and repacked the basket, except for two enticing slices of cake that they put in the refrigerator.

"I think last night is getting to me. Do you mind if I take a nap?" Kris asked.

"Would you like some company?" Tor said, winking at her.

"Only if you take that vow of celibacy."

"Not me," he said. "If you need me, I'll be up on the deck soaking up sun." He gave her a quick kiss and was gone.

Kris went down to the stateroom she had admired two days earlier and climbed into the double berth, propped up the pillows, and pulled a light comforter over her. Tired though she was, she was too anxious to sleep. She needed to get her mind off of Otto and Hans somehow, if only for a few minutes. Even trying to figure out where she and Tor were going in their friendship required more focus than she felt able to muster.

From the bookshelf next to the bed, she picked up a book called *History of Bergen and the Fjord Region*. She skimmed it, pausing at a section called "Historic Restoration." Black and white photos showed Bryggen, Håkonshallen, and Rosenkrantz Tower as they appeared in 1939, a year before the German invasion. Photos from 1944 showed the destruction near the wharf after the explosion in the harbor of the Dutch boat, the *Voorbode*. The roof of Håkonshallen was gone, that of

Rosenkrantz Tower shattered. The harbor looked as if it had been struck by an earthquake.

Kris thought about how often she had seen these buildings or heard others talking of them over the last several days—Andy recalling the explosion, Tor and Elsa each telling her about the buildings, Elsa and George talking about the picture of Bergen harbor. Yet, now seeing the photos was even more dramatic than hearing the stories. The buildings in a photo from 1946 looked practically as bad as in 1944. A photo from the 1960s celebrated the completion of the reconstruction of the damaged buildings.

She put the open book face down on her comforter and closed her eyes. In her mind she saw Elsa and George in the hotel library looking at the picture on the wall. George saying, "It is exactly as I remember it."

Kris yawned. She hadn't paid that much attention to the detail of the watercolor in the library. It would be interesting to study how the artist had captured post-war Bergen. She promised herself she would revisit the library when she got back to the hotel. She fell asleep and woke a half-hour later, refreshed.

Stopping by the galley on her way to the deck, Kris grabbed a bottle of ice water from the fridge and two plastic glasses. Tor was sprawled out on a mat on the foredeck, shirtless, the waist of his khaki shorts just below his navel. A *Fjordposten* propped against his head shielded his eyes from the sun. He snored contentedly. A fishing pole with a line over the side was anchored in a socket below the railing.

She had brought the cold water to drink, but the temptation was too great. She unscrewed the top of the bottle, tilted it, and let a few drops fall on Tor's feet.

"What the..." he muttered. His eyes sprang open as she turned the entire bottle upside down and poured it over him.

"Kelly's revenge!" she said, gleefully. She decided getting Tor's cold shower treatment after the sauna was worth the look of utter surprise and discomfort on his face.

"You...," he didn't finish whatever it was he was going to say. He flew up into a sitting position and grabbed her, wrestling her playfully to the mat. How very long it had been since a man had held her like this, kissed her like this. She ran her fingers along his cheeks, his beard, his broad chest. His warm hands stroked her back, then her midriff, then her upper thighs. Deftly he unbuttoned her blouse as she eagerly pressed her skin against his, hot not only from the sun but from excitement. But when his fingers touched the hook of her bra, she grasped his hand in protest, hampering his efforts to undress her.

"I can't, Tor," she said.

"You can," he said, taking her hand away and unhooking her bra anyway.

He rolled on top of her, supporting his weight with his arms on either side of her, but leaving her little room to maneuver. He kissed her long and hard.

Kris felt his arousal and fought her desire to give into his passion and her own. Finally she managed to turn her head to the side and break off their kiss.

"It's so good, Tor, but the timing's just not right. I'm sorry."

He froze for a long moment, resting his head on her shoulder, breathing deeply. Then he rolled off of her onto his side. "Why?" he asked, looking at her questioningly, his head propped up by his elbow. I know you're feeling what I'm feeling." He took her left hand in his and touched her wedding ring. "Are you still thinking about him?"

"No," she said adamantly. She realized that today Jim had completely vanished from her thoughts. But maybe her reactions to Tor were related to Jim. With her finger she traced the outline of the tattoo on his arm.

"I wasn't consciously thinking of him. A part of me wants to tear my clothes off and have wild, passionate sex with you."

"Sounds good to me!"

She put her finger to his mouth. "But Jim was my lover for more than half of my life and his betrayal hurt a lot. It's hard to get over that."

"And to get over him?"

"No, he's not the issue any more. You've given me feelings I didn't think I could have for another man. It's a question of being able to feel free to love and make love again—and having time for it. I don't want to be a one-night stand."

"Turn around," he said. Gently he pulled her bra back into place and clasped the hook, then kissed the back of her neck.

"Thanks," she said, embracing him.

The unmistakable whir of fishing line sent Tor leaping to the railing. Expertly, he reeled in a large trout, grabbed it, removed the hook and threw it in a bucket along side another. It flopped around and then was silent. He baited the hook again, threw the line out, and put the pole back in the socket.

It was getting warm. Kris tied the bottom ends of her blouse together above her waist, rolled up her sleeves, and put sunscreen on her face, neck, arms and legs. Tor accepted her offer to rub sunscreen on his back and shoulders. She tried to suppress her physical reaction to massaging his smooth skin, feeling his muscles beneath her fingertips.

The sound of a loud whistle startled them both. They looked across the bow and saw a cruise ship passing through the channel; sightseers lining its decks.

"Give a wave from friendly Norway," Tor said, putting his arm around her and waving his hand. "And hang on; those waves may rock us a little."

Kris marveled that the huge ship could navigate the narrow fjord. She and Tor watched the ship until it was out of sight and the water calm again.

"I think I should try my hand at fishing," Kris said. She took the pole out of the socket and held it over the side.

"You're holding it too stiffly," Tor said. He stood behind her and put his arms alongside hers. He covered her hands with his and flexed the rod. "Relax."

"When you're so close?"

He laughed.

"I think I've got the idea now," she said.

Tor let go, but instead of moving away, he remained where he was, his hands resting on the knot of her blouse. He kissed her ear.

"If you do that," she said, "how will I tell if it's you or a fish nibbling?" It was corny, but she had to say something. She wanted his attention and at the same time she didn't.

"You'll know," he said.

Just then her line was pulled taut.

"Hold it steady," Tor said.

She held on tightly to the pole, gritted her teeth, and reeled in the line until it was short enough, she thought, to swing it over the deck. She missed Tor's head by an inch or two. The fish wiggled in the air until Tor caught it in his hands.

"Here, hold it for me while I try to take the hook out," he said. Kris cringed; her hands slid along the slippery fish.

"You can't help if you close your eyes," he chided.

She opened her eyes and surveyed her catch.

"It's too small; it has to go back." He threw it over the side.

"I guess you call that being let off the hook," she said.

"Yes, for now, but he'll get caught another day," he answered, beaming.

They had coffee, tea, and cake at the table on the small upper deck.

"Now what are you so deep in thought about?" Tor asked.

"I was thinking about Yolanda's ring. The one that got stolen, supposedly."

"What do you mean?"

"I'm wondering if Hans stole it or if she gave it to him."

"Why would she do that?"

"I don't know. But she wouldn't be the first woman to marry an older man for his money and…"

"Cavort with younger men at the same time?"

"Yes."

"I think you've got it all wrong," he said. "But speaking of older men cavorting with younger women, when we get back to the hotel, some of the folks are going to assume we've been out for a romantic interlude."

"It has been romantic!"

"Hmm. Let's just say it's better for you if Hans and the people he's connected with see you"—he flexed his tattooed muscle—"as 'my woman.'"

Kris burst into gales of laughter. "You mean 'You Tarzan; Me Jane.'"

"Yeah."

She liked how his eyes lit up. "Well, since everyone thinks I'm married that'll give them something to speculate about—if they care."

When they were back in the pilothouse, Tor switched on the radio and called Oscar. "This is the loveboat," he said. "We're on our way back."

CHAPTER 28

▼

"Did you have a nice time on the fjord?" Inga asked when they stopped at the reception desk on their way back to their rooms.

"Wonderful," Kris said. "I feel much better."

Tor draped his arm around her shoulder. "Yes, we had a great time!"

From the look on Inga's face, she already thought she knew what they had been doing on the boat.

"Maybe you will be interested to know that tonight there is dancing in the lounge," she said. "Every Friday night we have a dance band. The band tonight is from Finland."

"Thanks for telling us. Maybe we'll go if we decide to leave the room," Tor said.

Inga gave them a knowing smile.

"Good job, Tarzan," Kris said pulling Tor by the hand toward the stairs.

"I like your eagerness to go upstairs," he said.

"You and Inga may think it's to the bedroom, but it's to the library."

"Why?"

"I want to see the Bergen picture again."

Kris was glad to find the library empty so that she and Tor could talk. "Here it is," she said, showing Tor the watercolor of Bergen. "But..." The picture mystified her. The artist's rendering of Bergen harbor was not dissimilar from how it looked now near the end of the twentieth century. The view was from the fish market looking across

Vågen—the inner harbor—to the Bryggen warehouses and the gray stone Håkonshallen and Rosenkrantz Tower with the little turret on its roof.

"This picture is old," Tor said. "Look at the date." In the corner there were the initials AW and the date 1940.

"I have to think," Kris said. She closed the door, then sat on the couch nearest the fireplace and stared into the empty hearth.

"So do you want to tell me what this is all about?" Tor asked, sitting down next to her.

"Didn't George say he was here in 1946?"

"Yeah, so?"

"But I heard him say that the painting is exactly as he remembers Bergen from when he was here before."

"So?"

"But that's not how it was!"

"What do you mean?"

"The explosion in the harbor in 1944 changed everything. I learned that from Uncle Andy and from you. Remember when you and I were walking down by Håkonshallen? We talked about it. You told me how devastating it was." From her bag, Kris pulled out the book she'd borrowed from the *Fjordstar*. "I found this book on the boat. Look at Bryggen in these pictures: 1939—now this photo resembles that watercolor, but here's the harbor in 1944 after the explosion. Just as you said. Look at Håkonshallen. Its roof is gone. Look at all the damage to Rosenkrantz Tower. Look at the mess. Even if by 1946 they had cleared most of the rubble, the buildings had just begun to be restored. This book says restoration wasn't completed until 1961."

"Hmm," Tor said. He studied the photos.

"I thought he was Jewish," Kris mumbled. She fell silent. In her mind she reviewed the events of the past several days, tested scenarios, felt her intuition leading her toward the truth in spite of the deep disappointment sweeping through her.

"It's all a fabrication. Just like with Otto. Tor, I think George is Klaus Brunner—The Elephant!" she said at last. She felt as if someone had just slapped her across the face.

"Whoa, Kris. That's a stretch!" Tor put his arm around her. "How did you get to that conclusion from an offhand comment about a painting?"

"Well, lots of ways. For example, even though Elsa said she thought she knew Yolanda from her London days, she seemed equally interested in George. And the travel agent said that Elsa referred to the Muellers—plural—as old acquaintances. I assumed Elsa really meant just Yolanda. But suppose she had also recognized George—or rather The Elephant?"

"But we saw your uncle's drawings. There's a resemblance to Otto, but not to George."

"Right. Not to George as we know him. A plastic surgeon could have pinned back those ears. He has a faint scar under his jaw; his protruding chin could have been modified. He had no fear of being recognized even here in Norway. He hadn't counted on being seen on television and Elsa recognizing him."

"But how could she recognize him?"

"Nils said that she had artists' sketches of how Klaus Brunner might look if his appearance had changed by plastic surgery or aging. If he looks like any of those renderings, seeing him on television would have been enough to pique Elsa's curiosity to follow him to the fjord. And I still think she recognized Yolanda, too. For all I know, maybe she's also a former Nazi."

"Too young."

"Well, maybe she is the daughter of one," she replied. "Bill and Rachel said that when they saw George hurrying to catch up with Yolanda in the meadow, he had come from the falls, as had she. But Yolanda had been in the meadow before with Grete. And I think I know where Elsa was all that time—I found the place yesterday. She must have confronted George, or George and Yolanda, with her suspicions. Why she chose an isolated spot where she was so vulnerable, I don't know. But maybe the Muellers—or at least one of them—are responsible for her death. George may have had the most to gain from it, but it's hard to know what a devoted wife might do."

"You're serious, aren't you?" Tor looked worried.

She nodded. "Damn! I've liked George ever since I met him. I've admired him. He's kind, he's charming, he's got the orphanage…" She felt sick. "George described Otto as a 'new' friend. I think he's an old friend—his brother."

They heard voices in the hall, followed by someone opening the door. Tor pulled Kris to him and kissed her passionately. She knew he wanted to cover up the seriousness of their conversation for whoever was coming, but the vigor of his kiss was real.

"Excuse me," Inga said politely. It was probably not the first time she had encountered guests in a private moment. "I must make some preparations for after-dinner coffee."

"That's all right," Tor said, "We were just getting ready to leave."

"Maybe you will want to check with the front desk. We tried to reach you in your rooms. Mrs. Kelly has a message from a Mr. Nilson."

"Thanks," Tor said, following Kris out the door.

*   *   *   *

"Who do you suppose Mr. Nilson is?" Kris asked Tor as they left the front desk with the envelope that had been left there for her. She waited until they got back to her room so they could read the message in private. She opened the envelope and took out the small piece of paper, and held it so she and Tor could read it together: *"Had the opportunity to come for overnight. Please come to room 315. Nils."*

"Now that's something—Nils traveling incognito!" Kris said. "Let's go see why he's here."

Room 315 was in their wing. It took Kris a moment to recognize the man who answered at first knock. Nils wore a sandy-colored moustache and toupee that filled in his receding hairline.

"I'm glad to see you both," he said.

"Likewise, Mr. Nilson," Kris said.

He motioned them away from the door to a corner table at the opposite end of the room, and gestured to them to sit.

"I had to see these people that you told me about. Otto Kohler and the Muellers. I have something to show you," he said excitedly. "I found Elsa's file on The Elephant."

He handed Kris a stack of computer-enhanced sketches of the notorious Nazi. One after the other she studied them and passed them over to Tor. It was amazing how many ways artists could morph a person's face. No matter how different the hair or other facial features, each still retained something of the face her uncle had drawn so carefully years ago. At about the tenth drawing, she stopped. The hair on this one wasn't wavy, but the face was close enough to that of George Mueller to have been his twin.

"I was right." She handed the picture to Tor. "Nils, have you seen him?" she asked.

"Yes, on the terrace. It is most certainly him."

"Well, Kris, you did it again," Tor said. Then to Nils he said, "A few minutes ago, she outlined to me the craziest sounding scenario, leading to her conclusion that George was The Elephant. I wouldn't have believed it if I hadn't seen this myself."

Kris smiled smugly. At last Tor believed her. "I think Elsa recognized him and confronted him," she said.

Nils nodded in agreement. "If she had been thinking clearly, she would never have taken such a risk. But she hated him so much! Did she ever tell you how Per was murdered?"

"Only that Per and a friend were trying to escape by boat, and The Elephant shot them—and she saw it."

"No details?"

"No, and I was reluctant to ask. She was never able to speak about Per without getting upset. I didn't want to cause her more pain."

"Then I'll tell you. Per and another of our friends wanted to join King Haakon and the army in exile in England. Their parents wanted them to wait, but they were determined to go. So they planned their escape by rowboat with the idea of rendezvousing with a fishing boat and going to England's Shetland Islands. Only a few of us knew of their plan; unfortunately, one of the group turned out to be a traitor, a Quisling, and told the Gestapo. Elsa was just a twelve-year-old girl, but she became suspicious of Per's activities. She followed him the night he and his friend planned to escape, and she hid in the bushes and watched. It was early spring and still very dark. Suddenly, she said, spotlights lit up the boat and the boys putting their things in it. Normally in such cases, arrests would be made and the suspects put in jail. That should have happened in this case, but it didn't. Brunner stepped into the light from an old shack where he and his men had been hiding, lifted his gun and shot them. Didn't even give them a chance to explain themselves. Elsa said she couldn't move. She thought she would also be killed." Nils paused and then continued.

"She said that after The Elephant shot Per, he simply put his gun away and began to throw stones into the sea as if he were out on a Sunday stroll. After that, she would see him on the street sometimes. She memorized everything about him: his walk, his gestures. She said she could never forget his face, never forget him."

"So, what happens now?" Tor asked.

"Nothing," Nils said. "I could run an exposé in the *Fjordposten* and get sued. The photo enhancement alone doesn't prove that Mueller is The Elephant. Even if I were to do a story and people believed it, the only result might be a public outcry for him to leave the country."

"Which he's doing tomorrow anyway," Tor said.

"But, how can we stand by and watch George get away with the murder of Elsa! And Hans with the murder of Odd! We have to tell Sheriff Bjornstad," Kris insisted.

"I have talked with the sheriff," Nils said. "He says George Mueller is a respected, wealthy businessman, a guest in Norway. That he can't charge a man with murder on the basis of computer-enhanced drawings. We need proof. An eye witness. Maybe, as you say, Odd was one, but he can't speak from the grave."

"There must be something we can do."

"We can't stop him, Kris."

"But he's a war criminal! What about the famous Nazi hunters—Simon Wiesenthal, the Klarsfelds? Can't we call them? Can't they do something?"

"I spoke to their representatives already," Nils said.

"And?" she said, impressed with his quick research.

"They said that it will take time. Now that they know who he is, they will get to him eventually and make life miserable for him. But even they can't prove that Mueller had anything to do with Elsa's death."

"So you're saying we should just forget about it? Just let this monster continue to live life as usual?"

"Did you hear what Nils said about the Nazi hunters?" Tor asked. "They will get George eventually. You just have to be patient."

"Easy for you to say." As soon as she said it, she regretted it and apologized. From their conversation on the boat, it was clear how deeply Tor despised what the Nazis had done to the family of his Jewish girlfriend, to his own father, to millions of others.

"You may have another possibility," Nils said. "One of my foreign sources told me today that there's a rumor that a wealthy Holocaust survivor in Switzerland is bankrolling an independent group of Nazi hunters."

"Who are they?" Kris asked, feeling renewed hope.

"Trained agents."

"You mean mercenaries?"

"I don't know. With Nazis, you don't need mercenaries; there are too many people eager to even the score. But it's a dangerous business; you can be sure there are plenty of risks involved."

"And, what happens if they find war criminals?"

"My source didn't know. Maybe they would hand them over to any country willing to try them."

"Or kill them without a trial?" Kris asked.

"I don't know," Nils said.

"Did you ask the people in Paris and Vienna about what you've heard?" Kris asked.

He nodded. "They say they have no knowledge of it."

"So how can we find this Swiss backer?"

"Maybe my inquiries will bring him to us," Nils said.

"But time is ticking away," Kris said anxiously.

"Sounds like a fantasy to me," Tor remarked.

"It doesn't matter if it's not really true," Kris said. "Don't you see? Elsa was upset that Nazis could live without fear, sure that no one was actively gunning for them anymore. But if they hear about a purported hit squad, it should make them squirm. Elsa would have liked that."

"Only if they don't break the law," Nils said.

"If the Israelis had been concerned about breaking laws, Eichmann would not have been captured," Tor said.

"That was a different era."

"Are you going to report this rumor in *Fjordposten*?" Tor asked.

"Sooner or later, for exactly the reason Kris just mentioned. But, first, I need more information." Nils put the pictures into a folder, then locked it in his briefcase.

"So, what do we do about George now?" Kris asked.

"Be very nice to him so he doesn't suspect that we know anything," Tor said.

Kris stared at her feet, unable to put her feelings into words.

"Remember the fish we had to let go today, Kris?" Tor asked, reaching his hand over to hers. She nodded.

"That's what you have to do with George. Let him go. He'll be caught another day."

"I'm going to call the Justice Department in Washington," she said. "I have a contact in the Office of Special Investigations. I talked to him for one of my research projects."

"Do you think OSI could get someone here in less than twenty-four hours?" Tor asked doubtfully. "They nail Nazis through legal processes. You might as well wait until you get back to Washington. Then you can talk to them. Tell them what you know."

Nils agreed. "Tor's right, Kris."

"Right now," Tor added. "Hans is the problem."

Slightly mollified by the idea of taking Elsa's cause back to Washington, Kris told Nils about her suspicions that Hans was behind the boulder attack that she experienced—the reason she escaped to the hut.

"You must tell Bjornstad," Nils said. "You could still be in danger."

"Not while she's with me," Tor said. "And I don't intend to let her out of my sight until Hans leaves tomorrow."

"You still need to tell Bjornstad," Nils said. "I told him I'd call him tonight. We'll do it together."

"Will you join us for dinner in Kris's room?" Tor asked. "The chef is preparing the fish I caught today."

They left with agreement that Nils would meet them in an hour, stopped at Tor's room so he could pick up a few of his things, and went to Kris's suite where they took turns showering and dressing for dinner. Tor had meant what he said when he told her he wasn't letting her out of his sight—or at least his reach.

CHAPTER 29

▼

After the delicious trout dinner, Nils called Bjornstad and Kris spoke with him at length. He was most interested in what she told him about Hans and assured her he would see what he could do.

Their next call was to Andy, who was eager for their return and anxious to get back to his sculpture.

Before Nils left for his room, Tor suggested he go to the dance. "We would like to introduce you, 'Mr. Nilson,' to the suspects. By the way, what's your first name?"

"Lars. And I don't want to meet them," he said with disgust.

"I know, but it's important they know that Kris will have an escort back to Bergen tomorrow."

"I have no desire to shake hands with a Nazi!" Nils said.

Tor badgered Nils to no avail. Finally, Nils said he would think about it and left.

At nine, Kris and Tor went to the crowded lounge. Kris recognized faces of guests she had seen in the dining room and around the hotel, but didn't see anyone she knew. They mingled while the band finished the tune it was playing. When they started the next piece, a waltz, Tor led her on to the dance floor.

"We came to dance, didn't we?"

For all the romantic moments they had had together, none had prepared her for the feelings that rippled through her as Tor held her close, their bodies touching, swaying, moving in sync as they danced. He kissed her neck and hummed with the music. They danced into the thick of the crowd. Tor must have felt her shake when she caught sight of Hans only a few feet from them. Tor embraced her more tightly, but the question she started to ask him was answered when Hans tapped him on the shoulder.

"May I have the honor of dancing with Mrs. Kelly?" Hans asked ever so politely.

"Hans, hello," Tor said, shaking his hand and unnerving Kris. He wasn't really going to let Hans cut in, was he?

Hans looked as if he thought that was the case.

"I'm sure Kris is complimented by your interest, but she's all mine tonight. Sorry. Perhaps after this dance, though, we could meet you at the bar for a drink?"

Hans was disarmed. "No, thank you," he grunted.

"Are you and Otto leaving tomorrow like everyone else?" Tor asked.

"Yes."

"Well, I hope you have a good trip," Tor said. He waltzed them away from Hans who disappeared into the crowd.

"Thank God, I'm your woman," Kris said.

Tor grinned.

When the band leader announced that the next dance would be a Scandinavian polka, many of the dancers returned to tables or the bar.

"Will you try it?" Tor asked.

"My legs are still a bit sore, but, hey, why not? I haven't danced a polka since I was about twelve."

"Don't worry. Just hang on."

The quick stepping, the whirling, Tor's literally picking her up off her feet from time to time, was a fun, aerobic workout. It left Kris's head swirling and her feet unsteady by the time they finished the dance. Laughing, they both wobbled to the bar.

"This is bad. We haven't even had any alcohol," Tor said.

"Allow me to change that," George said, appearing beside them. "Yolanda and I would like to invite you to have a drink with us." He motioned to a table near the door.

"Thank you," Tor said. He squeezed Kris's hand. "We'd like that."

Yolanda looked elegant in a low-cut white sleeveless dress and dangling gold earrings; her collection of bracelets jangled on her wrist. Her hair was pulled back and a pink silk rose tucked into her bun. "You both look very happy," she said.

"We are," Tor answered, pulling out one of the high-backed leather chairs for Kris.

"The best thing that has happened to me," Kris said, "has been Tor's coming into my life." She kissed him on the cheek.

The two Muellers gave them all-knowing smiles.

"My husband and I understand what it is to feel chemistry with each other," Yolanda said.

George nodded. "What would you like to drink?" he asked, signaling the waiter.

Kris asked for a soda.

"Where's Mr. Kohler?" Tor asked, after ordering a beer.

"He retired early," George answered. "He needs his rest."

"I hope we'll see him in the morning to say goodbye," Tor said.

"Yes, of course," George said. "You were out on the boat today?"

"Yes," Tor said, putting his arm around Kris. "Just Kris and me."

"And how was it?" George asked.

"Perfect. Or did you mean the boat?" Tor asked.

His humor had not gone unnoticed by George. "Yes, I meant the boat."

"It's perfect, too. We should have a good trip tomorrow. Unfortunately, Kris won't be able to join us."

George's disappointed look was very convincing. "Are you sure, Mrs. Kelly? We would welcome your company."

"I'm afraid I can't afford the time. I really need to get back to my uncle."

"It's a pity you can't come, my dear," Yolanda said.

Sure, Kris thought.

"I'm also disappointed that Kris can't come," Tor said, "But I hope, with your permission, Mrs. Mueller, that your husband and I can talk more about our common interests."

"Of course," she said.

"Very good," George said. "I am looking forward to it."

"There's Mr. Nilson," Tor said, signaling to Nils who chatted with a couple of people at the bar.

To Kris's astonishment, Nils's entire right hand was bandaged.

"Mr. and Mrs. Mueller, this is Lars Nilson," Tor said. He's here to escort Kris back to her uncle tomorrow morning."

"Good to meet you," Nils said. He acknowledged them with a nod and a shrug of his right shoulder.

"What happened to your hand, Mr. Nilson," Yolanda asked.

"A bad burn."

The Muellers expressed their sympathy.

"Surely a drink will make you feel better," George said. "Please join us."

"Oh, no, thank you. I have had a hard day. I need some rest." He turned to Kris and Tor. "Have fun. I'll see you in the morning." And left.

Tor chatted with the Muellers about the anticipated trip to Bergen, the potential for fishing. Finally, they all toasted a bon voyage.

When the band began to play "Strangers in the Night," Kris felt Tor's arm around her waist. "They're playing our song. Shall we?" he said, rising with her. They thanked the Muellers for the drinks.

Back on the dance floor, sheltered from the Muellers by other couples, Kris savored her closeness to Tor. She thought of Elsa. If she were here, she'd be saying, "You see, Kris, I told you to pay attention to Tor Olsen." But what would she say about them letting George Mueller get away? Coming to terms with Elsa's death would take her a long time; she knew that. Part of her ability to do so would be her success in helping Elsa's long-sought dream come true: to see Klaus Brunner, a.k.a. George Mueller, brought to justice. Once she got back to the States, she would talk with people in Washington, call Vienna, Paris, Jerusalem, Los Angeles, whomever she needed to, even try to find out more about the independent Nazi hunters Nils spoke of. She would do whatever she could to make sure George Mueller was not forgotten and did not escape what was due him.

She glimpsed Rachel and Bill—for once not dressed alike—dancing some distance away; both had their eyes shut. She leaned her head on Tor's shoulder and closed her eyes, too. She thought about the poignant circumstances that had brought Bill and Rachel together—him, the grandson of an American army veteran, and her, the granddaughter of a survivor of the Holocaust.

Tor hummed softly in her ear. Several hours before he had told her of his love for the daughter of Holocaust survivors. How ironic that these three people—Tor, Bill, and Rachel, no, make it four, she as Elsa's relative—whose families had been directly affected by Hitler's evils were in the same room as a notorious Nazi war criminal.

She and Tor danced almost at a standstill now, as did several other couples. Tor's hands rested on the small of her back; hers on his shoulders. It felt as though from their body heat alone they would meld into one. What had Tor said on the boat earlier? "It's easier to take risks if you're not attached to someone and vice versa."

Was this physical closeness without emotional attachment?

"It's a dangerous business; lots of risks involved." That's what Nils had said.

She pictured Oscar's reservations book and how the reservations for the Muellers, Otto, the Stephenses, Max, had all been made in March. Apparently even Tor's. And Inga had said Hasan had started working in March. She remembered the first time she had seen Hasan, she found herself thinking of the old TV series "Mission Impossible." Her thoughts flashed to the cabin, the first moments she saw and heard Tor, Max, Hasan, and Bill.

And then she knew in her gut that it wasn't ironic at all. Tor, Bill, Rachel, Yolanda, George, Max, Otto and Hans were not tourists thrown together by the coincidence of shared vacation plans. She, Elsa, Grete, and Odd were unexpected players in the drama that was unfolding. But who else was involved?

The day had been too long, the week too horrendous for her to think through what all this meant and what might happen next. But her instincts had proven correct before, and now they pounded at her.

The music stopped. Tor ended their dance with a kiss on her cheek.

CHAPTER 30

▼

"That was a great evening," Tor said when they arrived back in her room. "You kept calm, cool, and collected. I'm proud of you."

"You set the tone," Kris said. His confidence and command of the situation had inspired her. She had been worried about how she would behave around George now that she knew who he really was; but the imperative to not give him a clue that she knew, to believe that someday Elsa's dream would be realized and he would be caught, had overruled everything else. In the time since she and Tor had left the dance floor, Kris had decided that if her instincts were right, George would be caught sooner rather than later.

In her imagination, she constructed the Swiss-backed Nazi-hunting team: Tor, Max, Hasan, Rachel, and Bill. If she was right, the *Fjordstar* would not end up in Bergen tomorrow night. It seemed crazy, unbelievable! But unbelievable things had happened in the last six days!

"Like some music?" Tor said, going over to the desk where he had put a small CD player and some disks. "Any requests?"

"Sure. Bjork, Smashing Pumpkins, Pearl Jam, Rusted Root," she said. "That's about all I've heard with teenagers at home."

Tor laughed. "Best I can do right now is Grieg, Abba, or the Beatles."

"Grieg sounds relaxing." She watched him put in the CD, and waited until he had finished to ask him the question she'd held until now. "Not that it really matters, but I meant to ask you—before you came here with me, had you planned a rendezvous this week with someone at this hotel?"

"What?" He looked at her incredulously.

"Yesterday I discovered something that looked as if you made a reservation months ago for this very week."

"How in the hell did you find that out? Yes, I have planned to come here for a long time; to come by myself, that is, to do some hiking up on the glaciers. I could have told you, but then I thought…"

"With my suspicious mind…"

He grinned. "Yeah. And now, I think, also a jealous heart. I like that. It means you care."

Tor produced a bottle of wine and two glasses from the side of the desk and brought them to the coffee table. He placed them near the vase of fresh roses. "I hoped you would feel that this is one of those times to have something stronger than tea," he said.

"As long as you open it and pour it in front of me."

"Not in the mood for any lingonberry-type nightcaps?" he asked.

"That's right."

They sat close together on the loveseat. Tor opened the bottle of French Chardonnay, pouring a small amount in his glass first and tasting it. His head drooped, and he snored loudly.

Kris laughed.

His joke a success, he filled both glasses. "I'd like to propose a toast," he said.

"To?"

"To Elsa."

"Yes," Kris said. "To Elsa." They clinked their glasses together.

"*Skoal*," they each said to the other.

Kris took a sip of the mellow wine.

"And I'd like to propose another toast," he said. "This one is to friendship."

"To friendship," she said.

"*Skoal!*" He wrapped his elbow around hers so that as they sipped their wine, their arms were joined.

"Are you familiar with Grieg?" Tor asked.

"Not as much as I should be," Kris admitted, closing her eyes and listening intently to the music.

"This is one of the pieces he wrote for his wife. It's called 'I Love Thee.'"

"It's pretty."

"So are you, and so is the moonlight out there," he said. He turned out the nearby lamp.

Kris looked at the fjord, then at Tor.

"Kris, I'm not going to be able to meet you tomorrow evening in Bergen," he said.

She wondered if he had turned off the light for a more romantic ambiance or with the hope that it would be more difficult for her to see his face. In the last few days, she had learned to read the expressions in his eyes, and there was still enough light for her to wonder if she actually saw sadness in those eyes.

"It's my work," he said. He looked away from her as he set down his glass. "I have to go back earlier than I expected. And, I won't be able to attend the service for Elsa. I'm sorry."

"I'm sorry, too," she said. "But maybe it's just as well. It's going to be difficult to say goodbye to you; at least this way I only have to say it once tomorrow morning, not again on Sunday, and Monday when I leave."

"I want to see you again," he said, putting his arm around her.

"Same here."

"I told you that I like my life without attachments—it's easier that way."

"Easier, but maybe lonelier," she said.

"Hmm."

"You know people can feel strongly about each other without strings being attached." She wondered how that came to her out of the blue.

"For example?"

"I feel a really strong attraction to you," she said. "I enjoy being with you, but maybe one of the reasons is because you are so independent. I respect that. So if I put my arms around your neck like this"—she scooted toward him until her face was only inches from his—"and kiss you like this"—she kissed him sweetly on the lips—"it simply means that at this moment I'm showing you how I feel about you. In the same way that I'll wave goodbye to you tomorrow—the feeling will still be there, but you'll go one way, and I'll go another."

She moved on to his lap. When they stopped kissing and caressing each other, Kris had lost all track of time. And she knew she could never just say goodbye to him and go skipping off into the sunset.

"It's getting late," he said, his hands stroking her legs underneath her skirt. "We'd better get some sleep." He changed into shorts and Statoil T-shirt; she into a silk nightgown with a pajama top over it. She turned down the covers of the double bed. "You've got a big day ahead of you. You'll probably sleep better here."

"No. I'm a patient man. If the day ever comes that I come into bed with you, it's not going to be to sleep." He tucked her in and kissed her good-night.

While she watched, he made up a bed for himself on the floor in the living room.

"Why not sleep on the sofa?" she called.

"Too short."

"So let me sleep there, and you can sleep here."

"Out of the question. Good night."

She lay awake for a long time, looking at the moonlight shining through the window, thinking about Tor. She knew he couldn't see her tomorrow night because the *Fjordstar* was not going to dock in Bergen. Was he, in fact, a secret agent? Could this man she had spent the last few days with, to whom she had grown physically and emotionally close, who was so full of warmth and good humor, be also so filled with vengeance that he would be ready to kill someone like George Mueller? He had the build, the speed, the strength, the intelligence, the flexibility of lifestyle, to participate in a clandestine operation, but she wanted to believe he didn't have it in him to kill another person. But did she really know Tor at all?

She slept until five. In spite of the Nordic daylight already shining through the open curtains, she felt tremendous sadness—about Elsa, about Jim, about Tor. And at this moment her greatest sense of loneliness was for Tor. She slipped out of bed and tiptoed over to where he lay on his stomach, right arm outstretched. She slid in underneath the blanket and under his arm so that it rested on her back. He pulled her to his side, and she snuggled against him. Together they slept until seven.

They ate breakfast mostly in silence, not because they didn't have anything to say to each other, Kris concluded, but because they had too much to say. Across the dining room, the Muellers and Otto were eating together; Hans and Helga were a table away.

Kris's back was to the dining room entrance so it was the nod of Tor's head and the hush that fell across the room that prompted her to turn around. Sheriff Bjornstad, striking in his crisp, blue uniform, made his way among the tables. Kris felt as if she would stop breathing. Had he come to arrest George? Would he make it possible for Tor and the others not to become kidnappers? When he stopped at the Muellers' table, her spirits soared. If he were to arrest George, Elsa's killer would be caught, and Tor would be freed of responsibility. She was disappointed when she heard laughter from the group. She looked over to see Bjornstad shaking hands with Yolanda, George, and Otto, apparently wishing them all a good trip.

Next, he came over to her and Tor, greeting them with a "Good morning."

"Good morning," Kris said. "Sheriff Bjornstad, this is Tor Olsen."

"Glad to meet you," Tor said, standing and shaking hands with the sheriff.

The sheriff acknowledged his previous phone conversation with Tor and Elsa's father.

"If you're finished with your breakfast, Mrs. Kelly, I have some more papers for you to sign. I'd like you—and you, too, Mr. Olsen—to come with me for a few minutes, please."

Kris didn't even want to speculate on what the other guests must be thinking.

Bjornstad took them to room 315, where Nils waited. "Mr. Dahl has helped me to draw up these statements for you to sign," Bjornstad said. "He told me of your suspicions of George Mueller and Hans Schmidt. I believe we have enough information to bring Schmidt in for questioning, but I have nothing on George Mueller, and I do not wish to alarm him. I've arranged to have the police apprehend Schmidt when he arrives in Oslo later this morning."

"But what about George?" Kris asked. "He should also be arrested!"

Bjornstad shook his head. "On this one, we must tread very carefully. I cannot cause a scandal, which I would do if I were to arrest so distinguished a foreign visitor. I need strong proof that he did, in fact, commit the act you suspect. The day of your cousin's death, Mrs. Kelly, Kripos experts combed the ledge and the area around it. Their evidence might corroborate more definitive proof; but on it alone, I cannot make an arrest. I'm sorry."

Kris had grasped Tor's arm just above the elbow for support as Bjornstad spoke. Now she felt his muscles tighten; the Viking ship rocked ever so slightly.

"In other words," Tor said, "he's free to leave Norway."

Kris's heart sank.

The sheriff nodded, taking his leave.

Kris and Tor, agreeing to meet Nils in the lobby, went back to her room to get her things. It was a strange feeling, closing bags, looking around the room for any forgotten personal items, with this man with whom she had gone from being an acquaintance to hotel roommate in a matter of days. They'd been strangers; now they were more than friends and—given more time—could have been lovers.

"What are you going to do when you go back to the States?" Tor asked.

"Hug my kids. Try to make sense of my life. Do what Elsa would have done: not give up. I miss her terribly, but I'm going to carry on. Being with you has given me new strength."

"I want to give you something else." He put his hands on her shoulders and steered her forward until they stood in front of the dressing table mirror. "Don't move." He reached into his shirt pocket and placed a silver chain with pendant around her neck, next to the gold Olympic medallion from Elsa. The pendant was in the shape of a Viking ship.

"It's beautiful." She cradled the smooth silver boat in her hand. "This is always going to remind me of you and your tattoo."

"That's the idea," he said. "It's a remembrance of our time together."

He put his arms around her. She looked at his face in the reflection—his smiling eyes and his anticipation of the kiss he was about to deliver.

*   *   *   *

At nine-thirty, Kris, Tor, and Nils watched from the lobby as George and Otto said what appeared to be a tearful goodbye. Hans and Helga managed the loading of Otto and his wheelchair by automatic lift into the specially equipped van, while Yolanda and George looked on. Then, with Hans behind the wheel, the van pulled away. Kris felt her spirits lift; Hans was at last gone from her life or at least relegated to the bad memory part of her brain.

When the Muellers came back into the hotel, Kris caught their attention. "It's time for me to say goodbye also."

"Will you meet the boat this evening?" George asked.

"No, I'm going to be with my uncle."

George shook hands with her. "I'm sorry you cannot join us. I am happy we met, but I regret the circumstances. I hope that when you are back in America you will be able to forget the sorrow you have found here."

She thanked him; what more could she say? Now she, too, was an actress, pretending sincerity, regret at having to part.

Yolanda's handshake matched the distance in her eyes. "Goodbye, Kristina," she said, for the first time using her first name.

Max arrived in the lobby with bulging sports bag, two fishing poles, and tackle box in tow.

"Max takes his fishing very seriously," Bill Stephens said, as he and Rachel came from outside. The two, dressed in nautical shirts, jeans, and sneakers, looked ready for their voyage.

Max put down his gear. "So you are leaving, too?" he said to Kris.

"Yes, I'm going back to my uncle." She thanked him for all his help. "I haven't said goodbye to Oscar yet. Where is he?"

"Sick," Bill said. "It looks like he's got a virus."

"You mean he's not going with you?" she asked.

"It is most unfortunate," George said. "But with Tor and Hasan, we'll be in good hands."

"I'm sure you will," Kris said, realizing this must be part of the plan. Oscar had a hotel to run; he didn't have time for indefinite sea duty.

Again wishing Kris well, the Muellers left to make their final preparations for the trip.

Bill and Rachel accompanied Kris, Nils, and Tor to Oscar's Saab. "I really enjoyed meeting you both," Kris said. "And Bill, thanks again for your medical help."

"Anytime," he said.

They hugged goodbye.

Tor drove her and Nils to town. The interurban bus was already loading passengers.

"Be in touch," Nils said, shaking hands with Tor. He boarded the bus, giving Tor and Kris a few minutes alone. They moved to the end of the sidewalk, to the street corner where they had a full view of the fjord. Across the water, the hotel stood in relief against the mountains behind it.

"Well, Kris Kelly," Tor said, "I guess this is it."

How easily she had become accustomed to being in his arms; how quickly it was ending. His beard brushed her cheek, and he held her even tighter.

"Thank you for everything," she said when they ended their embrace. She took off her Olympic gold chain and medallion. "Here," she said, laying it in his hand and folding his fingers over it.

"But Elsa gave this to you," he said.

"Yes, and she would want you to have it. May it bring you good luck." She wanted to say more, tell him to be careful, but he had no idea she knew what he was planning to do.

Tor's eyes locked on hers. "I'll consider it a loan until we meet again."

The bus's horn sounded.

They shared a quick kiss. Then Kris ran to the bus. When she turned around, she saw him getting into the Saab; it was the beginning of a new journey for both of them.

CHAPTER 31

▼

"He's a good man," Nils said. "Elsa liked him."

"Yes."

"Your families go back a long way."

"Yes."

Monosyllabic answers were all that she could muster. He patted her hand in understanding, took out his newspaper, and gave it his full attention.

Kris wondered if she would ever see Tor again. He said he wanted to see her again, but what were the chances? He had chosen to be single, to be free to take risks. He was her opposite in many ways; she admired him. All her adult years, she had lived with Jim, had always been protected, the risks in her life minimal. If anything, she was inspired to learn to be independent, to take more risks. But she wasn't single like Tor; she was a mother even though her children were going off to college, and she was starting a new life.

She thought about Elsa and how she would have reacted to the kidnapping of George Mueller. She smiled, knowing if her cousin had been alive and known what Tor and colleagues were up to, she would have also been on the *Fjordstar*.

Kris and Nils spoke little as the bus wound its way up the mountain to Voss, perhaps because the things of which they wanted to speak could not be talked about in public. The train trip from Voss to Bergen—the reverse of the trip they had taken together with Elsa—was particularly poignant.

Yet Kris saw in her mind the end of the torturous journey of the past week. In two days she would be on a plane, on her way to reuniting with Laura and Charlie. Coming to terms with Elsa's death would take a long time; she knew that, but it would be easier thousands of miles away from here. Staying in a Bergen hotel the next two days would make it easier too. Before leaving the fjord, she had made reservations at a hotel recommended by Oscar; staying at Elsa's again by herself would be too lonely and sad.

When they arrived at the Bergen station, Nils told her he needed to swing by his office. Eager to make the switch to the hotel, Kris suggested she take a taxi to Elsa's, get her things together, and save him the wait.

"Are you sure?" he asked.

"Yes, of course. It's only for a short time, and besides lightning doesn't strike twice in the same place," she assured him.

Telling her he would meet her in half an hour, Nils hailed her a cab.

A few minutes later, Kris unlocked Elsa's front door. Checking the post box on the wall beside it, she found a package addressed to the family of Elsa Jenssen. It appeared to have been specially delivered rather than come through the mail. She took it into the house with her.

The scent of lavender greeted her, a bittersweet reminder that Elsa was gone but that in this place, for the last time, she could feel her presence. Kris had prepared herself for the emptiness of the house and for the eerie sounds she would probably imagine hearing. Hans's intrusion Monday night was still fresh in her mind; she rejoiced that he should be in police custody by now.

She set the package on the kitchen table and opened it. Inside a layer of Styrofoam was a videotape and a note: *"To Whom It May Concern: If you are reading this, then I shall be dead. I fear for my life. I saw Elsa Jenssen murdered, and this afternoon I foolishly tried to blackmail the murderer. I didn't think about the risk I was taking."* It was signed, Odd Engstrom.

"Oh, my God!" Kris gasped. She collapsed into a chair. Odd's message confirmed what she had suspected. Why had the parcel arrived only now? She studied the label on the outside wrap. A scribbled note at the top said, "Deliver to the family of Elsa Jenssen (and the address) if not claimed by sender by…" Kris checked the date, it would have been two days ago.

Kris took the tape into the living room, popped it into the VCR, and braced herself. The film began with some spectacular views of the fjord. She recognized the trail leading up the mountain from the youth hostel. Odd narrated here and there, but for the most part he tried to capture the sounds of nature—the singing of the birds, the ringing of the sheep bells as he reached the meadow. Then he apparently turned the camcorder off for a while.

When the video started again, the audio picked up the increasing volume of the waterfall. The camera panned up the mountain to the rushing waters above the falls, then Odd tried to capture the sensation of going over the falls. He tilted his camera through the ferns downward to the ledge where George Mueller, with elaborate arm movement, stood throwing rocks into the water below.

George's head turned suddenly; the camera picked up what he was looking at: Elsa standing just where the ledge jutted out from the trail, taking a photo of George. The audio did not pick up the voices, but the video showed Elsa talking animatedly to George, shaking her finger at him. Then she put her camera and a box she had set on the ground into her rucksack and triumphantly turned around and started to leave. George, who had already taken a couple of strides toward her, quickly took a couple more. He grabbed Elsa by her rucksack. Elsa slipped the straps off her shoulders and scrambled away, leaving George holding the pack. He tossed it to the side of the trail and ran after Elsa. He caught her by the arm and pulled her back on to the ledge. Elsa kicked at him and tried to pull away. Odd's lens remained trained on their struggle.

Brutally, with his left hand, George slammed Elsa's head against the rock outcropping on the inside wall above the ledge. Elsa fought back, pushing his hand off her head and into the rocks. She looked stunned, disoriented. Before she could recover, George swung her around and pushed her into the falls.

Kris held her hand over her mouth, sickened, the nauseous feeling in her stomach rising to her throat. She forced herself to keep watching the video. George left the ledge, then reappeared with Elsa's rucksack. He had something white in his left hand, no, it was wrapped around his left thumb. His head constantly turned back toward the trail, while he hurriedly stuffed a notebook and a black box into his own pack. Odd captured George removing the film then bashing Elsa's camera on the rocks before throwing it into the waterfall. Then, George looked up toward the top of the falls; perhaps he remembered there was a viewpoint. Apparently seeing no one, he shrugged his shoulders to arrange his backpack and left the ledge.

Next Odd appeared, the camera held close to his face, his expression both sad and frightened. "I made this video copy because I fear that I may be killed. I tried to blackmail George Mueller. I saw him kill Elsa Jenssen. Maybe I could have stopped him, but I was frozen by the scene. I thought it was just an argument. I couldn't hear what they were saying. I never expected that he would kill her. I didn't agree with her. She made me angry. But she was a human being who had as much right to live as the rest of us. I am sorry."

Tears poured down Kris's cheeks. Slowly the nausea passed. She wondered why Odd sent the tape to Elsa's family. Why not to the police or the news media? Had it been Odd who had called Nils Monday morning and then hung up?

Tor had said that the police would need an eyewitness in order to arrest George. The videotape was strong evidence and as valuable as gold. Kris put the tape into her bag, noticing for the first time the smell of cigarettes. Either Odd had smoked or maybe the package had absorbed the smell from someone else. Sniffing the air, she realized that what she smelled wasn't the stale odor of cigarettes, it was actual smoke. She whirled around. Hans, gun pointed at her, stood in the living room doorway.

"What are you doing here?" she asked angrily. She knew that her life depended on her ability to not panic. Bjornstad had said Hans would be arrested in Oslo. What had gone wrong? "I thought you were in Oslo."

"Otto and Helga went there. I have been hired to help you with your suicide. But first, you can give me that tape."

He took a step toward her; she backed away. "Stop, or I'll shoot," he ordered.

"I don't think so. George, I mean, Klaus won't pay you for that. Usually with suicides, people don't shoot themselves from a distance." She continued to back toward the dining area and kitchen. Hans would know that he had to guard two doorways; he stepped back into the hall.

In her mind, she could hear Elsa saying, "Remember Kris, you are a Jenssen." Jenssens didn't give up.

"Sooner or later, you have to come out one of these doors," Hans said.

"Not necessarily," Kris said, bluffing.

She stood in the doorway between the kitchen and dining room and picked up the receiver of the phone. It was dead.

"Do you think I would leave it in order?" he asked, standing in the kitchen doorway. She darted back into the dining area; he dashed back into the hall.

What chance did she have here alone with Hans? Eventually he might rush her, grab her, and that would be the end. Keep talking, she told herself. "You seem to have thought of everything. Can you tell me my motive for suicide?"

"You are sad about your cousin," Hans said.

"Why would that drive me to kill myself?" She could defend herself by throwing things at him. There were pots and pans in the kitchen that she could use. She edged back into the kitchen; he in turn appeared in the opposite doorway. with his gun aimed at her. If only she could get to the kitchen window and crawl out. Not a chance, she thought.

"Your cousin's death alone might not lead you to take your own life, Mrs. Kelly," Hans said. "But you are depressed about your husband. He has left you for another woman."

"How do you know that?"

"I have my ways."

"You read my letter to Elsa, didn't you? It was you here the other morning, wasn't it?"

For a moment, his smugness vanished. "Yes, but you knew that. That's why you have to die."

"No, that's not why. You already tried to run me down on Monday—that was before the break-in, before Odd died. Why?"

"Because George worried that your cousin had told you what she suspected."

Yes, of course, Kris thought. "Well, your suicide theory doesn't work. People at the fjord saw me with Tor—they know we're lovers. Obviously, I've gotten over my husband."

"Perhaps it is a guilty conscience then."

"I doubt that you know what a guilty conscience is."

She had to keep stalling, keep him distracted. If only there was something she could do to attract attention to Elsa's house. Nils had said that the police were still keeping an eye on it, so cruisers must be going by from time to time. What would seem unusual, out of place?

She kept her eyes on him, watching for his next move, at the same time relying on her memory of Elsa's kitchen to search for some signal she could use to call for help.

"You killed Odd, didn't you?"

"Yes, of course." He put his gun in his holster and reached for the knob of the kitchen door. Abruptly he pulled it shut, leaving her alone in the kitchen. Kris guessed he planned to come around now through the dining area and corner her here. But first he would have to secure the door. It was enough time. She grabbed the red tablecloth and quickly hung it from the window sash.

Hans pounded something across the outside of the kitchen door.

She shouted to him. "So your rock rolling and throwing didn't succeed, now you have to try something else."

"Correct."

She pulled two pots out of a cupboard, put one on the counter, and one in the sink, and turned on the hot water.

"What are you doing?"

She didn't answer, frantically searching for other weapons. She would establish her turf, her last stand, but she needed a barrier between her and Hans. If there had been a door between the kitchen and dining area, she could have closed it and tried to lock him out. But there wasn't, and he would appear in that doorway in seconds with the intention of closing in on her.

She pulled a bottle of olive oil from a cupboard and quickly dumped its contents on the tile area in front of the doorway, turned off the water and put the full pot on the counter.

A moment later, Hans stood at the entrance to the kitchen. Kris backed away toward the kitchen table, the refrigerator to her left, the end of the counter to her right, the window behind her.

"I had hoped you would die on the mountain," Hans said, raising his gun. His eyes were riveted on her, as if waiting for her to try to escape. "You know too much." He stepped forward and slipped on the oil.

Kris heaved the heavy mortar at Hans, hitting his wrist and knocking his gun from his hand. She pelted his upper arm with the pestle.

Grimacing, his arms flailing violently, he staggered toward her. She heaved the pot of hot water at him, disorienting him for a second—enough time for her to pick the gun up off the floor and level it at him.

"Don't move, Hans, or I'll shoot," she said, holding the gun steady, her finger on the trigger.

He began to slowly back away from her.

In the split second that followed, two police officers came from either side of the dining table. A startled look in her eyes must have warned Hans. He reeled, only to receive a karate chop to his shoulder and have his arm twisted behind him. He yelled in pain. The officers handcuffed him and forced him to sit down on a dining room chair, holding him there.

Kris recognized a third officer—Chief Finn Nygaard.

"Mrs. Kelly, you can put down the gun," he said, about to step into the kitchen.

Kris loosened her grip around the pistol and pointed it downwards. "Watch out for the floor."

Finn rolled paper towels over it and stepped onto his makeshift carpet. "You are very resourceful," he said. "You're safe now."

She handed him the gun.

After a lot of noises around the kitchen door, it opened and Nils rushed in, face flushed. He took her hands. "I'm so glad you're all right. I tried to phone you. I got concerned when you didn't answer, so I called Finn."

"When Bjornstad heard from the Oslo police that Hans was not on the helicopter," Finn said, "he contacted us. I sent my people to stake out the house, but apparently by then Hans was already inside."

"Hans confessed to me that he killed Odd," Kris said.

"He paid me to do it," Hans shouted.

"Who's he?" Nygaard asked.

"Mueller."

"Odd witnessed Elsa's murder," Kris explained. "He saw George Mueller kill Elsa, and that's why he was killed."

"How do you know that? Did this Schmidt tell you?"

"No. It's here." Kris handed Finn Nygaard the tape.

"I want to see that," Nils said.

"I'm not sure you should watch it," Kris cautioned.

Finn ordered his officers to take Hans into headquarters; then he put the video in the VCR and watched it with Nils.

Kris looked out the window at the town and across the water to Laksevåg.

"No! No! Oh, my God!" Nils cried.

She took a deep breath and then another. She couldn't allow herself to lose control, not now. She needed to think, to make a decision.

"What's that black box?" Finn asked, pausing the tape.

"Her tape recorder." Nils said. "She must have thought she could record a confession from him."

"His words would have been lost in the thundering of the waterfall," Kris said.

"We found remains of a tape recorder at the Engstrom place," Finn said.

"It's horrible. He's an animal!" Nils said when the tape finished. "You must arrest that man!"

"I intend to. Where's Mueller now?" the Chief asked.

Nils wiped his eyes and told him that Mueller was aboard the *Fjordstar* en route to Bergen.

"Who else is on the boat?"

"Mueller's wife, a few others from the hotel, and Tor Olsen," Kris said.

"Tor's on the boat? Good," Finn said. "Then, I'll put it under aerial surveillance for the rest of the way. We'll arrest Mueller when he arrives in Bergen this evening."

Kris shivered; her limbs felt icy cold. She fought back panic. What would Elsa have done in this situation?

Finn shook hands with Nils and said he'd be in touch.

"Finn," Kris's voice was not cooperating. She cleared her throat and began again. "Finn, George Mueller killed my cousin. We just saw that on the tape. He doesn't deserve your white-glove treatment. Why not arrest him now? As long as the boat is in the fjord, there's nothing preventing him from telling Tor that he'd like to get off at one of the towns along the way. He could disappear. I don't want that to happen, and I'm sure you don't either." There, she'd said it. Made her decision, for better or worse. Tor would never understand.

Finn studied her. "There are risks in trying to intercept the boat. Mueller may be armed, he may put innocent people in jeopardy if he sees police coming."

"But maybe there's another way of doing this," Kris said. Her thoughts ran faster than she could speak. "Tor and I...," she fumbled for the right words, feeling the color coming into her face.

"You mean you have succumbed to the Olsen charm," he said, giving her a knowing look.

"Yes." She didn't care if he thought she was just another name on Tor's list of conquests. "Everyone on the boat knows that Tor and I are very close. I said I couldn't go on the boat because of my uncle, but, suppose I didn't need to be with my uncle."

"And went all the way back to the fjord to be with Tor?" Finn asked dubiously.

"Love does unbelievable things to people," she said. "Look, consider me a crazy American. Isn't it conceivable that I would go to great lengths to spend more time with him? I could helicopter in, or come alongside the *Fjordstar* in another boat."

"She's right, Finn," Nils said. "I would believe that scenario for those two, and until you have him under arrest, you risk Mueller escaping—especially if he has any idea that he's suspected of murder."

And, thought Kris, if you wait for him in Bergen, he won't arrive, and you'll discover there's a kidnapping operation underway. Then Tor would really have problems.

"All right. I'll call Bjornstad. We'll track down the boat," Finn said.

CHAPTER 32

▼

The helicopter carrying Kris, Finn Nygaard, and one of his men headed north toward the mouth of the Sognefjord. In the hour that had passed since Hans's arrest at Elsa's house, the police had learned that the *Fjordstar*, after stopping for a while for fishing, had resumed its westward voyage and was only thirty miles from the open sea. Bjornstad and Nygaard had decided to intercept the boat while it was still in the Sognefjord.

The helicopter landed at a small fishing village, where a van met Finn and his entourage and took them the short distance to a waiting charter boat. Police patrols were ordered to stay out of sight.

Although Finn was dressed in jeans and sweatshirt as was she, it took her a moment to recognize Sheriff Bjornstad, in similar attire, standing on the deck.

"They're right where we expected," he said to her and Finn as they boarded. "If we head east, we should meet them in about ten minutes."

They were now in Bjornstad's county, and he was in charge. The captain of the boat was his assistant. Quickly Bjornstad reviewed the plan with everyone on board. His crew—his two men and the man who had accompanied Finn—would assist in Kris's transfer to the *Fjordstar*. Next, Finn, acting as the jolly second mate happy to be reuniting two lovers, would come on board to say "Hello." Then Bjornstad, out of sight in the cabin, would emerge.

Kris zipped up her jacket, put on her sunglasses, and braced herself against the stiff breeze blowing across the bow. She dreaded Tor's reaction. Finn had decided not to try to communicate with the boat until they were almost upon it, thus maintaining an element of surprise. Surely, Tor would know something was up the minute he recognized Finn's voice on the radio.

Kris spotted the *Fjordstar* at the same time that Bjornstad said, "There she is." He ducked into the cabin.

Finn picked up the radio microphone. "Hello, this is the *Anna Marie* calling the *Fjordstar*," he said in Norwegian. "Over."

"*Fjordstar* here, go ahead," Tor responded. Kris trembled at the sound of his voice. She hadn't realized how very much she wanted to see him again; on the other hand, what she was doing could well end their friendship forever.

"We're approaching on your port side. I have a passenger here who has hired me to bring her to you," Finn said. He motioned Kris to speak.

"Hi, Tor. Surprise!"

After a split second's hesitation, Tor responded. "Kris? Is that you?"

"Yes, I had to come. We have so little time left together."

"Request you go out of main channel so passenger can board," Finn said.

The *Fjordstar* turned toward the shore. Kris recognized George, Yolanda, Max, and Rachel on the foredeck watching the operation. Her heart leapt when she saw Tor coming down the ladder of the pilot-house; she guessed Hasan was at the helm. She waved. George and Yolanda waved back.

The *Anna Marie* came alongside the *Fjordstar*. Tor reached out to slow the rubbing of the sides of the boats. Bill Stephens and Bjornstad's two crewmen did the same.

When the boats finally settled next to each other, bobbing in sync, Finn Nygaard addressed Tor, "So you're the one she's come all this way for."

"I guess."

Kris looked into Tor's unhappy face.

Tor grasped Kris's hands to help her aboard. Finn gave her a boost, and she leapt from the *Anna Marie* to the deck of the *Fjordstar*.

"I couldn't wait to see you," she said louder than necessary. She threw herself at Tor as if she hadn't seen him in months, catching him off guard. She hugged him and spoke softly into his ear. "Just hold me and watch."

"No," he said. He disengaged himself from her hold, but she had provided enough of a distraction for Finn to board and start talking with the Muellers. The boat rocked as Max took a few quick steps toward him. He stopped when Sheriff Bjornstad leapt from the *Anna Marie* to face an astonished and indignant George Mueller. Hasan came running down from the pilothouse.

"What's happening here?" George demanded.

"George Mueller," Bjornstad said, "I arrest you for the murder of Elsa Jenssen."

George's face went white. "That's absurd!"

"Mrs. Kelly, I wouldn't...Mr. Olsen?" he said, looking for help.

Kris said nothing.

"I presume you have proof for this accusation," Tor said to Bjornstad and Nygaard.

"We have a videotape from the late Odd Engstrom that speaks louder than words," Finn said.

Yolanda's lips quivered.

"I want an attorney," George said.

"You can call one when we get you to headquarters," Bjornstad said.

Sheriff Bjornstad and Finn took George to the *Anna Marie*. Yolanda insisted upon accompanying her husband. Tor, with the help of one of Bjornstad's officers, helped Yolanda onto the other boat. Max transferred the luggage. And then it was over. The *Anna Marie* sped away.

"Damn!" Max said, swinging his clenched fists helplessly at his sides.

Kris felt the icy stares of the five people facing her.

"Do you want to tell us what happened," Tor said. She knew him well enough by now to know it was not a question.

She leaned against the railing of the boat; Tor against the mast. The others sat on various equipment; Hasan on the ladder to the pilothouse.

Kris looked from Tor to Hasan, Rachel, Bill, and Max, and started explaining.

"When I got back to Elsa's today, two surprises awaited me. One was a videotape from Odd, saying that he had seen George kill Elsa, had filmed it, and tried to blackmail George. But he failed, and he feared for his life. Somewhere he found a place to leave a package to be delivered to Elsa's family only if he didn't call for it within a certain number of days. That's why I received it today." She swallowed hard. "The tape shows George killing Elsa. He was ruthless."

"So, you called the police and gave it to them?" Bill asked.

"No, not quite."

"Hans was my other surprise!"

"Hans?" Tor said, aghast. "What did he do?"

"He came to help me commit suicide."

She told them of her cat-and-mouse game with Hans, how she finally got his gun, and then was rescued by Finn Nygaard and his men.

"Bjornstad and Tor both told me that, without an eyewitness, it was impossible to prove that George murdered Elsa. When I saw the tape, I knew we had the evidence we needed. Nils and Finn watched it, and Finn said it was enough. At first he thought he would just keep an eye on the *Fjordstar* and arrest George when you arrived in Bergen this evening," she said.

Max and Bill looked at each other. Tor's gaze was locked on her.

"I argued that there was always a chance that George would ask you to put him ashore, and then they might never catch him. So we came up with the plan that I was so eager to be with Tor that I chartered a boat to take me to him."

The group fell silent. Kris felt the tension. "I know what you guys were doing."

Everyone's eyes turned toward Tor.

"No, he didn't tell me anything," Kris hurried to assure them. "I figured it out by myself. You'd been planning this operation for several months. I got my first clue when I had a chance to look at Oscar's giant reservation book. I saw that you all made your reservations in March. Even you, Tor. Oscar erased your initial booking, but he didn't do a very good job. When Bill told me he and Rachel had come to the fjord at the spur of the moment, I knew he was lying. Oscar's book showed that their reservations were made in March. And, not coincidentally, all your reservations were made in that month within a matter of days from when the reservations for the Mueller-Kohler rendezvous were made. And, I learned that Hasan started working at the hotel in March as well."

Kris paused and saw her audience was waiting for her to continue. "As for Yolanda, I'm sure she is the Shoshana in Elsa's old photo. Tor, you didn't agree with me because you didn't want to raise my suspicions. But Shoshana is a Hebrew name; she must be Jewish. I believe Elsa recognized her. And I believe she also recognized George from the morphed pictures of The Elephant, which she had probably memorized. No wonder she was puzzled when she saw both Muellers briefly appear in the television interview at their hotel in Bergen. What would a Jewish woman be doing with a Nazi war criminal?

"None of you expected that Elsa would come to the fjord and confront George on her own—or end up dead for doing it. Her death definitely complicated your plan. For you, Tor, it was more than that—the ultimate and most horrible coincidence. You must have been doubly shocked when Nils told you of Elsa's death and where it occurred.

"How very difficult it must have been for you to grieve for Elsa, to try to help me, and at the same time, to try to protect an operation to which you knew she probably would have given her blessing."

Tor's eyes told her she was right.

"Probably you honestly believed it was an accident, and having me insist it wasn't created a nightmare for you. What would happen to

your team's plans if there were a media frenzy over suspicious circumstances related to Elsa's death? You tried to calm me—and discourage
my hunches—for my own sake and for the operation's."

Kris took a deep breath. "But you began to question things yourself
when the intruder broke into Elsa's house, and when we learned Odd
had died and all that evidence was found in his apartment. Oh, you
didn't mention it to me, but I'm sure you and the others were trying to
do your own investigation.

"When you heard about Elsa's long search for The Elephant, the
possibility must have occurred to you that she had recognized George.
That would have been an excellent motive for him to kill her. For one
thing, George wouldn't want his wife to find out his real identity. Iron-
ically, he didn't know that she already knew. That was the key: Shos-
hana/Yolanda must have been crucial to your entire operation and to
the actual identification of George Mueller.

"It was important that I not come on the boat today. Max, you
choked on your coffee Thursday afternoon just when George suggested
that I join you. Yolanda looked daggers at me so I knew she wasn't
keen on my companionship. None of you wanted me with you because
you weren't taking George to Bergen; you were going somewhere into
international waters—that's why Tor and Oscar were studying the
maps the day we had a brief tour of the *Fjordstar.*"

Kris fell silent and looked again at Tor. Her cheeks were burning;
her palms sweaty.

"Don't stop now," he said.

"You told me once about the time you spent in Israel, that you
know Hebrew. I've been trying to figure out what Hasan meant in the
cabin on the mountain. I thought he told you and Max to 'shake it.'
Right after that, he said, 'quiet.' Later I realized he didn't say 'shake it,'
but *sheket*—that's 'be quiet' in Hebrew. I learned that much during my
stay in Israel and apparently you did, too. When I opened my eyes in
the cabin that night, I saw four people: Tor, Max, Bill, and you,
Hasan."

Kris directed her next remarks to Hasan. "You wouldn't have uttered a word of Hebrew if even one person was not a member of the team. You simply thought I was still too far out of it to notice what was going on. And I was, more or less. You make a good Bosnian, but I bet you're Israeli."

"Max, you could be German, but you may well be Israeli—perhaps the son of German Jewish survivors of the Holocaust." She looked for some response from Max, but he remained uncharacteristically stoic.

"Bill and Rachel, the only thing I can really believe to be true about you is how you met. I don't know if any of you—other than Tor—are really who you say you are. Maybe your names are made up. It really doesn't matter. I admire you for wanting to bring a Nazi murderer to justice—though I'm not sure how you were going to do it. That can still happen. Who George Mueller really is will come out in his trial here in Norway. The case against Klaus Brunner isn't dead."

She was finished. No one said anything. After months of planning, their mission had been aborted—by her. These people had been willing to sacrifice their safety, perhaps even their lives, to bring a Nazi war criminal to justice, and she had, in effect, helped the Norwegian police take him away from them.

Kris didn't mind the others' silence, but Tor's ripped through her. He looked at her and then looked away.

"We'll take you to shore," he said; then asked Hasan to go up to the pilothouse.

It took only a few minutes until the *Fjordstar* docked next to an express boat in Lavik. Tor shouted to the captain, "Hold on, we've got a passenger for you."

CHAPTER 33

▼

Kris's welcome from Nils and Andy was far warmer than her departure from Tor. Uncle Andy gave her a hearty embrace. Even Nils greeted her with open arms. She described to them the dramatic arrest of George, leaving out the part about what the real intentions of the *Fjordstar* crew had been. She had gone with her conscience, made the decision she believed was right. She would have to accept the consequences.

"Thank God, it's all over," Nils said.

"*Ja,*" agreed Andy. "Come, Kristina, I want to show you something." She followed him to his workshop, where he unveiled his sculpture of Elsa. He had captured her essence—the determined look in her eyes, her high cheekbones, her upturned nose, her dimpled smile.

Kris was deeply moved. "It's truly Elsa. Uncle Andy, you have done a beautiful job!"

"Nils wants me to do one for the *Fjordposten* building," he said proudly.

"Yes," Nils said. "Andy is going to have a lot to do. Lots of thank yous to write, plans to make for the memorial service. I'm going to get him a secretary."

"Sigrid says she will help me."

"That's fine, there'll be plenty to do," Nils said.

"How's Grete?" Kris asked.

"Better. We've talked a lot of things over. We have a lot of work to do together—and with a therapist."

Kris was impressed. She remembered how Jim, so much younger than Nils, had scoffed at the idea of counseling.

"Grete loves me," Nils said, "and I love her in a way very different from how I loved Elsa. I have to start putting the pieces back together."

"*Ja*," Andy said looking at his sculpture. "That's okay with Elsa."

Nils's eyes teared.

"Kris, will you come back next month?" Andy asked.

She was going to be on a tight budget. Laura and Charlie would be away at college next month. How could she afford it? But had she thought that once she left Bergen, there would be no more Norway? "I'd like very much to come," she said, "but I can't promise."

"Tor will be here then," Andy said.

"How do you know that?" Kris asked. She wondered if her uncle was just doing some wishful thinking.

"He called me and told me he can't come tomorrow, but he shall come next month."

✳   ✳   ✳   ✳

On Sunday afternoon, Kris, Andy, Grete, Nils, fifteen journalists from *Fjordposten*, and some of Elsa's and Andy's other close friends sat in a circle in the meeting room at Andy's senior center. Plants, wreaths and fresh flowers were everywhere. A woman played the piano as people arrived.

Andy welcomed everyone and introduced Kris. Nils made a speech about his lifelong friendship with Elsa. When he sat down, he reached over and took Grete's hand. Sigrid tearfully recalled Elsa, then held up her gift to Elsa's memory—a completed blue-and-white-knit child's sweater, the one Elsa had been knitting. Sigrid said she and Andy would make sure it went to a refugee child from Bosnia. One after another, the mourners shared their memories of Elsa. Andy and Kris were last. She had practiced her Norwegian several times with Nils beforehand to make sure it would be flawless.

"There is so much I would like to say about my cousin Elsa, but, as many of you have said, there isn't enough time this afternoon to say everything. I first met her when I was just a young girl, but she remained like a mother to me for more than twenty-five years—she reached across the ocean and kept me in touch with my Norwegian roots. When my marriage fell apart some months ago, I was devastated. Elsa told me I must come to Norway to find my strength. And with her, I did feel strong. I felt so devastated when she died. I lost someone precious. I have felt such terrible pain—you all know how it feels."

There were several understanding nods.

"But throughout this past week it has been Elsa's voice that has kept me going, that has reminded me I am a Jenssen. Here in Bergen with Uncle Andy and Nils, and at the fjord with another friend of the family who cannot be here today, I have found the strength that Elsa told me I would find. This is Elsa's gift to me that I will take with me wherever I go."

CHAPTER 34

▼

On Monday morning Kris sat with Nils and Andy in the waiting area of Gate 23 at Bergen airport. At last, it was time to go home. She looked out the plate-glass windows at the jets on the wet tarmac and beyond to the landscape that she now knew so well from both the ground and the air. In her purse she had a packet of photos that Nils had given her. They had been on the roll of film that was under Elsa's pillow at the hotel, which Sheriff Bjornstad had gotten developed and passed on to Nils. Pictures of her and Elsa from the train to the Voss and other photos from their visit together in Bergen. In her arms, Kris held a bouquet of red roses, blue bachelor buttons, and white carnations surrounding a small Norwegian flag. This was where it was ending—where it had begun almost two weeks ago.

Perhaps her uncle, sitting next to her, was also thinking of the last time he was here. Suddenly he stirred and pressed his walking stick to the floor in an effort to stand. He smiled, his eyes looking down the concourse. Was he imagining Elsa? Kris followed his gaze.

She had wanted to assist her uncle, but the sight of Tor glued her to her chair.

Tor greeted Andy with a warm handshake and an arm to the old man's shoulder; then he shook hands with Nils.

"Do you mind if I have a few words with Kris alone?" Tor said. He grasped her hand and helped her out of her seat.

Kris held on tightly to Tor's warm hand and walked with him to a corner next to a large plant a considerable distance from her gate.

"This is probably as much privacy as we'll get," he said, embracing her. "I know you had to do it."

"But, on Saturday...," Kris stammered.

"On Saturday, I was damn mad. We had planned the operation for a long time. But, in retrospect, given the information you had, I wouldn't have expected you to do anything else than what you did."

"Where did you go?"

"Switzerland."

"Oh." She realized he had gone to face his sponsor—probably not a very pleasant encounter. "What did your friend there say?"

"He was surprised, to say the least. But he, like you, is convinced that at the trial, George's Nazi past will come out and justice may still be served. I believe it too. Now, I have something to return to you."

Tor fastened the Olympic medallion around Kris's neck. "Thanks for the loan. It did bring me luck." He rested his hand above her chest and held the gold Olympic rings and silver Viking ship pendant in his palm. "They belong together like this," he said, "Jenssen and Olsen."

Their kiss was warm, tender, and brief.

Earlier she had been upset about leaving Norway with Tor angry at her; now she wondered if that wouldn't have been easier. She had strong feelings for him, but she had another life waiting for her.

Boarding for her flight was announced.

Tor took her left hand in his. "You took off your wedding ring."

"Yes," she said. She had removed it the night before, using soap and water, and had wrapped it in tissue before placing it in her cosmetic bag. It would go in a safe deposit box when she got back home. "I have finally accepted the fact that my marriage is over. I'm ready to be on my own."

She looked down the concourse. Nils was motioning for them to return to the gate. "We'd better go," she said.

Tor held her back. "You know, your real acknowledgment that your marriage is over will be when you make love with someone else," he said. "I want to be that someone."

"Do you think we can do it by phone?" Kris said, affectionately rubbing his back.

Tor grinned.

EPILOGUE

▼

Bergen, a month later.

Propping the black-and-white polka-dot pillows against the headboard of the waterbed, Kris sat up to watch the local news on television. She had truly begun to get a sense of being on her own in Washington. Her divorce had been finalized. She had taken a job as a research aide in an academic center and enrolled in classes at American University. But now back in Bergen, in this comfortable apartment below the slopes of Mt. Ulriken, that life seemed very far away.

She focused on the television screen. "In Bergen today, in what was called 'a celebration of an amazing life,' Norwegians remembered journalist Elsa Jenssen," the commentator was saying. Clips of Elsa in interviews with famous people could be seen in the background. "In keeping with the celebration theme, the family of Ms. Jenssen requested that those attending the service not wear mourning clothes but rather what they would wear on a joyous occasion."

While a chamber orchestra played Grieg melodies, the camera, from its vantage point above the stage, showed a colorful crowd—a sea of red, white and blue with a few greens and pastels as well—gathered in Griegshallen, Bergen's modern concert hall. The narrator pointed out numerous dignitaries who had come to honor Elsa's memory. The camera panned to the center of the front row—to the prime minister in navy blue skirt and white jacket with a tricolor scarf, the King in military uniform, and the Queen in a red dress sitting next to Anders Jenssen, the father of the deceased. Uncle Andy looked proud and pensive in a navy blue suit. Pinned to his lapel and that of almost everyone in the hall were red carnations and mini-Norwegian flags which had been handed out at the doors.

The narrator identified *Fjordposten* Editor Nils Dahl, in gray suit and red tie, sitting on the other side of Elsa's father. To Dahl's left, his wife Grete in a tasteful rust-colored suit. And to her left, Kristina Kelly, Elsa's cousin from America, wearing a fitted blue-green suit. A chain around her neck held an Olympic gold medallion and a Viking ship, which filled the V shape of the top of her suit jacket. Her head was bowed; she was reading the printed program. The bearded gentleman to her left, in navy blue suit and tie, was identified as Tor Olsen, a Jenssen family friend. It was noted that Tor's father and Elsa's had been at Grini together.

Although no mention was made of the people visible in the row behind them, Kris saw two familiar faces. The first was that of Oscar Larsen, whom she had known only as the Fjord Hotel's proprietor—not as one of the few Norwegian Jews who survived Auschwitz. She had learned that he had changed his name and gone undercover long before moving to the fjord. He bought the hotel with the hope that someday he might help in the capture of former Nazis. Prior to the service, she had met the bald man who sat next to Oscar—one of Elsa's long-time Nazi hunter contacts, a retired Israeli Mossad agent who had been the mystery person Elsa called the morning of her death. Norwegian police eventually traced the phone number. He had not been at home when Elsa called, but she had left a message with his wife that she had located Brunner and would call back. She never did. That information would figure into George Mueller's prosecution.

The film zoomed to soundbites from the service, the prime minister's salute to a fallen citizen who had battled for justice, not on the battlefield but in the press; testimonials by a Lutheran pastor, a rabbi, and other clergy; the rich voice and haunting song of one of Norway's most popular female singers—and Elsa's favorite.

The report on the memorial service segued to an update on the upcoming trial of Klaus Brunner, a.k.a. George Mueller, Elsa's alleged murderer. His Nazi past had brought international attention to the case. Holocaust survivors were clamoring for his extradition to Israel. Norwegians who were fans of Elsa's and those who had lived through the Nazi period were demanding that the trial be televised.

Yesterday evening, the reporter announced, Brunner's brother Ernst, who had been living in Sweden under the name of Otto Kohler, had died of cancer. He had not been implicated in Elsa's death. However, his assistant, Hans Schmidt, was scheduled to stand trial for the murder of Odd Engstrom, a computer programmer and amateur photographer, whose murder was allegedly ordered by Brunner.

Mainstream press and tabloids alike dwelt on the compelling story of a star witness in the Brunner trial, Anna Shoshana Grizinski, a.k.a. Yolanda Mueller. As a child, Shoshana had been taken to South America by her British father, whose efforts to rescue her Jewish mother from Germany came too late; her mother had died in Auschwitz. Yolanda's father, a plastic surgeon working in the hinterlands of Argentina as a general practitioner, had been brutally murdered in 1947 by a patient when Yolanda was twelve. The patient had not known of the doctor's daughter. Neither did he know that she had seen his face before and after the surgery, nor that she was a witness to her father's murder. The patient had been Klaus Brunner. Forty-five years later, to bring about his eventual capture, the daughter had found her way into Brunner's bed. The commentator said that Mrs. Mueller would be returning to Venezuela and the orphanage that her husband had founded. He posed the question of whether Mueller/Brunner's nurturing of orphaned children could ever make up for the lives of children and adults that he had taken as a Nazi. The story gave Kris goosebumps. She pushed the off button of the remote control and turned to her companion beside her.

"How was she able to do it? To sleep with her father's murderer?" she asked. She trembled when she thought of what Shoshana had to do.

"There was no other way," Tor replied. "She had to get the crucial evidence."

"Such as?"

"Confirming that he had certain birthmarks on areas only a spouse or doctor might see."

"So why not a doctor?"

"For years they tried; no physicians, or anyone else on our side for that matter, could get to him. Yolanda could. She also found his Nazi party card with his photo."

But he doesn't look the same."

"The handwriting of the signatures is the same; it's been studied by international experts. And she found other documents that he had apparently saved for blackmailing purposes, but they incriminate him as well."

"How could she take them without arousing his suspicion?"

"When he was away on business, duplicates were forged. The originals were sent to Switzerland."

"Wouldn't it have been easier for her to just shoot him and take her revenge?"

"Maybe, but she wanted him to be tried for what he did."

"You mean you and Yolanda and the others hadn't planned to take George out to sea and kill him?"

"Not at all. We were counting on the Israelis taking him if we delivered him. We figured if we had him, they wouldn't refuse."

"For a price?"

"No, Kris. For justice."

"Poor Yolanda. She must have gone through hell," Kris said, sliding down from her sitting position and adjusting the pillow under her head. She felt the warmth of Tor's body next to hers.

"Yeah," he said. "But she feels that it was worth it. She says she forced herself to pretend that he had no past. In that way, she could be a caring wife, and he would never suspect her of being anything else. She may have acted with Elsa in England, but this was the performance of her life!"

"I hope she finds happiness," Kris said. "I couldn't have done what she did. I could only go to bed with someone I trust, someone I care about a great deal."

"And I wonder who that would be," Tor said, his whole face smiling.

Giving a mock sigh of frustration, Kris rolled on to him, feeling his welcoming response, his arms folding around her. She pressed her body against his. The familiar spicy scent of his after-shave reminded her of all the times they had been close, but never until today this close, this intimate. Together they rode the wave her sudden movement had stirred in the waterbed. Kris felt Tor's warm hand slip under the straps of her silk nightgown.

Jenssen and Olsen, Kris thought. Elsa would have approved.

Author's Notes:
The Story Behind *Hidden Falls*

Publishing a novel is exciting, but the true joy is in the research and writing. The process has been wonderful, sometimes bumpy, but enormously educational. I hope you have enjoyed reading *Hidden Falls*. These "Author's Notes" are my chance to acknowledge many people and to share this story of my story.

This novel has been 17 years in the making. I began writing it on a lined yellow notepad in 1987, reclining on a couch in our home in Princeton, New Jersey, recuperating from foot surgery. It was the first step of a very long journey and of the realization of my dream to "someday" write a romantic mystery novel that would embrace a number of key elements: my Scandinavian ancestry (this time, my maternal grandparents' Norwegian roots; and perhaps another time, my paternal grandparents' Finnish ones); my pride in Norway's resistance to the Nazi occupation; my outrage over the Holocaust and the Nazis who perpetrated it; and my belief in the necessity of Israel. My marriage into an Israeli Jewish family—and the experience of living in Israel— several years before my pen hit that notepad had greatly reinforced my dream and my beliefs. Having been so close to my own grandparents, I was always saddened by the fact that my husband had never known his—they perished in the death camps of Europe. The story behind *Hidden Falls* focuses a lot on Norway; however, the ongoing political crisis in the Middle East also served as strong motivation for my writing.

In 1980, I had "discovered" the setting I used for my novel. My husband and I—and our then-young children—lived for a few months in Bergen while he was on an academic exchange program between the University of Bergen and the University of Haifa in Israel. Professor Sean O'Fahey, my husband's host at the university, and Margaret O'Fahey and their children contributed greatly to our enjoyment of life in Bergen.

Our Bergen stay was my second trip to Norway. My first was to Oslo when I was in my early twenties. It gave me the opportunity to meet my grandmother's siblings and their descendants, all of whom made me feel at home. The experience touched me deeply and sparked lifelong friendships. When we lived in Bergen, I was thrilled to go to Oslo with our children and introduce them to their Norwegian cousins, continuing the ties that my grandmother and her siblings had nurtured ever since she left Norway at the turn of the century.

Also while we lived in western Norway, we toured the Sognefjord and its narrower offshoot, the Aurlandsfjord. I was smitten by the dramatic beauty of Bergen and the fjords to its north, which so much resemble parts of the Pacific Northwest where I grew up. The memory of that "Norway in a Nutshell" adventure stayed with me long after we left and settled in New Jersey.

A lover of Agatha Christie mysteries, I tentatively titled my book, *Death on the Fjord*. But raising children and developing a career takes time, and my novel evolved slowly. I received helpful critiques from fellow members of a writers group in Princeton. I longed to return to western Norway for further inspiration; in 1992, I made a brief return visit with my husband and children. And on I wrote. I appreciated the reading of sections of my novel by my Norwegian friend Bjorg Peterson and my young cousin Monia Nilsen.

My family's move from New Jersey to the Washington, D.C., suburbs in 1993 created a lull in my writing but opened up new opportunities to connect with the Scandinavian community here. I had already created my characters and plot, but I longed for more historical background. Shortly after joining the fraternal Sons of Norway (SON) Washington Lodge, I ran a request in its newsletter, *Capital Viking*, indicating my interest in interviewing a Norwegian woman who had lived in Norway during the Nazi occupation. I am indebted to SON member Paul Engelstad who put me in touch with another SON member, Gudrun Turner, a suburban Maryland resident. Gudrun shared with me many of her memories from the Nazi occupation of Norway and, in the process, we became good friends. I am grateful for her friendship and her encouragement of my writing and my interest in a period of history that had a profound influence on her generation of Norwegians. I miss her and deeply regret that she did not live to see the publication of this book. That is also my feeling about Rolf Holgersen, a Bergen native with whom Paul Engelstad also put me in touch when I traveled to Norway in 1995. But I'm getting ahead of my story.

Never having written a novel, I was ever-conscious of being a novice at fiction writing and sought critiques from experienced professionals. I am grateful to critic Courtney Henke and to two of my favorite authors, Dorothy Sohl and the late Caroline Llewellyn, who read my manuscript and provided encouragement and suggestions.

I decided to return to Norway in summer 1995 to revisit and further research the Sognefjord region and Bergen, and of course, to visit my Oslo family as well. My desire to hike in the fjord region led me to Sandra Lott Fisher, a Manhattan entrepreneur who booked hikes in Norway with experienced mountain guide Torger Møller Foss. Thanks to Sandra and Torger, I joined him and three British hikers on a gloriously sunny, warm August day for a ten-mile "jaunt" from Myrdal (on the Oslo-Bergen rail line) to Flam at the tip of the Aurlandsfjord. We hiked at our own pace, which allowed me time to be on my own to absorb the ambiance of the setting, the flora and fauna, dramatic rock formations, silence and sounds, and to savor the fresh air.

Hiking in the fjord country in August was something I had wanted to do as further research for my novel, but it became a means of catharsis. My mother had died in July. Though she had never visited Norway, she had passed on her appreciation of her parents' Norwegian roots and her love of nature to my sisters and me. She was in my heart every step of the way on that hike. At Myrdal, the water from the melting snow trickled into a narrow streambed, gained momentum, reached the rocky slopes and overflowed into waterfalls cascading down the mountain into the river that rushed through the canyon, and then gradually slowed and meandered through the valley before joining the great waters of the fjord at Flam. The sounds of the water—from where it began until it flowed into the sea—struck me as a metaphor for the stages of life.

I could never have written this book were it not for my late mother and father who gave me life, raised me with an appreciation of extended family and my Norwegian and Finnish-Swedish heritage, and a sense of humor; and who, by example, taught me that when the going gets tough, keep going. May their memory be blessed. And I am grateful to my sisters—Karen Anderson and Sue Hendrickson—for keeping me in touch with all of those things and for their loving support.

I owe deep thanks to Harald Hansen with the Norwegian Tourist Board in New York, who provided support for my domestic travel in Norway in summer 1995. He arranged for me to meet with a number of individuals in fjord country who generously shared their time and stories of the region. My fjord visits served as inspiration and confirmation of Norwegians' love of life and country. I was especially enamored with Balestrand, midway on the Sognefjord, where the local tourist office representative, schoolmaster, innkeepers, shopkeepers, and others took time to speak with me and tell me about their charming town, including its art-rich history. My thanks to Jon Gjeraker, proprietor of the Midtnes Pensjonat, for his hospitality, and to Gunnar Brevik, then Balestrand's assistant sheriff, who answered my many questions about police work in the fjord area. Thanks also to Leif Grinde and Jorunn Eitungjerde von der Leyen.

My thanks to Erna Turner, a travel agent at ScanTravel International in Vienna, Virginia, for arranging my travel to Norway on Icelandair. And *mange takk* to SON members Gunnar Grotos and Gunnar Eklund for referring me to Erna. I told Erna that I was writing a mystery set, in part, in an imaginary hotel in the Sognefjord region. She recommended that I visit the historic Kviknes Hotel in Balestrand because it would "be a great setting for a mystery." When I saw the hotel, I knew she was right, but I had already created my Fjord Hotel and my town. While I introduced some features of the Kviknes, the Fjord Hotel remained a hybrid—a combination of real hotels and my imagination, located not on the Sognefjord itself but in an imaginary town in the Aurlandsfjord. Special thanks to Sigurd Kvikne, owner/manager of the Kviknes Hotel, who showed me around the beautiful parlor rooms and told me about the Norwegian artists who painted the pictures that adorn those walls. Later, Sigurd and his sister Unni Marie provided further details for an article I wrote and submitted to *Scandinavian Review* in 1996.

In Bergen, I gained further inspiration from Rolf Holgersen, who, with his wife Kirsten, kindly hosted me for lunch at their home. Rolf recounted the days and years of occupation, and later took me on a walking tour of the town. At the Theta Museum, his sharing of his personal knowledge of the Resistance enriched my understanding of the exhibits and the times. On another day, I appreciated a chat over coffee with the prolific yet modest Norwegian mystery writer Gunnar Staalesen. Another treat was an impromptu tour of *Bergens Tidende*, Bergen's largest newspaper, with science reporter Inge Sellevag. My thanks also to my Bergen hostess Rita Grøtte for her hospitality, and to her and her husband Odd Magne for spending part of his valuable time-off from his job in the offshore oil industry to talk with me about the work and the impact on family life.

When after a week I returned to Oslo where I had begun my trip, my cousin Freddy Nilsen, an enthusiastic journalist for a suburban newspaper, *Asker and Baerums Budstikke*, had a big surprise for me—a front page announcement about my "forthcoming" novel, *Death on the Fjord,* with my photo, which he had taken while we were sightseeing the previous week. I was speechless, not knowing if I could ever realize Freddy's expectations that I would be published. My thanks to Freddy for his confidence in me when I didn't have it in myself, and to all the other Nilsens—May, Marit, Lillian and Bjorn—for the strong cross-Atlantic ties we share. May our younger generations continue this connection.

Returning to the United States, I worked on incorporating my research on fjord country into my book and assembling material for articles. Learning of my fascination with Balestrand, Gudrun introduced me to Odd Inge Ulvestad, a native son of Balestrand living in the Washington, D.C., area, and also a member of SON Washington Lodge. My thanks to Odd Inge for keeping me connected with Balestrand through his photos and postcards.

During the long gestation period of my novel, the Oslo peace process began (in 1993), with the Norwegians bringing Israelis and Palestinians together with the hope of finding a peaceful solution to the conflict between the two peoples, and that provided a valuable context for the story. In November 1995, Israeli Prime Minister Yitzhak Rabin was assassinated. I felt grief not unlike that I'd felt the day John F. Kennedy was shot. I wept watching his funeral at Jerusalem's Mt. Herzl Cemetery on television and listening to his family and world leaders pay tribute to him. This was the death of a peacemaker; would it also mark the end of the Oslo peace process? This historic event froze my novel in time. It would no longer be set in a vague year in the mid-nineties, but August 1995 when the peace process and Yitzhak Rabin were still alive and seemingly well.

In 1997, *Scandinavian Review*, a journal of the American Scandinavian Foundation in New York, published my article, "Balestrand: Between the Mountains and the Sea."

While taking courses at Georgetown University and freelance editing, I continued my roles as a wife and mother. In addition, I was active in SON Washington Lodge—a great group of people who share a love and appreciation of Norway and Norwegian culture. However, I told few fellow SON members of my novel writing, feeling I should wait until it was published. However, I did share my story with then-Lodge President Knud Knudsen, who offered to read my manuscript and give me feedback. Knud and his wife Liv had lived through and resisted the Nazi occupation of Norway. I was grateful for Knud's favorable comments on my novel.

With my son in college and my daughter about to go to college, I left freelancing and went back to work full-time as a writer/editor. My novel sat on a shelf.

In 1999 I was blessed to connect with a former Georgetown instructor and colleague from the Washington chapter of the Women's National Book Association (WNBA), LynnWhittaker, a literary agent with Graybill & English, LLC, in Washington. I am indebted to Lynn for her efforts, for her encouragement, and for her wonderful, professional editorial help. I decided to change the title of my book, and my husband suggested *Hidden Falls*. I liked the play on words. Lynn believed in my story and tried to find a commercial publisher for it. After several disappointments, we decided that my best chance would be with a small publisher. But I needed a second wind to start identifying and marketing my book to small presses. I dragged my feet, and time rushed forward.

In 2003, after learning of the rewards of iUniverse publishing from other writers, I became convinced that this was the publisher who could help me conclude my book odyssey. My thanks to authors Rasheed Newson, Bette Anderson, and Bill Neugent for sharing their positive iUniverse experiences.

I am grateful to many others who helped me on my research, writing, and publishing journey. Among them: The late Terry Offield, a geologist with the United States Geological Survey (USGS), spent a good amount of time with me at the USGS offices in Reston, Virginia, poring over geological maps and patiently answering my many questions about rock formations in Norway and elsewhere. The staff at Statoil in New York met with me early in my novel writing; and the staff at the Royal Norwegian Embassy in Washington were always ready with information whenever I asked. Elaine English of Graybill & English, LLC, in Washington, D.C., provided counsel at a time when I needed it.

Mange takk to Margaret Hayford O'Leary, chairman of the Norwegian Department at St. Olaf's College in Northfield, Minnesota, for helping me figure out what "Hidden Falls" might (or might not be) called in Norwegian. I take full responsibility for any errors I have made in the explanation of this or any other Norwegian words or terms.

Thank you, *tohdah rahbah*, and *tusen takk* to all my friends and extended family for the joy you bring to my life and for the interest you have shown in my writing. Special thanks to my friends: Liliane Willens, fellow SON member, for being a consistent and insistent voice urging me to publish *Hidden Falls*; Bonnie Belkin Baram for her enthusiastic support, thoughtful suggestions, and technical help; and Marcy Kahn, Susan Nugent, and Sheila Johansson for their willingness to read *Hidden Falls* and provide additional reader feedback. I am especially grateful to Michele Leber, a fellow member of WNBA and a former collection development librarian for Fairfax County, Virginia, for her positive feedback.

Finally, I can never adequately thank my wonderful family—my daughter Tamar, my son Elon, and my soulmate of 34 years, my husband Raphael (Rafi). You are my inspirations. Without the three of you—your love, support, understanding, expertise, editing, patience, and so much more—I could not have fulfilled my dream of writing, and publishing, a novel. Thank you for standing by me. I love you all so very much!

Carla Danziger

April 2004

Hidden Falls reader comments are welcome at carladanziger@yahoo.com. No attachments please.